PRAISE FOR THE NOVELS OF
COLLEEN GLEASON

"Intriguing, witty, and addictive…"
– *Publishers Weekly*

"Deliciously dark and delightfully entertaining…"
–*The Chicago Tribune*

"Gleason is really on a roll."
– *Publishers Weekly*

"Complex and filled with depth."
– *Midwest Book Review*

"…Gleason's publishing debut…turns vampire stories on
their ear with a decidedly dark, decidedly unsentimental
Regency heroine."
– *Detroit Free Press*

"Strong, vivid writing, clear and distinct characters, and
wonderfully delicious plot twists and adventures."
– *Front Street Reviews*

SANCTUARY
of
ROSES

COLLEEN GLEASON

ISBN-13: 978-1-929613-56-4

To my fellow Wet Noodle Posse Members:
at last the book that brought the blessing of you
to my life is in print!

Prologue

Tricourten Keep
England, 1132

"COME, MADDIE," Lady Anne of Tricourten urged. "We've only till the end of Seton's watch at the gate." Her voice, usually steady unless she was confronted by her husband Fantin, wavered as she glanced out the arrow-slit window in her solar.

Madelyne, though only ten, recognized the fear and desperation in her mother's eyes, and swallowed back her own terror. If her father found them, caught them leaving…nay. She would not allow the thought into her mind. Drawing the heavy cloak about her shoulders, Madelyne caught up its overlong hem and pulled the hood to cover her hair.

Anne opened the door of her solar, and, grasping her daughter's smaller hand in her cool one, led the way into the dark corridor. The edges of their rough woolen cloaks brushed silently along the cold stone floor, and the coarse material prickled Madelyne's neck and wrists. A mere torch lit the end of the corridor that began at the stairs descending to the Great Hall, where the sounds of drunken revelry reverberated among the rafters.

A great lump formed in the back of Madelyne's throat when they paused at the top of the stair. One more step and they would be in view of anyone who cared to notice two darkly-cloaked figures inching their way down the stone stairs and across the rear of the hall. Her mother's fingers clasped more tightly around hers, hesitating…and then she stepped forward and down.

Their descent was swift as they huddled along the stone wall, trying to blend with the shadows. Once upon the floor of the hall, Anne released Madelyne's hand and darted through a shaft of light thrown by a torch, stopping in a shadowy corner. She turned back to her daughter and gestured: *Come, quickly.*

Swallowing heavily, Madelyne looked out over the hall, where more flickering torches and the blazing fire at the other end lit the room enough for her to see the sweat rolling down the faces of the revelers.

Her father, Fantin de Belgrume, Lord of Tricourten, sat at the high table, holding a goblet aloft. His pale blond hair gleamed like wheat shifting in the sun, and his chill laugh sliced through the other noises to settle over Madelyne. She shrank back into the shadows when he looked toward the rear of the hall, fear rising in her throat. For a moment, all time halted and it seemed as though she could hear her heart pounding over the cacophony in the hall.

Relief washed over her when he shifted his gaze without pausing, and Madelyne suddenly became aware that her mother had moved further toward the door leading to freedom, even as she gestured for her to follow. Madelyne took a deep breath and hurried through the patch of light, gratefully melding into the dimness beyond the torch.

One of the hounds her father favored raised its head as she passed by, lifting the corner of its lip to show a sharp fang. Madelyne skirted around him, wishing she had a bone or aught to throw to the demon, and tried to ignore the low growl that rumbled in its throat. If the dog began to bark….

She forced herself to keep walking, and at last she reached a small alcove just adjacent to the door of the keep. Anne waited in this shadow, and, after a quick, hard embrace, she drew her daughter toward the large oaken door. It was slightly ajar to allow men-at-arms, hounds, smoke, and air to pass within and without the keep, and once through this entrance, they would be closer to freedom than Maddie had ever dreamed.

Thus 'twas with overwhelming relief that she followed her mother as she slipped through the opening and found herself huddled against the outside of the castle wall, blinking up at the quarter moon and starry sky.

"Praise Mary," Anne murmured, and, adjusting the small parcel she wore under her cloak, grasped her daughter's hand yet again.

The walk across the bailey to the side entrance, where Sir Seton de Masin stood his watch, was short. They stopped at the edge of the pool of light that spilled onto the earth, encircling the doorway. Madelyne stood to one side as her mother spoke in hushed tones to the red-haired man. She tried to ignore the starkness on the knight's face as he took her mother's hands in his, and Madelyne looked away when Anne tipped her face for the man to bestow a kiss on her lips.

A kiss of peace 'twas not.

Her mother's low tones became audible with emotion as she bid farewell to the man who would help them escape. "God be with you, Seton," she said, and Madelyne saw her caress his face with her palm. Then, as if she could no longer bear to look upon him, Anne turned to her daughter, once again taking her hand.

The door, heavy with thick wooden planks and iron bars and studs, inched open just enough for the two figures to slip through.

"Fare thee well, my love," Seton's voice carried quietly on the night's breeze. "God be with you."

ONE

IF THEY did not reach shelter soon, they would die.

The realization settled over him, wrapping him in calmness, even as the blood flowed from his wounds. 'Twould not be unwelcome, death, Gavin thought. His only regret would be his failure to take Fantin de Belgrume with him.

Rain poured from the gray heavens, thunder crashed with arrogance, and great, uncontrollable shivers wracked his body. The smell of blood and storms and death pervaded his nostrils. Sleepiness stole over him and his eyelids felt like massive weights.

"Gavin!"

The sound of his name, urgent, stole the calmness from him and he forced himself to sit upright in the saddle. Of a sudden, the desire to die was gone—the dark moment vanished—leaving the responsibility for the health of his knights foremost in his mind…and the bitterness of revenge burning in his heart.

"Gavin, look you there! 'Tis a gate!" Thomas Clervorne pointed with his bloodied sword. They'd not even had the time to clean their weapons, Gavin thought bitterly.

He turned in his saddle, knees pressing the shoulders of Rule, his war horse, and peered through the sheets of rain. Aye, there it was, barely visible through the trees and gray rain: a large, stone wall interrupted by a heavy gate.

"To me! *Á moi!*" Gavin bellowed, and the men he led—numbering only ten instead of the fifty he'd begun with—directed their weary mounts in his wake. Thomas had already reached the gate, and was pulling the rope that hung next to it as they gathered about.

The hollow sound of a bell tolling echoed, its tones eerie and distorted through the downpour. The men waited, their horses shuffling and snorting with the desire to feed and bed down. Gavin's head lightened as blood continued to seep down his side, providing the only warmth save that of Rule beneath his legs.

"Do those within have no pity?" Thomas growled, tugging at the rope more vigorously, and again the bell sounded.

At last, just when Gavin was preparing to curse those who resided beyond the gate for their inhumanity, his glazing eyes discerned a small figure making its way toward the portcullis. He pressed Rule forward, reaching the iron bars just as its inhabitant did.

"Aye, my lords? You wish shelter? An' who be ye?"

He saw that the figure was naught but an old crone, cloaked in dark garb and stooped with age. "Lord Gavin of Mal Verne, Lord Thomas of Clervorne, and ten men-at-arms, mistress." He had to concentrate to keep his voice steady and strong as a flash of light before his eyes told him he was weakening further. "We have wounded among us, and beg for shelter and, if you have it, care for our ills."

Even swallowing was painful, and, as he waited for the woman's response, the gate seemed to tip onto its side and then right itself.

Then the gate swung open, and the woman stepped aside. "My lords, you are well come to Lock Rose Abbey," she said in a strong voice that did not match her frail figure. "Come."

The men filed their horses through the entrance, then waited as she slammed the gate shut behind them. She shuffled along, leading them across a large bailey that had been cleared of the forest surrounding the stone wall, and paused at an outbuilding.

"You'll see to your own horses," she said without preamble, "as we've only one marshal and she is ill."

Gavin slid from the saddle, landing on his feet with a hard thump, and leaned against Rule. Standing made his head spin harder, and nausea well in his throat. Before he could take a step toward the stable, he felt an arm slide around his waist, bracing him. Thomas's voice registered dimly as it snapped, "Clem, see to Mal Verne's horse. Mistress, take us to a bed for him."

The wound in his side stung like boiled pitch, and Gavin fought back a groan as Thomas, weak himself from his own hurts, supported him through a seemingly endless walk.

Just as he felt the final vestiges of clarity leaving, Gavin saw the pallet meant for him and allowed his knees to buckle. His last impression was of the prickly comfort of a straw-stuffed bed.

"He has no sign of fever, my lord. I've packed the wound with a poultice and he must rest anon."

Gavin slowly became aware of the voices. The first was a gentle, female one, and 'twas followed by the rough, familiar one of Thomas Clervorne.

"He'll heal, then?"

"Aye, if the fever does not come."

Gavin tried to pry his eyelids open so that he could see the face that belonged to the silky, calm voice. She continued speaking as he struggled to focus. "Though the sword cut deep, the blood clotted well and we were able to sew the gap closed."

At last: his lids cooperated and he focused on the face of the one dabbing something cool on his sore arm. When he saw the visage bent near his, he nearly recoiled at the shock. The face did not match the beautiful voice.

'Twas that of an old woman: a long countenance with wrinkles woven in the skin and brown spots everywhere. Her eyes were watery and gray, and the lower lids gapped away to show deep, red pockets. She wore a wimple that covered her entire head but for the face that, though horridly ugly, carried peace in its expression.

"He wakes." This voice was old and thready, and emitted from the elderly woman's shriveled lips.

Then two others were at his side, looking down upon him. One was Thomas, Gavin's oldest friend, and the other was the Madonna.

Indeed, she had to be an unearthly being, for he'd never seen such beauty and serenity on the face of a mortal. Her eyes were luminous gray moonstones glowing in a perfect oval face framed by a nun's veil. High cheekbones created smooth hollows in fair, ivory skin, unmarked but for a small freckle near one eyebrow. The mouth that curved into a pleased smile was sweetly formed of soft pink lips that were neither too narrow nor too full.

"How do you feel?" It was the voice again, the mellow, soft one to which he'd awakened. The one that fit this face. "Can you speak, my lord?"

Gavin knew what he wanted to say, but he hadn't the energy to form the words. When she offered him a sip of water, 'twas all he could do to open his lips as she pressed a cup to his mouth. The wooden vessel felt rough against him, but the water slid, cool and smooth, down his parched throat.

"The others have been tended to." 'Twas Thomas speaking, almost as if he knew what his lord meant to ask. With effort, Gavin turned his head toward him. "John and Robert have the fever and are being watched, but the others have lesser hurts and will most like recover fully."

"Where are we?" Gavin forced the words from his throat, and they came forth like guttural groans.

"Lock Rose Abbey." It was the woman—the Madonna—speaking again. "I'm surprised you found us, for we are well-hidden—as is our intent."

Gavin vaguely remembered the cloying forest and how the gate to the abbey seemed to rise from nowhere. He nodded painfully, and managed to speak again. "Where is this place?"

"Deep in the forest, several leagues from Mancassel. Few there even know of our existence."

Mancassel. Gavin's fogged mind cleared enough for him to realize how far they'd traveled from the skirmish that had left them near death. His lips twisted.

Fantin de Belgrume could not have known they'd find shelter—he'd have expected that they'd perish in the wilds after he and his men left them for dead. Mayhaps that had been his plan: the ambush was not so much meant to destroy Gavin's troop in the depths of the forest, but to injure them enough, and far from any assistance, that they would die while searching for shelter.

'Twas only by the grace of God, then, that he and his men found themselves in the sanctuary of some abbey, and that he lived yet to kill de Belgrume. He smiled at the Madonna and asked one more question. "What is your name, sister?"

"Madelyne."

The beads fit comfortably in her hand, the irregularity of the rose-scented orbs welcome to the tips of her fingers. It was the first necklet of prayer beads she'd made after coming to Lock Rose Abbey, and Madelyne still prayed with it though she'd made many others in the decade since.

"*Ave Maria, gratia plena….*" The words flowed from her mouth without hesitation even as her thoughts wound down a separate path. Most oft when she prayed at matins, her thoughts centered on spiritual contemplation, rather than of men—such as those who lay wounded in the infirmary. 'Twas not often that outsiders—particularly men—came to the abbey.

Those who wished for shelter or sanctuary were welcomed, although they were kept from the portions of the abbey where the permanent inhabitants lived. In the guest house and infirmary, the furnishings were mean and simple. But in the abbey itself, the women lived in much more comfort. Mother Bertilde insisted that keeping the wealth of the abbey hidden kept not only their goods, but also the women, safer from the outside world.

Indeed, in the weeks after she and her mother had escaped from her father's keep, they had flinched at every sound of the bell tolling the announcement of visitors at the gates. Mother Berthilde, as serene and motherly those ten years past as she was now, pled them to feel safe in their sanctuary—promising that few knew of the abbey, and even fewer could find it should they wish to.

Despite the Mother's calming words, however, men sent by Fantin had indeed found the abbey only two fortnights after they'd left Tricourten. Madelyne still felt the sickness of fear she'd known when she learned her father's men were at the gate…until 'twas made known to her that Seton de Masin was the leader of the group.

Meeting secretly with her mother Anne, he brought tidings of Fantin's rage at their disappearance—and the promise that their whereabouts were safe in his keeping. Seton hid his meeting with Anne from the other men accompanying him. Thus they would carry the tale that the abbey had been searched with no result.

Madelyne's thoughts were interrupted as the soft swish of a skirt brushed the stone floor next to her.

"Mother Bertilde." Madelyne rose from the *prie dieu* at which she'd been kneeling and gave a brief curtsey.

The abbess glanced at the prayer beads with sharp blue eyes and murmured, "I didn't mean to disturb you, daughter, I meant only to see how our guests fare."

"The Virgin will understand," Madelyne replied. "They're resting comfortably, most of them. Two are ripe for a fever, but Sister Nellen watches over them and will wake me if need be."

Bertilde tucked strong hands inside the sleeves of her habit. She pursed her mouth, causing the fine, white hairs that grew along her upper lip to prickle outward. It seemed as though she needed to choose her words carefully, and, indeed, when she finally spoke, it was with precision. "They must be made to leave as soon as possible."

Madelyne stared at the abbess in surprise. "Mother—"

"Do you not turn them out until they are able to ride, but you must see that they leave at that time. I…." She closed her eyes for a moment, then opened them again. "They bring naught but disruption and danger to the abbey…I can feel it. The sooner they are without our walls, the more easily I shall rest." She fixed the gaze of her blue eyes on Madelyne. "You must also see to it that they are kept in the infirmary or at the stables, and allow them nowhere else within the abbey. If they wish to pray or to hear Mass, they may also come to the Little Chapel, but I'll not have them see any more of us, or of the buildings, than that."

Wrapping the prayer beads around her fingers, Madelyne could do naught but nod. She remembered with sudden clarity how cold and pained the gray eyes of their leader, the Lord of Mal Verne, had been when he opened them. A shiver skittered over her shoulders and she knew that Mother Bertilde was not wrong. This man brought power and the outside world with him, and somehow, this portended a change in the lives of those within the abbey.

She doubted that Mother Bertilde's precautions would protect them from whatever should come.

As the abbess left her, Madelyne renewed her prayers with fervor.

Two

THE DARKNESS *of fear slithered through her, constricting the breath in her throat.*

He held something long and thin, and it glinted in the firelight that tossed shadows over her mother's terrified face. The words that spewed from his spittle-flecked lips stabbed at her with their evilness, causing her to draw her knees closer to her chest as she huddled in the corner.

Screams echoed in the chamber where firelight danced happily as they endured his madness. Strange symbols that were carved into the stone floor melded into each other as the darkness and fear descended again, and again…and again.

No one could hear their screams, nor their cries for mercy.

Straps of leather…foul-smelling potions…the shrieks of a hooded hawk as it was denuded of its feathers…the crisp acridity of burning flesh…his laugh, smooth and low like the sound of far-off thunder….

Madelyne dragged her eyes open and pushed away the dream, reaching blindly for her prayer beads. The darkness of the nightmare hovered at the edge of her mind, and she frantically sought the words to keep it at bay. *Ave Maria, gratia plena….*

She mumbled the words automatically, inhaling the sweet, faded scent of roses from the beads. Slowly, the fear subsided and she became aware of the familiar surroundings of her cell in the abbey.

The barest hint of light speared the darkness, chasing away her dreams, giving shape to the forms of her trunk and the three-legged stool. A faint outline of the cross woven of willow branches hanging above the door, and the shape of the small tapestry that covered part of the opposite wall, comforted her.

Dawn was near, and Madelyne knew she wouldn't sleep again this night. Still shaken from the fierceness of her memory, she slipped slowly from her bed. Clad only in a fine linen chemise, she splashed water on her face from a low-sided bowl, and chewed on a sprig of mint. Her novitiate's habit, also made of well-woven linen, was naught but a simple, dark dress and an enveloping wimple that covered the two thick braids she wore.

Since she was awake, she'd see how her patients were faring, and relieve Sister Nellen from her night watch early. Tucking the beads into the hidden pocket of her gown, created solely for that reason, Madelyne left her cell and paced easily down the hall to the main entrance to the abbey.

Outside, the summer night was drawing to a close, and the gray of pre-dawn surrendered to the pale yellow of early morning. A thick scent of roses hung on the air, along with that of the rain that had passed through last eve.

Despite the fact that the forest crowded the walls of Lock Rose Abbey, within those walls 'twas as sunny and open as the King's Meadow. Gardens grew heartily, and the space was plentiful so that its inhabitants did not regret their lack of access to the outside.

She was so happy within those walls that rarely did Madelyne wonder what it would be like to be out of them.

In the infirmary, Sister Nellen had just finished changing the poultice on one of the injured men's arms. She looked up as Madelyne slipped through the door, her brown-spotted face creasing with wrinkles of welcome.

"Good morrow, Sister Madelyne," she greeted her in a low, raspy voice. "You are early, but 'tis good, as I am weary and wish to sleep a bit before the Mass. All is quiet."

"The fever has not come?" Madelyne looked toward the pallet of a man who stirred restlessly.

"Nay yet. He bears watching," Nellen stabbed an arthritic finger at him, "but there is no sign yet."

All of the men slept still, and when Nellen left, Madelyne wandered among the pallets to see to her patients, curious and fearful all at once. These men were fighting men—built strong and sturdy, with wounds and gashes, scars and swords. They lived death everyday, and she shuddered deep within herself at the thought.

She would never know the world in which they lived—that world of anger and battles and bloodshed, of greed and politics—nor did she wish to know it. Her life was promised to God in devotion for keeping her safe from the wrath of her father.

Madelyne paused beside their leader, the Lord of Mal Verne, and was drawn to look closely at his face. 'Twas not a handsome one, in truth, but one filled with hardness, pain, and determination. Deep lines cut through his cheeks—-not scars, nay, but lines of weariness and character. His brows were thick and dark, above deep-set eyes that lay closed in repose.

Madelyne saw the dark brush of stubble over his cheeks and around the square chin that jutted even in sleep. He sighed and shifted, his mouth moving in a silent comment, firming and then relaxing. She nearly touched it, that most beautiful part of him, but kept her hands tucked into her sleeves.

So odd, that feeling sweeping through her as she looked down upon him.

Madelyne turned away as the knight called John mumbled and rolled over, thumping his hand against the wall. Not one given to fancies or daydreams, Madelyne was grateful for the interruption of her inspection of Lord Mal Verne. She did not care for the tingle that started in her fingers when she'd thought to touch his lips.

After seeing that John had not injured his hand other than the scrape of knuckles over a stone wall, Madelyne busied herself chopping herbs for other treatments.

Some time later, when she turned away from the old wooden table, she saw that Lord Mal Verne had wakened. He sat partially inclined on the rough straw pallet, watching her with cool gray eyes.

"Good morrow," she greeted him calmly, 'though she felt a bit disconcerted that he'd been staring at her. "Does your side pain you?"

He shook his head briefly. "Nay, no more than any other hurt I've had." His gaze skimmed over the other men resting on their pallets, then returned to her. "The others?"

Madelyne nodded. "All are well. Most should be out of bed within a day." She added water to a shallow bowl filled with finely chopped bruisewort leaves and stirred it with a flat, wooden spoon. She would add dried woad and the paste would be used in his poultice. "I must look at your wound, and change the wrappings."

He grunted what she assumed was an assent, though it wouldn't have mattered to her if he hadn't—the poultice had to be changed. He rolled to one side and she stuffed a lumpy pillow behind his back to help him hold the position.

Working deftly, she pulled up the woolen tunic one of the sisters had found for him, exposing the neat linen bandage. Beneath, the clean slice through his flesh was an angry red line with a careful row of stitches crossing over it. Blood oozed slowly from the upper edge, but other than that, the wound had congealed and was not puffed with bad humors. Pressing it gently, she asked, "Does it pain you?"

"Nay."

Madelyne clicked her tongue absently as she pressed the cut to be certain more blood did not come forth. Then, with a flat, wooden utensil, she spread the warm, sticky mass of herbs over the wound.

Some of the pungent paste slid down his side, over bronzed skin decorated with other, healed, wounds, into the thick, dark hair that grew over his abdomen. She tried to catch it with the spoon, but it matted into the coarse hair and clung there. With a frown,

Madelyne finished covering the wound with the plaster, then lightly pressed a clean cloth over it.

"Do you not move," she told him, turning to get a damp rag. She felt him watch her, silently and steadily, as she brought back the dripping cloth, and was again conscious of the steeliness of his unwavering gray eyes.

"Ere I first saw you, I believed I had died and thought you to be the Madonna," he spoke, breaking the silence.

Madelyne glanced at him, a wry smile hovering at the corners of her lips. "And now, my lord?" She looked down, using the cloth to wipe away at the paste that had gathered in the hair on his stomach. His skin was warm and the ridges of muscle in his middle were smooth and hard under the cloth. When her hand brushed over bare skin, that tingle that had started in her fingertips returned. Her mouth went dry. The texture of another's flesh had never felt so warm, so soft and hard all at once…'twas foreign and stirring and she felt odd.

"Now? Now I wonder why one as fair as you would choose the cloistered life."

She jerked her attention from the sensation of touching his skin, raising her gaze to be caught and held by his. Pulling the cloth from his skin, she looked away and her scattered thoughts returned to order. "The freedom that we enjoy is not to be had anywhere but in an abbey."

"Behind stone walls you find freedom?" The derision showed in his face.

Madelyne turned away to retrieve clean wrappings, and when she came back to his side, she braced herself to look directly into those stone gray eyes. "Freedom from death and warfare, aye—freedom from the life you live all the day. And we have also the freedom to learn, to read and to write, to study…and freedom from the men who would rule our lives." Even as the tart words came from her mouth, she regretted them. She felt suddenly that if she spoke of the liberties allowed monastic women, they'd be taken away all that quickly.

He was silent for a moment, measuring her with his eyes, as her words hung between them. When he spoke at last, his tone was flat and scornful. "The good sisters have taught you well. Have you been here since birth, then? A youngest daughter sent with a dowry to the Church to ensure that her father will find his way to heaven?"

"I've been here long enough to know that I've more freedom behind these walls than not. I would never leave here." Unsurprised that he, a man, should not understand why she chose her life, Madelyne turned back to her work table. "Rest you now."

They would be leaving anon.

Mayhaps he would miss the serenity of the abbey, Gavin thought wryly as he sat on a large rock in the bailey. More like, he would forget it as soon as he rode without its walls.

He must return to the world, to the blackness of his vengeance upon Fantin de Belgrume…to the bleakness that awaited him, and to the anger that had become so much a part of him. No one waited for him without these walls, not even Judith—though his life had become naught but a tool to avenge her pain. Gavin would see her—and, yes, himself—vindicated, and then…aye, then he would happily succumb to the hand of death if he were so called.

A presence eased into his consciousness just as its person moved: gracefully, calmly. Gavin turned and looked up into the face of the nun he still thought of as the Madonna.

"You are well enough to ride," she commented in her low, quiet voice. "I've brought you a last draught to sip ere you leave."

She handed him a silver cup, engraved with likenesses of the roses that grew throughout the abbey. The sleeve of her habit slid back from her hand, exposing a slim, white wrist. A trio of freckles formed a small triangle on the delicate, blue-veined skin and he caught her fingers before she withdrew, turning her hand to look at them.

"Unusual." He looked up into her startled moonstone eyes. With a finger, he traced the three beauty marks, trying to recall why such a marking was familiar. Her flesh was smooth, and softer than anything he'd touched in many a moon. He felt the thrumming of her pulse under his thumb.

Sister Madelyne pulled her hand away with a firmness belied by the decorum of her movements and looked pointedly at his cup. "Do you drink that I may return the cup to the infirmary."

Gavin obliged, suddenly anxious to be on his way—away from the tempting tranquility of the abbey, and away from this woman whose inner peace caused her to be more beautiful than was right. The liquid tasted bitter, with an aftertaste of wood—but 'twas no worse than any other concoction she'd foisted upon him during his convalescence. He took three large gulps, then rested his tongue from the rank taste. The nun watched him, her hands folded at her waist, and he noticed a small rope of beads dangling from one wrist.

He peered at the black beads, then looked questioningly at her. "A necklet for a nun?" He was not quite able to keep the irony from his voice.

She looked down, then slipped the rope over her hand and proffered it to him. "My lord, 'tis only my prayer beads."

He took them, fingering the awkwardly-shaped nodules. They were made of some rough black material, and a faint scent of roses clung to them. When he raised his head to look questioningly at her, he felt a momentary dizziness that evaporated when their gazes met. "How did you come by these beads?" he asked, his tongue suddenly thick. "How are they made?"

"They are formed from rose petals," she told him. "I made them when I first came to the abbey." Her brows drew together. "How do you feel?"

Gavin blinked, feeling the dizziness once again. "I am well," he lied, trying to focus on the beads he still clutched in his hands. "How can one make beads from flowers?"

Her voice came from afar. "The petals are stewed for hours over a low flame." She leaned closer, her presence surrounding him, and he felt rather than saw her fingers brush over his forehead and into his hair. "Do you feel light of head, my lord?"

"Nay," he forced the words from his lips even as shadows dimmed the edges of his vision.

"God be with you," he heard that calm voice say as he slipped into nothingness.

$\mathscr{T}$HREE

FORGIVE ME, *Father, for I have sinned.*

Madelyne clenched her hands together and tried to banish the last memory of Gavin of Mal Verne from her mind. 'Twas her punishment, his haunting of her consciousness, for tricking him as she had.

Her fingers dug into the dry, unpolished wood of the *prie dieu* even as her knees pressed into its uneven hardness. A splinter shot under a fingernail, and Madelyne winced but made no move to dislodge it. The pain would be her penance…the pain and that surprising sense of loss now that he was gone from her life.

"Madelyne."

The sound of her name pulled her from more fervent prayers, and she looked up into the round face of Sister Patricka.

"The Mother wishes to speak with you." Patricka offered a hand to assist Madelyne to her feet. "Maddie, are you unwell?" There was concern in her blue eyes.

"Nay." Madelyne smiled at her friend—one of the only other inhabitants of the abbey who was near her in age. "'Tis only a guilty conscience that ails me."

"Ah." Patricka scrutinized her closely, and Madelyne looked away, fearing that her friend would see that more than a guilty conscience pricked at her. "Mother awaits you in her chamber."

Madelyne tucked her fingers into the cuff of her sleeves, the absence of her prayer beads painfully conspicuous as she hurried along a hallway to Mother Bertilde's office.

The door was closed. Madelyne knocked, then stepped back and waited with an inclined head. When the oaken door swung open, she was surprised to see her own mother, Lady Anne, inviting her within.

"Mama. Mother Bertilde." Madelyne gave a brief curtsey, then a quick embrace to Anne, taking care not to knock their wimples askew.

"You have spent much time in the chapel as of late." Bertilde spoke without preamble from her cushioned armchair. "Do you not tell me that your conscience is still plagued by that which needed to be done."

Madelyne lowered her eyes to look at the stone floor and curled her hands together. A twinge from the splinter still embedded under her nail surprised her, and she rubbed at the tender spot. She saw the glide of her mother's dark robe along the stones as she moved to sit near the abbess. "I regret that 'twas necessary to resort to trickery in dismissing Lord Mal Verne and his men from our abbey."

"'Twas necessary, Madelyne!" Anne spoke. "As long as Fantin lives, we cannot chance that word of our existence reach him. 'Twas necessary to remove those men from the abbey whilst they slept, likening the chance that they'll not find their way to return."

"But to drug them!" Madelyne looked at Bertilde, and then back to her mother. "They could not know who I am. And Mama, you remained hidden during their respite here. 'Tis impossible that they should recognize you! Father, if he lives still, cannot hurt us when there is no one to carry tales to him."

"He lives still," Anne said, her voice still and heavy.

"Madelyne, child," Bertilde said, offering her hand to the younger woman. "You speak aright—'tis most unlikely that Gavin of Mal Verne should be the cause of Fantin de Belgrume learning that you and Anne are here…yet, when those men came within these walls, I sensed that no good would follow. They are gone nearly a fortnight, and that fear has not left me."

When Madelyne took the large, capable hand, she was drawn into the abbess's arms, enfolded in the softness of her linen habit and hint of musky incense. The ease that usually came with such an embrace did not, and all at once, she felt tears sting her eyes. Mayhaps Bertilde spoke correctly and the safe idyll that she and her mother had found would be destroyed. The mother abbess was closer to God than anyone else Madelyne knew…mayhaps He had spoken to her.

"Madelyne…you did not talk of your past whilst you tended to their wounds, did you?" Anne's voice betrayed what must have been a most deep-rooted fear.

Because Madelyne understood her mother's dread, she didn't feel slighted by Anne's question, and she moved to put her arms around her. "Nay, Mama, I did not. You have impressed upon me the necessity of ne'er speaking of how I came to be here. I never shall." She felt the tremor in Anne's shoulders and pulled back to press a kiss to her mother's cheek. "I would never endanger either of us in that way. I will do anything to keep you safe, Mama. Anything." Her serious words became a vow, as if before God, spoken with conviction and certainty.

Anne seemed to gain control of the fear that had gripped her and slid her hands down from Madelyne's shoulders. Her fingers tightened around her daughter's arms with her next words. "Bertilde, and you, and I—and Seton, aye—are the only ones who know the truth of how we came here. If there are no others who know, then we must be safe. We *must* be." She repeated those last words with such fervor that a chill raced down Madelyne's spine.

It must be so, she thought. God must make it so.

"De Belgrume bested *you?*" The incredulity in Henry Plantagenet's voice caused even the scribe who sat in the corner of the royal chambers to look up. "*Mal Verne?*"

"Aye." Gavin's mouth firmed in annoyance at the reminder of his own incompetence even as the king drew his red-gold eyebrows together. The taste of defeat sat heavily upon him, as well as the ferocity to right that wrong. "I do not know how he learned of our planned assault at Mancassel, my lord, but 'twas obvious that he did, for we were set upon in a dense forest several leagues from there. No one could have known we would be there at that time. I begin to wonder if I have a spy in my midst, or whether de Belgrume is simply the most fortunate man alive. If I had not sent half my men on ahead to Mancassel that morn, we would easily have held our own, and I might now be presenting him to your Majesty.

"But, in the end," Gavin continued, "'tis de Belgrume who has suffered the greater loss—for I still live, though he surely believes I am dead."

"Aye, you have the right of it. His sword has long itched for you, and yet you continue to deny him that satisfaction. But still he makes war upon you!" Henry slammed his jewel-encrusted goblet on a nearby table as he strode past it. "'Tis the reason I gave *you* the task—he must be contained and he has continued to engaged you for years. It's only you who can put an end to this, Mal Verne. And I fear it is because he's never forgiven you for being Nicola's husband. Nevertheless, bring him to our custody, or when next you meet him in battle, finish the bloody deed!" The king turned, seemingly ignoring the fact that he'd just ordered one of his vassals to murder another one. He paced back toward Gavin, who stood next to a small table laden with bread, cheese, and wine.

"You know I should like naught better than to bring de Belgrume to his knees. He's taken much from me, and all in the name of his unholy work."

"'Tis unfortunate that the Church doesn't consider the study of alchemy blasphemous," Henry grumbled, snatching up a piece of soft white goat's cheese. "If it did, then at the very least we could ex-communicate de Belgrume for it…and at the best, he could be tried for treason and executed." His brows furrowed as he brandished the cheese. "Then I would be rid of him."

"Even the Pope sees no harm in one seeking the Holy Grail through alchemy…yet de Belgrume's obsession has completely be-taken his mind. His obsession has tipped him into madness." This was a familiar conversation, one they'd had many times over in shared frustration.

"When he first came to our court, he didn't strike me as one so obsessed," the king mused.

"Nay, 'tis true. When he first became known to me, and to Nicola"—Gavin did not pause at his wife's name, and 'twas a miracle it did not stick in his throat—"I bethought the man to be only an empty-headed charmer with a well-hidden temper. An odd man, but a harmless one. Yet, in these last six years, he's come to carry an eerie light in his eyes more oft than not." Gavin helped himself to a piece of pale yellow cheese. "I believe that the secrets of the Holy Grail continue to elude him, just as my own death has…and it's those failures which have ushered him into madness."

"Aye…de Belgrume laid his claim against you when he tempted Nicola from your side, long before this lunacy became madness. And then again there is that matter of your cousin's betrothed—Geoffrey? Geoffrey of Lancourt, was it?"

"Gregory, my liege. His name was Gregory, and, aye, he was betrothed to my cousin Judith. Another innocent lost because of de Belgrume. Aye…'tis as if he and I were fated to oppose the other in all ways." Gavin swallowed the mellow cheddar. "But he'll not best me again. I believe I've found a way to stop him." He slipped his hand into the leather pouch that hung at from his tunic.

Henry barely paused in his great, vigorous strides that brought him past Gavin once again. "And how is that?"

Gavin fingered the rough, unevenness of the beads in his pouch. "I mislike to speak of it yet, my lord. Until…until I've put all plans into place."

"I do not rightly care," Henry fumed, "as long as that man is brought under control, made to pay his taxes, and swear his fealty to me—I do not care how you do it!"

As always, it came down to the funds in Henry Plantagenet's mind. Despite the fact that there were other dangers in having a madman as one of his vassals. Gavin said naught but, "Aye, my lord. I shall." He swallowed the last of the wine in his cup. "By your leave, your majesty, I'll excuse myself to see to those arrangements."

"Be off." Henry waved a hand and returned to his pacing. "Keep us informed of your progress."

"Aye, my lord. Thank you, your majesty."

Gavin took his leave of Henry, relieved that the private meeting was over.

It had been no easy task to admit his resounding defeat to the king, but now he would redouble his efforts to stop Fantin de Belgrume. He'd declined to describe his stay at the abbey, and the hasty, manipulative dismissal those nuns had given him and his men—for that, too, stuck in his craw that they should be treated with such indignity.

Fortunately, the night in which he, Thomas, and the others had awakened in a glen with their mounts tethered nearby had been dry and warm—else they may have taken ill yet again. Gavin knew they had been drugged, and, indeed, knew the perpetrator of the deed. The serene Madonna-nun, who had so innocently given him the goblet from which to drink, had stayed at his side, watching him with luminous gray eyes while her potion did its work. Though he'd recognized a certain steeliness under her calm demeanor, he'd never thought to be the recipient of such callousness from his own healer.

Afterward, he may have thought all of it no more than hallucination, had he not found her prayer beads tucked into his pouch. An' it hadn't been until some days later ere he remembered the markings on her wrist and realized what that might mean.

He would seek out Judith, who served in the queen's court, to be certain his suspicions were accurate.

As always when he meant to speak with his cousin and childhood playmate, Gavin's heart weighed heavier. He relived again those moments when Judith realized what hurt he'd caused her. Those blue eyes had pooled with angry, accusing tears, and her long fingers had clenched into her own arms, drawing prickles of blood. She had bid him remove himself from her sight.

Ere that time they'd spoken but briefly, and though the accusation was no longer in her expression, he could see sorrow and pain still mirrored there. He grieved with her, but he could do naught about putting the anguish there except to have vengeance upon Fantin de Belgrume in her name as well as his own.

When Gavin, Lord of Mal Verne, was announced in the queen's court, the gossip and giggles halted abruptly and the ladies turned to watch in fascination as the tall, rugged man strode into the chambers. He went directly to Eleanor, kneeling to kiss her ring, and when a slight smile cracked his hard face at something she murmured to him, it was well-noted.

Judith, who sat in a nearby corner embroidering on a wedding gown for one of the ladies, stood as he rose from posturing over the queen's hand. She walked quickly to him, hoping to impress upon him her pleasure at his visit. Since she was very young, they'd been friends—although Gavin was nearly seven years older than she. He'd fostered under her father's care, and Gavin had been the elder brother she'd never had. This rift between them had caused her nearly as much grief as Gregory's death.

"Gavin!" She smiled and stretched out her hands to him, ignoring the interested looks cast from the other ladies.

Mal Verne had a reputation at court that caused a combination of attraction and trepidation among the ladies—they either discussed ways in which to breach that iron-like armor in order to captivate his heart, or 'twas declared that he had no heart to conquer. He turned, and though she had warmth and welcome radiating from her body, she saw that hesitation and apprehension still swam in his eyes.

"Lady Judith," he said formally, lightly taking her fingertips in his large, scarred hands. "You look well, as always. How do you fare?"

Disappointment swelled through her. He looked haggard and hard, his face set as if in stone, his gray eyes cool and flat as marble. 'Twas as if he allowed any emotion to come to bear, he would crumble.

Judith squeezed his hands, trying as always, to show that she'd forgiven him for that day years before…and, as always, he did not seem to comprehend, remaining remote and cool. "I am well, of course—how could I not be, here with the queen?"

She slipped a hand through the crook of his elbow, drawing him away from the curious ears and eyes of the ladies-in-waiting. "But you…Gavin, have you been ill?" She sat on the cushioned bench in a small alcove and looked up at his towering figure.

After a moment of hesitation, he lowered himself to sit next to her. "Naught but a small slice in my side from de Belgrume's sword," he said dismissively. "'Twas tended by a nun in a nearby abbey."

"You look weary." She tried again to bridge the span betwixt them.

"I traveled from York, and I have not rested ere I left. 'Tis no more than that." He formed his lips into a half-hearted smile. "Judith, I came only to ask of you some information—I do not wish to keep you from your duties, or your friends."

She swallowed and looked away. If only he'd let his guard relax, and put aside his feelings of guilt, he would see that she was pleased at his visit instead of being overset by it. Since Papa's death, Gavin was her only living relative, her only family…and he'd refused to acknowledge it since Gregory's death for fear of shaming her. "I would be most pleased to help you if I am able, cousin."

"You were fostered for a short time with de Belgrume's daughter, were you not?"

"Aye, Gavin, I know that I have spoken of that year in Kent on occasion. I was only twelve summers, and she no more than ten. She was there for only five moons before he sent for her to return to Tricourten. She did not wish to go." Judith clenched her fingers as she recalled the deathly whitening of her friend's face at the message. Though Madelyne spoke little of her father, 'twas obvious she disliked—even feared—him. "'Twas only some moons later that I learned she and her mother had drowned in the river near Tricourten."

"Drowned. Aye, that was the story I recall hearing as well." Something in Gavin's eyes gave Judith pause, and she looked at him more closely.

"What is it?"

"Did you not speak to me of an odd marking on her arm? I recall your musings once that the little girl had some unusual spots near her wrist."

Judith nodded. "Aye. Three moles near her wrist, just here." She demonstrated on her own flesh. "When she first came to Kent Castle, one of the maidservants made mention of it and spread the talk that mayhaps she was a witch, with such markings. But that notion was soon dispelled, for Madelyne was such a kind and sweet girl that none could think ill of her."

It seemed that a glint of grim humor flashed over Gavin's face at that, but 'twas gone so quickly that Judith was sure she had imagined it. He spoke again. "And how exactly were those markings placed?"

She showed him: one mole atop two that were aligned, creating the shape of a small, tight triangle. There was such satisfaction in his face that she suddenly realized what he was about. "You do not mean that she lives?"

His brows drew together in a sudden show of ferocity such that Judith was taken aback. "Aye, the wench does live. And it shall be through her that I'll at last get to Fantin."

"You'd not hurt her!" Judith forgot herself and the fragility of the tenuous bond between them and clutched at his powerful arm. Insult flashed over his face at her words, and she berated herself for causing it. But she'd not see another woman, especially Madelyne de Belgrume (if 'twas truly her of whom he spoke) hurt.

"Nay, Judith, I'd not hurt her." His voice was gruff as he closed his fingers over her hand to remove it from his arm. "But she will be a means to bring Fantin to heel."

The rough stones ground into his aching knees, but Fantin de Belgrume delighted in the discomfort. He would bear any such penance or pain whilst he prayed—for any distress he suffered now would be well repaid when his work was completed. Indeed, Fantin preferred to pray among the evidence of this work, there on the bare floor, within the sight and smell and feel of it, rather than in the chapel.

He twined his fingers together in supplication, finishing the hour of prayer that was as much a part of his work in the laboratory as the formulas and tonics and metallic brews were. Fantin began and ended every session in his laboratory in concert with God, knowing that without His guidance, he would never find the formula he sought…which had been promised him.

'Twas fitting, that he should be the one to receive the secret once given to the Magdalen—the fascinating, sinful woman who appeared as three different ladies in the Gospels: Mary of Magdala, Mary, the sister of Lazarus, and the woman who anointed Christ's feet with her tears and wiped them dry with her hair.

She was a woman who atoned for her sins—a wealthy woman, just as Fantin himself was wealthy. A wealthy woman who sinned through sexual pleasure…just as Fantin did. The woman from whom Christ had expelled seven demons.

Legend had it that this woman's bones—the bones of the Whore Saint, as Fantin preferred to think of her—were interred near Vézelay, in France. Coincidentally, it was the village near where his mother hailed, and was thus cause for her devotion to the Magdalen. Legend foretold that the blood of the woman saint ran in Fantin's own veins—and he knew that was the reason God had chosen him.

Pulling to his feet, relishing the pain that shot down his left leg and knowing that soon it would never bother him again, Fantin drew in a deep breath of pleasure and joy. The stale, earthy smell of the below-stairs chamber tinged his nostrils, and he inhaled deeply, drawing its energy into his being.

'Twas not a pleasant smell, that of brewing leaves, burning flesh and molten metal, he allowed—in fact, it was enough to curdle one's belly—but God had put it on His earth apurpose. Every aspect of His creation, every being, every creature served a role in God's world…and Fantin himself served the greatest of these.

He smiled, thinking on that as he returned to the table where the last task he'd been involved in—crushing the smooth, silky bark of a birch tree with flakes of silver and bronze metals—remained half-completed.

For years, he'd sought the secret of the Grail: perfect combination of chemistry that would create the substance whose mere touch would give him Immortality. It would change any metals to gold.

It would create for Fantin a life of power under which to serve God.

He sought and studied and prayed to determine the exact amounts of each element that would be required to complete the ancient process. Metals, wood, earth, water…fire…all or some of these elements would someday cohese, forming that miracle which Fantin sought—that miracle which had been promised him by his bloodline: the miracle of the Holy Grail and what some called the Philosopher's Stone.

Next to the bowl with curling birch bark and metal flakes, the corpse of an adder oozed blood into another bowl—a metal one, to hold the rich, wine-like liquid without absorbing its essence. Another element added to the mix…mayhap, it would be the answer this time.

The adder, Fantin reflected wisely, was the symbol of Eve's temptation, and a fitting conduit in his work bent on purification and transfiguration.

His laboratory, dug beneath the stone floor of Tricourten's Great Hall, had been Fantin's refuge and salvation since he realized he was God's chosen, and most especially since the loss of his beloved wife and daughter. Three long tables lined the chamber, which had more generous lighting than the hall above, due to fifty pitch torches lit by Tavis every morn and kept burning until late in the night.

Neat stacks of bowls—of every type of wood, rock, and metal—heaped at the end of each table. Goblets, skins, boxes, knives, pincers, spoons…all rested in the spot allotted to each of them, always arranged in a manner that would be most pleasing to God. Jars and pots of calendula, rosemary, woad leaves, belladonna, bergamot essence, dog's grass, ragwort, and hundreds of other useful plants sat on shelves against the large stone wall near the metal chains and restraints. He had taken care that the shelves remained well out of reach of the unfortunates who might make use of those chains—he did not wish to have his herbalry dashed to the floor by a disturbed or frightened guest.

Fantin used a stick to prod the small fire burning in a large metal cauldron set into the wooden table. The bones of the hare he'd skinned earlier had turned to ash among the sticks from an apple tree, and the charred wood glowed a wicked orange on the underbelly of the pot.

"My lord."

Fantin looked over at the berobed priest, who had just emerged from the tiny chapel built into the corner of his laboratory. His breathing quickened and sweat dampened his palms. He moved from the table toward the monk. "Father, have you word?"

Father Rufus, slender and thin-fingered, bore a sober look upon his narrow face. Weariness lined his cheeks, and the pasty whiteness of his skin bespoke of his many fortnights below-ground. "I've prayed long and hard and have at last received the answer which you seek."

Fantin gripped the stick, his fingernails digging into his callused palm, his breathing quick and shallow. "Aye, Father, speak! What is it that I must do to bring God's blessing upon me and revive the Philosopher's Stone?"

"You must continue with your work," Rufus told him. "God will not make clear the way until you have shown you are indeed fit for the deed. You must practice your work, you must continue to rid the world of its evils and temptations. You must study the writings of the ancients and you must continue to seek purification and transfiguration."

The dry wood cracked in Fantin's hand. "Is there naught more you can tell me, Father? I have been working for nearly twelve summers. Twelve summers, I have known I was the one chosen…and yet, I have not attained that promise. When shall I complete my life's work to be pure and holy and one with God?"

"Twelve summers, my lord, is naught but a drop in the sea for our God," the priest admonished him.

Fantin struggled with his rising impatience. He swiped the long sleeve of his robe over the perspiration that dampened his forehead, then folded his hands, once more, inside the sleeves of his robe. "Nine priests I have had, and not a one of you can interpret God's message."

"My lord," the priest replied in a voice raspy with disuse, "do you not fret. There is more. Prithee, you must show some patience. All good rewards from Above will come only to those who show patience and servitude and humility. Our God will send you a sign. A sign to show you the way. 'Twill appear very soon, mayhap this se'ennight. It is your duty to recognize the message, and follow the direction thus and the difficulty of your journey shall ease."

He stared directly into Fantin's eyes, and Fantin felt himself beginning to calm, to find clarity in the vision before him. The red light that had colored his world receded. Aye, the father had the right of it. He must watch for the sign. He must pray long and hard. He must continue the work of purification, the task he had been set to years before.

"Aye, Father…you have great wisdom," Fantin responded in his warm, smooth voice. He added a smile that, although it moved his face, did not reach completely within. He must remain patient, yet he felt his frustration…his need…growing stronger each day. The red light edging the corners of his vision threatened more oft than not as of late.

If only he need not rely on the priest and could pass his own days with prayer, mayhap he would understand sooner, mayhap he might more easily learn what he sought. Yet Fantin did not have the time to spend in prayer that must be spent, for he must manage his lands, and work his formulas, and conduct those other tasks that befell him as a mere mortal man.

The image of Gavin of Mal Verne slipped into his memory, suddenly, disturbing the calmness he'd managed to attain. Aye, at the least that task was complete. At any moment, he expected word that

Mal Verne had indeed met his demise—left wounded and far from help, where Fantin had last seen him.

It might not have been a direct order from God to send Mal Verne to hell, but Fantin knew it was what he must do. Mal Verne sought to disrupt his own work. He had taken Gregory from him, and Nicola—and if Fantin did not remove the man from this world, Mal Verne would continue to seek his own revenge upon Fantin. God helped only those who helped themselves.

Indeed, and 'twas surely a test of his mettle that Fantin had failed so many times during this journey. But the end was in sight, according to Rufus.

Fantin praised his God for sending him the skinny priest only three months earlier—for Rufus, more than any other, understood his task and his purpose, and acted as a holy conduit between Fantin and the Lord of All.

And when he completed his tasks as set by God, Fantin knew he would be graced by the formula for the Philosopher's Stone.

Fantin's hands no longer shook. He and the priest both would watch for the promised sign, and he would act accordingly. And God would find him worthy.

Four

SHE WAS in the garden when they came for her.

After two fortnights spent trying to banish him from her memory, Madelyne sensed his presence even before she heard the clink of sword against his mail chausses.

A shadow, long and heavy, fell across her lap where she was forming rose beads. The black mush of stewed rose petals covered her hands and arms and spotted an old gown. The air was heavy with the scent of the flowers, nearly as smothering as the weight that settled over her when she realized he'd come.

And yet, at the same time, a rush of something else flooded her when she looked up into his grave face. 'Twas almost welcome, seeing him again, feeling the command of his full strength as she had not when he was ill.

"My lord."

"Lady Madelyne. You do not seem surprised to see me."

That he used her title did not surprise her. Verily he'd discovered her identity and that was the reason he'd come. For a brief moment, panic surged through her, but she beat it back and wrapped her own strength about her. God would be with her, and…God help her, but she did not believe Lord Mal Verne would hurt her.

"Nay, I am not. What do you wish from me?"

He stood, looking down at her, his shadow casting darkness over her work. "What do you do there?"

Madelyne held up two small wooden paddles, grateful for a moment's reprieve before he should respond, and replied, "The rose petals have been cooked for days. Now, I take them betwixt these spoons and roll them into beads. See there." She pointed to a length of linen spread in the sun, dotted with perfect, round beads.

To her surprise, he reached into a leather pouch that hung from his tunic and pulled out the prayer beads she'd left with him before. "You've become more skilled in these last years."

"Aye."

She was surprised again when he hunkered down to sit next to her on the log bench. Now, his face was nearly on level with hers, and his nearness even more overpowering. Strength, warmth, intensity vibrated from his person—yet his eyes and his countenance remained cold and bleak. Madelyne had the sudden urge, so odd at this moment when he threatened her peace and well-being, to touch his face, to learn whether it was as unyielding as it appeared. She curled her fingers into themselves and willed her foolishness not to betray her.

"Why did you trick me? Why did you not allow us to leave with some dignity?"

She swallowed. 'Twas no surprise that a man of his power should be angered at such deceit. Using one of the flat spoons, she scooped up a small portion of the black stew and began to roll it into the shape of a ball as she chose her words to respond.

Gavin watched how her fine hands manipulated the paddles, noticing again the three freckles that decorated one narrow wrist. Her head was bent, and the edge of its veil obstructed much of the expression on her face, though he could see the length of long, thick lashes as she blinked. She had shown no surprise at his presence, nor mistrust, he thought. How could that be?

"We sought only to protect ourselves."

Her words, when they came, were as even and calm as the rhythm of her breathing. She looked at him, and he saw nothing but the gray depths of her eyes, clear and without deceit, without fear. For a fleeting moment, he wondered when last a woman had looked upon him without fear…and with such guilelessness. She had naught to hide, it seemed…but he knew that could not be so.

"Forgive us for acting in such a manner," she continued, "but, my lord, we did what we thought best."

"You removed us from the abbey so that we couldn't find our way here again, yet you aren't disturbed at my presence."

She blinked, and he could see the faintest movement of her lips as they tightened in the first indication of uneasiness. "'Tis true, I wish that you hadn't found your way back to the abbey…but now you are here, and there is naught I can do. Your presence portends little good for me, but I prithee…do you not hurt my sisters."

"I mean harm to none here at Lock Rose Abbey," Gavin replied. "I merely come in the king's name."

"The king? What has he to do with those of us here?" Confusion passed over her face, and she allowed the black-stained paddles to drop into the stew pot.

"His royal majesty, King Henry, demands the presence of Madelyne de Belgrume at his court." His words were more formal than necessary, and he spoke them distinctly and with a hint of threat to be certain she understood the gravity of the situation. "I have been appointed to bring you to him."

She remained silent, and Gavin waited impatiently for her outraged response. When she said nothing, he prodded her. "You do not deny that you are Madelyne de Belgrume, daughter of Fantin de Belgrume, Lord of Tricourten?"

"Nay." The breath she expelled was silent, but of such force that he felt its warmth on his face.

"Then you know you must come with me."

"Aye."

Gavin was caught by the clear steadiness of her eyes, and then they were shuttered as she lowered her lids. She took away the cloth that had rested on her lap, protecting her gown, and set it on the ground. There seemed to be little more to say.

Made a bit uncertain by the ease of her acquiescence, Gavin rose to his feet and extended a hand to assist her to hers.

Madelyne reached for it, then stopped, and, dropping her hand back to her side, pulled to her own feet. "I do not wish to stain you," she explained, spreading her blackened hands. "I will be thus for many days before it fades. Now, I must speak with Mother Bertilde. She does know that you have arrived?"

Gavin nodded, again struck by her clear practicality in what must be a moment of upheaval. "Aye. However, we must leave before matins, so do you not delay. I'll not be tricked again, and I'll not be held longer than need be." The annoyance he'd felt at being deceived by a bunch of women surged within him, and he looked at her sharply. "No tricks, Madelyne."

"Nay, my lord," she responded. "It is past the time of tricks."

Madelyne closed the door to her cell and leaned her full weight against it, covering her mouth with two shaking hands. She knew naught could keep the reality of Gavin of Mal Verne at bay, but she hadn't the strength to hold herself upright any longer.

Dear God, she had known…had *known* he would come…had known deep in the most secret part of herself that her peace would be destroyed by this man. And, God's Truth, she had prayed for it— prayed to see him again, prayed that he would find his way back to the abbey.

What had she done?

She choked on a sob and swallowed hard, hearing the grating sound of her dry throat in the dense silence. All in the abbey knew of his arrival, and knew the purpose of it. A hush of anxiety had fallen like a fog that smothered those within its walls.

Now, she must collect all of her strength and will and protect them all—most especially protect her mother. She must go willingly with him, she must find a way to keep him from learning of Anne's existence. The memory haunted her: of those days at Tricourten, of her mother's face, lined with worry and pain, with dark circles curving under her eyes and purple marks on her face and arms, and scars on her back.

Madelyne could never allow Anne to go back to Fantin, to that life.

A soft knocking at the door drew Madelyne's scattered, panicked thoughts under control and she thrust herself away from it. Turning to gather her few belongings, desperate to keep her fears hidden, she called, "Enter."

The door opened, but she did not turn from her trunk.

"Madelyne!"

To her surprise, it was Sister Patricka—not Mal Verne—who came into the small room. Before Madelyne could react, the other woman flew toward her, gathering her into her arms in a fierce embrace. "The Mother has told me you are to go with the men. I am going with you."

Madelyne pulled away to look into her friend's round, cherubic face. No fear or reluctance showed there, only earnestness and mayhaps a bit of apprehension. "You are to go with me?"

"Aye. There is no reason that I should stay here any longer—and I could not let you go alone. I have long realized I cannot take the final step and say my last vows. 'Tis not God's will. So I shall go as your tiring woman. If you'll have me."

Relief flooded through Madelyne, and she hugged her again, huddling her face into Patricka's shoulder. "Aye, Tricky, I would have you—if you are certain you wish to make that sacrifice. Only if you are certain."

Patricka nodded with such vigor that her wimple slipped to one side. "Aye, and an honor it would be."

Madelyne gripped her soft fingers, realizing that Patricka did not know how she and Anne had come to Lock Rose Abbey. "I cannot promise what will happen…there are many things you do not know, and that I cannot tell you at this time. But I vow that I'll keep you from harm ere I can."

"I have no fear of that, Maddie. The Mother did warn me that all was not as it seems. I place myself in your hands—and in God's. 'Tis my belief that I can do you more good at your side than here, clutching prayer beads in the chapel."

Madelyne gave a weak laugh. Tricky had a way of speaking that reduced complicated situations to such simple ones. "Thank you, my friend. Now, we must gather our things, for Lord Mal Verne does not intend to be kept waiting."

When she had collected those few items she intended to take with her, Madelyne gave one last sweep of the small room with her gaze. Would she ever see this cell again, kneel at the worn *prie dieu*, sleep on the feather-stuffed bed?

Squaring her shoulders, she pulled the bag made of loose cloth that held her few personal belongings. She adjusted her veil and smoothed her skirt, uncertain how she looked—for there was no mirror in her cell—and left the room for the last time.

Outside, in the bailey, the rest of the sisters had gathered to bid her farewell. Lord Mal Verne and his men-at-arms stood a discreet distance away, and 'though he watched her steadily, he did not speak as she and Patricka embraced their friends.

Only Anne did not appear, and for this, Madelyne was grateful. She had said a brief farewell to her mother after speaking with Bertilde, and that leave-taking had been fraught with tears and sobs. They could not risk the chance that Anne would be seen or recognized by the men.

Thus, the last arms to hold her, and the last face to be kissed, was that of Mother Bertilde. She pulled Madelyne tightly to her and whispered, "God be with you, my child. Our prayers follow you wherever you go. May you have the strength and peace to accept that which is your future."

Madelyne's face was wet with tears when at last she began to walk across the bailey to join Mal Verne and his men. Tricky followed, leaving a sea of red-eyed women behind.

She approached Mal Verne, who continued to watch with stony eyes, and whose gaze flickered to Patricka as they walked closer. "I am ready to accompany you now, my lord. This is Patricka, my maid, who will accompany me."

A twinge of satisfaction settled over her when she saw the disconcertion in his eyes. "Your maid? Nuns do not have maids."

"Patricka is my maid, and she does accompany me whither I go. I trust that you will be able to accommodate one extra female."

His mouth tightened ever so slightly—just enough for her to see that she had irked him with her cool response—and he turned abruptly, calling to one of his men. "Clem, the maid will ride with you." He started toward the small herd of mounts gathered near the stable.

Madelyne took that as a silent command to follow him, and she gathered up the hem of her gown to do so. Some of the men were mounted, and others stood in a small cluster, holding the reins of whuffling, stamping destriers.

At the sight of the huge warhorses, Madelyne's bravery deserted her.

The mounts stood many hands taller than she, with large heads and round eyes and huge, snorting noses. The hooves that fidgeted in the dirt or stamped in impatience were bigger than her face, and looked powerful enough to flatten a heavy oaken door with one thrust. Madelyne froze, unable to make herself move closer to the fierce creatures.

Mal Verne turned when he reached one of the larger, more spirited stallions, and frowned when he saw her standing aback. "Come, my lady," he bid her impatiently as he struggled to calm the vigorous horse. "You ride with me."

Madelyne's throat dried, and she didn't know if 'twas more from fear of getting close enough to the ferocious creature to sit upon it, or that she would be in such proximity to Mal Verne. It took every ounce of will to force to take a step forward, and then another, before the destrier reared slightly. His hooves slammed into the ground with a hollow sound, and Madelyne jerked backward, hand clutching at her throat.

"What ails you, lady?" Annoyance strained Mal Verne's voice as he gave off the reins to one of his companions and started toward her.

"I…do not ride, my lord," she managed to say steadily as he approached her.

"I did not think that you did," he said dismissively, continuing to look at her as if she were daft.

Madelyne felt the necessity to explain further. "I…do not like horses," she managed to say just before he wrapped one powerful arm around her waist, lifting her easily into the air. A faint shriek emitted from her mouth, surprising her before she pulled herself under control. "There is no need—"

Her words were stopped as he set her none-too-gently on the back of the dancing stallion. Before she could gather her bearings, she felt him leap into the saddle behind her. Suddenly, a long, firm thigh slid along her legs, which rested over one side of the saddle, and two hard arms enclosed her on either side. Madelyne fought to control a whimper of nervousness as the horse responded to the command of Mal Verne's legs, nearly leaping forward in its impatience to be off.

As the destrier stepped eagerly into a fast trot, Madelyne was jostled backward by the momentum, back against the hard wall of man. Her breath caught in her throat as she became aware that she was completely enclosed by Gavin of Mal Verne, completely in his arms and completely in his power…and they rode from the gates of Lock Rose Abbey.

Five

THE ABBEY was hours behind them and the sun dropping in the west before Gavin spoke directly to Madelyne. She seemed to have overcome, or at least concealed, her mislike and fear of riding.

When he leaned forward to speak into her ear, she straightened as if startled. "Tell me, Lady Madelyne, how did you come to the abbey, and leave your father to believe you and your mother drowned?"

She was quiet for a moment, in a silence he had come to expect from her—as if she took the time to carefully measure her words in response to certain questions. Her hands, stained from the boiled rose petals, clutched the pommel in front of her, and the corner of her veil flapped in his face as they jounced along at a brisk trot.

"I do not know how that particular story came about—I was only ten summers, and there was much my mother did not tell me. 'Tis likely the man-at-arms who helped us to escape created the tale of our drowning."

"Escape?"

"Aye, 'twas an escape from my father." He felt her move against him as she drew in a deep breath. "My father would fly into obscene rages when he prayed, and when he did, he oft beat and whipped my mother. One can understand why she would seek to escape him and that life…and of course, she would not leave me behind."

Gavin fought back a resurgence of loathing for Fantin de Belgrume as he raked a hand through his shaggy, overlong hair. Any man who would hit a woman was a coward, though verily there were many who did. There was no law against a man beating his wife—she was his property and his to do with as he wished—but Gavin could not stomach the thought of raising a hand to a weaker being.

Regardless, de Belgrume must have struck out at his wife once too often. Yet, 'twas not a common thing, women leaving their husbands—for there were few places for a gentlelady to go. And if a woman did leave her husband, she could be rightfully returned to him.

And, Gavin reminded himself ruefully, what was seen through the eyes of a ten-year-old girl could be misconstrued and misunderstood. If there was a man-at-arms who dared to assist in their escape, likely that man had a deeper, more intimate involvement with the lady of Tricourten than he should.

Gavin's mouth twisted and his chin jutted forward in remembrance of how it felt to be a husband who had been betrayed. 'Twas not any mean feat to comprehend how a man could be driven to such rage as to hit his wife.

But how did they come to the abbey, and what of the mother?

He leaned forward again in order to speak over the sound of thumping hooves and the ebullient conversations of his men. Her veil slapped into his face again, and he had the urge to yank it from her head so that his vision would not be obscured…and so that he could see the color of her hair.

Gavin sat back, upright, without asking his question. The color of her *hair*? From where had that thought come?

Then, as if that wayward notion suddenly opened a gate of awareness, he became conscious that her round bottom was nestled between the juncture of his legs…and that her breasts rose and fell with the rhythm of her breathing just above where his arms enclosed her slim body…and that if he were to move his leg, it would brush against her thighs.

Jesù, the woman was a nun! He scowled, annoyed with his wandering thoughts, and spoke to Lady Madelyne—Sister Madelyne, he'd best remember—this time without leaning forward. "And your mother? What befell her?"

"Mama died from a fever two autumns after we arrived at the abbey." He felt the slightest shift in her, a tensing, almost imperceptible.

"Where do we travel?" Madelyne's question, her first words to him that were unprompted, was so unexpected that he answered without thinking about why she changed the subject.

"We are a day's journey from my holdings at Mal Verne. Anight we shall sleep at a monastery near York." Though he had used the king's name to impress upon Madelyne the importance of her compliance, Gavin did not plan to make haste to Henry's side. In fact, the king had planned to leave Westminster in the week since Gavin himself took his leave. Knowing that the royal party traveled quickly and often unexpectedly, Gavin knew 'twas more efficient to send word to Henry and await his instructions, rather than attempt to track him down. As well, he'd not been to Mal Verne for nearly five moons, and 'twas nigh time he stayed there for a fortnight or more to see how his steward fared.

"Will we arrive anon? I fear my maid is becoming weary." Madelyne pointed with a black-stained hand to the pair on the destrier that rode just in front of them.

Gavin looked and saw that the young woman called Patricka had slumped to one side in Clem's arms, and that he looked as uncomfortable as she did. Urging Rule forward with his knees, he approached them and called to his man. "Do you wish to put her with someone else for a spell?" He looked closer at the young woman, whose face was upturned and her neck propped on Clem's meaty arm.

Patricka's round, cheery face was slackened in sleep, and her apple cheeks jounced slightly with each pace of the stallion. Her mouth, pursed into a berry-like swell of pink, parted just enough for a low snore to come forth, and her tip-tilted nose flared with each audible breath.

"Nay, my lord. There is no need to awaken the maid." Clem responded with a note of indignance, as if his vanity had been bruised by Gavin's suggestion that he could not manage the young woman.

"As you wish." Gavin raised an eyebrow, but forbore to comment further. "The monastery is no more than a half league ahead, and we will soon find our beds."

Madelyne forced her stiff legs to move. She could not recall ever being in such pain as she was, having spent much of the day in a saddle. Her back hurt from the effort of remaining sword-straight so that she would not brush up against Lord Mal Verne, and her arms ached from clutching the pommel.

She was grateful, however, that he'd chosen a monastery for their place to rest, as she was in deep need of a chapel, and some moments of peace.

'Twas after their meal—an unexciting affair, much plainer than that which had been served at Lock Rose Abbey—and after seeing that Tricky had slumped off to sleep in the women's quarters, that Madelyne had slipped from the room to find the chapel. One of the elder monks had pointed it out to her earlier, and now she crept like a wraith to its sanctuary.

Candles burned, filling the air with the smell of tallow and smoke, casting a warm yellow glow over the small room. Sinking to her knees on the hard stone floor—preferable than the wooden kneelers for keeping herself awake at this late time—Madelyne sought to find the words of prayer.

But, for the first time in her life, she could not find them.

Instead, she knelt, there in the presence of God, cloaked in her certainty that He heard and knew her random thoughts…and became lost in a whirlwind of images and reflections.

Had it only been this morn that she'd risen, as if it were any other day? Here, now, she found herself in the company of a strange man—one who stirred her with his strength and awed her with his control and authority—and who escorted her to the presence of the king.

She wondered how Anne fared, and if she worried her daughter would betray her presence. A tear stung her eye as she remembered the farewells they'd shared. Anne had wanted to go with her, but Madelyne, knowing how fragile her parent was, and that she was still haunted by the nightmares of her husband's abuse, had insisted that she remain at the abbey. Yet Madelyne would not have prevailed if Mother Bertilde hadn't intervened and insisted that Anne remain. Madelyne was relieved, for she knew her mother's constitution was not the heartiest…and she did not wish to worry about her mother's condition whilst she managed whatever it was that awaited her at the king's court.

What did it mean that she was called to the side of the king? Verily, he could not mean to send her back to her father. A sudden fear squeezed her middle. Why would he not? What other reason would there be that he ordered her to attend him? Nausea roiled in her stomach.

Dear God, I prithee, do You not send me back to my father. My Father in Heaven…Blessed Virgin…have mercy on me! Suddenly, the words came with fervor, and Madelyne opened her eyes to look up at the wooden crucifix and prayed.

Her thoughts shifted then again. And this man…this man who took her, who had somehow identified her…. Heavenly Father, protect me from him. *I will make my promise to You, speak my final vows with no further delay if You see fit to return me to the Abbey.*

Even as she prayed these platitudes, Madelyne knew she had to put aside the strange, bubbling feelings that Gavin of Mal Verne evoked in her. He could mean naught to her.

In sooth, she had no desire to feel for him, to live in his world. The Abbey allowed her the freedom to learn and to exist almost as a man, though cloistered. And now, this man threatened the path that she had followed for a decade, merely by appearing in her life with his power and command. She'd begun already to forget the admonishments her mother had impressed upon her, the warnings of the controlling, all-powerful hold a man had on a woman. Fascination and a deep, stirring need to know him had intervened quietly and subtly, and now Madelyne feared she would be lost.

Her hand shook as she remembered the fluttering in her belly as she sat encased in his arms, the horse jolting her against him with perfect rhythm until she had forced herself to sit uncomfortably upright. The smell of leather and the unfamiliar scent of maleness, of sweat and horse and clean chain mail, still lingered in her memory, as did the image of his strong, tanned hands holding the reins in front of her.

Madelyne took a deep, shuddering breath. She could not allow herself to feel this way. Any emotion toward this man was naught but her own naiveté, and was bound to be naught but a weak battering ram slamming against the stone wall of an arrogant, unfeeling man.

"What sin could you have committed this day that should bring you here such a late hour?"

Madelyne whipped her head around as her heart leapt into her throat. 'Twas as if her thoughts had conjured up the man, and now he stood just in the doorway of the chapel. Her limbs jittering from the startle, and her stomach roiling with guilt at being caught thinking of him, she pulled herself to her feet with slow, deliberate movements.

"Sin?" she asked calmly, tucking her hands into the sleeves of her gown to hide their trembling. "Nay, 'twas not a sin about which I spoke to God," she lied, mentally noting that she had yet another reason to seek a confessional anon. "'Twas for the soul of men like yourself, who have the hearts and lives of a warrior, and live only by bloodshed and power, and who destroy the lives of others without thought." She spoke flippantly, carelessly, of her own situation, so as to seem undisturbed. But when she saw his face blanch, she realized she had struck him as if with the self-same sword he carried in his belt.

His face hardened, and in the flickering light of the chapel, it settled like stone in an ominous mask, and for a moment, she was afraid. Then, she saw the pain under the steeliness in his eyes, and she closed her eyes briefly as her fear settled.

"Oh, my lady—Sister—'twas not without thought that I came to draw you from the abbey. 'Twas only after *much* thought that I chose to…destroy your life, as you have stated so bluntly."

"I did not mean to offend, my lord," she spoke quickly, unable to hold back the honest response to his obvious hurt. The first time she'd seen a change in that stony expression. "I truly do pray for your soul, and that of others like you."

A bitter laugh grated in the stillness. "Aye, my soul is indeed in great need of such concern."

He stepped toward her, and she had to make a conscious effort not to retreat. "Now, my lady—Sister Madelyne—we are up with the sun and in the saddle anon, and I shall not be as accommodating as my man Clem was to your maid if you should collapse in exhaustion. 'Tis time to return to your bed." He looked at her closely. "And do you not wander at night alone, else you wish to find yourself in need of more than a chapel for protection."

His meaning dawned on her, and she looked up at him in shock. "But, my lord, your men would not—"

"Only a fool believes he knows what a man would or would not do, especially when confronted with a beautiful woman."

Madelyne's heart bumped out of rhythm, then realigned itself. He did not mean it, she knew, that she was a beautiful woman. He only meant to warn her of her carelessness. And, indeed, she had been foolish to wander unescorted through the monastery. "I will return to my bed, then, my lord."

Lord Mal Verne stepped toward her and, to her surprise, offered her his arm. "And I will escort you so as to assure myself that you return unharmed. And that you plan no further tricks."

She reluctantly slipped her fingers around his forearm as she remembered seeing her mother do many years ago at Tricourten. Although her hand barely rested there, she was acutely conscious of the feel of the well-woven linen of his sleeve, and the steadiness of his arm beneath it. Her skirt brushed against his legs as they walked at a comfortably brisk pace back to the women's chambers.

When they reached the entrance to the chambers, Mal Verne stopped, pausing in front of the door, but making no move to open it. He looked down at her as she pulled her hand from his arm, and Madelyne found herself trapped by his gaze. Something glittered there, in the depths of his eyes, and it made her unable to breathe as they stood in a lengthening silence.

"Do you ever wear your veil—even to sleep?" he asked finally, reaching out a hand as if to touch it.

Unsettled by his odd question, Madelyne looked away, breaking their eye contact and the tension between them. His hand dropped back to his side, but he continued to look down at her. "Nay, my lord." She stepped back from him and raised her face to look up at him again, confused by his words.

She was shocked when his mouth curved into the slightest of smiles, chagrin lighting his eyes. "I have always suffered from the basest of curiosities…and I merely wondered at the color of your hair, that which you keep so well-hidden." Then, a flash of horror widened his eyes, but was immediately gone to be replaced by familiar, hard cynicism. "Unless 'tis the custom of the nuns at Lock Rose Abbey to shave their heads."

"Only those who have taken their final vows partake of that custom," Madelyne replied, suddenly glad that she had not yet done so. "My head is not shaved. And my hair is dark." She knew that only because it was long enough that the heavy braid she wore fell over her shoulder down to her waist, for she'd not seen herself in a looking glass since arriving at the abbey.

He stilled. "You are not a nun?"

"I will be a nun when I am returned to Lock Rose Abbey," she told him firmly, hiding her clenched fingers in the folds of her gown.

"Aye. When you are returned to the abbey." He turned abruptly and opened the door to her chamber, gesturing for her to enter. "I shall see you on the morrow, Lady Madelyne. I wish you a well-deserved night's slumber."

Fantin was mixing healing earth, dry apple wood ash, and chipped fragments of rubies when the sign he'd been praying for became known to him.

"My lord," the squire said nervously, executing an impeccable bow, "this missive has just arrived."

Turning away from the table at which he worked, Fantin dunked his hands into a small basin of water he kept for such a purpose. He did not abide dirt under his fingers, or stains on his clothing, or spills on his floor or tables—and most definitely did not allow his correspondence to have ink smears or blood specks.

Drying his pink, clean hands on one of the many cloths he kept about for that purpose, he glanced at the polished silver mirror that hung between two of the brightest torches. His handsome face—the one that drew women to him in embarrassing droves—was devoid of soot streaks, and his shining wheat-colored hair lay in gleaming waves, framing his face. 'Twas his one vanity—his hair. He did not restrain the thick, lustrous strands that Nicola had claimed reminded her of gilded moonbeams, despite the hazard it portended by oft falling into his face whilst he worked. Fantin was confident God would forgive him this one transgression, as it was such a minor trespass when one considered other sins—such as adultery and murder and slovenliness.

After assuring himself that his appearance was pleasing, he strode toward the boy, noting that his knees were fairly knocking at the thought of interrupting his master at work. Relieving the lad of the heavy parchment, Fantin deigned to bestow one of his warm smiles upon the boy, along with a nod of thanks. 'Twas thus to his private amusement that the boy fairly fled the room, relief gusting in his wake.

"The boy was like to piss his pants whilst coming here belowstairs, fearing to disturb your work, my lord," commented Tavis, his assistant—a slender, handsome man, not so much older than the squire who'd just fled the laboratory. He stood on the other side of the heavy wooden table, stirring a deep bowl of violet liquid that steamed and stank of belladonna.

"'Tis not so true, for he knows that should a message be delayed, he would find himself in worse straits than if he disturbed me at work." Fantin chuckled damply. "'Twas one of the first lessons you yourself learned, was it not, Tavis?"

Returning his attention to the missive, Fantin glanced at the seal and excitement surged through him. He resisted the urge to beckon Rufus from his incessant praying in the chapel—after all, should God speak, Fantin was determined that Rufus be available to listen.

He knew what this message contained, and if he pulled the priest from his holy duty, Rufus would only admonish him for what he'd called his obsession with Mal Verne. But now, at long last, that obsession had closed with Mal Verne's death, and Fantin could focus his complete attention on the purification of himself and preparation for the formula for the Philosopher's Stone. It was the sign he'd been awaiting.

"Who sends the message?" Tavis looked like an eager pup as he elbowed the bowl, sloshing the smoking liquid over the side. Dismay pinked his face as he grabbed a cloth to sop up the spill.

"Take care, you fool!" Fantin snapped, ire rising at the young man's clumsiness that seemed to rear its head at the least thrice per day. "I do not wish to have pig's blood and belladonna all over the floor of my chamber!"

His annoyed eased as he looked at his assistant, who'd cleaned up the mess and now had appropriately downcast eyes. Tavis might be overly eager, and more than a bit clumsy, but he was completely devoted to Fantin and his work and that in itself was worth the trouble of cleaning up after his ineptness.

"The message is from Rohan, the man I have in Mal Verne's employ." He broke the seal and began to scan the parchment as he continued to speak. "I expect this to be the news that—" Fantin choked off, his eyes bulging with incredulity and then in bare shock. Hot fury rose in him, heating his face and causing the hand that held the missive to shake violently.

At his master's high, keening cry of disbelief, Tavis froze, gaping at him with big, bowl-shaped eyes. "What is it, Master Fantin?" he asked in a thready voice.

The vein in Fantin's forehead throbbed furiously. Raking a hand through his hair, he looked at his assistant. "Mal Verne lives. He *lives!*"

Fantin clenched his fingers around the edges of the parchment, relishing in the yield of the brittle paper beneath his anger, wishing that it was Mal Verne's own neck beneath his nails. It could not be that he lived!

He sucked in a deep draught of air. He must retain control of his senses and force the red that suddenly colored his vision to ease away…he closed his eyes and called upon God to send him the calmness and clarity he deserved. If he was to undertake His Will, then He must give him the tools to understand it.

Fantin concentrated, taking two more deep breaths. The tang of smoke, and the acridity of burning pear wood and melting iron, seared his lungs, but it did not matter.

The missive vibrated in his grip so that he could barely read the words of the remainder of the message…but when at last he returned to the paper, he snatched in his breath. He could not believe the words he saw there. He read it thrice before the shock compelled him to speak. "Mal Verne claims to have found my daughter! My daughter is *alive*! It cannot be!" He stared at the paper, rereading the impossible words.

Tavis stared at him with his wide, dark eyes. "Your daughter is alive? But…is that not good news?"

Suddenly, at last, the familiar warmth rushed over Fantin, calming him and soothing his frayed nerves. Like a flash of lightning, a sharp thrill heightened his senses, and all at once he understood.

The sign! 'Twas the sign he'd been praying for!

"Rufus!" he shrieked, rushing to the chapel, "'tis the sign! My daughter lives!"

The priest paced from the small cell, his face sober as always, his hands tucked inside his sleeves. "Ah…I have been expecting such good news. The Lord has provided and now you can see the way."

"Aye!" Fantin could not remember the last time he had felt so relieved, so certain of his destiny. Warmth, beauty, love…all glowed within him at the knowledge that he'd been gifted thus. He smiled beatifically, caught sight of his own reflection in the mirror across the table from him…and admired the angelic, saintly glow that reflected in his fine-boned face.

At last.

That God should return his daughter—the pure, innocent manifestation of his flesh, conjoined with that of his beloved wife Anne—to him now…resurrected her, after so many years….

He was blessed. And without any doubt, he knew Madelyne would be instrumental in the creation of the Philosopher's Stone. She was the missing piece, now returned to him.

Of course. The warmth rushing through him was hot and full and arousing. "She has been serving God in an abbey and shall take the veil," he explained to the priest.

Rufus smiled. "All the better. Her devotion should not be wasted upon the needs of those sisters there—Lord Fantin, you must bring her here and she will serve God thusly for your purposes."

A warmth suffused Fantin as the truth of Rufus's words broke over him. "Aye, oh, father, you have the right of it! Madelyne, sprung from my own loins and that of her mother, is indeed the purest creation on this earth. 'Tis only fit that she act as the conduit betwixt myself and my God…for through her, He will speak and show me the salvation that I shall attain with the Stone!"

He smiled with a sudden spark of good humor. "'Twill be the greatest pleasure to welcome my daughter back to her home after so many years."

$\mathcal{S}$IX

"**LOOK YOU** there, Lady Madelyne." Lord Mal Verne pointed in a southerly direction as they reached the crest of a hill. "'Tis Mal Verne."

Madelyne turned obediently, and found herself looking across a small valley to another, larger hill, on which a rambling stone wall rimmed its height. Gold and black flags bearing the standard of Mal Verne fluttered over merlons that jutted like great teeth along the top of the wall. From her view, she could see the small figures of men-at-arms walking around the enclosure, and to the farthest south corner, she saw the heavy iron portcullis that blocked entrance to the bailey. The small buildings of the town clustered on a plateau below the wall, and down in the valley were healthy green fields ready to be harvested.

Lord Mal Verne kicked Rule, the warhorse, and, as if sensing he was near home, the stallion charged off the hill. Madelyne stifled a shriek as she was jounced abruptly to one side, nearly losing her grip on his mane before catching her balance, and she closed her eyes as they headed straight down the hill. She would have begun praying aloud had Mal Verne not given a short bark of laughter and tightened his arms on either side of her.

"Do you not fear, my lady. I have not brought you this far to have you fall beneath Rule's hooves!"

Madelyne pressed her lips together and sat even straighter in her seat. She would not show her fear…and she would not allow herself to fall! Those words became a chant in her mind as they careened down the hill, the other men in their party so close on their heels that she feared they'd be overturned, if not trampled, by their zealous companions.

It was not until Mal Verne shouted a greeting that rang in her ear that Madelyne's eyes flew open and she found that they had attained a more horizontal position. They'd covered the space between the two mountainous hills in such a short time that she was thankful anew that she hadn't watched as they hurtled past trees and down the slope.

"*À* Mal Verne!" she heard the men on the stone wall cry in response to their lord's hail. The party of knights was close enough to the castle wall that she could see their gold and black tunics, emblazoned with the now-familiar standard, and the sleeves of their chain hauberks glinting in the sun.

Mal Verne slowed the party to a trot as they reached the edge of the village, and Madelyne watched with interest as the peasants and tradespeople came to crowd the sides of the thoroughfare, waving at their lord. They were not fearful at all, even of the great destriers that pranced impatiently down the street—although Madelyne noted that the mothers took care that their children did not get too close to the horses.

Vague memories of riding through the town at Tricourten stirred in her mind, and the images were of naught but empty streets and shuttered homes. 'Twas clear that Lord Mal Verne was, if not well-liked, at the least not feared by the villeins who farmed his rich lands.

She felt movements behind her, him brushing against her back and causing her to sit further forward, as he nodded and gestured to the peasants. Though he did not stop to speak with any of them at length, he did call to several by name. She felt the weight of curious stares on her as they jounced along, and realized how odd it must seem for a nun to be sharing the saddle with their lord.

When they reached the portcullis, it lifted quickly and noiselessly—bespeaking of the care and maintenance that obviously went into its upkeep. Although Madelyne knew little of the ways of war, she was well-educated in the management of a household, for all of the sisters shared in the tasks at Lock Rose Abbey. She knew the value of a gate that raised and lowered without hesitation.

Then, before she had time to muse further, the party entered the bailey and rode to the massive stone keep that sat on the far end of the huge, enclosed yard. Marshals and men-at-arms swarmed the travelers and horses, accepting reins as the knights dismounted.

Madelyne waited as Mal Verne dismounted gracefully from behind her, then stepped around to the side of the saddle over which her legs were positioned. Instead of assisting her to dismount immediately, he gathered up Rule's reins and turned to speak with a stocky, black-haired man who looked to be perhaps a decade older than he.

"Robert! By the looks of it, you're fare better than the last I saw you, after that incident with the shield. Glad to see you aren't so black and blue. This woman is Lady Madelyne de Belgrume," he announced. "She is to be treated as a guest, but not allowed without the keep unescorted." Pointing a finger at a tall, blond man with a crooked nose, he commanded, "Jube, you shall be responsible for the lady's well-being in my absence."

Madelyne watched silently as her accommodations were discussed as if she weren't present. So this is how it would be in a man's world.

Mal Verne stood near enough to her that she could reach forward and touch the darkness of his shaggy hair. The sleeves of his mail hauberk shifted, jangling quietly as he gestured with his arm. He had not shaven for some time, and dark stubble grew over his cheeks and chin, adding sharpness to the planes of his face.

He turned to her without warning, his stone-gray eyes locking onto her gaze for a brief moment, causing her breath to heavy. Madelyne quickly looked away, down, and found her attention focused on his booted feet. Then all at once, strong hands spanned her waist, and she was lifted up and down from the saddle with a smoothness that indicated the ease with which he handled her weight.

Upon the ground, Madelyne staggered slightly before she gained her footing, swaying against his broad chest for the briefest of moments before she stepped back. He glanced at her as she steadied herself, and she managed a weak smile. Patricka, who, likewise had been assisted down from her mount, came to stand by her side, looking as lost and uncertain as Madelyne herself felt.

Mal Verne turned his attention to the stocky man named Robert and, as they began to speak in low tones, they started toward the large oaken door that led to the keep.

Madelyne and Patricka hesitated, but when the man called Jube gestured for them to follow, they linked arms and walked toward the massive entrance. Jube and a cluster of other men-at-arms traced their footsteps, while others melted away, most likely to return to their duties.

Inside the keep, Madelyne found herself dwarfed by the high-ceilinged Great Hall and the lines of crude, log-hewn tables that filled it. For a brief moment, a shiver of remembrance flitted through her mind, bringing with it the image of the smoke- and laughter-filled hall at Tricourten on the night she and her mother had escaped. Casting a sidewise glance at the dais where the lord and his guests would sup, Madelyne almost expected to see her father sitting there with his cronies as he played the lute and sang with the voice of an angel. Her apprehension settled when she saw that the table was empty, and she silently berated herself for her nervousness.

As long as she was in the king's care, Fantin could not hurt her. Thus Madelyne would do whatever she must in order to remain under the king's protection.

Still ignored by Mal Verne and his men, she took the opportunity to study the tapestries that hung on the walls, stretching to such a height that she had to strain her neck in order to see the top of the images, and then to look around at the people scurrying about their business. The rushes beneath her feet rustled, and although she saw one mouse dashing away when his slumber was disturbed, she noted that the keep seemed as well-kept as the bailey and stone wall.

Then, suddenly, she was aware that all were staring at her. She looked at Mal Verne, whose voice speaking her name had caused her to look up, and saw that he was giving her an impatient look.

"My lady, do you not wish for a bath and a change of clothing before supper?"

"Oh, aye," she gave him a grateful smile, and was rewarded as his stone-face seemed to falter for a moment.

Then, as if that flinch had not occurred, Mal Verne gestured with a graceful hand to very short, very round woman standing to one side. She had brilliant red hair pulled into a tight braid, with a wide yellow-white streak from her left temple along the length of the braid, which was wound into a bun. "Then you and your maid may follow Peg abovestairs."

Peg was at least two score years and had a motherly attitude that cloaked her like a comfortable cape. She gave a brief curtsey and waved the women behind her.

At the top of the stone steps was a balcony over which Madelyne could look down and see into the hall, and she paused for a short moment to do so. Then, gathering the skirt of her habit, she hurried to catch up with Peg and Tricky.

"My lady, this shall be your chamber whilst you are here." Peg threw open a door that led to a small but well-appointed room. "My lord sent a messenger on to announce your presence, an' we all hastened to make ready for you, just as we did the time his lordship's cousin came to visit when the leaves were ust turning gold and brown...or, alack, was it my lord's mother's sister that time?... now I shall have to ask Robena on that, for I fear my memory gets a bit slow now and again." Her rambling commentary was as welcome as the small fire that warmed the room, chill even in the midst of summer, and the large wooden tub that sat next to the hearth.

Madelyne stepped into the room just in time to avoid being sloshed by a pail of steaming water carried by a serf. She stood back and watched as a line of servants brought more and more pails, filling the tub, and leaving several more pails filled with hot and cold water to adjust the temperature.

Peg bustled over to the tub and, opening a small jar, poured dried flowers and herbs into the water. Then, she stood expectantly, her pudgy hands folded, and with a start, Madelyne realized she was waiting to assist her in disrobing. "Oh, nay, I do not—"

"We shall help you to bathe, my lady," Patricka said firmly, nodding at Peg. 'Twas as though some private message had passed between them, and before Madelyne could allow her modesty to rule, they advanced upon her and began to assist her out of her habit.

"Lord Mal Verne sent some of Lady Mal Verne's clothing for you to wear," Peg explained as Madelyne stepped into the tub. "Packed as 'twere in those oaken trunks, I shook out the wrinkles when I heard that you'd be in need of them. 'Twill be quite a relief from this plain gown and veil of yours, my lady, if you don't mind my saying so."

Madelyne did not know whether 'twas the sudden heat of the water or the notion that Mal Verne was married that caused her to gasp, but she ignored the sudden, inexplicable sinking of her heart and lowered herself into the rose-scented tub.

She looked over at Peg, who was chatting on as she showed Tricky several gowns of brilliant, jewel colors. At the least, she thought wryly, Mal Verne provided well for his wife. Even from her perch in the tub, she could tell the quality of the cloth and the intricacy of the embroidery.

She wondered, suddenly, if Lady Mal Verne, at least, was able to soften the harshness in his face and demeanor.

"Methinks this blue for the undertunic," Tricky was saying as she eyed Madelyne and then the cloth, and back again.

"You are well thought," nodded Peg, her jowls jiggling. "With her hair of such dark color, and her eyes like a pale moon—aye, she makes me think of mine own sister, whose hair was so long and thick as mine is. And my own auntie, well, 'twas her pride and joy this hair of our family, and when she had the ague, she must had it cut and how she bewailed that fate for days!"

The two women huddled together for a moment, throwing occasional glances over their shoulders at Madelyne. Tricky's arms gesticulated wildly, punctuating her bobbing head, and Peg nodded and murmured, nodded and tsked, and expounded on her reactions with rambling sentences of family anecdotes.

Madelyne, a bit discomfited with what she deemed as a conspiracy against her, sank into the tub and attempted to block out the two women and their chatter. A faint, wry smile did curve her face as she succumbed to the realization that Tricky had found her mentor, and that she, Madelyne, would likely be the pawn in her learning game.

The scent of roses filled her nose, for the first time ever not related to the duties of making rose beads. And, as if she was smelling it for the first time, Madelyne inhaled and closed her eyes, enjoying the sweetness of the floral scent. The steaming water was heavenly, such that she paused for a moment—albeit a brief one—to thank God for her safe arrival, and to contemplate whether 'twas a sin that she should enjoy such an earthly pleasure. Baths, although available at the abbey, were only occasional and never this warm and sweet. Most often they were a dip in the nearby stream, or a few hands of lukewarm water.

Tricky dug soap scented with basil and rosemary from a small crock, using it to clean under Madelyne's fingernails and to wash the grime and sweat from all parts of her body. Even the black rose-petal stains had faded when she was finished.

The loosing of Madelyne's braid after two days relieved the tightness of her skull, and the pleasure-pain of it had her sighing in soft delight. How wonderful it felt when Peg began to pour warm water over her thick hair, and how much more like heaven on earth could it be when she used her strong fingers to massage her scalp!

It was not until she stood in front of the fire, wrapped in a soft blanket, that Madelyne remembered the clothing. She held out a hand to stop Tricky as she approached with the blue undergown.

"Nay, Tricky, I cannot wear such fine clothing. You of all know that I'm promised to our Lord God, and that I cannot in good conscience don flamboyant finery. Peg, 'tis not my place to use that which belongs to Lady Mal Verne."

The two women exchanged glances, and Tricky nodded as if to give Peg permission to respond. "My lady, I am sorry, but your clothing has been taken to be washed. And, 'tis the lord's orders that you dress as befits your station, as the Lady of Tricourten. Wherever that land may be, certainly the women there do not see such simple gowns as flamboyant." She gestured to the overtunic, which was pale blue, embroidered with gold and silver threads. "This is but a plain gown, my lady, by standards at court. And verily, you will wear aught that is more up to date when you join the king."

Peg sighed, smoothing a hand over the embroidery that rimmed the edges of the overtunic, her eyes taking on a far-away look. "I remember that day when mine own baby Shirl went to care for one of the queen's ladies, and how she pored over the patterns and cloths and threads to be certain that she should dress in her finest, and that all that she brought with her for her lady was the most beautiful to be had from Lockswood, and even there at court 'twas as if she were naught but a country bumpkin. An' how my daughter worked to learn that new fashion, worked day and night, and…." Her voice trailed off and a look of confusion passed over her face. She glanced at the cloth she held in her hand, then at Madelyne, and the light of understanding came back into her eyes. "Ah, well, aye, my lady. You must be dressed ere supper is served, and this is all that you have to wear."

Madelyne's gaze strayed to the fine cloth, but she resolutely turned from it and walked over to the bed, where several other gowns lay strewn across it. "There must be something else that more befits a nun," she murmured, poring over the clothing. She paused at a pale yellow gown with little frippery. "I shall wear this, for 'tis more subdued and more suited to one of God's women."

"Nay, my lady," Tricky said, resting a hand upon her arm. Madelyne turned to look at her, surprise causing her brows to rise at the formal address. "Lady," Tricky said again with such ease, as if she had always addressed her as her better, "with all respect, you are not a nun, as yet…and you are the Lady of Tricourten. 'Tis God's will that you are here, and God's will that you bear the mantle of your position."

She showed Madelyne the blue undergown, the color of a brilliant sapphire, with delicate gold embroidery along the neckline and the laces of the tight sleeves. "That yellow will cause you to look aught but ill and sallow, whilst this blue will cause your eyes to take on its sheen. An' the cut of this is more flattering, as the sleeves will show the fine lines of your arms and draw attention to your height."

Annoyed by Tricky's sudden fashion expertise, Madelyne pursed her lips and frowned. "But—"

"Come now, my lady," Peg insisted, gently taking the pale yellow cloth from her fingers and urging her toward Tricky. "Though you are a bit taller than Lady Mal Verne, you are of a size. Now, 'tis not in our interest to anger Lord Mal Verne, either, so we shall fix you up rightly and send you down for supper anon."

With a sigh of capitulation, Madelyne acquiesced to the newfound fussiness of her maid and her mentor.

Her hair was black.

"Good evening, my lady," Gavin said as he struggled to contain his shock at the transformation of Lady Madelyne. Out of her habit and veil, and garbed in clothing that he thought had belonged to Nicola, Lady Madelyne de Belgrume was barely recognizable…and looked not the least bit nunlike.

"My lord." She gave a brief curtsey, bowing her head slightly, her thick, dark hair spilling over her shoulders and brushing the floor at his feet.

Some masterful person—Peg, he realized—had taken that thick, inky river, taming it into two thick braids that pulled back from his guest's temples…and left the rest of it to fall unencumbered down Lady Madelyne's back. When she raised her face and reached to place her fingers on his arm, he noticed a thin, gold chain that rested on her forehead and was woven into the darkness of her braids.

It was glorious hair.

With a start, Gavin realized he'd frozen, and she now waited for him to lead her to the dais upon which they would sup. "Come," he said abruptly, turning toward the high table and forcing his attention to matters at hand.

As the most high-ranking persons in the hall, he and Lady Madelyne were the only two seated at the high table. He took the lord's chair, the massive, walnut seat with a cushioned bench and without arms. She gathered her gown carefully, settling its folds over her legs, as she sat in Nicola's regular seat.

Gavin had just taken a sip from the excellent Bordeaux Mal Verne imported from Aquitaine when Lady Madelyne ruined his meal.

"I must thank your wife for allowing me to wear her clothing," she said, looking at him from behind her own wine glass. "Will she be joining us this evening?"

He felt the familiar anger and a bit of humiliation rise within him, and recalled those many, many evenings when Nicola sat to his left as Lady Madelyne now did. The woman had been a viper in his world, and he'd not known it until it was too late. "I do not speak of my wife," he said in the deathly chill voice he used whenever he meant to intimidate. "Nor does anyone else within my hearing."

Her eyes widened, innocent and luminous. Then she turned away, poking at the chunk of fish he'd placed in her bread trencher. "I did not mean to pry," she said steadily, but he noticed that there was the slightest tremor to her fingers as she reached for a crust of bread. Then, with a boldness that surprised him, she firmed her lips and continued, "Whatever reason you do not choose to speak of your wife is of no matter to me, but there is no need to leap upon me over the most innocent of comments." She did not look at him, but instead took a dainty bite of bread.

Gavin snapped his mouth shut on the apology he'd been about to make for his sharp, hasty words. Had the wench shed her nunlike modesty along with her habit and veil? He took another sip of wine to hide his chagrin as much as the admiration he felt at her temerity.

"I," she continued, this time turning to look at him with a spark of fire in her cool eyes, "meant only to make polite conversation with you, my lord. Thus, I shall leave it in your hands as to whether we have a silent meal or nay."

If he had not seen that her hand still trembled when she reached with great casualness for her wine goblet, he might have been angry at her continued audacity. But that bit of tremor eased his ire and he merely gave her a slant-eyed look. "But you have only tried one topic of conversation, my lady. Surely you do not intend to give up on me so easily?"

Mayhap it was the fact that he'd tamed the sharpness in his voice that prompted her to try again. However, her next words brought no more palatable a topic than Nicola had been.

"Then, my lord, perhaps you inform me of the purpose for which the king has summoned me, and when I shall see him my-self." Again, she did not look at him, but continued to pick at her food as though uninterested in his reply.

"If only my men were as unerring in their aim with a bow as you have been in suggesting topics of conversation that do not ap-peal to me!" He bit into a piece of cheese, chewed, and swallowed as he formulated his reply. "I have sent word to the king that you are in my company. As to the answers to your questions, I cannot say, but you will remain here under my guard."

This time Lady Madelyne looked at him. "Do you then—in the name of the king—intend to keep me prisoner here at Mal Verne? As I have seen no evidence of a writ from his majesty ordering my presence, I wonder if he is even aware of my existence. Or have you merely used his name in order to gain your will—whatever that may be?"

Annoyance flared within him and he looked at her sharply. "That would be treason, my lady. I do not tolerate such implications by anyone, be it man or woman—particularly one who is a guest in my home."

"A guest?" Lady Madelyne raised her fine eyebrows, adopting an innocent posture that grated on him. "I was not under the impres-sion that my status is that of a guest. If that is the case, then I am free to leave at my will—am I not?"

Gavin dragged his gaze that had somehow become fastened on her shapely mouth up to glare into her eyes. "Lady Madelyne, *if* you were given the freedom to leave—which I will not give—you would last no more than a night without these castle walls. Do not speak of such absurdity." He returned to demolishing his meal, certain that that would be the end of it.

But, still, she would not relent—and her tenacity was beginning to wear upon him. "Such may have been said to my mother and myself ten autumns ago, when we left Tricourten with naught but the clothing on our backs and a few simple jewels, my lord."

Gavin placed his goblet very deliberately on the table and turned to face her fully. He would not allow this wisp of a woman to goad him into losing his temper—but he knew he was nearing the end of his tether. "Lady Madelyne," he said tightly, "if it would end this discussion then, aye, I shall call you not a guest, but a hostage. Aye, a hostage of the king. And, lady, if you could read, I would show you the writ that orders me to bring you to his majesty."

"Very well, then, Lord Mal Verne. A hostage I am. And, as I am capable of reading not only French, but Latin and Greek, I should be pleased to peruse that writ of which you speak." She used her eating knife to spear a piece of turbot and raise it to her mouth.

Gavin snapped his jaws shut so hard that his jaw hurt. "Very well, my lady. On the morrow you shall see your writ. And methinks I should prefer a silent meal after all."

SEVEN

BUILDINGS FORMING the town of Mal Verne lay like little studs on the plateau below the castle wall. The orange sun had lowered to just above the horizon, and thick gray clouds had begun to fill the sky. A distant rumble of thunder came on the cool night air, and far off to the north, Madelyne could see a flash of lightning illuminate the belly of a heavy cloud.

The wind whipped up, tossing about her skirt and the hood she'd drawn over her head as she looked down from the castle wall. Jube, the tall, blond guard Lord Mal Verne had delegated to her, leaned casually against one of the merlons, talking with another man-at-arms who'd been assigned the night watch. He stood far enough away that she didn't feel smothered, but close enough that she was aware she was not free to come and go as she pleased.

Hostage. Madelyne clenched her fingers together under her cloak and closed her eyes. Innocent of the ways of the political world, she knew she was at a disadvantage in parrying to keep her freedom, to keep herself safe from the hands of her father. She would see that writ on the morrow, and mayhaps there would be a clue within to indicate what the king planned to do.

A large, wet drop splashed on her face, and thunder cracked more insistently. Still, Madelyne saw no reason to take herself within the confines of the keep that had suddenly become her prison. Jube looked over at her, his face placid, and when she made no indication that she was ready to move, he returned to his conversation. The wind carried a word or two from the men to Madelyne's ears. She heard mention of hunt and horses, and knew they discussed purely masculine matters—matters that were unfamiliar to her.

That trail of thought brought her to that which had been hovering at the back of her mind all the evening: Lord Mal Verne. The man was harsh and rude and unfriendly, yet she still had that self-same fascination for him. Mayhap the reason lay in the fact that though he snapped and snarled, she saw beyond the hardness of his face and the steely coldness of his eyes to the depths that hinted at more than that…suffering, perhaps, or fear….

Madelyne shook her head, dismissing those fanciful thoughts. Mal Verne was a man—a fierce, hard one, not unlike her own father—and 'twas foolish of her to think that she saw more.

She turned to summon Jube, suddenly ready to return to her chamber and to put those thoughts from her mind, but to her surprise, he and his companion had disappeared. Turning to look behind her, thinking that mayhap they'd strolled further along the wall as they talked, she found no one. Madelyne stepped nearer to the edge of the wall and looked down into the bailey, which had become nearly deserted and quiet in the last hour.

A movement behind her caused her to whirl, her skirts wrapping around her legs and the hood dropping from her head. "Lord Mal Verne."

There was no mistaking him, for even though the sun had nearly completed its drop beyond the horizon, and the moon was nowhere to be found, the light from wall sconces cast enough glow for her to recognize the form that shifted from the shadows. Tall, with thick, uncut hair that blustered in the swelling wind, he stood before her, his hands folded at the waist of his tunic. The reserved pose belied the vitality that ever exuded from him, and Madelyne, as always, felt it.

"If you wish to jump, the deed would be better done on the east side of the wall," he commented, stepping toward her. "There, the hill drops away to the cliffs of the sea. Rocks and the surf would make certain that the task would be complete, rather than leaving one a crippled mess."

"I would not jump," Madelyne replied, all too aware of the leaping of her pulse as he came to stand beside her. "'Tis a mortal sin."

He looked at her for a moment, his plain, sculpted features made almost handsome by the half-light. Then, his lips—full, wide and hard—curved into the faintest of smirks. "Ah, aye. How foolish of me to forget. One can wish for death, can court it in battle or elsewhere—but one cannot take matters into one's own hands and expect salvation."

Madelyne did not know how to respond to those words, for she sensed another layer to them—an almost melancholy sentiment. Instead, she continued to stare out over the darkening land.

Mal Verne stood next to her, unspeaking. Yet she was as aware of his every breath as she was of her own pulse beating through her veins. His hand rested on the waist-high stone, and she saw how long and thick his fingers were, how the veins and tendons and scars sculpted the back of it. How solid his wrist looked next to her own dainty one.

He broke the silence at last. "If you did not climb up here to elude Jube for the purpose of taking matters into your own hands and jumping, what was it that prompted you to come out in the midst of a gathering storm?"

Madelyne looked at the lightning that flashed in the north, closer now, then down again at her own hand resting next to his on the wall. Slim and pale, her fingers took up barely a third of the width of one stone brick, while his hand covered nearly the whole of one. A flash of memory caught her by surprise—an image of a hand, powerful and wide as Mal Verne's, raised in violence and darkness.

The remembrance was so strong that she took an involuntary step backward, her hand pulling to her chest to clutch at her cloak. He turned his head quickly to look at her, question and something akin to concern flashing in his eyes. "What is it?"

Feeling foolish at her reaction to a mere memory, Madelyne forced a smile and waved her action away. "'Twas naught but a night beetle that flew in my face," she replied lightly. "It startled me."

Mal Verne looked at her curiously for a moment, then relented and allowed her out from under his delving stare when he turned to look back toward the storm. "May I escort you below to your chamber now, my lady? The lightning draws near and you are at risk at this height."

Madelyne arched one brow but continued to look out over the land. "And what happened to my own personal guard, Jube? Is that not his duty, my lord?"

"I dismissed Jube, sending him to take his place out side of your chamber door." Mal Verne's voice rumbled low, not unlike the thunder echoing in the distance. "If you had planned to end your life thus, I preferred to be the one to witness it—as you are under my care in the name of the king." The stress on those last words was not lost on Madelyne. In that moment, she realized she believed him when he claimed he acted in the king's name.

And, she also knew the odd disappointment that 'twas not his desire to seek her company that had led Mal Verne to find her on the wall. "Very well, then, my lord." She turned abruptly to take his arm and found his stare fixed on her in such a way that caused her breath to hitch in her throat. For a moment, he was unmoving and she halted, confused and riddled with an odd heaviness in her limbs.

The moment froze—thunder crashed behind her, lightning zinged through the clouds, the smell of rain was in the air, and the brick felt rough and hard beneath her fingers—as he reached to touch her. His hand hovered in mid-air for a second, as if he hesitated, then rested warm and heavy on top of her head. His fingers smoothed over the side of her skull, bumping over one thick braid, and slid along the heavy tresses that were tucked under her cloak.

Madelyne hardly dared breathe. No one had touched her that way…ever. Certainly not a man. Certainly not the man to whom she now played hostage. Her heart thumped madly, but for all of that…nay, she was not truly alarmed. Why did he not frighten her—this large, stony, gruff man?

"You have beautiful hair," he murmured in the same low, rumbly voice he'd used a moment earlier. He stepped toward her, his presence surrounding Madelyne like a cape. She felt the wall behind her and looked up into his eyes, inscrutable in the dimness. Her heart thundered in her chest and her mouth dried as the heaviness of his gaze sent heat coursing through her.

Then, suddenly, it was as if something snapped. He fell back, his hand slamming to his side, and the urgency gone from his gaze. "'Twould have been a sin had you cut it." His words were fact of the matter, and made in a sharp, almost cutting voice. "Now, lady, may I take you below where you will be protected from the storm?"

Her head spinning, and her face warm with the flush of mortification, Madelyne could do naught but nod. Disdaining his proffered arm, she turned her back to him and, clutching a handful of skirt, started toward the stairs.

'Twas just as well that he did not sleep well that night, Gavin would realize later with some relief.

This first night back in his own chambers should have been one of comfort and rest. For the first time in many a moon, he was not forced to unroll a traveling pallet onto cold, hard ground, or to sleep on a lumpy, hay-filled pallet in a chamber he shared with a myriad of other snorting, snoring, snuffling men.

Rosa had bathed him and would have serviced him further had he wished, but Gavin declined, desiring only his own company. He stood at the window slit, clad in his chausses with loosed cross garters, watching the lightning brighten the sky as if it were midday. The wall beneath his fingers shuddered as thunder crashed above.

Mayhap he should have availed himself of Rosa's offer, else he would not have made such a fool of himself upon the wall with Lady Madelyne…and likely he would be sleeping soundly instead of watching the rain trail off from its brief, thrashing downpour.

Clean wetness filled the air, tingeing his nostrils and cooling his bare chest as he leaned on the bottom of the arrow slit and looked out over his domain. Yet, in the darkness, he could see only the perfect oval of the nun's fair face, upturned to him with wide eyes, darkened by the night shadows. And her lips…*Jesù*…they were full and wide—made for kissing, he'd thought in one absurd moment before he'd remembered who she was.

Even now, his own mouth twisted in disgust. Madelyne was the daughter of his dearest enemy, as well as a woman prepared to embrace religious life. She could have no idea that her innocent beauty was enough to make a man hot with desire…even a man who had not touched a woman other than the occasional whore or serving wench for seven years.

Gavin pushed himself away from the window and folded his arms over his chest, pacing to the fireplace to stoke up the smoldering blaze. The sooner he turned the woman over to Henry, the better off he would be.

He poked at the charred logs that glowed with orange embers, releasing sparks and tiny tongues of flame. The short rainstorm had cooled the summer night and his chamber had become chill, yet he was not yet ready to seek the warmth of his bed.

When he received notification of where the royal court would be stopping for the next months, he would pack up his guest—and her erstwhile maid—and take them to Henry himself. And then, he would never have to see the woman with her calm gray eyes again.

The king would likely make her a royal ward, keeping her under his care or that of the queen in order to control the actions of Fantin de Belgrume. It was well-known of de Belgrume that he had greatly mourned the loss of his daughter and wife, and verily he would be more easily brought to heel knowing that his daughter yet lived. Mayhap the king might even find a way to relieve de Belgrume of his fiefdom, thereby putting an end to the madman's resources.

Gavin nodded to himself and replaced the long metal pole he'd used to tease the fire, refusing to give credence to the niggling guilt at the back of his mind. She would be better off at court, he told himself, ignoring the echo of her own explanation as to why life

in the abbey afforded her more freedom. A woman such as she—
beautiful, with lands aplenty through her father—was not meant to
while herself away in an abbey.

Peste! He stalked over to the window again. What did he care
of her future? He had a task to do—to bring her father under control—and the king expected nothing less of him to do so. If he felt
guilt by taking her from the solace of Lock Rose Abbey, that was
merely a sign of his own weakness and an uncontrollable factor in
his doing his duty.

He stared unseeing over the world below, catching out of the
corner of his eye the impression of dawn starting to lighten the sky.
The cool tang of rain-filled air had evaporated, to be replaced by a
bitter acridity of smoke. Gavin sniffed, frowning, then turned his
attention to the town below.

Where the darkness should have yielded only the faint gray out-
lines of cottages and huts, a yellow glow flickered on the west side
of the town.

By the time Gavin reached the village, crowds of peasants and
men-at-arms had gathered in the streets. Three of buildings were
ablaze, and sparks and flames leapt and jumped with such vigor on
the gusty wind that 'twas only a matter of time until the next buildings caught afire. Though dawn was beginning to give natural light
to the sky, shadows danced eerily over the faces of women and children who stood to one side of the street, watching as the men threw
bucket after bucket of water onto the flames.

Soot and black smoke whorled from the buildings, mingling
with the moist air and choking the bystanders and fire fighters.
Gavin pushed his way through the crowds of people to join his
men near the blaze, quickly taking a place at the front of a line that
passed the leather buckets to and from the town well.

Clem stood next to him, handing him dripping pail after dripping pail. He swiped at his sweating face with a thick arm, smearing
black ash over his cheek and temple.

"'Twas lightning struck the house here," he told Gavin as he whirled to shove a full bucket into his lord's middle. He turned away to get another, then spun back to take the empty and pass on the full. "It must have smoldered below the roof for some time, else—" He turned away again, then back, "the rain would have put it out."

Gavin grunted in agreement, forbearing to point out that the brevity of the storm, fierce as it was, had likely contributed. The thatched roofs of the peasant homes were particularly susceptible to such dangers. It had happened more than once in this village alone—lightning had struck, passing through the roof into a house, setting the interior ablaze before anyone realized it.

"Did all get out safely?" he asked Clem, slamming an empty bucket into the man's hand.

"Aye, I believe so…although—" He turned back as Gavin turned toward the fire in the rhythm they had established, then they returned face to face. "Robert the Cooper has a bad burn."

A sudden wind blustered, sending ash and smoke billowing into the faces of the fire fighters. Gavin ducked, holding up an arm to ward off the black fog. Something stung him fiercely on the shoulder, and he slapped a hand there to brush away the sparks that landed on his bare skin. He cursed himself for neglecting to pull on a *sherte* before leaving the keep, but there was no time to stop now.

"This way!" A voice shouted, and the mass of fire fighters stumbled, shifting several steps in one direction to move out of the wind's changed path.

The buckets kept coming, but the wind would not allow them to gain an advantage. Soon, the walls of the first building collapsed inward, sending up a shower of sparks and ash. A spray of orange coals scattered over Gavin, stinging like tiny needles that he didn't have the time to brush away. Already, a fourth building was beginning to smoke in the hay-like thatch of the roof.

With a shout that had grown rough because of the sooty air, Gavin pointed at the coil of smoke coming from the building. He beckoned for two of the lines of bucket-passers to turn their attention to this new danger, then, with a quick nod to Clem, he slipped out of his own position and started toward the group of women and children.

Pointing to the wife of the smith, he said, "You—Sally—get you those children who are old enough, and whatever women can be spared from watching the young ones, and throw water on this house next. If we have God's luck, we shall keep it from spreading further."

He was just about to return to his place in line when an agonized scream reached his ears.

He turned to see a woman running toward the fourth of the burning buildings. "My son! Barden! My son!" She would have dashed into the blaze had Gavin not thrown out an arm and caught her around the waist.

When she looked up and recognized him, even that did not stop her from struggling to get free. "My lord! My son's home! My son and his wife!" she shrieked—a mournful, wailing cry that tore at Gavin's heart. "I cannot find them! They are burning!"

"They are there?" he asked, looking at the building, gauging how badly it was burning within. His glance flickered over the mass of people that worked as one body, passing buckets and tossing water. It was unlikely that Barden and his wife had not been awakened by the activity. Thus, if they were within the house, they were most certainly dead. "Stay you here." He started toward the house.

"My lord—" her shriek of mingled gratitude and horror followed him as he started toward the small home.

Gavin was near enough to feel the blistering waves of heat from the building next door when a hand closed over his arm. He shook his arm to loosen the grip, and turned in annoyance to see a familiar, soot-covered face. "Lady Madelyne!" he exclaimed, stopping. "What are you doing?"

"Nay, my lord, you cannot go in there!" she tightened her grip on his bare arm, seemingly heedless of the sweat that made her fingers slip. She was dressed in a long, stained gown, with the bulk of her hair pulled back into a thick braid. Sweat dripped down her own face, which was flushed from exertion and speckled with ash.

"I must see to her son," he said simply. "'Tis my duty. I am the lord, and I am foresworn to protect my vassals." He started away again.

"Nay! My lord!" Moments later, she was after him again, carrying a bucket of water. "Wait."

He turned, more annoyed. "You cannot say me nay, Madelyne. I must—"

"I would not. But, here, take this to cover your mouth and head." She handed him a length of cloth, and he saw that she had torn her gown to her knees. It was wet and cool, and she helped him to wrap it around his head and shoulders, leaving a flap to pull over his mouth and nose. "Have a care!"

Her words followed him, even over the crackle and hiss of flame and the calls and shouts of bucket-passers, and for once he did not ask himself why he should have a care for his safety. Instead, he paused at what once was the door of the house, wrapped the wet cloth more tightly over his head, and pulled up a piece of it to cover his face.

He kicked out at the sagging door of the house, shoving it into an interior that was dim. Smoke did not billow out, which bespoke of the fact that mayhap the fire had not progressed as far as he'd feared. Gavin stepped inside gingerly, watching for fallen timbers and other pitfalls.

The house was little more than a hut, and it did not take much effort to scan the room with his gaze, even in the dimness of the interior. At first, he saw naught but the flames that licked the ceiling, kissing the walls and dropping an occasional tuft of fire onto the floor. Then, back in a corner, he saw a large, unfamiliar shape.

Stepping over a fallen beam, he skirted the edge of the building to avoid the fire in the center, and approached the lump. It was a piece of the wall, and had folded inward, collapsing onto a pallet, leaving an opening just next to the blaze outside.

With a grunt of triumph, Gavin stepped over a collapsed stool and, continuing to hold the cloth over his face, used one hand to push the wall up. It sagged, bowing in the center, but held together so that he lifted it up enough to see the two people it had covered.

Though he could not tell if they yet lived, he dropped the cloth from his face to push the wall away, and it fell outside of the hut, landing against the next house that burned. The smoke suddenly speared into his nose and mouth, and Gavin found himself needing to duck near the floor. Fighting the cough that welled inside his lungs, he replaced the cloth over his nose and reached to grab the woman's arm with his free hand.

He grasped her wrist, half lifting her off the floor, and slipped his arm around under both of her arms, then began to push his way toward the opening where the wall had collapsed. He was just reaching it when he realized the fire next door was too close for him to make it out safely, and he was forced to turn.

By now, the smoke was burning his eyes so that they were hardly tearing any longer and he could see little but blurred shapes. It was hot, and sweat made him and his grip slippery and clumsy. He took several steps toward the door before stumbling and nearly falling to his knees.

Nay, Father, do not take me now!

The thought came from nowhere, but came with a galvanizing strength, and Gavin felt a burst of energy beat back the fatigue he'd been feeling. He took two more steps toward the door, and was just about to reach for the edge of the opening when a loud crash filled the air. A sudden wave of smoke and flame buffeted toward him, and the last thing he saw was the roof tumbling toward him.

Eight

FANTIN DE Belgrume awoke with a smile on his face.

At last, his destiny was clear. He felt light and free and very sated, only part of which was due to the warm body that slumbered next to him.

The only disappointment, the only thing that kept him from being completely serene was the knowledge that Gavin Mal Verne still lived. The mere thought of the man caused Fantin's insides to roil with anger and hatred—but the added knowledge that the evil man had Fantin's own innocent daughter in his possession served to make him near mad with the bloodred fury that seemed to rear in him more oft as of late.

An obsession…mayhap Rufus spoke aright. In the dawning light of day, abovestairs and away from the beckoning power of his laboratory, Fantin could admit that his venom toward Mal Verne was perchance more of a distraction than it should be.

Did he indeed allow his need to annihilate Mal Verne sway him from his holy work? Aye, it could be true.

Yet, he could not allow the man to keep him from his purpose, and Mal Verne, should he have the chance, would destroy Fantin's life and any opportunity to finish his work. 'Twas self-preservation, Fantin acknowledged as he trailed a finger along the sweeping curve of Retna's spine.

As the woman next to him shifted, brushing against him in her sleep, Fantin could not help but recall the many times Mal Verne's own Nicola had done the same. The woman's body had been sleek and sensual, and she fancied herself in love with Fantin. He, in turn, had believed she was the woman God had provided him in the replacement of his dead wife Anne. Mayhap not as pure, but worthy to bed with Fantin and become one with him. After all, God had given the earthly pleasures of coupling to all humans, and, like his patron, The Whore Saint, Fantin did not deny himself that release.

It had been no hardship to avail himself of what Nicola, Lady Mal Verne, offered the first time he'd met her at court. Fantin had had merely to give her his measured, haunting look from the lute over which he labored with such melancholy, and to sing of beauteous maids and the perfection of the love bestowed upon them by their champions …and the woman had been lured in like a mule following a carrot.

Of course, being wed with a gruff, silent, stupid man such as Mal Verne should drive any woman to one with the charm and striking countenance that Fantin possessed, he reflected as his lips shifted in a self-satisfied smile. God had blessed him well, indeed, in making him attractive to both women and men…at the least, those of whom he *wished* to have find him attractive, and to follow his way and support his work.

Retna opened her eyes, hazy with sleep, and allowed the blanket to shift nearly to her waist, baring herself to him. Fantin looked at her, the stirrings of lust returning to his nether regions, and considered whether he should make love with her once more before sending her to her fate in the laboratory.

'Twas a messy fate, but necessary.

This was, in fact, his weakness. The physical coupling with a woman—any woman—who did not bear the same purity that God had bestowed upon Fantin was the vice that he must battle, the cross he must bear, the temptation that he must set right. He knew he compromised his gift, his Purpose, by enjoying the flesh of whores and women who gave their bodies to any man who asked— true whores, or even the ladies of court, such as Nicola Mal Verne. She had not been the pure woman he'd believed, and that had caused Fantin much grief.

Yet, David had had his Bathsheba, and God still gifted him with his kingdom. Aye, David'd had his punishment, but Fantin did not fear that. So long as the Lord continued to show him the way to the formula for the Philosopher's Stone, Fantin could manage any penance that might be foisted upon him.

If Anne had not perished…. Ah, Anne, his wife, the one woman who possessed untouched innocence and was chosen as he was. The one woman worthy of his physical love.

Fantin had searched for one to replace her these ten summers past, and had never found one worthy of him. Nicola had been his greatest error, enslaving him with her whoring ways whilst causing him to believe she was innocent and pure.

Until he found the woman God meant for him, his transgressions would only be forgiven if he removed the temptation—the sluts, the whores—from his sight, from his life…from this world.

Only then—when he found perfection in a woman and needed to look no further—would he be forgiven his transgressions.

Madelyne heard the horrifying crash as the roof groaned and folded into the house where Mal Verne had disappeared. She shrieked and ran toward the collapsed building as smoke poured forth. Jube, who had shadowed her since she left her chamber, was right on her heels, shouting for Clem and Arden to assist. He pushed her to one side, giving her a curt command to stay there, as he approached the rickety structure.

She stood there obediently, gnawing on her fist, watching the three men dash toward the building. A small crowd of women and children, led by the woman who had alerted Mal Verne to the missing people, clustered behind Madelyne.

Jube, followed by Clem and then Arden, stooped and gingerly pushed through the entrance to the house. They disappeared into the smoke.

Madelyne saw flames beginning to flicker through the roof, and she clenched her fist tighter, her attention fastened on the building. What if all of them were lost?

After what seemed like an age, a figure stumbled through the entrance, dragging a heavy burden, and was followed by two more soot-blackened men, carrying a body between them. Madelyne's heart pushed up into her throat as she ran forward into the circle of heat blasting from the house. The first man was Arden, and he pulled his burden well away from the building, letting it drop onto the ground as he sagged against a nearby tree. One quick glance identified the lump as a woman, her skirts mussed and torn, and her face and hair cut and bleeding.

Madelyne saw that she was being attended to before rushing on to meet Clem and Jube, who carried what she feared was Gavin Mal Verne between them. They staggered, choking and coughing, with their heavy burden, to the perimeter of the crowd of people before allowing the body to sag onto the ground.

Madelyne was on her knees in an instant, sinking onto the stone-covered ground next to the limp, blackened body of Lord Mal Verne. She felt immediately for a pulse, touching the side of his neck and gasping with relief when she found it. Then, she placed her palm flat on his bare, scarred chest and bent her ear near his mouth and nose to ascertain whether he yet breathed. When she felt the rise and fall of his chest and heard the raspy breath coming from his nose, she sat back and scrambled to her feet.

"We must get him, and the other injured, to the keep immediately," she commanded unnecessarily, gesturing to a man-at-arms she did not know. The alarm had already been raised for the lord of Mal Verne, and two men-at-arms were preparing a litter for him.

A sudden gust of wind buffeted Madelyne's shortened gown and caused the flames to billow more furiously. She looked at the next home in line for the fire, and saw that it too would be up in smoke shortly. Scanning the line of houses that would be the next victims of the fire, she saw they were built so close together that the chain would continue, flattening most of the village if the flames were not subdued.

Madelyne looked over at the first of the buildings to catch fire, and saw that the line of bucket-passers had adjusted their efforts from that one to the others, since it was long past saving. They seemed to be able to do little to contain the blaze. Mal Verne would awaken, God willing, to find that his whole village had burned.

Suddenly, just as she was turning away to join the group of men carrying the injured up to the keep, Madelyne had an idea. Grabbing Clem's arm, she spoke rapidly into his face, glad to see that he had seemed to recover from his rescue mission in the collapsed building.

"If the fire is not stopped, the whole town will burn," she told him. "It leaps from house to house, and we cannot stop it. Why do you not destroy the next two houses so that the flames have nowhere to go, and then they will be contained."

He looked at her as if she were mad, but then a dawning light crept over his face. "Aye, my lady, 'tis a good thought! It is too bad for those who live in those houses, but 'tis a better option than seeing them burn." His voice, though rough and raspy from smoke, showed his enthusiasm for the idea.

She started to resume her walk up the path to the walls, and he stopped her with a brief, gentle hand on her arm. "Thank you my lady, and care for Lord Gavin if you can save him. He may not have the will to live, but you must infuse it in him, for he has traveled a long and hard road." With that, he lost the remains of his hoarse voice and became encompassed in a fit of coughing.

Madelyne touched his arm in response. "I shall do what I can for Lord Mal Verne. And do you come to me when this is over and I will give you aught for your cough." Then, she turned away and began the trek up to the keep.

❧

It was she, his Madonna, the first thing he saw when he opened his eyes. Gavin's lids were painfully heavy, scratching over eyes that were gritted like sand, but there was nothing wrong with his vision.

Her pale oval of a face reflected concern and determination. Its beauty was marred by a thick streak of soot over one high cheekbone, running along the length of her face to the chin, and tiny flecks of black over her forehead and nose. Wisps of night-colored hair framed her high forehead and caressed the curve of her jaw.

A sudden fit of coughing caught him by surprise and she immediately rested a cool, soothing hand on his chest as if to help subdue it.

She turned to the table, then back. "Drink this," she offered, slipping her fingers around the back of his neck and bringing a cup to his lips.

He drank thirstily, feeling the cool soothing taste of mint slide down his throat. When he drank, he smelled its camphoric aroma and felt his lungs begin to expand more easily. As the heaviness of his breathing subsided, he became aware of a throbbing pain on his leg, and a more subtle ache to his head. As if reading his mind, Lady Madelyne spoke.

"I have wrapped your leg with a poultice to ease the burn there. You have other cuts and scrapes, but I do not believe they are much more than nicks to you." She smiled. "It appears that the ceiling landed on your head when it collapsed, and though it most likely aches, it does not seem severe."

He crooked his lips slightly. "It seems that no matter what it is that befalls me, you appear upon my awakening to care for me."

Her smile faded and she stepped back. "'Twas a foolish thing you did, Lord Mal Verne. Though you accuse me of attempting to take mine own life, you should make a meal of your own words! 'Twas naught but foolishness, rushing into a burning building as you did!"

"Foolishness." Whatever tenderness he may have felt for the Madonna-like woman before him disappeared at her reprimanding tone. "It may be no great loss to you should a villein perish in such a way, but each life given by God is sacred—"

"Indeed it is," she interrupted calmly, her level voice somehow overriding his. "Including your own, my lord. If you had been killed for your rashness, would not the lives of more have suffered with the loss of their liege, their protector? 'Twould have been more prudent to have assistance in your quest, do you not think so?"

So great was Gavin's surprise at the concern clouding her eyes that he did not take umbrage with her pointed words. "I am used to taking such risks," he replied in his rough, scratchy voice. "'Tis my duty."

Madelyne nodded, leaning toward him with a cloth that she used to dab at his pounding head. "Aye, my lord, 'tis your duty. And is it your duty to wish for death as you take those risks?"

Gavin stared at her, suddenly caught in the moon-like pools of her gray eyes. She was so close that her warmth and serenity covered him like a thick blanket. The cloth on his face was cool and soothing, and he was surrounded by the scents of mint and smoke and, beneath it all, woman. "I did not wish for death this time," he admitted, hardly aware of what he was saying, so strong was the sudden urge to pull her to him.

Madelyne stilled, as if she sensed his churning emotions. "Death would not become you, my lord," she said at last, brushing gentle fingers down the side of his face. "And methinks you would leave much sorrow behind you in this world."

Nine

MADELYNE PULLED another offending weed from a patch of lavender, tossing it onto the stone pathway behind her. The day was beautiful, with a full, bright sun casting warmth over all the earth, and the scents of herbs and flowers carried on a gentle breeze. The garden at Mal Verne had long been neglected, and she had taken to spending some of her day among the calendula, peppermint, thyme and ladies mantle.

She'd been at Mal Verne for nearly a fortnight, and had fallen into a bit of a routine. After the fire, which had destroyed one portion of the village, the news of her ability to treat injuries became known, and Madelyne found herself in some demand for such tasks. Thus, she allotted the morning hours immediately following Mass to receiving the villagers and seeing to their hurts. Through Jube, Lord Gavin—as she'd come to think of him—had given permission for her to use a small storeroom built off the kitchen for her infirmary. When asked why the villeins did not seek the services of the town leech, Jube replied that news of her years at the abbey, and proximity to God, lent her abilities more credence in the eyes of the townsfolk.

After her time spent with the villagers, Madelyne was often approached by Mal Verne's steward, Jonnat, with issues that would normally have been handled by the Lady of Mal Verne.

The first time Jonnat came to her with problems caused by infighting among the seamstresses, Madelyne did not know how to respond. "How does the lady of the household handle such problems?" she asked in confusion.

Jonnat looked at her, confusion mirrored on his own face, and snapped his jaw shut. She saw him dart a glance around, then return his attention to her. "The lady—we do not speak of her within the lord's hearing…or otherwise."

Madelyne barely refrained from rolling her eyes in frustration. Whatever the absent Lady Mal Verne's role in her husband's life, it seemed much too extreme that her name not even be mentioned within the household. However, she forebore to respond. Instead, she took it upon herself to visit the solar where the seamstresses worked. With a few pointed questions and some veiled suggestions that the lord would not be pleased to be bothered with such trifles, Madelyne was able to smooth out the problems and get the women back to work.

Jonnat was so grateful—for, apparently, he'd been unable to handle the catty, spiteful women—that he made it a practice to approach her with other such feminine related problems. Madelyne did not begrudge assisting the man, who was a bit elderly and prone to confusion when faced with feminine wiles. And having lived among only women for so long, Madelyne was well-versed in such conflicts—for even in the abbey, there was occasional jealousy and gossip.

Thus, it was not until after the midday meal that she found the time to escape to the chapel for some moments of reflection, and then to God's other home, the outdoors, to bury her hands in the soil and encourage the struggling plants to grow.

Since the fire, she'd seen little of Mal Verne himself. Though he'd been burned heartily by a fallen ceiling beam, he'd insisted on rising from his bed the following day—overriding her protests—and going down to the village to supervise the rebuilding of the burned out homes. She'd heard from Tricky, who had the information from Clem, that Lord Gavin had declared that no home be built closer than twenty paces to the next.

A sudden high-pitched giggle pierced her ears. Madelyne pulled back onto her haunches and looked toward the high growth of boxwood, which was shuddering much too violently to be simply the breeze passing through. Just as she turned, the bushes next to the thick boxwood hedge parted, and Tricky stumbled through. She had her skirt clutched in her hands and she was looking behind her, another giggle tumbling from her mouth, as she dashed toward the pathway.

Upon seeing Madelyne, she paused, raising a finger to her plump, berry-like lips, and, eyes twinkling, ducked behind a rosemary bush.

Heavy crashing announced the arrival of someone larger and stronger than Tricky, and Madelyne watched in faint amusement as Jube burst through the hedge several paces from where her maid had appeared. He skidded to a halt in his tracks when he caught sight of Madelyne and froze, looking acutely uncomfortable.

"Hail there, Jube," Madelyne said, pulling a small growth of oregano from the midst of the lavendar patch.

The tall blond man stood, tugging at his tunic and brushing dirt and leaves from the sleeves of his *sherte*, then shifted his weight from boot heel to boot heel. He looked around covertly, but did not move. "Good day, my lady," he said at last, glancing toward the rosemary bush.

"I wondered where you'd gotten off to," Madelyne commented idly.

"Ah, yes, my lady. As I knew you would be occupied for some time here in the garden, I went to see to…mmm…some other business." He rubbed his prominent nose, then pinched the spot where it bent to one side. "Er…has anyone happened along here recently?"

She bit her lip to hide a smile. He tried so hard to sound casual, but his gaze continued to dart around like a butterfly. "Nay, not that I have noticed." She avoided looking toward the rosemary bush, which vibrated briefly. "I have been very busy, though, and may not have seen someone if they passed by quietly."

"Mmmm." Jube clearly did not know how to react, and 'twas obvious that he was torn between his duty to watch over her, and his desire to learn where Tricky had escaped.

Madelyne took pity and dismissed him with a wave of her hand. "Go you and finish your business—I shall be here yet until the sun reaches the top of that apple tree."

He smiled at her, and, passing a hand over his thin hair, gave a quick bow. "Thank you, my lady. I will return then." He started to go, then turned back. "If anyone should pass this way, you may… mmm…never you mind." And, with a faint flush staining his pale face, he bounded off down the path with the grace of a plow-horse.

No sooner had he gone than the rosemary bush shuddered in earnest and Tricky blundered out of hiding. Her face was flushed with enthusiasm and her honey-colored hair straggled in messy wisps, springing from the confines of its braid. "Many thanks, my lady!" she said.

Madelyne's amusement grew. "An' what kind of chase do you lead him on?"

Tricky sank down on the ground next to her, reaching for a tuft of grass that grew amidst the thyme. "He thought to kiss me, and I thought to foil his plans!" She tossed the grass to one side, heedless of the fact that it missed Madelyne's head only by a slight margin.

"If he has overstepped his bounds, you need only tell me," Madelyne told her, looking at her shrewdly…while at the same time, wondering what it would be like to have a man think to kiss her. Lord Gavin's face popped into her mind, and she bit her lip. Had he mayhap thought to kiss her on the wall that first eve at Mal Verne? And if he wished to, why had he not done so?

Madelyne suppressed the sudden shiver of heat that slid up her spine, then resolutely dismissed the thought. A man such as Gavin Mal Verne would want naught to do with a mousy nun such as she…and, dear Lord, she'd forgotten—he was married! She pursed her lips, renewing her silent vow to return to life at the abbey as soon as possible. She'd been with out its walls for less than a fort-night, and already she was tempted to stray from God's path!

"'Tis naught for you to be concerned with," Tricky was say-ing earnestly. "Jube has behaved only kindly toward me, and I have no quarrel with his attentions." She beamed, plucking a daisy, and began to pull its silky white petals from their yellow center mooring. "He loves me, he loves me not …"

Just then, a dark shadow fell over the two women. Tricky looked up, squeaked in surprise, and floundered to her feet. "My lord!"

Madelyne raised her face, shielding her eyes from the sun that blared behind him, but did not move from her position. "Good day, Lord Gavin."

"My lady." He cast a brief glance at Tricky, who had begun to melt away into the nearby shrubbery. "Patricka." He looked around, then down at Madelyne, who had shifted so that the sun did not blind her. "I do not see Jube, my lady. Is he not nearby?"

Madelyne saw Tricky's sudden intake of breath and replied mildly, "He was here only a moment ago, my lord. I believe he stepped away to…tend to some personal matter."

"Ah. Chasing some unsuspecting maiden most likely."

Madelyne stared up at him, aware that her surprise was openly on her features. Had he actually made a jest? She looked closely at his face, but saw no indication of good humor in his eyes. He plucked a stem of peppermint and began to chew on the leaves.

Tricky stepped backward once more, trampling on the boxwood. "With your leave, my lord, my lady," she babbled, "I shall find Sir Jube and inform him that his presence is requested." Without waiting for a response, she turned and crashed into the thick brush and disappeared.

Lord Gavin peered after her for a moment. "What ails your maid, Lady Madelyne?"

She shrugged slightly and returned to her task of pulling up the oregano that had begun to sprout throughout the garden. Her hand trembled, and she felt her heart leap into her throat when he crouched down beside her. Out of the corner of her eye, she could see his scuffed brown boots and his strong tanned hand resting on the dirt. He was too near, and she could not think clearly.

"You've spent much time setting right the gardens of Mal Verne, as well as guiding old Jonnat in his tasks. The villagers speak highly of you and your healing skills, and I wish to thank you for all you have done."

Madelyne kept her gaze trained on the plants in front of her, afraid that if she looked over and was caught in his stare, he would see what in her eyes she did not wish for him to know. "I am not used to being idle," she replied. There was a silence and she nearly gave in to the urge to look at him, but instead kept her attention trained on a ladybird that scuttled along the stem of a daisy.

"I wish also to thank you for tending to me, and to my hurts. How fares the woman we saved from the fire?"

"Lettie is doing well. Barden's mother, Coria, has taken her into her home and cares for her."

"And how fares she with the loss of her son?"

Madelyne brushed some dirt from her skirt. "She has become accustomed to the loss, my lord, and though she grieves for him, she has found strength in caring for Lettie and the child she carries." Now she had the courage to look up, and she was surprised to see him staring into the distance, his face carved in emotionless stone.

"I had hoped to save them both," he admitted, still gazing, unseeing, toward the horizon. Then, as if comprehending the words she'd spoken, he whipped his gaze to hers. "Lettie carries a child?"

Madelyne nodded once, suddenly shy under his heavy gaze. "Aye. She had only suspected before the fire, but now she has told Coria, and together the women have learned to deal with their grief by focusing on the coming baby."

"I shall send her a cow and some hens," he murmured to himself.

Madelyne returned to her task, and felt rather than saw him as he sank further to the ground, sitting next to her so that the toe of his boot nearly brushed her skirt. What he could hope to accomplish by his presence, she did not know, so, emboldened, she turned to ask. "My lord, is there aught that I can do for you?"

As she spoke, he reached out and caught a flyaway strand of her hair, tucking it behind her ear. Madelyne froze, her heart thumping in her throat, as his fingers brushed her ear and the side of her face. "Nay." The single word was carried softly on the breeze and hung there for a moment until he spoke again. "I wished only to seek the serenity of the garden, and the calmness of your presence after a day of much activity."

Shaken, Madelyne forced herself to return to her weeding. What could he mean? Still acutely aware of his presence, she felt him reach for and pluck another stem of mint, and smelled the crispness of its scent as he chewed on it.

"You prefer to be out of doors," Lord Gavin commented in a dusky, rumbling voice.

"Aye. 'Tis the best place to enjoy the world God has given us. To smell the clean air, to enjoy His creatures and the green things He has created…." Madelyne glanced at him, then quickly back to the clump of oregano that grew in the midst of the mint. "Even when it grows where we do not wish it to," she continued, gesturing to the oregano as she pulled it from the earth. "One must stop and give thanks."

Lord Gavin looked at her in such a way that made her feel as though he'd never before seen her. "And I—'tis something I rarely think to do, my lady. The times I spend in this world are on the back of a horse, or brandishing some blooded weapon…and rarely have I a peaceful moment such as this…to smell the mint and to touch the soft leaves of the rosemary."

There was silence for a long moment, again, and just as she was about to speak, the sound of footfalls thumping down the path reached them. She and Lord Gavin looked up to see Jube, accompanied by Clem and Tricky, hurrying toward them.

"My lord, a missive has arrived from the king," Clem announced, brandishing a parchment with the sovereign's red wax seal on it.

Lord Gavin took the message and broke the seal, heedless of the pieces of red wax that crumbled to the ground. "Does the messenger await a reply?" he asked as he unfolded the paper.

"Aye. He is to join us for supper and stay only the night, then return to his majesty with your response."

Madelyne watched as he perused the letter quickly, and saw his countenance still and settle into the harsh features she was familiar with. All trace of ease faded from his face, and when he looked up, even his dark brows had drawn together in a fierce black line. He looked at her, and his eyes were stone cold and flat. "The king requests your presence at his court."

A pang of fear shot through her, and she managed to subdue it with a swallow and a slow breath. 'Twas only the royal order that she had expected, yet Mal Verne seemed inexplicably disturbed by the missive that he had certainly anticipated. Without thinking, she touched him, resting her fingers on the hard muscles of his arm. She felt him start beneath her hand, almost as if he wanted to pull away from her touch…and she dropped it immediately. "What is it? Is there more?"

He had folded the parchment and stuffed the stiff paper into the belt of his tunic as he rose to his feet. "Your father has learned of your presence here at Mal Verne, and he has expressed his concern for your safety and his desire to see you."

The shaft of fear pierced her again, and Madelyne felt light-headed. Her father. Fantin. She grasped a handful of skirt and pulled awkwardly to her feet. Quelling the panic that threatened to overtake her, she replied carefully, "When must we leave?"

He measured her with his gaze, then flickered his attention to Jube and Clem. "On the morrow. His majesty expects us at Whitehall with all haste."

Peg would accompany them to court.

The older woman and Tricky had taken charge of the packing, leaving Madelyne to do naught but sit near the fireplace and be subjected to a discussion of her clothing, fashion, and personal attributes as if she weren't present.

"Nay, child, not that violet! 'Twould make her look as lost as the drabness of a plowed field," Peg admonished Tricky, who had held up an undergown of the offending color. "Verily, my sister's daughter by law could wear such a color as that, for she has hair a pale wheat color. But for one such as my lady, why, only the reds and greens and golds, and mayhaps a blue or so, will do for her.

My brother's daughter's mother was known for her beautiful blues woven in cloths made for the ladies of the courts in Paris. Aye, she would pick the flowers and cut their stems, leaving only the blue leaves before she would stew them in a pot—for days and days, he would tell us…and the smell would be enough to turn yer stomach, it would…and I suppose she must cook them out of the house, else….." Her voice trailed off, and she paused, looking at Tricky, who had been listening avidly, and then at Madelyne, and then down at the cloth she clutched in one hand. "Hmmph…aye…. hmm." She turned, folding a golden undergown and laying it carefully in the trunk.

"I cannot take all of this clothing," Madelyne protested, gesturing at the mounds of cloth on the bed and stools. "Will not the lady miss it when she comes here?"

Peg looked at her in bewilderment. "What are you speaking of, child? The lady is not coming here—at the least, if she were to do so, she would have no use for clothing!" She gave a short chuckle, then sobered. She picked up another gown. "Did you not know? Lady Nicola is dead, my lady."

"Lady Nicola? Lord Gav—Mal Verne's wife—is dead?" Madelyne felt a sudden, foolish unburdening of her heart.

Tricky sprang off the stool on which she'd perched for a moment's rest and placed her hands on her round hips. "Aye, 'tis so, my lady. Did not Lord Mal Verne tell you?"

Peg snorted, casting a sidewise glance at the other two. "Lord Gavin speaks not of his wife, nor will he allow any of us to speak of her in his presence."

"Aye, 'tis why, then Clem spoke so quickly and softly in my ear when I asked him." Tricky frowned, folding her arms over her middle, and pursed her lip into a pout. "An' I bethought he meant to steal a kiss by doing so."

"Tricky! Clem tried to kiss you as well?" Madelyne could not suppress the niggling annoyance that her friend should suddenly be the target of affection of two different men, when she had not—

Had not what?

Caught the attention of the mighty lord of the manor? She huffed out a breath of air and bit her bottom lip. Marry, she was a fool to entertain such fantasies!

Her maid was shaking her head. "Nay, Lady Madelyne, it 'pears I was mistaken that he sought to kiss me." She appeared slighted by this realization and returned her attention to delving into a new trunk of old clothing.

"Well, there's no sense in bein' put out by the fact that he ain't kissed ye yet," Peg wagged a motherly finger. "Kissin's a good thing, but ye don't wanna be too free with'em. 'Course…it's the best way to know true love." She held up a ruby-colored gown and shook it out. With a nod, she added it to a trunk filled with clothing. "When the right man kisses ye, ye'll know he's the one! Mark my words. I've had my share of kissin' and only my Peter was the one who made m'head spin like a top!"

Peg pushed down on the lid of the trunk that overflowed with gowns and overtunics, shoes, hose, and several cloaks. "Aye," she puffed, sitting heavily on it, and brought them back to the previous topic, "My lord Gavin is quite the closed-mouthed ogre about the lady. Tricky, fetch those ties there—beyond the bed clothes."

Madelyne joined the other two women as they struggled to wrap the ties about the bulging trunk. Curiosity got the better of her, though, and she asked, "What happened to Lady Nicola? And why will Lord Mal Verne not speak of her?"

The older woman smoothed a hand over her bright red hair with the pale yellow streak. "I served Lady Nicola as her tiring maid at court, ye know, and I saw how it happened."

Tricky plumped herself on the floor next to the trunk, tucking a cushion beneath her rump. "What was it that happened?"

"Well, 'twas oh, nigh on seven years past…nay, six summers. Lady Nicola accompanied Lord Gavin to the court of the new King Henry and Queen Eleanor as they went to pledge fealty to our new rulers. She was a beautiful if foolish lady, and had been married before she was wed with Lord Gavin. She oft complained to me that the lord traveled overmuch, fighting in battles and that he did not woo her as he should."

"Well, 'tis no surprise. Lord Gavin is not the wooing sort," Tricky snorted. "'Tis obvious even to me, who has been in an abbey since I could walk!"

"Tricky!" Madelyne could not disagree, but she would not have spoken such a thing.

"Nay, my lady, 'tis true. And since the death of his wife, Lord Gavin has been e'en less gentle." Peg took up the story again. "At any rate, I was with Lady Nicola on the first she saw him…not Lord Gavin, mind, but the man who would be her lover.

"Even to these old eyes—well, they weren't so old six summers past, but old enough that a fine face and figure won't easily turn them—er…ach, aye, yes, even to these eyes, the man was fine and courtly. Not so tall, but taller than Lady Nicola…and his hair brushed his shoulders like a moonbeam." When Tricky snickered, Peg pulled from her reverie to glare down at her. "Those were the words of Lady Nicola, and not my own, know you well.

"Aye, she did moon for him, and wail over his manners, and his sapphire blue eyes, and the skill with which he played the lute… and she waited until Lord Gavin was called home to Mal Verne. She begged for him to allow her to stay with the king and queen's court…and Lord Gavin, sharp though he might be, cared for her enough to allow her to stay."

Peg stopped, and when Tricky humphed in impatience, she shrugged. "'Tis easy to guess the rest, of course. Nicola found her way to the man's side, and he wooed her with his smile and his beautiful voice—I'll not argue that when the man sang, he had the voice of an angel—and his gentle charm. In Lady Nicola's eyes, he was all that Lord Gavin was not."

Madelyne felt a stab of pain for Mal Verne. The man might be a warrior, and a rough one at that…but surely he did not deserve to be dishonored by his own wife because he did not sing beautifully. 'Twas no wonder that he did not wish to speak of her.

"Did Lord Gavin learn of her betrayal? She did betray him, did she not?" Tricky asked, adjusting her bottom on the pillow like a child in the throes of a bedtime tale.

Peg nodded sagely. "Aye. 'Twas not until later that my lord learned of her fancy… months later. And aye, she did betray Lord Gavin by bedding with her lover during their time at court. Lord Gavin did not learn of the depth of her unfaithfulness until he came to bring her back to Mal Verne." Her eyes became troubled and she patted the streak of yellow in her hair again. "Quite a row, there was…the lady would not leave, and my lord insisted that she go. She loved *him*, she said to Lord Gavin, and she wanted only to be with *him*."

Drawing her eyebrows into irregular ridges, Peg paused for a moment as if to gather the threads of the story. "I did not hear it all, but another of the maids claimed Lady Nicola insisted that her lover was a man of greatness and holiness …hmph, I said when that was told me…a fine face and lilting voice do not make a great man! And one who would couple with another man's wife is no holy one in my mind!"

"Did Lord Gavin make her leave with him?" Tricky asked. Madelyne did not know whether to be amused or alarmed at the glow of interest in her friend's eyes.

"Aye. He took her back here to Mal Verne. A fortnight later, a missive arrived for her. 'Twas from her lover, of course—his name she never spoke in my hearing. She planned to ride out and meet him, so they would leave together."

Peg sighed, and stood suddenly, shaking out her skirts. The pleasure of tale-telling evaporated from her face, and Madelyne recognized sorrow blanketing her features—but was the sorrow for Lady Nicola or for Lord Gavin?

"The rest I do not know," said Peg. "There is no one but his lord and her lady who do. All that has been told to us is that she left here in the dead of night—escaped his wrath, some say—and Lord Gavin went after her. When he returned, 'twas with word that she was dead from a fall off her horse."

Coldness gripped Madelyne's heart as she remembered her own flight with her mother. What would Fantin have done if he'd learned of their escape and caught them? The thought sent a wave of emptiness and fear through her. "And no one knows what happened?"

"Nay. None but the lord and the lady herself. And she ain't speakin'."

Ten

RULE WAS eager to be on the road again. Gavin was not.

In fact, he was in a most foul mood, and his men had given him a wide berth since leaving Mal Verne that morning.

The solitude—at the least, as much isolation as one could have when traveling in a group of men-at-arms—suited him fine. He'd begun the journey riding at the rear of the party, keeping Rule to a handy trot as they left Mal Verne and started on the road to Whitehall. It would take four days to reach the king, even traveling as quickly as he planned, since the roads were mired with mud from the heavy rains that had fallen in the last sevennight.

The carts carrying the bulk of their luggage would have a slower time of it, but there was no help for it. Nor could he have allowed the women to ride in a cart because of its slower pace. The king's message had made it clear Gavin was to make all haste to bring Madelyne de Belgrume to his presence.

He remembered the fear that turned her face ashen when she learned de Belgrume knew of her presence, and of his desire to see her. It had not been an insignificant expression—it had been true horror and panic. Gavin brooded, wondering what it was that she feared and if it was anything he could protect her from. Then, frustrated he shoved a hank of hair out of his eyes.

He was not the permanent protector of Madelyne de Belgrume—he was merely her escort to the king's side, after which he would be free to never see her again.

His attention wandered over the backs of his men until it found the mount carrying Jube and Lady Madelyne. Gavin tightened his hands on Rule's reins and forced himself to look away from the slim figure cloaked in a midnight blue wrap. She rode behind Jube, and he could see the wrist-thick braid that disappeared into the neckline of the cape where her hood had fallen back.

He clearly remembered the feel of her settling on the saddle in front of him, his thighs locking around her and her head jouncing just in front of his chin as they rode along. That memory was precisely the reason he'd refused to share a mount with her again, and was just as strongly the reason he'd made certain she sat behind Jube, rather than in front of him.

And, verily, it was also the reason for his nasty mood.

Annoyed at the distraction, he jabbed his mail-covered heels into Rule's side, and the steed surged forward with a sudden leap. They clipped quickly along, weaving expertly among the others in the party, to the head of the group where Gavin's three scouts cantered along. Glad to put Madelyne de Belgrume behind him, he manipulated the stallion so that he could talk with Leo, the leader of his scouts.

Fantin gripped the reins of his dancing mount and jammed a heel into its side. The bloody horse was causing the bush to shake and would alert Mal Verne and his men to their presence long before the ambush he planned.

After praying and fasting with Rufus for two days, Fantin understood: God wished him to return Madelyne to Tricourten immediately.

It had become clear there was some purpose she must play in his quest—for her reappearance was the sign he'd been awaiting. Not only must she return to his fold because she was his daughter, his flesh and blood, and he *owned* her…but because she must play a part in this purpose with which God had burdened him so generously.

Whatever Madelyne's task, it would be revealed to him in God's Time.

With a hiss, for he did not know how much longer 'twould be before Mal Verne's party approached this curve in the road, he captured the attention of his thirteen men-at-arms who stood ready to swarm into their path. He cocked his head, catching the eye of Tavis, and ordered, "Go you back on the road and look for signs of their approach."

He had no need to wait for the king to make his decision regarding the fate of the girl—or even to grant him an audience. The wench was his daughter, and he would have her if he pleased.

The message he'd sent to Henry served only to cause him to appear complacent—to allay any suspicions the king might harbor against him and his Work. And thus when he appeared in the royal court, demanding to see his daughter, Henry would only be able to tell him that she'd disappeared again. And no one would fault Fantin for his anger against the king for allowing Mal Verne to lose his daughter again so soon after she'd been found. He licked his lips, feeling their pleasing plumpness—due to the herb-scented goose fat he smeared on them each night—and smiled.

The king was no better friend to him than Mal Verne was—and his whore of a wife as well. They would be among the first to feel his wrath when he completed his work and had the Stone in his grasp.

Eagerness rising within, he swallowed the smile and manipulated his stallion away from the group of men, taking a post further up the road. Mal Verne would die today, and Madelyne would be back in the care of her loving father…as she should have been for the last ten years.

He grinned there, silent in his glee, and thought of the destiny that awaited him once his daughter was in his custody.

And he gave a solemn prayer of thanks.

'Twas a capriciousness very unlike him, Gavin thought as he bent toward Rule's head, just missing being slapped in the face by a heavy branch. He patted the smoothness of the steed's neck, digging his fingers into the thick mane. An exhilaration filled him as the stallion leapt over a small creek, galloping at full speed through the thick forest.

They'd left the traveling party in favor of chasing a stag in hopes of having venison for supper—and to give Rule a few moments to exert his stunted energy. Gavin grinned, enjoying the feel of the wind buffeting his face. It had been overlong since he'd enjoyed himself so, and for a few moments, he felt young again—as if he'd shed the weight of his past, his mistakes, and that of those he'd loved.

The white tail of the deer was just visible as it bounded over a fallen tree, and Gavin leaned forward, urging Rule to go faster as they drew closer. He reached back for the spear he carried, readying it for the fatal thrust, crouching low as Rule sprang over the fallen trunk.

Suddenly, a scream rent the air, far distant but chilling to his ears. Gavin jerked his head toward the sound, hearing its echo even over the thrashing of Rule's hooves through the brush. *Madelyne.*

Gavin yanked back on the reins, kicking his mount frantically, and the destrier spun on its rear legs with the practiced grace of a warhorse. They reversed direction instantly, and he pressed forward, hugging Rule with his powerful thighs and urging him on with commands in the stallion's ears.

They burst from the forest onto the road moments later and swerved in an easterly direction, following the path of the travel party. Hooves thudding, Rule did not hesitate as he galloped furiously toward the sound of swords clashing in the distance.

Gavin swallowed back the dryness of fear at the unmistakable sound of battle, and froze all thoughts of self-rebuke from his mind. He would curse himself later. Now he must keep his wits clear in order to subdue their attackers.

Bellowing a clear battle cry, Gavin drew his sword as they rushed into the midst of the skirmish. He engaged one of the attackers, who wore a helm to cover his face and had been about to strike Clem and Tricky. A quick glance away from his opponent revealed no sign of Madelyne, and Gavin summoned all of his strength and rage to plow his sword through the chest of his adversary. He wheeled Rule about and cantered around the perimeter of the melee, which seemed to be dying down now that he'd reached it. In fact, those that remained were men from Mal Verne, with the exception of three bloody bodies that lay unmoving on the ground.

"Madelyne!" he shouted, rising on his heels in the saddle.

"She is taken!" cried Clem between gasps of air. He clutched his side even as he held Tricky in place on his lap. Gavin took in the sight of red staining his friend's arm and fury escalated within. "They came upon us from nowhere, and took my lady right from behind Jube!"

Gavin fought the urge to rush pell-mell in the direction Clem pointed, and halted for a moment, his chest heaving with heavy breaths. "Jube!" he shouted, then looked where another man pointed.

The tall blond man stood to the side of the road, his sword hanging at his side, violence darkening his features. The destrier that Gavin recognized as Jube's was on its side, its gut slit open and spilling entrails onto the dirt road.

"They made certain I could not save her!" he shouted furiously, rage roughing his voice. "By the rood, I'll murder the man who took my Blazon!"

"*To me!*" Gavin roared, calling his men to cluster about him. "You who cannot fight, do you ride ahead to Prentiss Keep and relate this stealing of the lady to Lord Markhand's captain of the guard—ask for reinforcements. We go east and will see them as they come to join us. Those who can, follow me!"

Rule leapt forward and the others fell in behind. Fortunately, the ground was soft from the rains and left a clear pattern of tracks along the easterly road. Gavin and Rule kept a generous lead from the remainder of the party—approximately eight of the fifteen men with which they'd left Mal Verne.

As they thundered down the road, Gavin forced himself to focus on reaching the kidnappers and saving Madelyne. The man he'd killed had worn no standard or livery that could identify him. It was likely he was part of a band of thieves that preyed on travelers. Mayhaps Madelyne been targeted and taken to be held for ransom. If that were the case, then she would not be harmed.

The tightening of his chest—the fear that he was wrong, that there was some other reason for her kidnapping—grew and he urged Rule on further.

Madelyne swallowed the fear that bubbled in her middle, nauseating her. Mayhaps 'twas the stench of the man who carried her on his mount in front of him that caused her stomach to turn, but most likely it was the horror that she was no longer in the safe hands of Gavin Mal Verne, and had been catapulted into a worse fate than that of being taken to the king.

Her hands were bound tightly in front of her with a rough rope, and she clutched the mane of the horse in hopes that she would not lose her balance and be trampled under its hooves. The man behind her—she'd heard his name given as Arneth—breathed heavily, leaning forward and billowing stale breath into her face.

Lord Gavin.

She thought his name, praying that he would have heard her scream and was even now racing to save her. She did not know who had taken her, nor had the four men who accompanied her captor said anything to disclose the reason for her kidnapping. She had seen through the whirlwind of fear and fighting that some of the men who'd ambushed them had been left for dead, and the others had been separated, retreating in a different direction.

Suddenly, they changed course, wheeling off the road and into the underbrush. She heard a grunt from Arneth, and the reek of his breath buffeted more strongly as he shouted, "We are followed! Break away!"

A leap of hope lunged in her chest, and she wrenched her head to look back. Arneth's face, drawn together in ugly intensity, loomed inches behind her, his gray teeth bared in concentration. Madelyne jerked away from the ugly proximity and felt her seat slip. Bracing her aching legs against the side of the horse, she struggled to regain her balance even as she heard the man chuckle in her ear.

Dear God, please let that be Gavin. Please let him find me. Madelyne prayed with more vehemence than she'd ever thought possible on those nights at the *prie dieu* in Lock Rose Abbey. *I will cease these errant thoughts of him if You will grant me this.*

She felt Arneth shift behind her, and then heard his exclamation of surprise. Loud thrashing, heavy breathing, shouts and the unmistakable sound of steel being slid from within steel filled her environment…and then suddenly, it was over.

A howl reverberated in her ears as she felt a jerk behind her, then the loss of Arneth's weight in the saddle as he tumbled to the ground. She clutched at the horse, a cry escaping her lips as she began to slip, and then suddenly, she was lifted—plucked easily from her seat—and slammed onto the front of another saddle.

She did not even need to look behind her to know that it was Gavin whose powerful arm held her steady in the seat in front of him, and whose brawny thighs enclosed her. Her heart still thundered in her chest even as they slowed to a canter, and then a trot, and finally to a standstill in the middle of the forest.

If there had been others in the chase, they had left them far behind, and the stillness of the wood caught up with them as they stopped in a small clearing. The only sound was his rough breathing mingling with her own.

Gavin said naught, and she, too, had remained silent, trying to catch her breath and slow her heart. He slid from the saddle, his feet landing on the ground in two rhythmic thumps. When he turned his face to look up at her, raising his arms to lift her from the saddle, Madelyne nearly recoiled in shock.

It was Gavin Mal Verne, and yet it was not.

If she had thought him to have a mask of stone for a face before, she had not a clear idea of how that truly should look—for now his countenance was still, angry, and hard, and his gray eyes blazed with intensity and ferocity as his chest heaved with exertion.

His wide brown hands slipped under her bound arms and lifted her down with a gentleness she had not expected.

"I cannot plead your forgiveness enough, my lady," he said stiffly, his flat gaze inscrutable. "My foolish actions and lack of attention to your person were disgraceful and inexcusable." He looked down at her hands, which were beginning to gray due to the tightness of her bonds. His mouth pinched and she saw his face darken. In a trice, he had sliced the hemp at her wrists and began to chafe them gently.

The pinpricks of circulation returning to her fingers caused her to pull away and shake her hands. "Lord Gavin, I am in your debt for your protection of me—"

"Do not be a fool, my lady," he snapped, spinning away to stalk toward Rule. "'Tis I who am indebted to you, and 'twas my folly that caused you to be in this state."

He gathered up the trailing reins of the well-trained destrier and, with a quick pat on his nose, led the horse toward Madelyne. Mal Verne's thick dark hair sprung wildly about his face, brushing the heavy black brows that drew together in angry points while curling softly about his ears and throat. The cord of his neck throbbed and thrummed with his furious pulse, and his sensual mouth leveled into a thin, hard line. "Come now, I will get you back to the others where you will be safe."

He stepped toward her, and the energy that surrounded him engulfed Madelyne even as he reached to touch her. Pushing aside her earlier bargain with God to cease her deviant thoughts of Gavin Mal Verne, she looked up at him and replied, "I cannot be any safer than when I am with you, my lord."

Her heart swelled in her throat and her stomach turned a little flip when he paused, his hands resting on her shoulders. The harshness in his features eased into derision and weariness clouded his eyes. "If you imagine that, Lady Madelyne, then you are even more of a fool than I believed." He made ready to lift her, but she stopped him, reaching out to place a light hand on his chest. It felt solid and warm beneath the shifting, chinking of his mail.

"I am no fool, my lord," she replied, suddenly annoyed at his persistence on that track. "An' if that is all you think of me, then—"

"Nay, Madelyne, that is not all that I think of you," he whispered, and suddenly he pulled her to him, his mouth slamming down onto hers.

Those lips that had moments before been hard and unyielding became soft and coaxing as they closed over her mouth that parted in surprise. They molded to hers, hot and smooth and slick, tasting of mint and sweat and man…Gavin. Gathered up against his solid chest, Madelyne felt the bumps of the mail and the bands of his arms holding her close, his hands cupping her head from behind. She fitted against his tall length, thigh to thigh, belly to belly, mouth to mouth. Her hand moved up to touch his thick, damp hair, and her fingers brushed the heat and moistness of his neck.

Her world spinning, Madelyne kissed him back, tasting him, tentatively caressing his mouth while his lips devoured hers—demanding from them, from her—leaving her breathless and her eyelids weighted closed. A fiery heat built within her, surging into her middle and down, lower, to pool there where they fitted, hip to hip.

One of his arms slid to the base of her back, crushing her close, lifting her up against him as his mouth continued to coax and caress hers. She felt a thrill of surprise when his tongue slipped inside her, bringing all the heat and sleekness of his desire. He sighed into her, giving a short shudder, and dragged his lips away with a soft, deep-throated moan.

Gavin stared down at her, breathing heavily, his fingers sliding from the back of her neck to rest on her upper arms. He gazed at her for a long moment with hazy eyes, a myriad of emotions playing across his face before the harshness settled there again.

"As I said, Lady Madelyne, a fool is not all that I think of you." His words were rough and hard. He continued to look at her with eyes that had cleared and flattened to match his tone as he gathered up Rule's reins. "I'll not apologize for that—nay—but I'll see that it does not happen again. Now, you will put your misguided self into my passable care until we reach Prentiss Keep, and then we shall start off for the king's court with a rested band of men and no more of my transgressions."

Eleven

FANTIN'S HOWL of rage ricocheted off the walls of the small room, followed by the clatter of tin goblets, eating knives, and metal platters as they tumbled to the floor. "Imbeciles!" he shouted, eyes bulging as he stalked fore and aft amongst his men. "Each of you! All imbeciles!"

He could not even take pleasure in the way they cowered before him, for pure rage empurpled his vision. Madelyne had been within his grasp…the Stone so close he could taste its power…and now he sat empty-handed in some bloody, primitive tavern with naught but godless cretins to serve him. Unblessed, they were, and he, foolish as he was, had brought them into his employ, thinking to share with them some benefit of the Gift once it was his. But now, nay. Nay.

"Out of my sight! All of you!" he ordered, heedless of the proprietor's worried face peaking around the doorway.

The men fled—those who were left of the thirteen—and Fantin slumped in his chair, fighting to regain clarity over the haze of fury that fogged his faculties. These rages that befell him at moments such as this, and with more frequency now that he came closer to the fruits of his labor, affrighted him with their vehemence and strength. Rufus had cautioned him to work to control them, else he might become too impatient and suffer God's displeasure. Thus, Fantin raised his eyes to the heavens and prayed for a moment, allowing the comfort of this familiarity to wash over him.

He barely finished his words of supplication when his mind wandered back to the moment…the moment when he had seen her, seen the girl and recognized her—before slipping away from the small battle to allow his men to finish. In an attempt to maintain anonymity, he'd left the actual seizure of Madelyne to his trusted man Arneth, choosing to keep for himself the pleasure of killing Mal Verne—of putting an end to the man who stood always betwixt Fantin and his work. But to his surprise and fury, the bloody coward had not been present when the ambush took place.

God's bloody teeth! The fury threatened to rise within Fantin again, rattling his nerves and stringing his muscles tightly. How could he have come so close, only to have her swept away? Never again. *Never again* could he trust those fools to do what he must do for himself!

His fist closed around a knife and he stabbed it into the scarred wooden table, burying it as deep as the first digit of his finger. His shuddering breathing rasped in the sudden silence, and his fingers opened and closed, opened and closed around the hilt of the knife.

His breathing slowed again, and at last he was able to reach for his goblet of wine—he disdained ale, for it was the drink of mean serfs—and drink heavily, draining it with several gulps.

Could he have been wrong? Could he and Rufus have misunderstood?

Or…mayhap it was another test.

Aye. Another test. He nodded and sank to the floor, to his knees, to prostrate himself there.

He must ask forgiveness…for failing. For allowing the bloody heathen Mal Verne to best him. For allowing his rival to once again stand in his way, to keep him from completing his work.

The stone floor bit into his knees, but Fantin reveled in the pain. He knew he must bear it, enjoy it, *worship* it. He must find some other painful penance to bear, now that he had failed his God again.

Curling his fingers into the edge of the rough table, Fantin dropped his forehead to the wood with a loud and painful thump and stared down at the floor with vacant eyes, praying, begging, pleading…silently and violently…for something. For God to speak to him, to guide him.

Tears filled his eyes. He tried so hard…so hard to be the man God had chosen him to be. To fulfill his destiny. To be all that God wished him to be. A drop fell to the floor, dampening the dust below, and seeping into nothingness.

At last, when he looked up, he saw a flicker of movement at the doorway—the wisp of a skirt as it fluttered past. "Hail! Wench!" he called, suddenly thirsty…and famished.

The skirt paused and returned to view, and with it came a comely wench with a low-cut, but soiled, bodice. She sauntered in to the room. Obviously she was either unaware of his high ire only moments before, or, now that it had subsided, was unafraid.

"My lord, how may I-a be helpin' ye?" She flashed him a coy smile and came to stand next to his table, generously showing her cleavage to its best advantage.

The ample mounds of her pushed-up bosom threatened to erupt from the tight bodice, and he saw them vibrate with her movements.

And he *knew*.

God had responded to his pleadings. Here was his penance. "Come hither, my lovey," he invited in his smooth, rich voice. He smiled.

She bent forward, and, eyeing her cleavage, he reached to slip a long finger into the deep crevice between the globes. She allowed him to slide his hand down to cup a heavy weight, sighing and smiling in the same way all whores did…the way Nicola had, and Retna.

"Eey, my lord, I see what 'tis y'r wishin' for." She grinned, showing three holes where teeth had been and moving around the table to stand next to him. "Wit' such fingers as you have, I can bet at the pleasure you give. An' let's see what we have to work with, now."

"Aye…let us indeed." Fantin did not relish taking the filthy whore to his bed…but 'twas God's will, and, in truth, his desire flared there beneath the table. After doing this task, he would serve his penance and mete out the punishment God had chosen…upon himself and the woman.

Gavin's jaw hurt. His teeth ground into each other, jarring slightly with the rhythm of Rule's sure-footed trot, as he focused his attention on the road in front of him—looking over the dark head that rocked below his chin and sent a faint smell of something floral to his nose.

He refused to think about the thick, shininess of that bare braid, or to admit that with one slight movement of his arm, he would brush against her ribs. Instead, he concentrated on what he should have been doing instead of chasing stags through the wood: delivering Madelyne de Belgrume safely to Henry's court.

He would not allow himself to be distracted by the memory of those lush lips beneath his, and the way her lids had slid closed over luminous gray eyes, fanning thick black lashes over her fair cheeks.

A spear of desire shot through his abdomen and for a moment he was helpless to the memory of her soft curves pressed against him and the tentative slide of her tongue over his. In sooth, he had committed his share of sins in his life…but surely this was too great a penance even for those.

He shifted uncomfortably in the saddle, then gritted his teeth as the movement brought him in contact with Madelyne's rigid back. She'd been more silent than usual, ducking her head when faced by him whenever they'd met in the day they spent at Prentiss Keep, and now that they had been back on the road again, she and Patricka kept to themselves when not ahorse. The bit of spirit Madelyne had begun to show since leaving the abbey had disappeared, leaving her little more than the silent, serene nun he'd taken from Lock Rose Abbey. Verily, he'd frightened the wits from her with his clumsy, forceful assault in the wood.

He almost regretted it—that succumbing to his base urges— but, in all truthfulness, he knew he would do it again if he had to do it over. It had been so long that he'd embraced or kissed a woman that did not smell of the farm, or did not need to scratch the fleas and lice that infested her hair. And surely it was only that novelty causing his mind to spin with the memory of a soft, scented noblewoman in his arms—nun though she was. With a frustrated rake of fingers through his hair, Gavin vowed to find a clean, willing woman when they reached the king's court to flush this haunting memory from his mind.

He was pulled from his internal ruminations as Clem rode up next to them. Gavin was mildly surprised to note that he was not sharing a saddle with the dimple-cheeked maid Madelyne had insisted upon bringing and he raised an eyebrow. "Where is your charge, man?"

Clem's face ruddied slightly and he gave a curt gesture. "She insisted that to save my arm from further injury, she should allow it to rest as it healed. She rides with Jube."

Gavin glanced back to see the pair in question, then returned his attention to Clem. "Does your arm pain you, and did you welcome the discharge of that custody?"

The other man straightened in the saddle, flickering a glance toward Madelyne. "My lord, you know that I would not shirk my duty. The mistress stated that she wished to spare me the pain of holding her in the saddle. I could not argue with her logic."

"She is no light of feather," Gavin agreed.

"'Twas no strain for me to hold her, my lord." Clem replied with indignation, "But if she prefers the company of Jube, then who am I to say her nay?"

Gavin shot a surprised look at his man, noticing that his wide, kind face was set in a shuttered expression. He seemed most irked that the chubby maid rode with Jube, but mayhaps it was only that he felt his mastery had been challenged by her fear of injuring him. Gavin frowned. Clem was not normally one to care what a woman would think of him—Jube was more likely to flirt and woo and court a maiden than Clem. And Gavin himself rarely even smiled at a woman, yet he'd smiled at Madelyne...sought her company... kissed her in the deep woods....

Sighing, Gavin shifted again in the saddle. It seemed his thoughts always came back to the woman who rode with him.

Praise God they would reach Whitehall this night, where he could discharge himself of Lady Madelyne and return his attentions to that which truly mattered.

The Court of Henry the Plantagenet was more hectic and crowded than Madelyne could have imagined. She forgot to sit forward in the saddle, away from Lord Gavin, in her amazement at the activity just within the bailey at Whitehall. And she did naught but gape like a peasant.

There were squires and pages dashing to and fro, dressed in the livery of the king, the queen, and other nobility. At the least, ten marshals rushed to greet Mal Verne's party as the horses picked their way through the crowded bailey to the stables. Men-at-arms strode through the yard in loud, boisterous groups, swords and mail clanging to the rhythm of their steps. Clusters of merchants hawked baskets of fruit, vegetables, and small cloth items, and Madelyne even saw peasant boys and girls chasing chickens, sheep, and goats about.

Gavin dismounted near the stables, and before reaching to assist her down, he turned and barked orders to three nearby pages. "Make it known to his majesty that the Lord of Mal Verne has arrived," he commanded one young boy. To another, he said, "See that lodging is prepared for Lady Madelyne de Belgrume near the ladies' chambers—on the order of the Lord of Mal Verne." And to the third, he added, "Send word to Lady Judith Kentworth that Lord Mal Verne has arrived. I will see her anon."

He turned back to Madelyne and, fitting his hands around her waist, lifted her from the saddle to the ground in one fluid movement as she wondered who Judith of Kentworth was. Before she even steadied herself, he had turned to Clem, giving curt orders about the care of the horses, the deliverance of the baggage that followed, and lodging for the men.

Madelyne stood to one side, watching him—his face intent and hawkish, his thick dark hair shifting with the wind, his stance tall and commanding. This was the Gavin she had first experienced— the harsh, shuttered man with nary a hint of humor or softness in his persona. She'd thought mayhaps that had been only a shell that had begun to crack in those days at Mal Verne, but now, it seemed that she was wrong. That gentle moment in the garden when he brushed her hair behind her ear, and confessed that he'd sought her out to enjoy her presence…and the bold, sensual kiss they'd shared after her rescue: those moments did not belong to this man, here and now. Mayhaps they'd been only of her imagining.

"Lady Madelyne." His deep voice rumbled, tinged with annoyance, catching her attention over the cacophony of other arrivals and making a flush rise in her face.

She looked at him without flinching for the first time since he'd kissed her in the wood, and she struggled to appear unmoved. "Aye, my lord?"

He offered her his arm without another word, and reluctantly, she slipped her fingers over the sleeve of his mail hauberk. They'd taken several steps toward the castle entrance before he deigned to speak to her again. "'Tis unlikely the king will grant you an audience before the morrow, so I will send for you when he does. You may be called to serve her majesty in the mean while, and if that should happen and I cannot attend you, seek out Lady Judith of Kentworth. She is very kind and she will help you in my stead."

All at once, panic swamped her. Madelyne swallowed, barely noticing that they had entered the castle called Whitehall and that they were making their way down a stone hall filled with people. Some called acknowledgements to Gavin, and others eyed them with blatant curiosity. A small group of ladies passed by, dressed in bright, sumptuous gowns, and looked in askance at her as they offered cooing greetings to her companion. Madelyne took small comfort in the fact that his response to them was as cool and unemotional as 'twas toward her, for her mind was on the matter at hand.

He was going to leave her here—at court—alone.

The stab of trepidation returned and she struggled to contain her panic. He wouldn't leave her if it wasn't safe, she told herself as he manipulated them silently down the hallway. She might be new and naive to the ways at court, but she would learn them.

Remaining here, under the care of the king and queen, was far preferable to being turned over to her father. A shiver raced through her, and although Gavin glanced down, he said nothing.

As they walked along the hallway, Madelyne renewed her private vow to do what she must to remain under the king's care…and to return to the abbey for her final vows should the king release her.

"The ladies' chambers are there," Gavin spoke, coming to a halt at the commencement of a side hall. He paused, stepping away from Madelyne and allowing her fingers to slip from his arm. He appeared to be looking for someone, and she backed toward the wall, tucking her fingers into the sleeves of her overtunic to hide their trembling.

A faint musty smell from the damp masonry reached her nose, and she wrinkled it slightly, hoping that her lodgings would not be so chill. Gavin gave her a brief look, followed by a short gesture indicating that she should stay there, then started down an adjoining hall, craning his head this way and that.

Feeling bereft and out-of-place, Madelyne tried to make herself as unobtrusive as possible, leaning back into a small corner. She watched in silence as people continued to pass by, giving her nary a glance as they chattered, argued, or laughed.

A familiar squeal of laughter reached her ears just as Gavin reappeared at her side, and they turned as one to look down the hall from where they'd come. Madelyne felt her companion spew out a long breath, but he said nothing as they were accosted by a breathless, bright-eyed Tricky, who was flanked by Jube, Clem, and Peg—as well as several serfs toting trunks and cloth bags.

Tricky ignored Gavin and went directly to Madelyne, taking her hands with soft, pudgy ones, and giving a sketch of a curtsey. When she rose to her full, diminutive height, her face was shiny and apple-cheeked. "There you be, my lady! I made certain to wait for our trunks that they be delivered to the right chamber." Glancing at Gavin, who hadn't done much to hide his faint annoyance, she spoke, "'Tis said my lord has enough influence in his majesty's court to procure a private chamber for you, my lady."

Madelyne looked at him in dismay. It had not occurred to her that she might have to share a chamber with some of the other ladies of the court, and she waited, holding her breath, for his response.

"Do you not look so unsettled," he responded with a gentler tone than she'd anticipated. "'Tis the reason we wait here—I expect the page to return with word of your chamber—a private one for you, my lady, as your maid seems to think you warrant such."

"Aye, and costly 'twill be too, my lady. But 'tis the least can be done for you that you do not have to share a chamber with the other ladies." Tricky cast a brief yet pointed look at Gavin.

Madelyne's dismay turned to confusion. "Cost? But…what cost would there be—his majesty has requested—nay, ordered—my presence here. Surely it is not expected…." Her voiced trailed off as she saw the impatient look on Gavin's face.

"Lodging is available at no cost if you wish to sleep in the women's quarters, on a pallet on the floor, with the other scores of women and children who follow the court—"

Tricky interrupted boldly—not unlike a terrier fiercely defending her mistress against a lion in his den. "My lady cannot stay in such a public place! Lady Madelyne, 'tis the very least can be done for you to arrange for a private chamber since his majesty has required your presence here."

"But at what cost?" she asked, acutely aware that she had no funds with which to pay for her keep. Her chest tightened as the reality closed over her: she was completely at the mercy of the ways of the court, and with no money, she was even more vulnerable. "I haven't—"

Gavin cut her off with a curt sweep of his hand. "Do you not concern yourself with such matters. You shall be lodged here, and clothed and fed in the manner befitting the Lady of Belgrume. The expenses will be managed by Clem—send you to him any costs you incur."

Madelyne's voice left her as she stared at him in a combination of horror and outrage. "Lord Mal Verne, I cannot accept that you should bear the expense of my stay at court." She twisted her hands, still tucked in the sleeves of her overtunic, but kept her voice quietly even.

He glanced at her as though she were a fly buzzing about his ear, his brows knitting together in a dark line. "You were brought to court under my care, and will remain thus until the king relieves me of such duty—thus your expenses will be borne by Mal Verne." When she was about to speak again, he gave her a quelling look, his face hard-planed and dark with annoyance. "Do you not fear—Mal Verne can easily bear any expense you might incur. I'll hear no more on the matter."

He turned away to speak with Clem, leaving Madelyne to glare at him in angry futility. The man had the unlikable penchant for snapping at one when he wished to hear no more of a conversation. She withdrew her hands from her sleeves and folded her arms across her middle, turning from him in frustration. She did not intend to be a burden to him—or to anyone else. She would return to the abbey as soon as she gained permission from the king. What reason could the king want her—a nun—to stay in his court?

An unexpected shard of pain caused her to curl her mouth as Gavin's words penetrated her thoughts. A duty she was to Gavin of Mal Verne—and naught more than that. When the king relieved him of his care of her, she would not see him again.

Whether that be a blessing or a curse, she did not know.

$\mathcal{T}$WELVE

"NAY, 'TIS not right," Madelyne protested as Peg held a length of garnet-colored cloth alongside her face to check the color with her complexion.

The maid ignored her as she and Tricky clucked about, discussing colors and styles with the seamstress who had appeared at the door of their chamber the morning after their arrival.

"'Tis like the night sky!" Tricky breathed, sighing over a vibrant blue cloth shot with silver threads.

"Aye, mistress, and silver stars and moons embroidered on the cuffs," nodded the seamstress. Madelyne realized in annoyance that the woman had learned to disregard her protests almost immediately, turning her attention to the short, plump women who fluttered about their lady. The seamstress's eyes gleamed with satisfaction as yet another bolt of cloth was added to the growing pile of silks and linens and wools.

"'Tis not right," Madelyne spoke again, this time with more vehemence. "It's too much—the cost will be too great, and I do not need all of these gowns!"

This time, her objection was not ignored. Tricky turned to her with flashing eyes, surprising Madelyne with the indignation in her expression. "My lady, when I agreed to come with you, I vowed to care for you to the best of my abilities—to protect you and to serve you. I cannot allow you to dress in rags, or in clothing that belonged to another woman in another time. You must be dressed as befits your station, and you must adorn yourself with jewels and gold—else you will be eaten alive by the wild cats here!"

Madelyne blinked. How had Tricky become so seasoned with the ways at court, and from where had this stubborn streak come? "I am but a simple nun," she replied, "and I do not believe that you *agreed* to accompany me…I believe that you gave me little choice in that matter." A wry smile suddenly caught at her face—mayhaps that stubborn streak had always been there, but hidden by a veil and prayerful hands.

"You are no nun yet," Tricky reminded her boldly. "And until such time as you make your last vows and shave your head, you must bear the mantle of your position. Even you, my lady, must wear the pretension of the Lady of Tricourten if you are to have a chance here."

The seamstress bobbed her head vigorously. "Aye, my lady, you must listen to your maid—she has the right of it. And the Lord of Mal Verne has instructed me to clothe you in such a manner. I cannot disregard his wishes." The expression on her face revealed that she was not so much afraid of his lord as she was loathe to lose the business.

Madelyne frowned and didn't reply, trying to forget her sudden aversion at the reminder that she would shave her head. She could demand that the women go, and leave her to her simple, borrowed clothing…but mayhaps that would be no more than slicing off her nose to spite her face. She would need every bit of influence in her favor if she were to gain permission from the king to leave his court, and to survive her stay whilst she was there.

She sighed, and the others, seizing the opportunity of her tacit approval, returned to their animated discussion of her clothing. The seamstress left, and by that time, Madelyne was at peace—albeit temporarily—with the arrangement. It would be a temporary allowance, and when she returned to Lock Rose Abbey, she could don the familiar gowns of black and blue linen. Absently, she allowed her fingers to trail over the smoothness of a pearlescent silk, reveling in its sleekness. 'Twould be no hardship to slip into the softness of a tunic made from this cloth, she mused guiltily. Snatching her hand away, she turned to the small fireplace and forced herself to say two paternosters and one prayer to the Blessed Virgin in penance for her frivolous thoughts.

Madelyne had barely finished when a knock sounded on the door. She started for it, but Tricky gestured her back and opened it just enough to peer out. She withdrew back into the chamber and announced in a voice heavy with formality, "My lady has her first visitor. Lady Judith of Kentworth requests an audience with my lady."

Madelyne rose to her feet, smoothing her gown. "Tricky, please let her in." She stepped toward the door to greet the woman who breezed in, followed by a young page and two maidservants.

"Lady Madelyne." As she swept in, the other woman brightened the room with her smile and fiery, golden-red hair. She paused from taking Madelyne's hands into her own. "Do you not remember me?" Her laugh tinkled into the room as she moved forward, nearly stepping upon a stack of discarded bolts of cloth. "Our summer of fostering in Kent?"

The memory struck Madelyne with the force of a gale wind and she could not help the smile that burst over her face. "Judith? 'Tis you?" Before she could speak further, she was enveloped by her childhood friend in an exuberant embrace and she felt tension ease from her body.

Judith stepped away, holding her by the fingertips, and appraised her bluntly. "Aye, Maddie, how you've grown into a beautiful woman! But we must do away with your clothing!"

Before Madelyne could protest that she had much too much with fussing over her dress, Judith spurred into action and began to issue firm, simple commands. "Fetch you my ribbons and girdles trunk, Mellie," she said to a maidservant who'd accompanied her. "Onda, I will need to see Mistress Blaine—send to her to see us before the midday meal." Thus, each of the companions were sent away—including Tricky and Peg, who wished to accompany Onda on her mission—and the two women were left alone.

"At last," Judith said, casting her a bright smile.

"Please, sit," Madelyne found her voice and was determined to regain control over her future. She would gladly admit her deficiency in fashion and dress, and capitulate to those who knew better. But in other matters, she would not be overruled. Before she had a chance to speak and establish this, Judith waved a hand at her as she plopped onto the bed.

"I trow, 'tis most difficult to think up excuses to send them away that they do not wonder why I should be so urgent in the matter. 'Tis just that I wished for a moment alone with you—as you are guarded by that little dragon—to speak on these long years." Her face, beautiful in its own right, softened from the smile into one of quiet sadness. "Dear Maddie, you cannot know how ill I felt when I learned you'd been drowned these ten years past. And you cannot know the hope I felt when Gavin shared that he'd found you yet alive."

At the mention of Gavin, Madelyne felt an odd wrench in her stomach and she stood abruptly. This beautiful woman, with the red-gold beacon of a head and sparkling green eyes, was the one he'd told her to seek if she needed assistance. She spoke of him with familiarity and warmth, and though she shouldn't care, Madelyne couldn't keep back the unhappy thought of what Judith of Kentworth meant to Gavin of Mal Verne.

"Lord Gavin told me I should seek you out should I need assistance, but I did not know that it was you of whom he spoke," she replied carefully.

"How did he come to find you? How did you come to be alive?"

Madelyne gave a simple version of the escape she and her mother had made ten years earlier, careful to repeat the tale that Lady Anne had perished some years after reaching the abbey. "Lord Gavin came upon the abbey which had been our refuge, and after the sisters treated his wounds and those of his men, we released them." She thought it best not to refer to the trick she'd played on Gavin. "'Twas only a fortnight later that he returned with an order from the king demanding my presence at court." She looked questioningly at Judith. "I do not know why his majesty has ordered an audience with me."

A flash of surprise flitted across Judith's face. "King Henry has requested your presence? But Gavin told me—" She stopped abruptly and bit her lower lip. For a moment, she looked uncertain, and Madelyne watched her steadily, her heart freezing.

Then Judith clapped her hands together in chagrin. "'Tis always my loose tongue that puts me into the fire!" She shook her head, and a thick coppery braid swung around, falling over her shoulder.

"What did Lord Gavin tell you?" Madelyne asked with a calmness she did not feel.

Judith sat upright on the curtained bed, still gnawing at her lower lip. "He came to me to ask if I recalled the markings on your wrist," she gestured to Madelyne's left hand, the wrist barely exposed by the tight sleeve of her undertunic. "'Tis how he came to recognize you, if you did not know."

Madelyne inclined her head, trying to subdue the churning in her middle. "What concern was it to him?"

"Your father and Gavin of Mal Verne are sworn enemies," Judith told her, her eyes wide and solemn. "Gavin has vowed to crush Fantin de Belgrume, and he has the support of the king in this."

"King Henry has given his permission that Lord Gavin should kill my father?"

"Nay, not to kill him—'though, in truth, methinks Gavin would not hesitate to do so should he have a permissible reason. His majesty wishes only that de Belgrume, who has waged reckless war on other barons to steal their lands, should be brought under control."

It suddenly became clear to Madelyne how she'd been manipulated. "Lord Gavin has brought me to the king to suit his own purposes then," she said flatly. "The king has not requested my presence—'twas only to suit Mal Verne that he has done so."

Judith must have seen the coldness that settled over Madelyne's features, for she reached out to touch her friend's hand. "Maddie, Gavin does not mean you any harm—"

Madelyne drew away. "I do not know that. I do know that I'm here against my will, having been taken from the sanctuary in which I sought refuge—in which I was happy—for years. In this world, this man's world, I lose the freedoms I had in the abbey: the freedom to write and read, to manage my own affairs within the abbey, and the freedom to answer to no man except the king—who knew me not until Lord Gavin blazoned my presence to him."

She wrapped her arms around her waist, fighting the fear and anger that swarmed her. She had been a fool to believe the man meant her no harm…a fool to consider that a man might have more than his own interests at heart. Lady Anne had warned her over many years…and every word her mother had spoken had flown away in the presence of Gavin of Mal Verne.

"I am to be used, then, to bring my father to heel—or to his death." Her voice was dull and her mind numb. "Then Lord Gavin spoke true when he named me hostage. I am to be a tool, a carrot to dangle in my father's face." All hope of returning to her private, simple life at the abbey disintegrated, and she stood abruptly, moving to look out of a small arrow-slit window.

"Madelyne—" But before Judith could finish her sentence, a rap sounded at the door, followed by the announcement that the maidservants had returned.

Madelyne turned to answer it, pausing with her hand on the leather strap. "For what reason does Lord Gavin seek such destruction of my father?"

For the first time, Judith's eyes shuttered and her face lost its inherent glow. "He seeks to avenge a wrong he believes your father has done me, and to atone for Gavin's own perceived sins toward me. And…for the other cause he has to hate your father—you will have to ask Gavin yourself."

Although Madelyne pressed her for more information regarding Gavin's relationship with her father, Judith did not feel she should divulge more details. She would do nothing to promote Gavin's own feelings of guilt.

She made certain to remain in Madelyne's chamber until dinner, so that she could escort her proud friend to the hall where the meals took place. She'd been pleasantly surprised that Gavin had arranged a private chamber for her, but vexed that he had not visited his charge since leaving her there the day before. Thus, Madelyne had not ventured from the room, and had relied on her maids Patricka and Peg to procure bread, cheese, and wine for her meals.

"You must be starved!" she exclaimed when she learned of Maddie's simple fare.

Shaking her head, Madelyne replied with a quiet smile, "Nay, Judith, I am most content with the simple meals, for that is how we supped in the abbey. 'Tis true, I may find myself more overwhelmed than comfortable in the royal court." A glint of humor lit her luminous eyes and Judith smiled in return.

She patted her lightly on the cheek. "Maddie, somehow I sense that you shall garner strength and boldness that you did not know you have when confronted by the whirlwind of the court. At the least, you shall have myself, who knows much of what goes on here—and what I do not know, I most usually can learn." She took a last, appraising look at Madelyne, who, with her help, had shed her outdated gown and was garbed in a more stylish mode of clothing.

Madelyne was an exceptionally beautiful woman, Judith thought to herself—not for the first time. With her fair, smooth skin and midnight dark hair, she would likely cause a stir among the queen's ladies—as well as among the noblemen and men-at-arms who were part of the court. Now that she wore more fashionable clothing, the snipes and darts borne from jealousy would not carry the added sting of belittling her clothing or branding her a country mouse.

Judith had chosen an emerald green undergown from her own wardrobe for Madelyne to wear. Although she'd initially balked at the form-fitting skirt that laced up the side and along the sleeves, Madelyne had acquiesced and now wore that, covered by a floor-length overtunic of sapphire blue. Onda, Judith's tiring maid, had shown Peg and Tricky the intricacies of braiding Maddie's thick dark hair and looping it in stylish snoods over each ear. The snoods also belonged to Judith, and they sparkled with tiny gold beads nestled against the black masses of braids.

"Absolutely breathtaking," Judith told her, cocking her wrist to place a forefinger on her pert chin. "You will turn every head, and they will wonder who you are."

Madelyne blanched, her hands going automatically to touch her hair. "But I do not wish to attract attention!"

"Now, Maddie," Judith chided, linking an arm with her, "you cannot hide your beauty, and you shall soon be known to all anyway…so 'tis best to do it under your own terms. Come, we mustn't be late."

Brushing aside the unhappy expression on Madelyne's face, Judith propelled them out of the chamber, leaving the maids to scurry behind in their wake.

Upon reaching the hall where the masses of people who followed the royal court ate their meals, Judith paused, stretching onto her toes to look over the gathering. She hoped to spot Gavin and insist that he sit with them at table, or, at the least, that he settle them in a place near the royal dais. Aside of that, she intended to sharpen her tongue on him for leaving Madelyne to her own devices. A sigh caught at her, and Judith lowered from the balls of her feet onto her heels. She meant to take Gavin to task—if she found him—but their relationship was tenuous and fraught with tension, and 'twas likely he'd only turn cold and blank and proceed to act unerringly the gentleman, accepting the reprimand and his fault in the matter.

Her lips pursed. If only he'd show some emotion other than anger or blankness! Judith squeezed Maddie's hand and began to pull her through the crowd, heading toward the royal dais. There had been a time when Gavin laughed and joked, and his face warmed with smiles and caring…a time before Nicola, before Gregory…and before Fantin de Belgrume.

She threaded her way between the rows of tables, tugging Madelyne behind her. Suddenly, she felt the cool fingers slip from hers, and Judith stopped, turning about. "Maddie, are you—" She swallowed her words when she saw Gavin standing there, his face dark and unreadable as ever.

Madelyne had frozen and, having drawn her hand away from Judith, had folded her hands demurely over her waist. "Why, Lord Gavin, 'tis a surprise to see you. I thought you must have left the court."

Her words, quiet, calm, and without a hint of rancor, delighted Judith and made it unnecessary for her to make the selfsame point to him. The kitten does have claws, she thought, hiding a smile.

He gave a small bow, his gaze traveling over Madelyne from head to toe, then flickering to Judith. "I see that you are none the worse for your first day at court," he replied mildly, returning his attention to Maddie.

Judith stepped toward him, taking his arm with a firm grip. She looked up into his face and directed a bright smile laced with temper at him. "Madelyne had not ventured from her chamber since yestereve, and I bethought 'twas nigh time she found her way to sup with the rest of us."

Gavin had the grace to show a bit of shame as he made another slight bow to Madelyne, offering her his arm. "Many apologies, my lady," he said. "I did not mean to leave you unattended for so long, but my services were required elsewhere and I would have sent word had I known how long I was to be occupied."

Madelyne glanced at his proffered arm, but made no move to take it. Instead, she cast a cool smile at him and responded, "Do you not fear, my lord, 'twas not your presence that I felt lacking, but the desire to sup on more than bread and cheese. With Lady Judith to assist me in that, I should only need from you an introduction to his majesty, and you shall need to dance attendance upon me no further. Unless I am to play some momentous role in your vengeance upon my father?"

Judith swallowed back an exclamation of surprise at her friend's direct and powerful censure, and looked at Gavin. His countenance remained stone-like and immovable as always, although she saw a flare of surprise widen his eyes for a brief instant before he turned a frigid gaze onto herself. "You have ever the loose tongue, do you not, Judith?" Annoyance set in his face and his lips firmed into chiseled marble.

Then he turned back to their companion. "Lady Madelyne, I will be pleased to see that you are made known to his majesty. As to your role in the vengeance that I will have upon your father…it remains to be seen how you will figure there. Now, ladies, with your permission, I will escort you to your seats and I will leave you to your own devices."

*T*HIRTEEN

GAVIN SLUGGED back a gulp of foamy ale. It burned the back
of his throat, warming its way down to his belly, and settled there,
heightening the faint haze that softened his mind. Someone guf-
fawed in his ear—'twas Thomas, laughing at his own jest—whilst
another companion snorted with mirth, spewing ale from his
mouth and spraying Gavin's cheek.

With a swipe over his face, Gavin laughed too, automatically,
then took another drink. He leaned an elbow on the split log table
that was sticky from spilled ale and reminded himself again not to
look in the direction of the high table. If he did, it would seem as
though he were looking at Judith and Lady Madelyne.

Aye, if he turned that way, it might appear that he was interested in what the ladies were doing, or as though he cared whether
they had been joined by any of the noblemen who visited the king's
court.

He wasn't interested and he didn't care.

On the morrow, he would make certain that Lady Madelyne
had her audience with King Henry, and he and the sovereign would
determine the best way to notify de Belgrume that his daughter
was in their custody. Then, he, Gavin, need have naught further to
do with her, and he could return to Mal Verne, knowing that de
Belgrume was under the king's control at last.

He tightened his fingers around the wooden ale cup. Allowing de Belgrume to live was not his preference…but in this, he must obey his king until Fantin misstepped again. Then, Gavin vowed, he would be waiting for the opportunity to finish what had been started seven years earlier.

The sweet sound of a lute caught his ears, wafting over the dull roar of the diners. Forgetting that he didn't want to look that way, Gavin turned toward the high table where Henry and his queen, Eleanor, supped. Instead of seeking the musician, his gaze found and settled on the willowy figure of Lady Madelyne only three tables away. She'd been seated facing him, but now had half-turned toward the lute player, giving Gavin a covert view of her profile.

He couldn't pull his attention away. She looked so calm and serene, beautiful in her composure in the midst of the energetic, rowdy crowd. He saw the slim, white column of her neck—bared now that the thick masses of braids had been gathered above her ears—and watched the curve of it shift innocently as she strained to look between the crowd to see the musician. The bareness of her neck seemed almost obscene to Gavin, for she still had the aura of an innocent, virginal nun, and the baring of such skin was too intimate for a protected woman.

He frowned, tasting his ale again, but still unwilling to look away. He could still taste the sweetness of her full mouth beneath his, and had no delay in summoning to memory the feel of her soft curves molding beneath his hands. Desire that he had suppressed sprang to life, sending waves of heat pulsing through the core of his abdomen, and lower.

He swore silently, then buried his face in the ale cup again … but his gaze remained fixed on Madelyne.

Judith chose that moment to glance in his direction, and Gavin looked away too late. He felt his neck warm as he jerked his eyes away, pretending to look at the lute-player. His time would be better spent looking for a willing maidservant in the stead of gaping at a holy woman.

With renewed firmness, he turned away, his gaze scanning the rearmost tables for the comely maidservant he especially sought when at court.

"Who is the woman there?" asked Lord Ferrell, one of the men with whom he was seated.

Gavin swung to look at him and caught the eye of Thomas, who had a brow raised in question. Gavin gave a sharp nod, and his friend replied, "'Tis Lady Madelyne de Belgrume, Ferrell, lately arrived at court."

"De Belgrume?" Ferrell's bushy eyebrows twitched in confusion. "The get of Fantin de Belgrume? I did not believe he had an heir." He turned to look toward Madelyne again, and Gavin could easily discern the thoughts that bumbled through the man's head. "Did he not have a daughter who perished some years ago? And a wife too? Do you not tell me...." his voice trailed off and he stared at the woman, his eyes slitting as his brows twitched. "'Tis not the selfsame woman, is it, Thomas? Where has he hidden such a beauty all these years?" He made to stand, brushing crumbs from his tunic and swiping a hand over his wiry gray hair.

"Sit down, Ferrell, and stick your pecker back in your breeches," Gavin drawled, shifting his shoulders to alleviate the tension that was gathering there. "The wench came from an abbey—-she is promised to be a nun."

Ferrell looked at him blankly, then returned his gaze to Madelyne. "'Tis a good jest, Mal Verne, but I vow, I've never seen a woman who looks less like a holy woman than that wench."

"I brought her from the abbey myself," Gavin told him, a bit of steel creeping into his voice. "She's under the protection of the king."

Ferrell frowned again, then sank back onto the bench where he'd been seated. "Bloody shame," he said sadly, bringing his cup to his mouth and slurping. "Bloody damned shame."

Gavin's mind echoed those thoughts, and he swiveled to cast a last glance at Madelyne's table. His momentary relief vanished when he saw Lord Reginald D'Orrais laughing as he took a seat next to her.

∽

'Twas heaven…pure heaven.

Madelyne sighed, pushing away the knowledge that, strictly speaking, it was a blasphemous thought, and closed her eyes. Strong fingers kneaded her skull, threading through her hair and loosening the ten braids that had pulled her scalp taut for hours. The dull ache gave way to relief and she sighed again, resting her head in the palms of her maid's hands.

Tricky's chatter flowed in and out of Madelyne's consciousness just as her nimble fingers brushed through Maddie's long hair. "…Never seen such food! I could barely choose betwixt the rabbit, the capon, and the roast goose…an' when they brought forth the stuffed pigeons, I thought I'd eat to bursting!" She reached in front of Madelyne for a comb carved of wormwood with bits of mother of pearl inlaid amongst the etchings on its side.

"How did you come by such a pretty comb?" asked Madelyne curiously. It slid smoothly through her hair, running over her shoulder and along the length of her back, past the edge of the stool on which she sat.

"'Twas a gift," Tricky replied smugly, maintaining her rhythm of long, sure strokes. "Whilst Clem and I were gone to seek aught for you to break your fast, we chanced upon a merchant showing his wares. I made such a moon-face of myself that he had no choice but to buy it for me." She giggled girlishly, jerking Madelyne's hair in her distraction. She froze, smoothing her fingers solicitiously over the tender spot. "Ah, my lady, forgive me. I didn't mean to hurt you."

Madelyne laughed softly at her friend's enthusiasm. Since leaving Lock Rose Abbey, it had become clear to her that Patricka was in no manner suited for the life of a nun…nor was Madelyne any more certain that she was cut of a maid's cloth. "You didn't hurt me, Tricky, 'though such inattention could do so in the future. Nevertheless, you have worked such magic on my aching head that I would forgive you in a trice even if you had pulled my hair." She sighed, smiling, suddenly in a delightful mood. "I shall remember not to ask you of your paramours whilst you have a brush in my hair anon."

"Paramours! Hah!" Tricky nearly caught the comb in a tangle again, but caught herself in time. "Mayhaps one could name Jube such, but I do not care for that malcontent Clem at *all*. I wish only to torture the man, for he does naught but stand about and glower at me. I do believe he could be taking instruction from Lord Mal Verne."

Madelyne felt her eyebrows rise at such a blatant criticism, but she could not fault Tricky for accuracy in her observations. Indeed, she had felt the weight of Gavin's surly stare that evening. Firming her lips, she reminded herself that 'twas she who had cause to be furious with him, rather than the other way around. Despite the fact that her heart had jumped into her throat when she'd turned to see him, and regardless of the acuteness of the memory of his lips tasting hers, Madelyne knew she couldn't trust those flighty emotions. She could not trust *him*.

For some reason, that realization pained her more than leaving the abbey. Emptiness and unease settled around her, and the back of her throat hurt when she swallowed. Before the surprise tears could materialize, she stood and Tricky let the comb slip from her hair. Fighting sadness, Maddie walked toward the tiny fireplace, her eyes fixed on the orange flames. Peg had set the fire and it burned calmly in its little enclosure, whilst Peg herself snored on a pallet in the corner.

"Methinks my lady has attracted her own paramour," Tricky said slyly, shoving her comb into a small linen pouch. She pulled on the strings to tighten the opening of the bag and glanced at Madelyne.

"What do you mean?" Maddie asked, startled. A warmth that had naught to do with the fire suffused her face. She folded her hands in front of her and sat on the stool near the fireplace, looking over at her maid.

"Lady Judith had the right of it when she said you would attract attention," Tricky responded, busying herself by folding one of the tunics Judith had loaned Madelyne. "I saw many people staring at you, my lady—"

Madelyne relaxed. "'Twas no more than curiosity, Tricky."

"Mayhaps from some, aye. But the tall man who sat next to you had more than curiosity in his face." She spoke matter-of-factly, turning to open a trunk where the other tunics were stored.

Tricky could have no idea that her casual words sent Madelyne's heart sliding into a heavy ball in her stomach. "Lord Reginald? Why, he…." She allowed her voice to trail off. He had been very attentive once Lady Judith had consented him to sup with them, his soft lips pressing lightly to the back of her hand upon introduction. His blue eyes glowed with warmth and humor, and his mouth quirked in a ready smile above the deeply cleft, square chin. "He merely wished to find a seat near an acquaintance of his," she continued firmly, recounting the excuse he'd given them upon approach.

"Mmm." Tricky continued her business of arranging the bolts of cloth and other materials left by the seamstress. "From the back of the hall, where Peg and I sat, he appeared to spend more of his time conversing with you, my lady, than any other in the vicinity."

Madelyne took a deep breath to calm the churning in her stomach. "I did nothing to encourage Lord Reginald," she said, defending herself without wondering why she should do so—most especially why she should do so to her own maid. But Tricky had been her friend before taking on the subservient role, and, in truth, aside from Judith, Madelyne had no one else to confide in.

Then, with a sinking heart, she recalled her forward actions of resting her fingers lightly on the edge of his sleeve as she leaned toward him to comment on a nearby juggler, and the overbright smile she rewarded him with upon his own jests. And, she remembered the sharpening of her breath when Lord Reginald touched her hand, or offered her a tasty bite of venison…and the increase in her pulse when he smiled at her so.

Mayhaps Tricky had the right of it. Madelyne bit her lower lip and reached for the rose-bead string of prayer beads that hung from her girdle. She would pray on her knees this eve in penance for her coy actions, and she would beg The Lord and The Mother that they would give her strength to keep from straying from her path. "Lead me not into temptation," Madelyne murmured, fingering the beads.

"Pardon, my lady?" Tricky's head popped up from where she had been stuffing clothing into another trunk.

"Nay, 'twas naught," Madelyne replied, looking down at her beads. This was the first time she'd meant to use them since leaving the abbey, though they had always hung at her side. She had prayed oft to The Father and the saints, and she attended Mass once a day or more…but she had avoided using her beads since Lord Gavin had taken her from Lock Rose Abbey.

She wondered suddenly whether he still had those beads she had given him on his first visit to the abbey…or whether they had been destroyed or lost. It had surprised and moved her that he still carried them when he came back to the abbey.

Her fingers worried the strand of scented beads, feeling the roundness of them and the tiny scores made by the little paddle she'd used to form them. Gavin's serious face loomed in her memory—the harshness and unyielding planes of his countenance melding into the intense, blazing expression that had been there in the glen, when he'd kissed her. His mouth had been so persuasive, so demanding…her body turned to liquid again, now, at the mere thought of it. She still remembered the thickness of his damp hair, smooth and heavy under her fingers, and how tall and hard he'd been…how safe she'd felt.

Madelyne shook her head violently as if to chase the remembrance away. How could she be thinking of such a thing? She was meant to be a nun—she had vowed her life to God—and she should be on her knees begging forgiveness for her transgressions of this evening, not mooning over the memory of another sin.

Sin.

Dear God, it did not feel like a sin.

Fourteen

"**YOUR MAJESTY…LADY** Madelyne de Belgrume."

Gavin watched as Madelyne glided forward and sank into a deep, graceful curtsey. He stood to the side in the king's private court room, near the clerk, and leaned against the table at which the clerk scratched royal edicts onto parchment paper. He had arrived at Madelyne's chamber a short time ago to escort her to Henry's presence. She'd spoken little to him, and he'd returned the favor in kind.

Madelyne rose upon the king's invitation, and pressed a kiss to his ringed forefinger before stepping slightly back. Her graceful neck was bare again—long and slim and white, with tendrils of stark blackness wisping about her nape—and she wore a fine gown of goldenrod covered by a pale yellow overtunic. The lack of jewelry was the only indication of her status as a nun and not the well-landed heiress she could aspire to be.

"Your majesty, I am grateful for the invitation to your presence," Madelyne said in a clear voice.

Henry stood next to his massive oaken throne, his golden-red hair glinting in the sunlight that streamed through three wide slits in the wall. "We are as pleased to offer the invitation as you purport to be grateful." He stepped away from the chair and across the dais to place his hands on the back of the empty throne that belonged to Eleanor. "'Tis our understanding that you have sought sanctuary in an abbey? For ten years?"

Madelyne nodded. "Aye, your majesty, my mother and I found refuge there after leaving Tricourten." She clasped her hands in front of her.

Gavin frowned. "Your mother is dead, as you told me, Lady Madelyne." He stepped away from the table on which he'd been leaning and took several steps closer to Madelyne, so that he could see her face.

Henry flashed a look at him, then transferred his stern stare to Madelyne. "Is this true? Your mother no longer lives?"

"Aye, 'tis true. Mayhap I was not clear in my answer, your highness. My mother and I made our way to Lock Rose Abbey, and she perished some three years after we arrived there."

"Why did you not return to your father at that time?" Henry paced across the dais, in front of the two thrones, his steady gaze focused on Madelyne.

Gavin saw her draw in her breath, oh so slightly, and then slowly release it before she replied. "Your majesty, my mother and I left Tricourten because she bore the ill will of my father, and the weight of his hand. I dared not return, for fear that he would take out his anger on me…and, in sooth, I had not the means to return, nor did I know where Tricourten was. I was only ten summers, your highness, when my mother and I left."

Henry pursed his lips, pinching the lower one with his right thumb and forefinger. "'Tis not uncommon for a man to beat his wife to guarantee her obedience…still, we do find it rather ambitious that your mother was able to plan such a successful escape. By all rights, Lady Madelyne, you should be returned to your father's care."

Gavin saw her face turn to white, and her mouth pinched at the corners. He felt something akin to sympathy for her: she obviously had a great fear of Fantin de Belgrume.

"Your majesty, I pray that you would reconsider such a thing." Madelyne's voice, though calm, was a bit breathless with anxiety. "I have spent these last ten years in an abbey, cared for by the good sisters, and I have chosen to embrace the life of a religious woman. Indeed, I should never have left had you not requested my presence."

The king raised one eyebrow, glancing at Gavin archly. Returning his attention to Madelyne, the king asked, "You are a nun? You have taken your final vows?"

The long white column of her throat constricted. "Nay, your majesty, I have not shaved my head and taken my last vows, though 'tis my intent—"

"You have not yet taken your vows? Verily, you are not a nun." Henry waved her protest aside with a large, beringed hand.

"Your highness," Madelyne began, "'Tis my intent—"

"Your intent has laid unmet for ten years, my lady." His gaze was as shrewd as his words were pointed, and Gavin felt a bit sorry for her. "You have had ample opportunity to make those vows, and as you have not seen fit to do so, then we shall make the choice for you."

Her eyes widened and her face became even paler. "You would return me to the custody of my father?" Her hands were clenched in front of her, the knuckles graying as her fingers curled together.

"Nay." Henry stepped down from the dais and across the room to a small table where he poured himself a goblet of wine. "Gavin, serve yourself and Lady Madelyne," he commanded, stalking back onto the dais.

"Nay, Lady Madelyne, we shall not return you to the care of your father. In sooth, 'tis our plan to keep your wardship under our care until a proper protector—a husband—can be found for you. In the mean while, 'twill keep your father from razing the lands of our other barons and causing war among them whilst you are our guest at court."

"But, your majesty," Madelyne started desperately, ignoring the goblet of wine Gavin offered her, "please have pity—I have made a vow to God that I shall dedicate my life to Him!"

Gavin saw her eyes glisten with unshed tears and trepidation tauten her face, and he nearly reached out to touch her. How terrible it must be to have one's fate seized, he thought, suddenly realizing how accurate she'd been when she told him of the unusual freedoms granted to women in cloistered abbeys.

The knowledge that he'd been party to—nay, that he was responsible for—destroying that freedom she'd obtained crested over him like a dash of cold water.

Henry had turned to Madelyne and now looked at her with steely blue eyes. "My lady," he responded in his firm, monarchical voice, "we do not attempt to naysay God, but, as we have made clear, your dedication to Him has not been formalized, and thus we take that as a sign, from God Himself, if you wish, that 'tis not His desire that you do so. We shall hear no more upon it, Lady Madelyne." His voice had grown impatient, and he slashed his hand in the air as if to cut off any further protestations on her part.

"As you wish, your majesty." Madelyne stood humbly, shoulders straight, gaze slightly downcast, hands balled together at her waist.

There was a prolonged silence as the king sipped again from his goblet, and it was broken as he set the cup down deliberately on a small table near his throne. "Lady Madelyne, you are now a ward of the king, and you shall fulfill your duties here in our court by serving her majesty, Queen Eleanor. We shall collect a fine from your father—Burland!" he called over to the scribe who had continued to huddle over a table, scratching at his parchment throughout the entire exchange. The scribe's head popped up and he blinked blearily. "Burland, send you a notice to Fantin de Belgrume that we are assessing a fine as recompense for taking on the wardship of his daughter, Madelyne."

Gavin caught the glint of humor in the king's eyes and could not resist a small grin. Henry did not miss the slightest chance to add to the royal coffers in any legitimate manner he could fabricate. Fantin would be murderous with rage when he received the notice, and there was naught he could do but pay it.

He sobered as he looked at Madelyne again. She stood rigid as a statue, as cool and smooth and beautiful as a marble figure, silent as the men interacted about her. Again, a pang of guilt thrashed him, but he pushed it away. He was not responsible for the fact that she'd neglected to make her final vows, and that was the only reason she found herself in the current predicament.

"You are dismissed, my lady. We shall expect to see you with the queen's ladies hereforth."

"Thank you, your majesty." Madelyne made a graceful curtsey, then turned and walked stiffly toward the door at the other end of the room.

Gavin caught a glimpse of her set profile, but she did not look in his direction as she stepped past.

He looked at Henry, whose own gaze followed Madelyne from the room. "'Twould be a sin for one as beautiful as she to take her holy vows," Henry murmured with a wink at Gavin.

Madelyne heard the king mumble something behind her, but she was so close to tears that she dared not turn to see if he yet spoke to her. A low rumble followed the king's comment, and she presumed it was Gavin's response. She did not look behind to her to ascertain whether Gavin followed. She would find her own way back to her chamber rather than wait for him.

Holding her head high, she braced her shoulders at the door to the hallway. A page stood at the high oaken portal, opening it as she approached, and stepping aside so that she could find her way into the perpetual crowd that gathered out side of the chamber.

People milled about in the large, open area, and Madelyne hurried through the throngs without noticing any of them. Dimly, she heard the page announce the king's next audience, and then heard the door close firmly behind her.

She still clutched her golden skirt in her hands, but kept her attention focused on the floor made of large gray stones as she hurried blindly away from the people. She paid no mind to where she was going, knowing she would likely become hopelessly lost in the vast warren of corridors and passages…but at the moment, all she wished was to *get away*.

Her inattention caused her to stumble into someone, and she stepped aside, looking up to murmur an apology. When she raised her eyes up the tall form of the man standing in front of her and saw his face, she froze. All sensation fled her body, leaving her light of head and numb.

"Madelyne. How good it is to see you again." He smiled brilliantly, but she saw the odd gleam in his wild blue eyes.

She could not speak at first, just gasped for air as fear and loathing rushed through her heavy limbs. Where had he come from? "What do you want?" she managed to say with amazing calmness. "Were you following me?"

His smile turned chill. "Is that any way to greet your father?"

Madelyne noted with alarm that they seemed to be in an unusually deserted corridor, and her heart swelled into her throat. She raised her chin, taking care to keep her voice low. "You are my father only by an accident of birth. I wish naught to do with you, my lord, so please step aside." How could others miss that madness, that obsessive light in his eyes?

Fantin's hand snaked out to close around her arm before she could move past him, tightening into an immediate vise. "I'll not suffer such words from you, Madelyne." He jerked her once, quickly, but enough that her head snapped back. "Now, you'll come with me, daughter. After ten years, 'tis more than my right to take you under my care."

Quelling the nausea of fear, Madelyne jammed her heel onto her father's slippered foot and yanked on her arm. Although he grunted in pain, his grip was too tight and he curled his fingers around her arm even tighter, causing her to cry out in pain. "Let me be!" she cried, now hoping that someone would hear their altercation. Surely there couldn't be any place in all of Whitehall that was deserted for long.

"Be still!" he growled, propelling her down the empty hall, away from the faint noise of people. Her gown caught around her legs and she tripped, falling against the rough stone wall even as Fantin wrenched her arm to keep her on her feet. "I'll have none of your tricks!" he snarled as she slammed up into the wall from the force of his yank. Pain burst in her shoulder and along her arm.

"Unhand the girl, de Belgrume." The steely voice cut through the air like a sword and Madelyne's knees went weak with relief.

"Step aside, Mal Verne!" Fantin whirled toward Gavin, a hand going to his belt and returning with a glittering dagger. "I'll not have you in my way in this."

As Fantin manipulated them around, Madelyne saw Gavin through the fog of pain that had enveloped her. Even in her half-dazed state, she saw the rage blaring in his eyes.

"I said unhand her." Gavin's voice was calm, but the violence lacing it sent a frisson of fear down Madelyne's spine.

Fantin held the dagger steady in his outstretched hand. The grip on Madelyne's arm lessened as his attention swerved to the other man. "I suppose you think I ought to thank you for finding her for me, Mal Verne," he sneered, "but 'twas truly God's working and not any deed of yours."

They froze like two hounds taking each other's measure, then suddenly Gavin moved. Fantin gasped in pain as the younger man's foot came in contact with his wrist, and the dagger flew through the air. With one quick movement, assisted by the surprise and pain that immobilized Fantin, Gavin grasped the man by the front of his fine tunic and slammed him up against the wall.

Madelyne was able to pull free, and she retreated from the two men, rubbing her aching shoulder and bruised arm, and trembling from head to toe.

"She is under the protection of the king," Gavin gritted from between clenched teeth as his hand closed over Fantin's throat.

"The king?" Fantin's voice had a decidedly unmasculine squeak to it.

"The king," Gavin affirmed in a calmer voice. He made as if to release him, but then it was as if the anger swept through him anew. Madelyne could tell by the renewed consternation on her father's face just when Gavin's fury returned. "Methinks I ought to put an end to this now," he murmured in a terrible voice. "I ought to have finished you long ago."

Fantin's face flushed darkly when the band of fingers constricted, just as his own had around Madelyne's arm. "Your lack of success in doing just that is legendary, Mal Verne," he managed to gasp.

"What makes you believe you'll succeed this time? 'Tis I who have God's strength behind me!"

Madelyne saw Gavin's stone face darken, tightening murderously, and she muffled a gasp as she saw his intent. "Nay, Gavin, nay! Do not! 'Tis not right!"

It was a long moment, and Madelyne fairly stopped breathing—but in the end, Gavin relented and abruptly loosed his grip on Fantin's throat. The man slumped to his knees, pure loathing settling on his face, as he looked around Gavin to shoot a poison look at Madelyne.

"Do you not fear, daughter—we shall meet again when you do not have your cowardly protector about. I'll not let anyone stand in the way of our reunion—mark me well." He struggled to his feet and smoothed a hand over his high, silvery-blond mane. Shooting a glare filled with loathing at Gavin, Fantin jeered, "Once again, sirrah, you have managed to hide behind the skirts of the king to get your way. Enjoy it whilst you have that advantage, for the king's might is naught compared to that of my Lord's."

His face just as dark and furious, Gavin forbore to respond. Instead, he merely watched as Fantin scuttled away. As soon as he was out of earshot, he turned to Madelyne. "'Tis no more than you deserve," he snapped, glaring at her as she rubbed her shoulder. "Do you not go unescorted through this castle—or anywhere—Lady Madelyne, or the next time, I may not be able to intervene. Have I not already warned you of that folly?"

"Once again, I owe you my thanks," Madelyne replied from between lips stiffened to keep them from trembling. He was right in his anger and fury; he had warned her.

"Come. I'll see that you reach your chamber with no further incident." He offered her a solid arm, and she winced when she raised her hand to accept it. "What? My lady, are you hurt?" Gavin stopped and peered searchingly at her.

"Only a bit of an ache on my shoulder," Madelyne replied evasively, still stung by his sharp reprimand, and stunned by all that had happened so quickly. She turned to continue walking, but he whirled her back to face him.

"Wait." The command gentled his voice as firm fingers gingerly felt along her arm, up along her shoulder. "I did not know he'd hurt you," Gavin said, his mouth tightening when she winced at the probe of his forefinger. He looked down at her, and Madelyne recognized concern in his gray eyes. Their gazes met and held fast as the world slowed.

Her breath caught in her throat and she suddenly became acutely aware of the warmth and heaviness of the fingers that were now caressing her arm. Despite the haze of disbelief and bewilderment that had benumbed her since her audience with King Henry, Madelyne felt her pulse leap. Heightened sensitivity blaze throughout her limbs. When Gavin's other hand, large and brown, reached up to tuck away a lock of hair that had fallen from her coiffure, she thought she might stop breathing.

Her lips parted slightly, fulling, as Madelyne looked up at him, and she saw his eyes flare wider for an instant before they narrowed.

"The king has the right of it," Gavin said in a low voice, "you are much too beautiful to be a nun." His hand, which had hovered, raised, now lifted higher to slip a lock of hair behind her ear. He brushed along her jawline, sending warmth to suffuse her face.

Then, his words registered through her foggy mind and sanity reigned. "Too beautiful?" Madelyne stepped away, backing into the damp stone wall, then shifting to the right. "What has beauty to do with anything?"

Chagrin flooded his face and he dropped his hand back to his side. His features realigned into the familiar stone mask and his eyes took on a sardonic gleam. "'Tis no secret our king has an eye for comely women," he replied.

Madelyne tucked her fingers into her sleeves and turned away. "Then more's the pity for her majesty the queen. And again, I ask, Lord Gavin," she said, purposely using his title to reaffirm distance between them, "what has beauty to do with a woman's religious vocation? Must I mutilate my face or shave my hair in order to be allowed to do that which I wish?" She swallowed heavily, barely able to keep her voice from breaking in frustration.

"That would be a very foolish thing to do," he responded quickly. "His majesty has already made his decision, and 'twould serve no purpose to harm yourself so—only to cause yourself pain." He took her arm firmly—the one that did not pain her—and tucked it into the crook of his elbow. "Come, now, lady. I shall return you to your chamber so that your hurt can be seen to."

FIFTEEN

DESPITE THE fact that he'd just left Henry's presence, Gavin was readmitted to the king's courtroom upon his request. The courtier who had dismissed him an hour earlier swung the large oaken door open once again, bowing Gavin into the large room.

"Aye, Gavin, what is it that brings you back so soon?" Henry griped, glancing up from a parchment missive that still had a bit of blue wax clinging to it.

"De Belgrume is here. And he nearly relieved you of the wardship of his daughter." Rage still simmered in his hands, causing them to clench and unclench in memory of Fantin's soft neck.

"What? Here? In my court?" Henry bolted from his chair. "How can that be? He has been banned for two winters!"

"I do not know, but he would have made off with Madelyne had I not arrived on the scene as I did. I can only suspect that he was waiting without for an opportunity to grab her. You know as well as I the number of spies in this court." Gavin stepped aside as his king stalked off the dais and past him to thrust the parchment he'd been holding into the face of his secretary, who sat, shoulders scrunched, in the corner.

"And did you do no damage to the man?"

Gavin's mouth tightened. "I nearly sent the man to his grave. My hands were thus about his skinny neck."

"Nearly?" Henry bellowed. "Why in the blazes did you not rid me of that pestilence—and yourself of the same man who has taken so much from you?"

"I could have, my lord…but she begged me stay my hand, and I did."

"Surely she does not care for his health. There was fear in her eyes when I mentioned his name."

"She is murderously afraid of the man, and moreso now that she has felt the madness again. But she is a nun—or meant to be—my liege, and she does not believe in wanton killing. She…prays for the souls of men of violence. Those such as you and I."

Henry gave him an assessing look. "You stayed your hand at the throat of your deepest enemy because a woman begged you to? You, Mal Verne—you who have been made a cuckold, a near-murderer, a laughing-stock by that man?" He scratched his wiry copper hair, shaking his head. "I would have rewarded you greatly should you have relieved my kingdom of such a pestilence."

Gavin swallowed annoyance at the reminder of de Belgrume's sins upon himself: all of them, and, too, the damage done to his cousin Judith. "Ah, but then you—in your infinite quest for justice—would have had to throw me in the dungeon for murder," he reminded the king.

"Many in the land know de Belgrume is mad—with all of his talk of finding the secrets of the ancients and turning metals into gold."

"Aye. The man has the flame of madness in his eyes that was not there even six moons ago. He spoke as if he was doing the Will of God, as if he had some power from the Almighty behind him," Gavin replied, his face settling into soberness. "Many might know he is mad, as you have said, but others do not believe it, and are tricked into believing his work." He didn't need to mention Nicola or Gregory as two who had fallen to that trap.

"We know he has been the cause of deaths, and unnecessary warring in the south," Henry countered, sloshing wine into his cup. "And there is more, we suspect—but cannot prove."

"Aye. He is a wily man, taking care to protect himself—else you would have incarcerated him long ago. With no proof, I would be labeled the murderer of an innocent man." Gavin frowned and directed the conversation away from his own shortcomings and to the purpose which had brought him there. "Madelyne needs to be protected, or he will try to take her again. That's the reason I came back to your presence, your majesty…not to have my actions questioned yet again."

Henry raised a brow at Gavin's tone, but merely replied, "Ah yes. The fair Madelyne. A source of excellent revenue for us now… but we will need to find her a husband sooner than I had wished." Henry drank deeply, glancing at Gavin sidewise as he raised the cup. "It could be a possible task for you."

Gavin froze, then forced himself to breathe again. "Nay," he said. "You know I have no wish to wed again. And in particular, no wish to wed a nun. Do—"

Henry was stroking his moustache vehemently, his eyebrows raised high. "Gavin, 'tis not like you to jump to such conclusions. I meant not for you to wed with her. I well know that Nicola's infidelity ruined you for any other woman. I meant only for you to find the best man to be her husband. One who can protect her from the madman, and one who does not mind wedding with a nun—a beautiful nun, might I remind you—in exchange for the fiefs that she will inherit when my lands are rid of Fantin de Belgrume."

Gavin steadied himself against the heavy chair that belonged to Eleanor. "Ah." He felt foolish at his rash words, then suffocated by the thought that in searching for a proper husband for Madelyne, he would not yet be freed of her presence. Yet, he could not naysay the king when Gavin was the one who'd brought the problem to him. "As you will, my lord."

"So I leave you with yet another duty, Mal Verne. Two things I ask of you to take some of the weight from my burdened shoulders: find a husband for the nun, and rid me of de Belgrume. Do you not let me learn that he is still here at court! I will not have that madman slithering about my castle!"

"Aye, your majesty."

"Tavis, you have the right of it." Fantin's vision swam pink and damp as he dug each of his ten long fingernails—with which he used to pluck the strings of his lute—into his thighs. "I had the girl within my grasp, and Mal Verne interfered."

The rage still threatened to erupt within him, though he'd kept it at a simmer by fasting and praying for more than a day. Yet, Rufus was not here to lead him in his pleadings to God…and thus far, he'd received no response, no acknowledgement from Above. Was God angry with him for failing yet again?

Nay. He could not believe that. He would not believe it. He, who had given his life for this quest in the name of the Lord, would not be forsaken by Him.

"'Twas a great chance you took, entering the king's court," Tavis continued, offering his lord a goblet of wine. His eyes, round and dark and serious, reminded Fantin of the young Gregory, who'd also served him thus.

'Twas yet another reason he hated Mal Verne. Not only had the man had Nicola before Fantin, but Mal Verne had also taken from Fantin the young man he'd thought of as a son—slaughtering him in a battle at one of his holdings.

Tavis waxed eager, but he did not have the cunning and intelligence Gregory had possessed. Had he not been the betrothed of Mal Verne's own cousin—Judith—was that her name? Fantin frowned, trying to recall. It had been so long ago. Nearly four autumns, and the details of that time remained foggy in his mind. All he knew was that Gregory had been taken from him. By Gavin of Mal Verne.

"Aye. None saw me, save Mal Verne and my daughter…yet, I'll not risk being seen at court again." The king had banned him long ago because of an incident in which Fantin had tried to gather a cluster of Henry's own priests to join his holy quest—yet the king still continued to collect rents and taxes from him.

Fantin would not suffer long that indignity. Nay, he would not.

"I'll leave my man Seton de Masin here, and also his cohort James of Mangewode to spy upon the workings here," Fantin decided. "I must return to Father Rufus, for mayhap he will have the answer I cannot find."

"If we return to Tricourten, my lord, how then will you have your revenge upon Mal Verne?" asked Tavis. "You know he will be here for some time."

"Aye. Yet whilst he hides behind the skirts of the king, you and I shall plan his demise. And keep a watch over my beloved daughter. Mayhap…"

Fantin thought for a moment, his thoughts settling into something clearer. The pink had faded. "Aye, 'tis best. I will stay here for a time—and you with me, Tavis. Instead, I will send de Masin and Mangewode back to Tricourten with a message for Rufus. We'll wait here, in the town, out side of the court where we shall remain unknown. Thus, news of the king will reach us more readily, and de Masin can return with communication from Father Rufus."

He liked that plan. It felt right. Perchance God wished him to stay nearby the king and his whore, Eleanor of Aquitaine. Of all the women on this earth, she—with her sultry beauty and beckoning smile—had tempted and turned many. She had divorced her first husband, the king of France, a holier man than Henry could ever hope to be. The Whore Queen had led women on a farce of a Crusade to the most Holy of Lands, dressed in breeches like a man. Rumor had it that she and her uncle had fornicated whilst she was married to Louis of France….

A bolt like lightning struck him, and Fantin stilled. The thought shot through him, and his breathing hitched faster, yet his heart rate slowed. The trembling of his hands ceased as the surety, the knowledge flowed through him.

'Twas so clear, so perfect, so attuned to his calling that Fantin knew this would be the final step in his work.

At last his God had spoken. He understood why he must stay at court. And how his daughter could be of help to him. And why he had not managed to seize her yet.

His lips shifted to one side. With one achingly beautiful act— and in the name of God—he would destroy Mal Verne and commit the final task in this journey on which he'd been sent.

And then at last the secret of the Stone would be made clear to him.

The stone floor was cold and hard beneath her knees, and Madelyne shifted yet again to relieve the pressure. How long she'd been there, in the chapel, she did not know…but the rays of light that had been a dim moonbeam through the narrow windows were now strong golden streaks staggering across the uneven floor.

Her beads were a comfort in her hands, but there was little else to bring her ease. All that lay before her was the darkness of unknowing, uncertainty, and fear.

"Dear Father," she prayed again, as she had so many times those last hours, "I wish only to do Your will…to live to serve You. I place my life in Your hands…I ask that you show me forgiveness for failing You and the vows I have made to You…."

Madelyne's voice trailed as despair and fatigue overcame her. Now, as had been the case for hours, there was no lifting of response in her breast…no certainty that her prayers had been heard…no fulfillment of knowing that her life was strong and had meaning.

Had God turned from her, knowing that she'd failed to abide by the vows she'd meant to make? Or was this a test, challenge for her to overcome. And at the end of the challenge, should she meet it, would there be the comfort of knowing that she'd done His will—whatever it would be?

Could it be that He wished for her to wed? To love a man and wed with him?

A faint scuffle reached her ears, and a booted foot stepped into the realm of her downcast vision. She raised her head without hurry, swallowing the first innate fear that it was her father, and looked into the slightly shadowed face of a man too slim to be Gavin Mal Verne.

"Lord Reginald," she said, tempering the surprise she felt. "Do you come here to pray?" As he extended his hand, she accepted it and allowed him to assist her to stand.

He smiled, a soft quirk of tenderness. "Nay, my lady, I but came in search of you. Your maid directed me to you here…she lamented that your absence had been noted but that she had a fear of leaving the chambers to come in search of you."

Madelyne raised her brows in surprise. "Tricky had a fear of leaving the chamber?"

"A large, burly man had been posted out side of the door," Reginald told her, slipping her hand smoothly into the crook of his arm. "'Twas only because your maid had sent for me that I gained audience with her. She called him Clem, and he allowed me to speak briefly with her."

"My maid sent for you?" Madelyne felt a flush rise over her cheeks and pulled her arm from his, clasping her hands in front of her abdomen. Whatever Tricky's purpose in doing such a bold thing, she would receive a tongue lashing from Madelyne at the first opportunity. Such a transgression was not to be tolerated, even from the sunny-faced Tricky. "Please accept my apologies, Lord Reginald, for my maid's interference—"

"Nay! 'Twas no fault of hers. She but responded to a missive I sent when I did not see you at supper last evening." His smile was gentle and friendly. "I merely missed your presence and wished to have the opportunity to walk with you in the garden betimes."

Disconcert flitted through her, and Madelyne did not know where to look—anywhere but into the warm, searching blue eyes. "Lord Reginald, I—"

"Forgive me, lady, but you are finished with your novena? I should have asked you first—I have no wish to disturb your prayers."

She allowed a small smile at his concern. "Aye, I have made my petitions many times…whether they will be heard begs yet to be known." Her smile faded, and she felt for the prayer beads that hung from the kirtle around her waist.

"Surely you are hungry. Your maid appeared to be much concerned about your lengthy absence, bewailing that you had not broken your fast." Now he took her arm again, and pulled it into the warmth of his elbow. "Please, let me help you to find something to eat."

"My thanks, Lord Reginald, but in truth, I have no wish for food. I fast today."

"And my thanks to you, D'Orrais, as well."

The deep voice coming from the shadows of the chapel caused Madelyne's heart to surge into her throat, where it settled, thumping with fervor. "Gav—Lord Mal Verne," she said, turning toward him, pulling her hand again from Lord Reginald's arm.

Mal Verne came forward, and she saw from his stony face that he was angered. When he spoke, however, his words were simple and even. "I do thank you, D'Orrais," he said again, "for seeing to Lady Madelyne's safety. 'Though she is under the protection of the king—and myself—" he spared a quick, meaningful glance at her, "she appears to need some direction to cease wandering through the keep of her own volition."

Lord Reginald nodded his blond head briefly, glancing at Madelyne as though to assure himself it was permissible to leave her with Gavin. "I didn't know that the king had a special interest in Lady Madelyne."

Gavin's eyes were steady and cold. "Aye, the king and myself have great interest in her well-being…and, as well, there are other parties who have interest only in her non-well-being. I thus warn you that she will be well-guarded until such time as a permanent protector is chosen for her."

Now, he turned to look fully at Madelyne and his words were for her. "Have you finished your prayers, my lady? If not, I beg that you will complete them in the privacy and safety of your chamber. Come with me." Gavin did not wait for her assent. He grasped her wrist—albeit gently—and she had no choice but to allow him to direct her to the place he wished her to go.

That place was outside of the chapel, outside where the sun blazed down and serfs, knights, tradesmen, and pages hurried about their business in the large bailey of Whitehall. Madelyne blinked rapidly as her eyes watered, adjusting to the brightness. She stumbled as Gavin gently pulled her across the trampled ground.

He didn't stop, nor did he speak to her—or to anyone else—until they re-entered the keep. He guided her along the halls until they reached a private alcove, where he gestured for her to take a seat.

"Surely you did not mean to seek me out in the chapel, and interrupt my prayers to bring me here?" Madelyne asked, sitting on a wooden bench. A tapestry hung on the wall above her head, depicting King Henry's coat of arms.

"Nay, I didn't know you were in the chapel. Foolish woman. Again that you should be unprotected so soon after your father's attack upon you yesterday. Until I received word from Clem that you had been gone since last eventide, and that your maid had sent D'Orrais in search of you, I didn't realize you'd gone missing." His face had hardened with annoyance. He appeared prepared to continue, but Madelyne thought it timely to interrupt before any passersby might hear his angry words.

"I do not fear harm when in a chapel, and in the presence of God," she told him, smoothing her skirt, noticing the dirt that stained where she'd knelt in the sacristy. "Aside of that, and more practically, the priest was present during my entire stay, leaving just before Lord Reginald arrived. Surely you do not believe I would be that foolish, Lord Gavin?"

"I'm relieved to learn that you weren't alone," Gavin replied. "But I must reiterate again that it is not safe for you to wander about alone, or to be alone anywhere in this court. Even in a holy place. Your father is here—unbeknownst to the king—and he is a dangerous and desperate man. I cannot continue to protect you if you do not take care."

Madelyne looked directly into his eyes. "I have seen the king, he has taken from me my freedom and my desire to devote my life to God, and thus you no longer have reason to have concern for my person, Lord Mal Verne."

"I have been instructed to find you a husband, my lady," Gavin told her in a harsh voice.

Madelyne's gaze flashed to his face at this announcement, but he wasn't looking at her. "You are to choose my husband?" she echoed. "What special talent have you that you should be thus privileged?"

·"The king has ordered it of me—-that is the talent that I have," he responded, his words softer now, and his gaze returning to her face. "Until then, I will keep you safe—and help you find your way and comfort here at court, now that you, as you have so aptly described, lost your freedom." He thrust a hand into his thick hair, yanking his fingers viciously through so that it stood wildly about his head, making him look even more formidable. His annoyance seemed to evaporate with this gesture, and his next words gentled. "My lady, for the loss of your freedom and the disruption of your vows, I am truly sorry. 'Twas never my intention to place you in such a position."

She considered him for a moment.

To her surprise, she was not angry. Nay, she'd come to accept it—and him—after this night of prayer and day of fasting. Nay, she was no longer angry with him. But disappointed, sad, and disconcerted—and frustrated with the futility of her position and the loss of her freedom.

"I accept your apology, Lord Mal Verne. Yet my acceptance is with the knowledge that, though you regret my inconvenience, if you had the choice to make again, you would make the same decision." He began to speak, and she raised a slim white hand to stop him. "Prithee. 'Tis the man you are, Gavin, and there is naught I or anyone could do to alter that."

"And what kind of man is that?" he snapped.

"A man of honor, of right, of vengeance…and, aye, of blood…. That is the kind of man you are. And the man you will ever be. Just as I," she sighed, and looked down at her trembling fingers, "…I will ever be a daughter of madness, of despair, and one destined to seek peace and serenity—all the while fighting to keep those self-same tendencies from my blood."

"Madelyne…." He reached for her, then his hand dropped. "Aye. You have the right of it, my lady. You may not be schooled in the ways of politics or court, but you are a woman far too wise in the ways of men."

Sixteen

"THE BLOOD of madness runs in her veins, say they."

"She wishes only to take her vows and live cloistered for the rest of her life. What man would take to wive such a woman?"

"The lady must be as comely as a horse to desire only solitude!"

The catty tongues had already begun to wag, thought Judith as she sat demurely in the queen's solar. Her relaxed posture and benign expression belied the anger and disgust that seethed within her at the nastiness abounding. She had not expected anything different, of course, knowing that many of the ladies of Eleanor's court were self-centered and vain, but their words served to spark her own indignation.

Before she could decide whether it would be detrimental to Madelyne to speak in her favor so soon, the door to the large, open chamber swung inward, allowing entry to a young page and the source of the raging gossip.

Judith, who had deliberately chosen to arrive prior to Madelyne instead of escorting her there, sat on a hassock near the queen, surrounded by some of Eleanor's favored ladies. Looking about the solar, she saw it as Madelyne must see it, entering this world for the first time: ladies dressed in bright colors, settled in groups about the room. Some sewed on embroidery, others shared a table of cheese and wine, still others sat with a lute. Two women pushed, tapped, and pulled on looms in a corner, weaving new tapestries for the great hall. The chamber was large and filled with sun, for on this warm day, the large rectangular windows were uncovered and allowed a comfortable breeze to flow through.

She flashed a brief smile, catching the eye of her childhood friend, as Madelyne followed the page who led the approach to her majesty. *Be strong, Madelyne.*

"Lady Madelyne de Belgrume," reported the page.

The women, who were scattered about the chamber, trickled into silence and cast sharp, interested stares at the lady who stood quietly before the queen.

Judith knew it had taken Tricky a concerted effort to dress and coif Madelyne in an appropriate manner—richly garbed in a new gown ordered days earlier, with a few jewels provided by Judith herself, for the woman still preferred the simple attire of a nun. But in her dark red bliaut, fitted along the wrists and waist under the loose crimson overtunic, Madelyne looked every inch the lady and ward of the king that she now was. Her thick black hair was wound and coiled in an intricate pattern of plaits around the crown of her head, with gold netting woven about and through it. Her lips were dark red as well—mayhap from nervous nibbling, Judith thought to herself. But Madelyne's fair, elegant face was serene as she curtseyed smoothly to Eleanor.

Whatever she was feeling was well-hidden behind that peaceful countenance.

"You are well come to my service," said the queen, a beautiful woman in her own right—and, Judith knew, astute enough to recognize that this new addition to her ladies in waiting would provide more than a little disruption. "You come to us from an abbey, I understand. Tell me a bit about your accomplishments there so that I may learn how you can best serve me." She smoothed her hand over the jewel-encrusted skirts that splayed over the heavy chair on which she sat.

"Aye, your majesty," Madelyne replied in her clear voice. "Whilst there I learned the healing arts, and became the most learned in the herbary. I tended a small garden of medicines as well. The nuns taught me to read and write Latin and Greek, and we studied many of the holy papers. I have learned some mathematics, though I confess 'twas not to my liking and I did not fare as well in those studies, and also some geography. As to embroidery and weaving, I am well-learned there and rather enjoy the rhythm of such tasks." She curtsied again.

Judith saw a narrowing of eyes among some of the ladies, and smirks of condescension from others. Lady Artemis de Trubell, who sat in a cluster of women away from Eleanor, tossed her ink-black head and smiled coolly. "You are well-suited to joining our queen's court, Lady Madelyne, as we spend overmuch of our time discussing Latin and Greek writings. And, of course, French and Italian as well."

A soft titter erupted from her clique of companions and Judith bit the wayward tongue that itched to lash out at Artemis. She wasn't surprised that the first attack had come thus, but it would do Madelyne no help if she interfered at this time. The queen, also, would remain silent, as it was not her practice to intervene among her ladies' spats. As she'd once told Judith, if that were the case, she would spend the whole of her days doing only that, and then would be seen as choosing favorites. Eleanor did, indeed, have her favorites, but they were subtly selected from ladies as intelligent and self-assured as she herself.

Madelyne turned politely—not enough that her back was to the queen, but just so that she could see the woman who'd spoken—and smiled. "I am very pleased to hear that, for I was led to believe that most of the writing and reading here at court was provided by scribes. I could not imagine needing to rely upon others to read my own private missives or study the Word of God."

Judith blinked, fighting to hold back the smile that tugged incorrigibly at the corners of her mouth. Was Madelyne sincere in her response—did she really believe that the ladies studied many languages?—or did she know that Artemis's comment was laced with sarcasm and mockery? Most of the ladies of the court did not read, or write, French—their own language—and certainly had no knowledge of any other tongue, written or spoken. 'Twas a lucky thing for Madelyne, whether she made her response in innocence or not, that Eleanor herself was an exception to that. The queen was, indeed, very well educated. Judith herself had only learned to write French once she arrived at court, and only because she had asked it of the queen.

"I am certain we shall have the opportunity to test your skills in Latin," spoke Eleanor, interrupting the moment. "Many of the messages I receive from my uncle in Rome are written thus. I am not as well learned in Latin myself, so mayhap you will assist me with them."

"Of course, your majesty," Madelyne curtsied again.

"For now, you may sit next to me. You may stitch on this embroidery and tell me more about life at the abbey."

"Of course, your majesty," replied Madelyne. "But, may I ask of you to hear tales of your journey to the Holy Lands? I have read maps of that place, but wish to know more of it from one who was there."

A palpable holding of breaths hushed over the room, and Judith clenched her fingers into her piece of embroidery. Eleanor did not take well to having her particular wishes diverted.

"A lady with her own agenda," murmured the queen.

As Madelyne sank obediently into her place next to the queen, she appeared to have no idea that she had perhaps offended her liege lady.

Eleanor looked down her elegant French nose at Madelyne as though assessing her lady's actions. "I should like to hear about your life at the abbey, Madelyne de Belgrume, and then, if it please me, I will tell you about Jerusalem and the other places."

Judith released her breath and picked up her own stitching, pleased that the queen was not offended. She could not hear the conversation that ensued between Madelyne and Eleanor, but noted that the queen appeared to be interested in the tales relayed to her, nodding her head in agreement and smiling at moments in a rueful manner.

The morning passed quickly, and the whispers, though still rumbling in the fringes of the group gathered about the throne, were not overt.

Several knocks on the chamber door, and consequent entries, did not give the ladies pause until a page entered, requesting that entry be allowed for Gavin Mal Verne. Judith looked quickly toward the entrance and saw the tall, dark form of her cousin as he strode in. A hush fell over the ladies as he passed through, his swift movement stirring the air and the hem of his tunic flapping against his powerful thighs.

"What brings you to my presence, Lord Mal Verne?"

He bowed to the queen. "The king has sent me to escort you to his chambers, your majesty."

Eleanor rose, and, standing on her dais, still had to look up at his hawklike, impervious face. "How foolish of my husband to waste the talents of a good man by sending him on an errand meant for a page. Nevertheless, I will accept your escort." She glanced about the room as she smoothed her skirts. "Your little nun has made herself quite entertaining to me this morrow," Eleanor commented as her eyes rested upon Madelyne.

"I have no doubt of that." Gavin's reply was impersonal, and Judith saw that he barely flickered his attention to Madelyne. "Your majesty, shall you accompany me?"

With a nod, Eleanor turned and walked quickly from the room, her jewel-laden skirts dragging behind her, as Gavin followed with nary an acknowledgement even to Judith.

"That man is fearsome," whispered one of the ladies as soon as the door closed. "I am like to have nightmares just seeing him!"

"'Tis said he killed his wife in a fit of rage. Is that true?" asked Lady Beatrice, a newer addition to the court.

"Of course it's not true," snapped Judith, standing abruptly. Her embroidery slid to the floor, and she stepped over it to approach the others. "Lady Nicola died from a fall off her horse."

Artemis slanted a brown-eyed look at her. "That is what Lord Mal Verne has said, but what else would such a man say should he be the cause of her demise? And what else would you say, Judith, if other than to defend your cousin? 'Tis most likely that he helped her in that fall, as I have heard tell she cuckolded him for another man!"

"'Though how you could still speak well of the man after your own tragedy, caused by Mal Verne, I cannot know," added another lady—Renee of Hintenston.

Judith felt as though she'd been punched in the middle. How did these cats know of Gavin's involvement—innocent as it was—in the death of her betrothed?

"He is not always quite so fearsome," purred a low voice from the corner. Lady Therese, widow of Lord Grayerton, looked up from her loom and her smile glinted slyly.

Judith frowned. She'd heard rumors, of course, that Gavin had been seen in her company, but she did not put much credence to it. Therese, well-known among the court for her overt sexual appetites and boastful comments, was much too coarse and conspicuous for Gavin's tastes.

"You would consort with such a man?" squeaked Beatrice, her blue eyes wide with alarm and admiration.

Therese, a diminutive, curvaceous woman, rose from the loom and stepped into the center of the room. "Dangerous men are much more exciting than those milksops like Reginald D'Orrais," she told the younger girl airily.

"Exciting or nay," Artemis said pointedly, "that man turns my blood cold. And one who would be seen with him is likely to soon find a cold grave. Just as his wife did." She turned suddenly to Madelyne. "Especially little nuns."

Renee and Beatrice tittered. Artemis stepped toward Madelyne, who remained in her seat by the queen's throne. "It must be frightening for you, little nun, to find yourself in such a vast world—so different from your cloister. Do you take care that you do not find yourself caught up in a world that you cannot manage."

"Many thanks for your concern, Lady Artemis. I have found naught to fear in this court thus far. Only the cats with sharp claws who seek a scratching place have drawn my attention. I shall deal with those cats as I did with the mousers at the abbey: leave them outside in the cold."

Judith settled in her seat. Madelyne might appear to be fragile and naive, but there was a solid shell of serenity about her that would keep the barbs from striking deeply.

Seventeen

"YOUR NAME is spoken with such fear and reverence in the ladies' court," Therese said into Gavin's ear as she settled next to him that eventide.

Dinner was finished, and the platters of food had been removed by serfs and pages pushing between the rows of trestle tables. Ale and wine continued to flow as the court settled in for the evening's entertainment.

"Most of the ladies fear you, but you know that I see you for what you truly are."

Gavin tore his gaze from Madelyne, who sat among a cluster of nobility near the front of the great hall. "And what is that, Lady Therese?"

"A man with great passion, and a man who knows what he desires." She pushed her generous breast against his arm and only many years of training to control his reflexes kept him from flinching.

He saw Madelyne turn slightly in her seat, away from the jongleur that danced while juggling goblets on the front dais. Her eyes scanned the crowded hall, and Gavin shifted himself away from Therese just as Madelyne's gaze rested upon his. Their eyes met for a moment and suddenly his linen *sherte* and tunic felt heavy and hot. Then she turned back to her companions and Gavin took a large sip of his ale.

"Lady Therese, did I not see the queen beckoning to you?" asked Clem, who sat across the table from them.

"Her majesty?" Therese nearly tripped on her own gown in her anxiousness. "Excuse me, Lord Mal Verne, but I must go."

"Many blessings upon you, Clem," said Gavin when she had gone.

His man's face wrinkled in a wry smile, then settled into his usual dour expression. "A pox on all women, I say!"

Gavin raised his brows, but his attention had wandered back to Madelyne. Now, Lord Reginald had taken a seat next to her. Gavin's jaw tightened and he watched intently to see what—if any—response she would give him. A smile, he saw, a brief one, and then her attention returned to the jongleur.

He became aware that Clem had been muttering on for a long moment about aught—and that fact that he was still speaking regained Gavin's full attention. "What is it, man?" he asked, looking at his companion.

"Ye cannot ever trust'em! And when you think they're comin' forth with what they want, and ye got'em over their mad, then they get all mad about somethin' else!" Clem took a long draft of ale, as though this unusually long speech had dried his tongue.

Gavin stared at him. "There is some comely wench who has captured your heart, then, Clem?"

"My heart? Nay! 'Tis not my heart she's captured—'tis my ears and feet! The maid of Lady Madelyne—that woman Patricka—plagues me with her demands and orders. While I guard the lady's door, the maid runs me willy-nilly with her silly tales and her calls for me to move this, and reach that, and open this, and foolish things such as that. I begin to feel like a nursemaid to that wench!"

Gavin remained silent, nodding his head, drinking his ale, peeking at Madelyne, and allowing Clem to bluster on. Strange as his unchecked tirade was, it saved Gavin from the necessity of having to respond.

"'Tis Jube whose eye has been caught by that maid—'tis not mine," Clem said sourly, pausing to take a gulp from his goblet.

Swiping a hand across his mouth, he continued, "It should be he who guards the door and runs household errands for that woman!"

Gavin, who'd seen Madelyne rise and begin to walk in his direction, quickly returned his attention to Clem—just in time to hear his last gripe. "Very well. If it will cease your moaning, you are then relieved of guard duty and I shall place Jube there during the day, henceforth. He may have his fill of the maid as long as he does not shirk his duty to watch over Lady Madelyne."

Clem opened his mouth to speak, then snapped it shut. "Many thanks my lord," he said gruffly, and buried his face in his goblet.

"Hail, Lady Madelyne," Gavin said, standing as she approached him. Her head was bare—still so strange to him to see that beautiful hair uncovered, despite the fact that she'd worn it thus since their arrival at court. Long strands of dark hair, wrapped in gold cord, hung from each temple, whilst the rest had been coiled and braided and gathered at the nape of her neck. Her gown trailed on the floor, the wide sleeves of her overtunic nearly brushing its hem, while hints of the tightly-laced bliaut underneath showed the lush curves of a very un-nunlike body.

Hiding his surprise that she should have sought him out, he continued smoothly, "I have just informed Clem that Jube will take a stint at the guard duty out side of your chambers for a time—during the day. At night, of course, Rohan will continue to pace out side of your doors."

Madelyne gave a slight curtsey, glanced with a smile at Clem, and returned her attention to Gavin. "Aye, thank you my lord." She felt the weight of his stare as his eyes scanned her from head to toe. Warmth crept up over her throat and face and she looked away in order to regain control over her suddenly scattered thoughts.

"I trust that your first day in Eleanor's court was uneventful?"

Madelyne nodded, and the strange feeling ebbed. "'Tis nothing like the abbey, but I am certain I'll adjust. I have little choice, at the least until I am wed." The words stuck in her throat, but she must get used to saying them—and accepting them. For, barring some act of God, it appeared that her destiny was set.

Gavin shifted, and his face held a slight grimace. Good, she thought, 'tis right that he should feel some small discomfort after the result of his actions upon me. "'Tis the reason I have come to you," she told him. "May we walk from here—'tis so loud—to talk? I have something I must ask of you."

He nodded. "Of course, my lady." He extended his forearm and she slipped her hand under and around it, cupping the sinewy, firm muscles under her fingers. He was warm and solid as she bumped against him while he pushed the way through throngs of people, leading her out of the hall. "Shall we go out side of the keep, or would you prefer to find somewhere within? We cannot go to your chamber of course."

She looked up, surprised and pleased that he should ask. "May we go outside? 'Tis been long since I have breathed the moon air."

His eyes softened, then crinkled at the corners. "The moon air. Aye, of course. Let us be off."

His pace was slower now that they were out of the hall and away from the people. Gavin brought her through the entry way and past the guards posted at doors as tall as three men. Their bodies were closer now, shoulders brushing as they walked—his stride long and smooth, mismatched against her shorter, faster one.

Once outside, Madelyne slipped from him and stood on the hard-packed dirt, turning her face up to the moon. It was only a sliver on this night, but the stars were many and the air was chill and crisp after the cloying, food-soaked, smoke-filled, sweaty space of the great hall. Her lips moved in a brief, silent prayer—one of thanks and admiration for this moment of beauty—then she turned back to Gavin.

He was there, arms crossed over his broad chest, leaning against the shadowy gray stone wall that stretched above him. He watched her, and her stomach lurched like a rusty drawbridge.

"What is it you wish to ask of me?" his voice carried easily to her, even over the sounds of busyness that surrounded them: the ever-present pages and squires, serfs and men-at-arms, going about their duties in the bailey.

"I…." She stepped toward him, then stopped. Something hung there, palpable, yet enough to make her stomach squeeze again. "Lord Gavin, you said that the king has asked you to find me a husband."

"Aye. Please do you not ask of me to disobey the command of the king. You must know that is the one thing I cannot—or will not—do for you."

Her lips tightened. He did not know her at all. She'd thought that perhaps….ah, she was foolish to think thus. "I would not ask that of you, Gavin." Her throat dried as she realized she'd used his given name.

"Then what is it?" His voice became rougher.

"'Tis only that I ask that you…have no hurry to find a husband for me…and that you have a thought to select a man…who…."

She did not know how to form the words. His stare was so heavy upon her, so steady, that all coherent thought disintegrated. She could only look at him, into those penetrating gray eyes, clear and open there in the starlight. The world receded and there was nothing but a wide space between them—a space of dirt, and a more cavernous space of violence and bloodshed versus peace and hope.

"Who will…?" He sounded annoyed, and he looked away, breaking the fragile connection. "Who will let you go back to the abbey? Who will not wish to beget an heir upon you? Who will what?"

Madelyne stepped back, straightening her posture. "Who will have some care for me. Who will not hurt me. Who will not order my every action, my every breath." She pivoted from him, stalking away, her hands trembling and her eyes filling with wetness. She hated that her voice had broken at the end.

"Madelyne."

She kept walking, ignoring her long skirts tangling about her feet, blinking rapidly, until the shout above stopped her.

"Who goes there?"

"'Tis Gavin Mal Verne." His voice boomed behind her, up at the guard who looked down from the corner of the wall that surrounded the bailey. He was close to her now, and she stopped, turned to him, her face shadowed by the tall wall. She clutched her light wool skirts, crumpling the fabric up into her palms to keep her hands still.

"You may pass." The permission wafted down from above, but neither Madelyne nor Gavin cared.

"Madelyne—"

"Please." She held up her hand to him.

"Nay, I will speak." Anger wavered in his voice. "Do you think that I would give you to the first man who asked? To a man who would hurt you? Foolish woman. Have I not done you enough damage already? At the least I owe you a husband who will be a better man than your father was."

He passed a hand over his forehead, as though to wipe away the ire. "Madelyne, the reason you must wed is so that you can be safe from your father. He wants to take you back, and he'll keep trying—he tried in the wood, during your travel here, and he tried under the king's very nose! The king and I know that he is mad, that some religious fervor burns within him and he seeks to harm others—mayhap yourself. If naught else, he will be incensed that you were taken from him some years ago, and be most unwelcoming to you.

"I will find you a husband only because the king has ordered it. One who will protect you…who *can* protect you. And one who will be worthy of your lands—which will come to you when your father is gone. And one who will have some care for you."

He stepped toward her, close enough that she could see the rise and fall of his chest and the movement in his cheek as he paused in his speech. When he spoke again, the words softened against her. "I do not believe it will be such a challenge to find one who will care for you—but more of a challenge to find the man worthy of keeping your father at bay. You are a lovely woman, Madelyne, and you will make a fine wife."

She looked up at him and her heart nearly stopped when one of his large rough hands came to cup her chin, to slide slowly over the side of her face and throat. The memory of the kiss they'd shared blazed into her and she stepped toward him, into his hand, and felt the firmness of his fingers as they closed gently around her jaw. They touched her hair, at the back of her neck, and an amazing shiver coiled around her ear and down the side of her neck.

"Madelyne, you tempt me so…." he said in a taut voice, closing his eyes. She did not move, just felt the trembling of his hand on her jaw, cupping around the nape of her neck as the rest of the world moved beyond them.

Gavin opened his eyes, and when he did, she saw a steely resolve glinting there in the moonlight. He dropped his hand from her face and stepped back. "I apologize if I have made you uneasy, my lady. I cannot seem to keep myself…in check…when I am with you." He gave a little, impersonal bow that made her want to stamp her foot in frustration.

What was wrong with him—with her—with this whole situation?

Madelyne drew her brows together and clutched her skirts with both hands. "Gavin, you've done naught for which you need apologize—at least, tonight, here, now. I may be a naive, shy woman who is not learned in the ways of the court, but the barest touch of a man is not about to cause me to turn tail and hie back to the castle screaming rape. I know to expect much more than that on the night in which I find myself wedded and bedded.

"You may escort me to my chambers now, my lord." She pushed past him, purposely brushing against his rigid arm because her patience had been lost and she didn't understand why she felt so frustrated and disappointed.

$\mathcal{E}$IGHTEEN

THE MORNING air hung damp with dew and alight with the risen sun. Gavin breathed deeply as Rule trotted across the drawbridge toward the forest. Once past the guards at the entryway, he gave the horse his head and the stallion leapt into fluid motion.

Hooves pounded and the fresh air blasted into his face as Gavin urged his mount on. Over a creek and around the bend of a pathway they flew, startling pheasants and gray hares from their hideaways. His bow and quiver hung over his shoulder, but he was not yet ready to put them to use. For now, he needed to ride…to put distance between himself and Whitehall and all that it held.

He rode at breakneck speed, but it was not enough to put the images from his mind. He'd nearly kissed her last night. He'd wanted to touch her and he had…but it had taken every bit of restraint to keep himself from pulling her to him and into his arms.

How could he dream of touching her when he knew she preferred a life with the Lord…and certainly would not relish a life with the man who'd taken that right from her. Madelyne deserved better than a man who lived only to kill, who dreamed only of violence upon another…who could not fathom a life without the need for vengeance.

He would never marry again. He'd remain alone, wreak his punishment upon Fantin, and then retire to Mal Verne to live until the king would call him to arms again. And thus and so it would be until he was too reckless and was himself killed.

And Madelyne....

Gavin pulled back on the reins. Rule trotted to a halt and they stood, silent and still in the wood that was devoid of birds singing and the crackle of animal movement. Silent and still, it surrounded him and closed his thoughts in upon him as he slipped his fingers into the pouch that carried the rose prayer beads.

Madelyne would find herself wed anon—as soon as he could find a suitable husband for her and the king gave his blessing. She would wed and bed him, as she so bluntly reminded him last night. Gavin's heart iced over as the images formed in his mind: of the apprehension that would be on her face, of large hands on her pale body, loosening her hair so that it fell to her hips, of a heavy figure poised over hers...of Madelyne kneeling in abject prayer on a stone floor—sobbing. His hands trembled on the reins.

If he did nothing more, he would make certain to select a man who would be gentle with her—one who would not destroy her serenity or her peace. One who would have sensitivity for the woman who would be a nun.

He cursed Henry for burdening him with this mission.

And then he cursed himself for creating it.

"Do you hunt with us on the morrow, Lady Madelyne?"

"Nay, Lord Reginald. I do not ride," she told him. "I had no opportunity to learn at the abbey...and, in sooth, I do not care for horses. They make me nervous."

He smiled kindly at her, covering her hand with his. "Lady Madelyne, I can understand that. Horses can seem like fearsome creatures...but in truth they are not. They need a gentle hand and can be as tame as a kitten."

She looked at him with skepticism. "Aye, as you say. I will choose to believe you, but will remain admiring horses only from a distance."

Reginald chuckled and tightened his fingers over hers. Madelyne gently pulled away from his grasp under the guise of raising her goblet to drink. She didn't know how to feel about his overt attention, and was even less certain how to act when he flirted with her.

Lady Artemis sallied over and found a seat next to Reginald. Madelyne greeted her politely, but held her breath as she waited to see whether the cat's claws were extended. "Good evening, Lord Reginald. We have missed your presence in the queen's court as of late. Will you be hunting with us on the morrow?"

If Madelyne had felt any sort of possessiveness toward Reginald, she would have felt the hair at her nape rise as Artemis looped her hand around his arm. As it was, she took notice, but had no reaction—likely to the other lady's dismay.

He glanced at Madelyne. "I have not yet decided."

Artemis raised a black eyebrow into a dark slash. "And you, Lady Madelyne? I should love to see you ride."

"Nay. I do not ride, Lady Artemis, as you may have surmised." Meeting the double-edged comment with acknowledgement of its slice was her only defense at this time.

"Lord Gavin is a fine rider," Artemis added shrewdly. "He is known for his ease in the saddle."

"Is that so?" Madelyne could not explain why the mere mention of the man should make her heart pick up speed. "Then I am sure he will be on the hunt."

"I am sure he will…." Artemis let her voice trail off as she looked pointedly across the room.

Madelyne followed her gaze and saw then the meaning of her words. Gavin sat, *tête-à-tête*, with the woman named Lady Therese: heads together, and bodies close enough that their shoulders brushed. As she watched, he tilted his head at something she said and gave as much of a smile—and a bark of laughter—as Madelyne had ever witnessed on his stoic face.

Strangely bereft, she turned back to her companions and smiled, determined to make light of it. "Mayhap he will have better luck in the wood on the morrow." Then, suddenly exhausted, she placed her hands on the table. "I am tired and will retire to my chambers now."

Reginald rose immediately and assisted her to her feet. "Lady Artemis, please excuse us. I will escort Lady Madelyne to her chambers."

"Nay, my lord, that will not be necessary," Madelyne protested, feeling the heavy weight of Artemis's stare now upon her.

"But of course. You cannot traverse this court without escort, and as your customary guard dog is otherwise occupied, the pleasure shall fall to me."

Madelyne acquiesced, only because she was too weary to argue, and walking alone through the dark warren of halls did not appeal to her.

Reginald offered her his arm, and she took it, wrapping her hand around his elbow as she had done with Gavin the night earlier. Reginald's shoulder rose a bit higher than Gavin's had, and his forearm was less bulky and warm, Madelyne noticed as they made their way down the halls. She took care that their bodies did not touch as they walked, and noticed that his stride stayed in check so that she nearly matched his steps.

When they reached her chamber door, she was surprised to find Jube still in attendance. "Good evening, Jube," she said with a nod. "I bethought to see Rohan here by now."

Jube bowed from his immensely tall height and responded, "He should arrive anon." His attention flickered to Reginald. "Where is Lord Gavin?"

"He remains in the hall," replied Madelyne lightly. "Lord Reginald kindly offered to see me here in his stead."

She began to open the door, but Reginald gently stopped her. With a glance at Jube, he said quietly, "My lady, 'tis unseemly that I should enter your chamber alone with you…but 'tis near impossible to have a private conversation with this giant hovering nearby."

Startled, Madelyne glanced at Jube and saw that he was sidling toward them. Looking back at Reginald, she saw the earnestness on his face, but also determination in his eyes. "Mm…Jube? Would you please step down the hall a trice? I should appreciate a bit of privacy for a moment."

He glowered in surprise, but complied, stepping away just far enough that he was out of earshot—she thought—but close enough that it could barely be considered private.

"Yes, my lord? What is it you wished to say to me?"

Reginald stepped closer to her, standing so that his back blocked Jube's view of Madelyne. She felt enclosed by him, with the wall behind and Reginald between her and Gavin's man. "I have heard that the king wishes you to wed," he told her. Taking her hands, he raised them, looking down seriously at her. She felt neither threatened nor apprehensive…just curious and more than a bit shy as he continued, "I have decided that I will place my suit for you to the king. If I am granted thus, we will wed." He pressed his lips, soft and gentle, onto the back of her hand.

Madelyne's heart thumped harder. "I was to be a nun," she told him. "But I was brought here to the king for another purpose."

"You will make a fine wife," he replied, in an echo of the same words Gavin had used the night before. "I wished only to tell you that I hope you will be mine."

Frustration rose within her. Was this how it was to be outside of the abbey? All of her life's decisions made without regard for her feelings and desires? Lord Reginald was a comely, gentle, kind man…but he did not seem to hear what she said.

Did any man ever hear what a woman said?

"It appears I have no choice in the matter," she told him, reminding herself of that as she spoke. "I can do only what the king requires of me, and all I can wish for is a husband who will have a care for me."

Reginald stepped closer, brushing a hand over her cheek. "I vow, if the king shall approve my suit, I will have a care for you, Madelyne. And I will court you and woo you so that you won't regret that you didn't take your vows."

She nodded. "Aye, Lord Reginald. I thank you for your kind words." Pulling away, she turned to grasp the handle of her door, noticing that Jube had somehow inched his way close enough to hear their words. She wondered how much he'd heard, and then realized it didn't matter.

"Good night, my lady," said Reginald as she opened the door.

"Good evening, my lord. Good evening, Jube," she added.

Madelyne pushed into the chamber, closing the door behind her, and turned to see Tricky pacing the floor, muttering in agitation.

When her friend saw that Madelyne had entered, she froze and crossed her arms emphatically over her chest. "Good evening, my lady."

"What is it that ails you, Tricky? Where is Peg?"

"Peg is supping with Lady Judith's maid Onda. I returned to the chambers to await your return, and to have a word with Clem— only to find that he has cried off and asked Lord Mal Verne to relieve him of the duty of guarding you." Her full lips firmed into a tight line.

Madelyne looked at her in surprise. "But 'tis Jube for whom you have a care, and who has taken Clem's position. Does that not please you?"

Tricky snorted and moved to stoke the fire. Even in the summer, the castle chambers were damp and cold at night. "Of course. I do not miss the grumblings of that malcontent Clem when I step out of the room. But I had aught I wished to speak with him on, and now he is gone."

"Certainly you can send for him if your need is that great," Madelyne replied, shaking her head. "Tricky, I do not understand why you are so overset."

The plump maid collapsed on a stool. "I meant to talk with Clem upon my return, but he wasn't here." She stood just as abruptly as she'd sat. "I'm sorry, my lady, for burdening you with my silly complaints when you are waiting for my assistance!"

She began to help Madelyne disrobe, chattering all the while. "'Tis said that you are to be wed anon," she said. "All of the court speaks of the shy woman from the abbey who will have a husband chosen for her."

Madelyne felt the coldness settle over her again, and sat slowly on the stool recently vacated by Tricky. "Aye, my friend. It appears to be so. The king will not allow me to return to the abbey, and he has decreed that I must wed. I have prayed long and hard over it—you know that, Tricky. Yet, there appears to be no way other than to abide by the king's wishes." She felt the weight on her head lessen as her maid pulled the pins from the coils of hair and they opened, falling straight.

"My lady…you have agonized long over what you cannot control. You must embrace your new life with a bold face and courage."

"You have the right of it…and deep in my heart I've come to believe that is what God expects of me."

"Aye, the matter has been taken from your hands by the king—the highest power on this earth other than the pope. You are right to believe it is God himself who pushes you in that direction. You are not meant to devote your life to Him. I know now that I am not meant to either." Her last words were softer, but firm. "I will not return to the abbey, Madelyne. Indeed, I should wish to remain with you for as long as you desire—in whatever capacity you wish."

Madelyne turned in her perch on the stool, looking up at the befreckled face of her companion. "Tricky, of course you may stay with me. Indeed, I am gratified that you should wish to…and I will relish having a friend rather than a maid at my side." She reached for her hand and squeezed.

Patricka smiled, tears springing to her eyes in big, large drops. "Thank you Madelyne. I am meant to be your maid, though. I hold no title and have no other attribute to commend me. I truly wish that, for you are a friend as well as a mistress."

"Indeed. As you wish—but you must call me Madelyne when we are alone. I do not wish to have that distance between us."

Tricky hugged her from behind, then returned to the task at hand. "Now, Madelyne, tell me what you feel for handsome Lord Reginald. 'Tis said throughout the court that he woos you and presses his suit to the king. There are others who would do the same, you know, but he is the most vocal. 'Tis believed that he would be a good match for you."

Madelyne swallowed back the lurch of her heart into her throat. "Lord Reginald has said the same. I do not know what to think.

He is kind and gentle. I don't wish to wed, but if I must—which I know that I must—it would not alarm me were he chosen."

"Has he kissed you yet, my lady?" asked Tricky mischievously.

"Kissed me? Of course not."

"Oh." Tricky sounded disappointed. "I was certain he had. Do you not wonder what it would be like to be kissed by a man? I wondered for so long, and now it has been by two men I have been kissed in this last fortnight."

"I do not wonder what 'twould be like, as I *have* been kissed." Madelyne stood to slip her sleeping gown on. Then, realizing what Tricky had said, she added in surprise. "*Two* men? Tricky, you have been kissed by two men?"

At the same moment, Tricky paused from tying the back of Madelyne's gown to peer around into her face. "If Lord Reginald has not kissed you, then who has?"

Blood rushed to Madelyne's face. "I should have said nothing," she stammered. "'Twas foolish to speak of—it meant nothing. Who is it that you have kissed besides Jube?"

"That naysayer Clem," Tricky said in disgust. "But that was long since passed, and he has been naught but rude and edgy since then." She sighed, then giggled. "Poor man…he does not know that he is meant to wed with me, so he fights his desires. He believes 'tis Jube I love, and I have half a mind to let him think so betimes—the man is so thick-headed!" Even as she spoke, Madelyne saw her reach for the wormwood comb that Clem had bought her.

"You are going to wed with Clem?" Madelyne asked, glad to have deflected Tricky's interest in her own kissing experience—and bewildered by her friend's sudden change of heart. "Were you not complaining what a malcontent he is? Were you not grousing that you do not wish even to speak with him?"

"Oh, aye, but 'twas only because I was angry with him, you see…the man does not know yet that we will wed. He believes only that he is annoyed by me…little does he know that 'tis love he feels and does not know how to scratch that itch!"

With a little frown on her apple-cheeked face, Tricky resumed her duties and began to drag the comb through Madelyne's long tresses. "'Tis glad I am that Jube kissed me too, else I would never have known that Clem—the oaf—is the man for me."

"What do you mean?"

"'Tis in the kiss, Maddie. Do you remember what Peg said—'tis by the kiss that you will know. And he will know too—the kiss that makes your head spin. Jube's kiss was nice and pleasant, but it stirred my insides little more than a wisp of a breeze…but Clem… ohh, Maddie, 'twas like I was caught in a storm on the ocean and could not find a secure holding for the life of me…and I became hot and fluttery…." She yanked too hard with the comb, pulling a short yelp from her mistress. "I am sorry, my lady!" she apologized, and silence ensued as Tricky concentrated on combing her hair without balding her mistress as Madelyne mulled over her friend's words.

Then, as Tricky replaced the comb on its table, she turned to look at Madelyne. "Who is it who has kissed you if it was not Lord Reginald?"

Again, heat swarmed Madelyne's face. "Nay, Tricky, I do not wish to tell. It was nothing."

"You must tell me Madelyne. I want to know!" Tricky planted her hands on her hips and stood in front of her, glowering. "If I am to be your maid, I must know all so that I can advise you and look out for your best interests."

Madelyne, though not convinced by her maid's argument, drew a deep breath. Part of her wished to tell…someone. "Lord Gavin. 'Twas Lord Gavin."

Tricky squeaked in shock. "Lord Mal Verne kissed you?"

"Be still!" Madelyne snapped, looking toward the heavy door. Could Jube—or Rohan—hear what was being said?

"Lord Gavin kissed you?" Tricky had lowered her voice, but now stared at her assessingly. "I should never have guessed that, my lady. That puts quite a different light on things."

"What?" Madelyne asked. "What do you mean?"

But Tricky did not reply; just looked at her shewdly, brows crinkling and lips settled firmly, nodding her head as though some great mystery had been revealed.

Nineteen

"I'VE SEEN nor heard nothing of de Belgrume," Gavin told the king. It was evening, and he sat in a large cushioned chair in the king's private bedchamber.

Henry paced, as always, hands clasped behind his back. "He has been too quiet and I fear that he plots something. I much prefer to know where he is and what it is he does."

"I cannot disagree," Gavin replied. "But he seems to have disappeared and is nowhere to be found here at Whitehall. Mayhap he has taken his twisted self back to Tricourten for a time…but I do not believe that is likely."

"How come you on your task of finding a husband for that little nun?" Henry changed the subject.

Before Gavin could reply, a knock came at the chamber door and a squire entered. "Her majesty has arrived and awaits your pleasure," said the young man with a short bow.

"Indeed, I have been awaiting her for the last hour. Bid her enter." Henry waved his hand impatiently. "How can it take a woman so long to prepare for bed?" he grumbled.

"When one is preparing for bed with the king of the realm," a husky voice said from the doorway, "one must do the preparations justice."

Garbed in a fur-lined satin robe, Eleanor crossed the room. Giving a brief curtsey to her husband, she then raised a cheek to him. He kissed it and grasped her hand, bringing it to his lips. "Madame, you are beautiful as always," he told her. When she glanced curiously at Gavin, the king explained, "I shall be only another short while. Please, sit…and mayhap you will have an opinion on the matter at hand."

He gestured to Gavin, who had risen upon Eleanor's entrance. "Your majesty, may I pour you some wine?"

"Only if 'tis from Aquitaine," she responded with a coy smile.

"Of course. The king has only the best of all vintages," he said smoothly, nodding pointedly in her direction to include her in the compliment.

She was delighted. "Gavin Mal Verne, I did not expect such an agreeable response from you. The ladies speak of you with such apprehension…half of them would swoon if you so much as looked at them, they fear your black moods so much." She laughed and took the goblet that he offered to her. "Now I know better and will not allow them to speak thus."

Gavin wasn't certain how to respond, so he merely nodded again and, after she sat, he, too, sank into a chair. Henry continued to pace, fussing with his tunic, a sheaf of parchments, his goblet of wine…whatever it was that caught his eye and allowed him to expend energy.

"Do you hunt with us on the morrow?" Eleanor asked Gavin.

"Aye, your majesty. I didn't know that you planned to join us."

She nodded regally, her blond hair gleaming in the candlelight. "I and several of my ladies will join you. I look forward to fresh venison or mayhap a wild pig if all goes well."

The king seemed to pull himself from the frenetic activity of pacing the chamber back to his companions and his own agenda. "So, Gavin, have you found a husband for Madelyne de Belgrume? The sooner she is wed and bed, the easier I shall feel—for de Belgrume will have no cause to disturb my court. And of course I shall assess a significant brides-price for her hand," he added, tugging at his beard.

Eleanor drained her goblet. "My solar is abuzz with the rumors that John of Kilharten plies for her suit, while Reginald D'Orrais appears to have the favor of all, including the lady herself."

Henry whirled, his overtunic spinning from his body like the petals of a flower. "And you—madame…who is your favorite to wed with the woman who would be a nun?"

"Reginald is a fine man—if a bit young, but fine enough for the likes of Madelyne. She will give him no trouble, and he is smart enough to keep her from the hands of her father."

"Gavin? Do you have a thought on this or will you continue to stare blankly at your hands while we make the decision?"

"I had not given D'Orrais much thought, my liege. As her majesty says, he is young…but smarter than Kilharten, who cannot tell his hand from his foot in the dark. Still, D'Orrais has little experience with a large fief such as Tricourten, and may not have the ability to keep it producing the rents you are accustomed to." Gavin knew that attacking the king's coffers was the most effective way to sway his opinion.

"Aye. Hmmm…well, you must make an assessment. I have too many other burdens to see to. I cannot bother myself much longer with this trite situation. Make a recommendation by three days hence, or I will make it easy and give the nun to D'Orrais. He isn't a bad choice—'tis your task to see that he is the best choice. Unless you find a compelling reason not to select him, 'twill be D'Orrais."

Henry looked pointedly at the chamber door. "You may leave us now."

Gavin bowed to the king, then for the queen, and took his leave.

The hall was dark—it was well past midnight—and he wended his way back toward the chamber set aside for several of the nobles such as himself.

Reginald D'Orrais…'t could be worse, had the king leaned toward Kilharten, or any of the other lascivious or stupid men who made up the court. At the least, D'Orrais was gentle with his horses—something that was a sure indication of his propensity toward others. And he was not stone dumb.

Madelyne appeared to have some fondness for the man. He seemed always to be at her side…and had even escorted her to her chamber on two occasions, as Jube and Rohan had reported. Gavin supposed he would be considered handsome to a young maid such as Madelyne—most especially to one who had had little interaction with men due to her days in the abbey.

He rounded the last corner, thinking little about where he was going, but focusing his attention on what could be wrong with D'Orrais—and why he would not be a prime choice for Madelyne—and hurtled straight into a warm, soft person.

"Lord Gavin," murmured a familiar voice. "What a pleasant surprise."

"Therese?" he responded, refocusing his thoughts. "What are you doing out of your chamber at such an hour?"

She placed her hand on his arm, smoothing it up toward his shoulder. "I had hoped you would return this evening that we might have some moments to…talk."

"Talk?" Gavin repeated in confusion. Then, her very insistent hand moved over his chest and, tugging his arm, propelled him toward her.

"Nay, you are correct. Talk is not what I would prefer from you," she murmured, pressing her lips against his.

It was a testament to his confusion and distraction that Gavin did not feel the weight of the eyes staring from behind him as Therese pulled him into a dark alcove.

"There! 'Tis off through that underbrush!"

Gavin bent low over Rule's neck as the destrier thrashed through bushes and bramble in the wake of the dogs and a wild boar that was now their quarry. Thomas's mount nosed up beside his, and he could hear the crashing of the others just behind them.

Gripping his lance tightly, Gavin shouted, "I'm to the left!" and Rule veered off toward that direction in response to the pressure of his thighs. A low-hanging branch whipped toward him, and Gavin ducked in time to feel only the scrape of twigs over his bare head. Wearing a helm during a hunt was uncomfortable, but distaining one left a man vulnerable to being toppled from a mount or having a scratched face.

Gavin rose slightly in his saddle as Rule pounded through the wood, the stallion relishing the chase as much as his master. The baying of the hounds echoed shrilly in the air, and he saw the dark rump of the boar as it leapt over a small creek.

Some of the others in the party had split off to follow Gavin, while the main group continued on in the boar's path. "There! Again!" shouted Lord Ferrell, coming up from behind.

"Aye!" Gavin gave a short wave, bending low in the saddle, and feeling the exhilaration surge through him. Even if he didn't get a shot at the boar, the thrill of the ride and the wild danger was enough to satisfy him.

Ferrell's horse took a leap over a small bush and dashed ahead of Gavin and Rule, its rider throwing a white-toothed grin as they passed. "First!" he called back, letting Gavin know that he would take the initial shot and his friend should be prepared to follow with a second.

"Go!" Gavin shouted. He didn't need to kick Rule to urge the horse faster. They were bounding over fallen trees and between thin saplings at breakneck speed. Green and brown blurs passed on each side, broken only by splashes of bright sunshine where it streamed down into the forest in erratic patterns.

The hunt was dangerous—most especially for those in the lead, and even more so when it was a cornered boar they sought. Riding at top speed, dodging the pitfalls of a forest, and clutching a lance at the same time made it as hazardous as fighting a battle. The boar itself could be erratic and fast, and Gavin had seen more than one fatal swipe of a horn gouge man, horse, or dog.

The cry of the hounds grew more urgent, and he knew that the boar had been cornered. Shifting his lance, Gavin stood again in his saddle as Rule careened toward the noise and the scent of fear.

Just as Rule, nostrils flaring and breath streaming in hard pants that matched Gavin's own zeal, leapt over a fallen log, Gavin felt his left leg give way. In an instant, the world tilted and he was falling, rolling, crashing, out of control. A shout registered in his tumbled mind, pain seared along the shoulder and arm on which he'd landed, and a high-pitched squeal that meant danger to his ears shocked him to continue rolling back to his feet.

Dizzy, out of breath, Gavin groped for support at the log over which Rule had leapt and found himself facing a red-eyed, well-horned black boar. His fingers closed reflexively, but the lance was long gone during his tumble, and the boar was already charging.

Shouts and the thudding of hooves penetrated his mind as Gavin reached for a heavy stick. He swung at the tiny-eyed, black-bristled face as it barreled toward him. He connected with the flat nose that was close enough he could see water dripping from it, and an enraged squeal rent the air as Gavin stumbled away from its flailing hooves and overpowering stench.

Just as he hauled himself upright, another shout and a shriek of rage echoed in the clearing…followed by a second shriek that became almost a moan at the end. Thomas rode up at that moment, tossing Rule's reins to Gavin. "Are you hurt?" he asked as his friend heaved into the saddle.

"Nay," Gavin replied, breathless, as he gathered his wits about him enough to look at the scene before him. The boar lay on his side, shuddering its last breath, with three lances piercing its hide. The dogs sniffed eagerly, and were being called back by the masters even as the hunters clustered in more closely.

"What a fall!" Ferrell loped over on his mount. "What happened?"

Gavin suddenly remembered and slid off his saddle. "I felt the stirrup give way as Rule jumped," he told them, and held up the broken leather stirrup. "If I had not been standing for the leap, I'd likely have kept my seat," he frowned. "But it could not have broken on its own."

"Could you have sliced it with your lance?" asked Lord Michael d'Gloetherin.

"What fool do you think I am?" he snapped, suddenly feeling the pain in his shoulder and arm. "I manage my weapons and would not make such a foolish mistake. And, if I'd been so careless, or someone else had been close enough to be so, would not Rule have been cut as well?"

"Aye. And you have great care for your saddle and Rule," Thomas added gravely. His eyes met Gavin's and their suspicions mirrored each other. Fantin.

King Henry rode up at that moment. "Mal Verne—are you hurt? I did not see the fall, but I am told 'twas most magnificent." His infectious smile flashed as he saw that Gavin was unhurt.

"Though I would not wish to repeat it, I would agree that it would be hard to match it ever again." Gavin grunted in pain as Thomas jostled close enough to touch his shoulder. "I'll have some care to my arm when we return, but it does not pain me overmuch. Shall we ride on?"

"Nay. We return. The others found two deer and a wild pig, so we are in need of no more," replied another hunter.

Gavin would not have admitted it aloud, but he was thankful for the reason to return to the castle sooner rather than later. Now that his energy had ebbed and they rode along at a much less dangerous pace, the throbbing in his shoulder increased enough to make him grit his teeth and keep his conversation to a minimum.

A sudden thought bloomed in his mind, soothing his discomfort: he would return and seek out Madelyne to care for his hurt.

In the past, when he'd received small injuries, he would have squirreled out one of the king's squires or pages who could plaster on a paste of putrid herbs and wrap his injury—as would any other man injured in such a way. But now, he would impose upon her to see to his needs.

Her long, narrow fingers would smooth on some paste that likely smelled awful but cooled and appeased the injury. She'd wrap it gently and mayhap offer him a tea or infusion to drink to ease him in his sleep. And he'd think, yet again, of her as a calm, quiet Madonna…and smell the scent of her as she bent to him…and feel the warm heaviness of her touch….

The clattering of hooves across the wooden bridge leading to Whitehall pulled Gavin from those oddly disturbing thoughts, and the proximity to the woman in question brought upon more disconcerting ones. What if she didn't want to take care of him? She was not obliged, and he had no right to ask it of her. He shouldn't ask it of her. She owed him nothing and soon she would belong to Reginald D'Orrais.

The frown settling between his brows must have been a fierce one, for Thomas trotted over and said, "It appears that you are in more pain than you displayed in the wood. Allow me to have Rule brushed down and stabled for you. Seek you help in taking care of your injuries."

"I'm fine," Gavin replied gruffly, sliding down from his saddle. Clem appeared and 'twas with great relief that he handed the bridle to him. "Thomas, you have enough to do. Clem can take care of Rule for me." He looked at his man. "Do you know where Madelyne is? I have a need to speak with her."

Clem shifted as he fought to keep Rule from storming toward the stables. "I believe she is in the orchard garden. At the least, 'tis what her maid told me when I last saw the harpy some half hour past."

Gavin forbore to acknowledge his man's uncharacteristically caustic comment. Instead, he gave Rule a last pat of thanks for being so beautifully sure-footed, and said, "My thanks Clem. I'll be off to locate Lady Madelyne."

Though he started off with alacrity, Gavin slowed his footsteps as he approached what was known as the orchard garden. What fool was he that he should impose upon her—even that it should occur to him to seek her out to care for his needs? Indeed, why had it been such a natural, unconscious thought that he would go to her? She owed him naught but disdain, and, in truth, he was beholden to care for *her* far more than she would be answerable to *his* well-being.

Gavin's steps faltered as he found himself entering the garden—which was, in reality, more of a grove of trees and benches than any true orchard. She would be sitting with Judith, mayhap, and some other ladies who did not hunt, and he would thus approach like a young boy with a scraped knee.

Distaste filled his mouth and he whirled abruptly to leave. He would seek comfort from some other lady who might care to deliver it. He thought fleetingly of Lady Therese, who had kissed him well and soundly in the alcove the evening before…but then decided he preferred to find a squire taught in easing war wounds instead.

He'd taken two more steps back out of the garden when he heard his name called behind him. Cursing under his breath, he turned back to see Judith hailing him from near an apple tree.

"Gavin! Are you hurt?" she asked, reaching to touch his arm.

"Nay…only a small injury," he told her, glancing beyond her shoulder to see if Madelyne followed. Dirt and blood must have dried on his face for Judith to have guessed at his accident.

"If you seek Madelyne," Judith spoke, reading his mind, "she sits back under the pear tree."

"Nay, I…we just returned from the hunt, and I am dirty and wet." He turned to go, realizing how filthy and sweaty he must be.

"She sits with Reginald D'Orrais," added Judith casually. "All the court knows that he is to be named her betrothed on the morrow."

Gavin looked at her, but she had turned to wave to another lady-in-waiting who hurried past the garden gate toward the castle. Judith looked back at him. "I must go, for I am promised to the queen now that she has returned from the hunt." She hurried off, leaving him to stare after her with an angry tightening in his belly.

D'Orrais. The man might be plying suit for her hand, but it had not yet been granted to him, and he presumed overmuch.

Gavin clenched his fist and wheeled back into the garden, setting his teeth in line so hard his jaw hurt.

He would remind Madelyne that she was not yet betrothed and that sitting in the garden unchaperoned would only lead to damaging rumors about herself. She was not accustomed to court life, and could not realize that such simple actions were often the cause of much destruction.

Gavin fed his anger thus, stalking toward the corner of the garden where the pear tree grew.

He came around the bush into a full view of Madelyne and Reginald D'Orrais. They were in an intimate embrace.

TWENTY

WHEN REGINALD'S lips covered hers, Madelyne stilled. She neither moved closer nor further from the man whose arms slid around her shoulders, and whose mouth pressed to hers.

'Twas a soft kiss—nothing like the one she'd shared with Gavin in the wood—and Madelyne felt as though she waited for something more to happen. It did. Reginald pulled her closer to him and fitted his mouth more tightly to hers, angling his head and drawing her face toward him.

Warmth trickled through her and she allowed her hand to reach tentatively to touch his shoulder. It was pleasant, she thought dimly. Neither frightening nor disturbing, she realized with relief. He would be her husband, and it did not alarm her when he kissed her. Nor did it cause her veins to jump and her body to soften into a mass of warmth as Gavin's kiss had done.

Their wedding night would be different, she knew, with much more than a gentle kiss to occur. Would she feel the same…*nothing* then, or would Reginald's touch make her limbs feel light and her skin jump?

She vaguely noticed that Reginald's fingers brushed the side of her face as he pulled slowly away. "Madelyne," he whispered, "I would that you are mine."

Then he drew her to him, more forcefully this time, his mouth plastering against hers so fiercely that her breath caught. Her heart raced now, as she tried to assimilate this new experience, and determine how she felt about it.

Then, abruptly, Reginald pulled away, allowing her to settle back into her place on the bench.

"I beg your pardon for interrupting, D'Orrais" came a voice she knew very well—a voice calm, deep, and frigid.

Madelyne's stomach flipped as she twisted around to see a tall figure—Gavin—standing with his back to the sun, looking down at them. She could not see his face, as the sun was bright and it shadowed his countenance, but his stance bespoke of the barest of control.

"His majesty has just returned from the hunt and it is my understanding that he wishes to speak with you," he continued in that cool voice.

Reginald, who had not removed his attention from Gavin, stood immediately. "My thanks, Mal Verne." He turned to Madelyne, taking her hand and bringing it swiftly to his lips. Pressing against them softly, he spoke, his mouth moving against her skin, "Mayhap 'tis the news I have been waiting for. I shall find you at supper, then, my lady."

"Of course," Madelyne spoke, finding her voice. Had she expected Gavin to be angry with Reginald for kissing her? Why would she have assumed he'd feel the same annoyance that she'd felt when observing him and Therese together?

But he was not angry at all—instead, he came bearing glad news for her suitor.

The thought left her empty and bereft, and she stood as Reginald started off.

"Nay," Gavin commanded, his hand coming out to grasp her wrist. He directed her back to her seat. "I wish to speak with you."

Now she saw it, as he sat next to her on the bench: the darkness smoldering in eyes the color of tempered iron. She noticed, too, the bloody scrape along his cheek and the dirt streaks along the side of his face and arm. "What has happened?" she asked, reaching automatically to touch the dirt on his sleeve. "Have you been hurt?"

"'Tis naught of your concern," he responded, pulling back as her fingers brushed the rough fabric of his tunic. She saw him wince as he moved, and knew he was in pain.

"Gavin, you are hurt—"

"Madelyne, do not attempt to sway me from my purpose! Your concern for my hurt is a meager balm at this time—"

"Your purpose?" Her interruption surprised him, Madelyne observed with satisfaction—she was not so much the shy little nun she once had been, thanks to his own actions. "Your purpose was to inform Reginald that the king wished to see him, and now that task is completed—"

"'Twas a falsehood," Gavin said flatly. "The king does not wish to see him—'tis my task to give him the news that he may wed you."

Emptiness swelled within her, but she pushed it aside in favor of growing irritation. "What then is your great and lofty purpose, Lord Mal Verne, that you should interrupt my peaceful seat in the garden with your anger and annoyance?"

"Ah…yes, I did interrupt, did I not. I cannot in truth apologize to you, my lady, for coming upon you as I did and attempting to salvage your reputation." Anger flashed anew in his gray eyes. "Do you not know he only wishes to brand you as his own? 'Tis why he kisses you in the public garden where any may see it—and thus wonder about your virtue."

Madelyne recoiled, and then annoyance surged through her. "'Twas only a harmless kiss," she responded evenly, realizing that she must speak her mind. "He has been courting me gently, and never attempted such a thing before today."

"Madelyne, I—do you love him?" His voice was rough.

"Love him?" She had not expected such a question…'twas almost as if he had some care for her. Mayhap….Resolve built within her. "Why would I *not* love him? He is kind and gentle and treats me with respect…and he is most certainly not hard upon the eyes! What woman would not love such a man…most especially a naive little nun who knows naught of a man's world?"

She tilted her head to look at him steadily while trying to keep her gaze from resting upon his beautiful mouth: the only part of his face that appeared pliable.

Now, as he returned her stare, Madelyne felt surrounded by his presence. Gavin's body so close to hers on the bench suddenly made her feel as though they touched—when they did not. His thigh rested just next to hers, thick and ridged with muscle, his cross-garters and hose sagging below the knee.

"Do you like his kisses? Do you wish to marry him?"

"His kisses were…adequate," she replied coolly, taking care to keep her voice steady and nonchalant. "It has been my experience that one kiss is the same as another…would you not agree, Lord Mal Verne?"

She looked away with great casualness, forcing herself to focus on the tiny green apples that grew just beyond their bench.

All at once, large, firm hands closed over her shoulders and she was hauled toward him and into a solid, imposing chest. Gavin's face—dark and hungry—blurred toward her, his mouth descending upon hers before she could draw a breath.

A rush of something surged into her belly—flipping it, squeezing it—catching her by surprise, and she leaned toward him intuitively. Her eyes slid closed as she sagged against him, feeling every part of her body come alive as his mouth devoured hers and she kissed him in return.

His lips, soft now that they weren't plated with annoyance, fit to her mouth, caressing and demanding in turn as Gavin slipped his hands around her back. His fingers molded against her shoulder blades, warm and firm through the fabric of her gown. Still half-seated, she fit closely to his chest, at last remembering to breathe… and gathered in all of his masculine scent: sweat, blood, power and something raw and wild.

Everything drained away: only he remained, and the warmth dancing through her veins as he tempted her mouth open with his. This new sensation—slick, warm, urgent, as his tongue moved with hers—brought a faint moan from the back of her throat. Gavin pulled away enough to press light, tender kisses on the side of her mouth, her cheek…then, cupping her face in his palms, brought his mouth back to hers.

Madelyne remembered her hands, tucked between them in her lap, and reached to touch his neck. Her fingers brushed damp, dark hair as they curled to embrace the back of his head, then moved almost immediately to know his thick, broad shoulders. Her fingers closed over his arms, pulling him to her, wanting to feel the muscle and strength that surrounded her. Under her hand, he jerked, a grunt of pain escaping, and Madelyne pulled away, struggling to return to herself.

"What is it?" she asked, her lips full and clumsy, her chest rising and falling rapidly, still close enough to brush against his. Once again, she felt the hard bench beneath her and realized that the garden flourished around them. For a moment, she'd lost track of where, and when....

He looked down at her, his eyes now soft andglazed, his lips full and moist. A pang of heat came from nowhere, shooting down to the place between her legs as she recognized some intense emotion in his face. Gavin breathed as though he'd been running, and his hands returned to the bench beside him as he shifted slightly away. "I should offer my apology—" He held up a hand to stop her as she drew in her own staggering breath to tell him that he could offer his apology to her backside "—but I will not."

Then, as though he himself was returning to place and time, Gavin moved again, placing more space between them on the bench. Some of the sharpness returned to his features—but a sense of peacefulness remained, too, Madelyne saw, even as she wondered why he would shutter himself so quickly from what had just occurred. Despite the fact that she wanted to revel in the kiss...to explore what it meant and if it made him feel as soft and happy and unfinished as it did her...Madelyne accepted that he was not yet ready to do so.

"Gavin, you must allow me to see to what it is that ails you," she urged, reaching to touch him again. This time, he did not pull from her reach, but nodded, and she felt that that was some small accomplishment.

"I fell from Rule during the hunt," he told her. "My shoulder and arm are likely bruised more colorfully than Eleanor's jewels, but

I do not believe anything is broken. I would welcome any attention you might be willing to give my injury—or, if 'tis too much trouble, I can seek out another healer to treat me. ”

"Gavin, how can you think I would see you in pain and do naught to help? Of course I will see to it."

He looked back at her, those gray eyes probing more deeply than his kiss. "Nay, Madelyne, I did not know whether you would care to ease me when I have caused you much greater hurt."

She reached to touch his face, but pulled her trembling hand back before connecting with his dirt-streaked skin. "I cannot hold against you that which makes you who you are—a man of vengeance and honor. Nor would I withhold my care for one who is injured. You need not fear asking that of me, for I will gladly serve you thus. I see no reason that Lord Reginald would object to my caring for my appointed guardian," she added, watching him carefully. "I do not believe, however, that he would approve of any further kisses between us. Most particularly since I have changed my mind."

The change that passed over his face was astonishing. Eyes, cheeks, mouth, skin all appeared to tighten, harden, darken before her eyes. "Aye, Madelyne, D'Orrais could have little to say were you to see to my needs, but 'tis true that he would likely object to any kiss other than one of peace to pass between us."

He stood abruptly. "You may have no fear—I shall not place you in such an awkward position again. It grows late, and I must bathe the blood and sweat from my body. Allow me to return you to your chamber so that I can go about my business." He offered her his arm.

Madelyne took it, frustration and annoyance coloring her mood. "Thank you my lord," she told him, resorting to chilly formality as she could think of no other way to express her irritation.

He looked down at her, then began to propel her toward the front of the garden. "What is it you have changed your mind on, my lady?" he asked carelessly as they strode along at a pace faster than she would have wished.

"I no longer am of the opinion that one kiss is the same as another." Madelyne did not look at him, and did not take any pause in her steps. She continued to walk toward the keep as though she had not just laid her heart out for him to step upon.

And Gavin did not make the merest of pauses himself. His strides went on, unbroken as well—as though he'd heard nothing.

TWENTY-ONE

"WHAT AILS Lord Mal Verne?" Tricky asked, looking up into Clem's stoic face.

He shrugged, his large shoulders moving with rugged grace against the stone wall at which he leaned. Tricky pulled her attention away from those broad, capable shoulders and found her interest wandering over the meaty arms that crossed over his middle and then back up to be trapped by his gaze.

She felt her heart pick up speed. He was such a large man, and when he looked at her like that—with a combination of irritation and flat disinterest, but so heavily that she felt her chest swell—Tricky felt light-headed and the need for support. She groped for the bench and sat upon it, focusing her attention on her feet and the arrangement of her skirts over them.

"He nearly threw himself down Jube's throat when he brought my lady back to her chamber this day," she continued, feeling the need to fill the silence that yawned between them. "He scolded him for allowing Madelyne to be unchaperoned in the garden—but I know that she was not alone. Lord Reginald…" She stopped and felt the familiar squiggly feeling she got in her stomach when something interesting was about to happen—like when Lord Mal Verne had arrived at Lock Rose Abbey to take Madelyne away with him. A smile tugged at the corners of her mouth and she chewed over her theory for a moment.

"I'm certain that Jube was most obliging when you offered him comfort in the face of our lord's ill temper." Clem looked idly at the fingers on one hand, then glanced briefly at Tricky.

"Aye…the man has a charm about him that would wither the most dispassionate of women," Tricky responded lightly. Why was the oaf forever talking of Jube when she was with him? "While you, sirrah," she stood, moving close enough to him that she could tell that he held his breath, "are naught but a malcontented killjoy." She stepped closer, effectively trapping him between herself and the wall. "I wonder," she mused, running her fingers slowly up along his arm, "what it would take to lighten your mood…."

Clem pushed himself away from the wall—and away from her—and stood at his full height. Not as tall as the blonde Jube, but much taller than diminutive Tricky. "I must see to my lord Gavin, for he was injured during the hunt this day. Mayhap that is the reason for his ill humor."

She could not help but notice the rapid rise and fall of his barrel chest. "If you believe that his injury from the hunt is the reason for his poor temper, Clem de Ardethan, you are the veriest fool I know!" She poked him in the chest with her index finger, noting how hard and firm it was. "Look you more closely at what transpires and you will see that there is more to it than that! Did you not know that Lord Mal Verne has kissed Lady Madelyne?"

The expression on Clem's face was one of such disbelief that she thought for a moment he would dissolve into a fit of laughter. Then, irritation flashed across his face. "A kiss between them? Pah! Even if it were true, 'twould mean little more than a moment of foolishness on his part!"

"Is that, then, what a single kiss betwixt a man and a woman signifies? A moment of male foolishness?" Angry now—after all, Clem had kissed her one time, and the man was dense besides!—Tricky slammed her hands onto her soft hips. "I vow that makes you the veriest of fools, Clem de Ardethan!" She whirled, stalking off down the corridor, away from the man who—she hoped—stood gaping after her.

Tricky fumed as she rushed back to Madelyne's chamber. Men were so foolish—so thick-headed!

When she arrived there and found her mistress seated next to the fire, Tricky did not hesitate to share her frustration with Madelyne.

"Clem is the veriest of fools! I can see it in his eye that he desires to kiss me…yet he makes the greatest of excuses to walk away!"

Madelyne set her embroidery down and looked at her with unblinking gray eyes. "Tricky are you so sure this is true—or do you only speak of wishes?"

"Oh, nay, Maddie…'tis in his eyes and was in his kiss. It's just that men seem to fight it when true love smacks them in the backside. Lord Gavin—'tis happening to him too, you know. He doesn't know what to do with his feelings for you."

"What nonsense you speak." Madelyne's attention was fixed closely on Tricky. "Lord Gavin does not care for me—he is about to give me in marriage to Lord Reginald."

"Oh, nay, Maddie…'tis not so. Mark my words…you will not be wedding with Lord Reginald."

"We have had the betrothal contract prepared," Henry told Gavin as he drummed his fingers on the table next to him. The ever-present goblet of wine rested near his elbow, and a plate of dried apples and a hunk of bread next to it. "All that remains is to tell young D'Orrais and seal the betrothal. The wedding can take place immediately after—mayhap this Sunday." Henry chuckled. "He'll owe my coffers twenty gold pieces and two years service of fifty men for the privilege of wedding with the nun."

Gavin drank from his own goblet, draining it, then moved to refill it. A strange gnawing scraped his inner belly, and neither food nor drink seemed to alleviate it.

Henry rose and paced over to where his scribe sat, scratching busily upon a parchment. The man could not speak, although he could write and hear well, so Henry preferred his attendance over all other scribes at court. "A missive to Fantin de Belgrume, informing him of his daughter's impending marriage, and the assessment of a fine for our services in arranging the betrothal, would be in order as well, do you not agree, my lady? One hundred gold coins should suffice." He chuckled complacently.

"Aye," Eleanor purred from her seat in the formal court chamber where Madelyne had met with the king only a se'ennight earlier. "All the court—the ladies most especially—gladly await the announcement of a wedding celebration. Indeed, the sooner she is wed and bedded, the easier I'll be. I like the girl—she's no Therese, the foolish slut," she cast a shrewd glance at Gavin, who quickly took another drink of wine, "thank the saints, but she's caused enough havoc among my ladies that I am ready to have her out of my sight." She smoothed her gown, then looked up. "Gavin, my darling, would you please pour me some of that wine you have been hoarding?"

"Of course, your majesty." He found his voice and moved to do her bidding.

"Gavin, have you summoned D'Orrais? 'Tis nigh time we had this arranged." Without waiting for a response, Henry stood and stalked to the door leading from the court room to the main alcove. He flung it open, bellowing for a page to attend him at once.

Eleanor watched in amusement, then returned her attention to Gavin. "Well, my lord, 'tis the moment you have long sought. You shall thus be relieved of your duty to Lady Madelyne, and free to return to your lands—or to your warring, whichever it is that you interrupted to bring her to our presence." A sly light colored her eyes as she curved her lovely mouth into a smile. "You have served us well, Lord Gavin, now, and these years past. I am quite sure that my husband would agree, would you not, my lord?"

Henry, who had sent a page scuttling off to fetch Reginald D'Orrais, returned to his wife's side and, resting a hand upon her shoulder, nodded. "Of course. Mal Verne knows that I value his service." He paced over to the table and picked up a piece of apple, shoved it into his mouth, and chewed like a cow.

Eleanor glanced at Gavin, who stood lamely to one side. The queen spoke true…his desire to be free of the responsibility of Madelyne's well-being was upon him. Yet….He looked at Eleanor, and she caught his eye, tipping her head slightly.

Suddenly, it burst from him. "I would wed Madelyne de Belgrume." The words were out before Gavin could bite them back, and he stood, silent, as shocked by the statement as Henry appeared to be.

"What?" the king roared, slamming his hand onto the table and the edge of the plate. The platter flipped onto the floor, scattering food beneath the moving feet of the king. "Gavin, what in the bloody hell are you talking about?"

"D'Orrais cannot hope to compete with Fantin's wiles," Gavin explained, the words rushing from his suddenly loose tongue, the facts and arguments all lining up as if he'd long thought them. "Nor does he have the experience or knowledge to manage a fief such as Tricourten at the level of rents you expect, sire. As well, you have bid me find a manner in which to contain de Belgrume, and I believe that wedding with his daughter would give me ample opportunity to do so." He paused, then added, "And, most practically, 'tis time I married again. I must have heirs, and a wife who can minister to me when I am hurt or ill would be an asset as well."

Henry smiled slyly. "You would indeed have a time of it begetting an heir on that nun. She is—" He abruptly stopped when he saw the black expression on Eleanor's face. "Aye, well, then, Gavin, forgive me if I appear to be more than a bit… stunned…by your pronouncement, as you have bewailed the burden of seeing to that young woman for weeks now. And now, when you have the chance to unload yourself, you request to be shackled to her?" He shook his head, but a grin tickled behind his beard. "Do you fancy yourself in love with the maid?"

"Of course not," Gavin replied, gripping his goblet more tightly. "As I explained, it is the most fitting of solutions. As you charged me with the task of finding her a husband, I hereforth make my recommendation."

Henry looked at him, exchanged glances with his wife, and nodded. At that moment, the throne room door opened, and a page announced Reginald D'Orrais, who entered just in time to hear Henry's words. "Aye, then, Gavin, you may have Madelyne de Belgrume to wife. And a very generous fine to your liege as for the privilege."

Twenty-Two

WHEN GAVIN departed the throne room, leaving a flabbergasted and glowering Reginald D'Orrais behind, he knew his first action must be to speak with Madelyne.

As much as he had been shocked by his own actions, and needed the opportunity to assimilate this new event himself, he must talk with her before D'Orrais—or some other wagging tongue of the court—did.

At the least he knew he wouldn't find her with D'Orrais this time. Gavin's mouth flattened into a humorless smile. If the man stepped foot near her again, Gavin would put him out of his misery.

This thought checked his rapid footsteps—only for a moment, but enough for Gavin to reflect on how strongly and quickly the possessive urge had come over him. He rather found he liked it.

As he neared Eleanor's solar—where he was sure he would find Madelyne, as 'twas midday—Gavin's footsteps slowed. What would she say? What could she say, he reminded himself. The king had made his decision and they would wed.

How would he tell her? Would she wish to have Reginald in the stead of himself? She had appeared accepting of that eventuality…yet, there was the kiss they shared.…He knew that Reginald's kiss could not have affected her the same way his own had. After all, Gavin himself had interrupted them, and he'd seen nothing of glazed eyes or swollen lips when they broke apart.

Still. 'Twas he, Gavin, who had dragged her from her life in the abbey, and he was certainly not such a prize as the young, handsome, gentle D'Orrais….

He'd reached the door to the solar, and the page waited expectantly for him to speak. "I seek Lady Madelyne de Belgrume," he told him. It was unnecessary to identify himself.

When he stepped into the chamber in the wake of the page, the room—scented with the myriad of perfumes of the ladies and studded with their colorful apparel—skittered into silence. His gaze immediately found Madelyne and he saw that she sat near Judith. She was clad in a soft gray gown and white over-tunic, both trimmed with blue and yellow embroidery. Her gleaming ink-colored hair coiled intricately over her ears, pulled back softly to frame her fair, oval face. Their eyes met, and he felt the unmistakable bump of his heart shifting out of line…and then back…as he realized that she really belonged to him. He felt Therese's eyes upon him, and heard snatches of whispers and sighs as he strode to his betrothed's side.

"My lady, I wish to speak with you," he told her with a brief bow. He glanced at Judith, who looked at him with an unreadable expression in her eyes. It was leaning toward a frown, with a tinge of disappointment woven within. He wondered, fleetingly, what his cousin would say when she learned the news.

Or mayhaps she already had, and thus was the cause for her disappointment.

"Of course, my lord." Madelyne rose as she spoke, her stomach squeezing. He had come to bring her the news of her betrothal. Tricky had been wrong. Her hands trembled slightly as she put aside her embroidery.

She felt a sudden rush of the past, remembering the day he'd come to take her from the abbey. She'd been sitting, engrossed in her work, in much the same manner that morning…and, like today, his very action of taking her from her work would serve to cause ripples throughout her life.

His presence arrested the room, and his person—tall, garbed in dark blue and forest green—towered among the women. It was as if the chamber held its collective breath when he entered, apprehension and respect exuding from all corners. Yet, Madelyne knew that the harsh, dark persona was a wall that had been built and she grieved that others could not see past it. With a brief glance at Judith, whose attention was focused, not on her but upon her cousin Gavin, Madelyne slipped her hand into the crook of his arm.

"Reginald was attending me when he was called to the king's side," she told him, once the eager ears of the ladies were behind them.

Gavin looked down at her, pausing there outside of the solar, searching her eyes. She had difficulty meeting his gaze, and looked away. "I have come with word as to what transpired in the king's chambers with your suitor," he told her. "Let us go to a private place and I will tell you all."

She nodded, but said nothing as they made their way through the warren of halls, and then outside through a door she had not known existed. Around a hidden corner Gavin took her, past several small buildings, until they reached a small gate, well-hidden around a far corner of the keep.

With a grunt, he unjammed the iron lock and pushed the heavy gate open, gesturing for Madelyne to precede him. She stepped through, and found herself in a small garden, shaded and green and silent. The dull clang of the gate closing prompted her to turn in alarm, but Gavin was there behind her in the garden, standing with his hands at his back. Looking at her.

His face was unreadable—sharp-planed as always, but his lips settled in almost a smile, and his eyes, darkened by the shadow of the corner of the keep, fastened in a steady look upon her.

When she did not move, nor speak, he spread his arm in a wide gesture to encompass the small courtyard. "I bethought you would find peace and comfort here. Few know of it, and you will find it private and a place to enjoy as you will. 'Twas Mathilda's garden, when she was queen, and it has mostly been forgotten."

Madelyne pulled her gaze from his and turned slowly to look about the garden. 'Twas small, and half-shaded by the castle wall, which, along with some other buildings she could not identify, enclosed the whole of the garden. Several trees—fruit trees, she thought, spying green bulbs of unripened apples and pears—enclosed a small stone bench. Plants that she easily identified as lavender, basil, thyme, rosemary, calendula, and other herbs grew in pleasing disarray among narrow pebbled paths. Obviously uncared for over time, the garden spoke of casual neglect and it called to her.

She turned back and saw that he'd taken steps toward her. Her heart thumping steadily in her breast, reverberating into her throat, she offered a smile of thanks. "My lord, 'tis very thoughtful of you to think of this. I had been missing my own gardens—and those at Mal Verne—since our arrival. But…surely you did not bring me here for any purpose other than to discuss my future." Her smile faded as she recollected what that future would be.

"In truth, I brought you here for two reasons, Madelyne," he told her, gesturing to the bench. "The first was because I knew that it would please you to have a private place to go…and to be among God's beauty. I have not forgotten your joy at Mal Verne when you spent time in my gardens." He cleared his throat, glancing at the bench again when she refused his invitation to sit. "'Tis a betrothal gift to you…of a kind…as I thought you would prefer it to jewels or other adornments."

Madelyne's heart swelled painfully in her chest and tears threatened to sting her eyes. The foolish man…did he not know how bittersweet this gesture was? Refusing to look at him, she reached for a stalk of lavender, pulling her fingers along its stem. The sweet scent was released into the air as she rubbed the small indigo flowers between her fingers, trickling them onto the ground. "And the second reason?" she prompted, allowing a tinge of annoyance to color her words.

Gavin looked away. "I wished to tell you what transpired in the king's chambers in a place safe from prying ears." He pushed his splayed fingers through the wild mass of hair on his head, then his hand dropped to his side as he took a step away.

"Why do you bring me here to tell me what I already know?" she asked yanking a bright yellow calendula flower from its scraggly green stem. "What all the court knows—that the king has presented Reginald with my hand and the betrothal papers are to be finalized." She began to dismantle the peppery smelling bloom, scattering bright yellow petals on the ground.

"Madelyne, please sit."

"I shall stand, thank you my lord. I have been sitting all the day. Please, I wish to hear what it is that you must say, so that I may return to my work."

His chest rose as he took a deep breath; then the words rushed out. "The king changed his mind. He has decreed that you are to wed with me."

It was a moment before his words penetrated. Her body went cold, and then warm. Rushing with warmth. "You? I am to wed with you?"

He stepped toward her, capturing one of her hands with his own. "Aye, Madelyne…the court will soon know that you and I are to wed and that D'Orrais's suit was declined by the king."

"But…why?" she asked, curling her fingers in his palm, her heart bumping along madly.

"He believed I would be the better man to keep you safe from your father…and to manage the lands at Tricourten, when they become yours." He tugged her closer and found her other hand. "Madelyne, I am pleased with this arrangement…'tis my hope that you will not find it too much of a disappointment." Though his words were stilted, she saw the uncertainty in his eyes.

"I do not," she told him, stepping closer to him. "I do not find it a disappointment." His presence engulfed her…the faint, basic scent of him—something sharp and clean—and the heat of his person. His fingers tightened around hers and he bent his head to press his lips to hers…gently.

Warmth streamed through her, as, soft lip to soft lip, they pressed together…breathed together…sighed together. Madelyne's lips curved in a gentle smile under his. Tricky had been right.

"Do you find my kisses amusing?" asked Gavin, pulling back just far enough to look into her eyes—and for her to see the faint amusement in his own. Beautiful, dark eyes in which she felt like drowning, they were….unshuttered and open with emotion, soft and bathed in a gentle light. This was a Gavin she'd not seen before.

She stepped back, her fingers remaining clasped in his rough hands. "Nay, 'tis not you whom I find amusing, but my maidservant…and her unerring wisdom."

"Tricky?" He sat on the bench and gently tugged her to sit beside him. The sides of their bodies touched, and he transferred both of her hands into one of his large ones. With the free hand, he reached to touch a tiny wisp of hair—one she'd not even felt escape from her coiffure—and smooth it back over the top of her head. "What is her unerring wisdom?"

Madelyne leaned slightly into his hand as it slid from the crown of her head to cup the side of her face. She would not tell him all— she must keep some secrets—but some little hint might be amusing. "My maid is determined that she will wed with your man."

Gavin, his face relaxed from its familiar sharp planes into an almost handsome appearance, reached to pluck a daisy from behind her. "That is no secret she has an eye for Jube…though I would be well-surprised should he decide to wed, as his favorite past-time is to chase light-o-skirts." He offered her the flower.

She took the daisy, brought it to her nose, then looked up at him from behind the petals, suddenly filled with joy…and something else, deep and warm and unfurling inside her. As if recognizing her feelings, his eyes darkened. His lips parted as he leaned toward her, pushing the flower from his path.

"Nay," she smiled under his mouth, "'tis not Jube but Clem that she will wed." She kissed him back, now, reveling in how simple it had all become. She loved him and they would wed and they would kiss like this every day.

A shiver of comprehension flitted through her. So this was love, she thought, pressing her mouth to his, feeling his hands as they came around her body to pull her close—as their breaths joined, mingling with their mouths and mixing with their sighs.

"Clem?" he said, pulling back as though the words had just made their way to his consciousness. "Never. He cannot stand the sight of her."

Madelyne looked at him, as sure now that Tricky would have her man as she'd been certain she would not. "Aye, my lord Gavin, they will wed…for Tricky has a faultless way of knowing."

"And what would that be?"

"I would not tell you that. Just mark my words and when you learn that I'm right, you may beg my forgiveness for disbelieving me." She allowed herself one of her rare, capricious smiles and was rewarded by an expression of pure desire—there was no mistaking it—that washed over Gavin's face.

"Madelyne," he whispered, pulling her to his chest; not to kiss her, but to hold her ear to his heartbeat, "have I told you that you are the most beautiful woman I have ever seen?"

His arms around her, gathering her to him, her head settled under his chin, and her own hands splayed over his muscular back, Madelyne felt a security that she'd never felt before. She closed her eyes and smiled.

Twenty-Three

THE NEWS spread like wildfire through the court: Gavin Mal Verne was to wed again, and to the shy little nun who was his sworn enemy's daughter.

Reginald D'Orrais took his loss with self-deprecating grace, which found him favor with the ladies. And his slightly injured air—a sensitivity attributed to his broken heart—only garnered him more favor with them.

"He appears to be recovering quite well," Judith commented to Madelyne as she surveyed her friend—soon to be her cousin-by-marriage—in the gown she would wear for her wedding on the morrow. "Maddie, you look stunning! Gavin will be unable to catch his breath when he sees you!"

Madelyne peered at herself in the polished mirror that Judith kept in the corner of her chamber. "Did Nicola look beautiful on their wedding day?" she asked. She had been fighting the curiosity for days—weeks, really, since her arrival at Mal Verne—and now she felt she had the right to know what had happened to Gavin's first wife. Judith would know, and would tell her the unvarnished truth…and she would live with whatever it was she learned about her husband.

"She was beautiful, aye, in a brittle, golden sort of way…while you, Maddie…you are the cool, sensual, exquisite moon to her brassy, harsh sun."

"What happened to her, Judith? I have the right to know now that I am to wed with Gavin. All that I have been told is that she took a lover…and that she died on the eve she went to go to him."

Judith settled back on her stool, looking at her in surprise. "You do not know the whole of it then." Her greenish-brown eyes scanned Madelyne, and what she saw there must have convinced her to speak the truth. "Her lover was your father, Maddie."

Madelyne could not contain a gasp, and she felt the warmth drain from her face, leaving it cold and pale. "My father? But…my father is mad!"

Judith took her hands into her warm ones. "Aye. He is mad. But betimes he was a great favorite of the court—at the least, for those who did not know him well. I know from your own words that he laid a heavy hand to you and your mother…and that the smile he bestowed upon the ladies hid only the poison behind it. He spoke of his work with such fervor that he was praised by all— even the priests.

"Work?" Madelyne felt a crawling in her belly. "Aye…his work in that below-ground chamber….I knew only that it was a dark, frightening place…but I do not know what work he did that would have caused praise from the priests."

"Aye, you must have been too young to understand….Your father is an alchemist, in search of the Holy Grail—the Philosopher's Stone…which he believes will give him everlasting life. He claims that through his devotion to Mary Magdalen a vision was made known to him in which God revealed the secret of the Holy Grail. He even believes that the saint's own blood runs in his veins!"

"My father? A holy man? Never…nay, my God would not reward him thus. 'Tis just the proof that he is mad. How is it that you know so much of my father…and yet I know so little?" Madelyne tried to pull the threads of her whirling thoughts together.

"Gregory was my betrothed, the one I was contracted to since birth. He was a boy I'd grown up with. He'd fostered at my father's house, as had Gavin, and they were friends—although Gavin was the elder by three years. My Gregory made a foolish decision and became swayed by the fantasies of your father, and he tempted

Gregory to his side with promises of immortality and power. The same as he has done with many a man. And when they beseiged a keep that belonged to Gavin, a great battle ensued…and in the course of which, Gavin struck down Gregory."

"Oh, nay!" Madelyne sank onto Judith's bed. "Gavin killed your betrothed! Judith, I am so sorry…."

Judith nodded her head, but her eyes were clear. "Aye, 'tis true. Gavin did nothing wrong, Maddie….I know that—he sought only to defend his own, and his people, and he did not know it was him, covered in his helm and filthy with dirt. Gregory, in his foolishness, led Fantin into the keep through a way only he knew because of his relationship with me….aye, Gregory made a terrible mistake and he paid the price. I have long forgiven Gavin, Maddie…but I do not believe he has forgiven himself."

"And…Nicola? Was she too struck down…?" Madelyne could not speak the words, though fear simmered in her heart. Nay, Gavin could not also have the death of his wife on his conscience…by accident or design.

"'Tis said she was leaving Gavin to go to your father…she raced across the fields and into the forest, and Gavin followed, trying to stop her. He tells me that she fell from her mount—that the horse took a jump it should not have, and she tumbled from his back. I believe that is the truth, Maddie, but there are some who believe that Gavin—in his rage—took his hands to her neck and broke it himself because he could not stand the thought of losing her to another man." She stopped, looking directly into Madelyne's eyes."

"He has too much honor to do such a thing," Madelyne told her quietly—knowing that her friend needed to hear her affirmation for Gavin.

"Aye, he does. I believe that. And that is why it has been such agony for me to see him as he has slid into this blackness which has surrounded him since the death of Nicola…and that of Gregory. If I could see that anguish wiped from his face, I'd be happy again. Mayhap you will be the one to help him do so."

"Mayhap I will." Madelyne sat with her hands quietly in her lap. On the morrow, she would wed him—this man whom she knew not well, but one who'd shown her both gentle and harsh sides.

"It is my greatest hope that you will, Madelyne. 'Tis my belief it is God's will that you have been turned from your intent to be a nun so that you might save the soul of a good man."

"My daughter is to wed with *Mal Verne?*" Fantin's heart roared in his chest and for a moment, his head felt as though 'twas lifting from his shoulders. He slammed his palms onto the table in front of him to keep his balance and stared in disbelief at the man who carried the news.

"Aye, 'tis so. The king—with a bit of prodding from his queen, as Mal Verne tells it—has gifted him with your daughter."

Yet another reason the queen must be punished. Fantin's eyes pounded as they bulged in his face.

This cannot happen.

He could not allow it to happen. To have his beautiful daughter—the product of his love with Anne, the manifestation of their pure joining—wed with the rough, dangerous, Mal Verne....

To have the sacred blood of the Magdalen polluted by that of his sworn enemy Mal Verne.

Never.

Fantin reached blindly for his goblet of wine—a watery, poor vintage, but he could not expect better at this hole where he lived in the town out side of Whitehall. At the least he wasn't forced to drink ale or water. He choked down five huge swallows before replacing the cup and stared at his man.

"They wed on the morrow?" Fantin could barely force the words from his mouth, dry and raspy from the nasty wine and his own fury.

"Aye. The court is awash with joy over the celebration."

An emptiness surged over Fantin and he sank onto his chair. There was no way he could halt the wedding...even he, in his pulsing, pounding need, knew this.

All could not be lost. There must be a way. There must be a reason for this. To have his get consummate a marriage with Gavin Mal Verne….'Twas all he could do to keep from screaming.

If she was to help him, his daughter could not be sullied—dirtied—by the touch of a man, any man…but most particularly that of Mal Verne. As the product of the pristine relationship between himself and Anne, Madelyne was meant for more. She'd been resurrected from the dead, after a fashion, and destined for holiness.

Somehow, he must wrest her from Mal Verne—most especially before she was got with child. Madelyne was meant to play a role in his work, and Fantin would not allow himself to be stopped.

On the even of their wedding night, Gavin found his betrothed on the battlements atop the castle of Whitehall. He knew this because Rohan had sent the word to him, but then remained to watch over his lady.

She stood near the edge, looking out over the darkness that yawned before her. Her night-dark hair had come loose from its coils and fluttered like so many banners in the healthy breeze. She'd turned her face up to the slice of moon that hung among the dancing stars.

"Surely you do not find wedding with me such a challenge that you should jump, choosing death instead of me," he said quietly, purposely echoing similar words he'd said to her on the battlements at Mal Verne. Tonight, he spoke only partially in jest.

Madelyne turned regally. "I knew that you would find me here."

Her smile gleamed in the darkness, and he was overwhelmed with longing. When had she turned into such a siren?

"What do you here?" he asked, stepping toward her so he could be close enough to feel her warmth. It was amazing: the warmth that emanated from her was not just a physical one…'twas one that enveloped him and made him feel manly, strong, and protective.

Her shoulders moved gracefully. "I wished only to look upon the land from here…and to think. My life will change greatly on the morrow." She turned to face him, the uneven stone wall at her back.

"Aye." His word hung quietly between them.

"I've forgiven you for taking me from the abbey," she offered, reaching to touch his face. It was the first time she'd felt the smoothness of his cheek, and she rested her hand there, allowing her fingers to soak up every sensation of warmth and the harsh, short hairs that had sprung up since that morning's shave. "I look ahead to my life with you and at Mal Verne. I've come to believe God has directed me in such a way that I could not balk it."

He wrapped his arms around her waist, still conscious of the soreness in his shoulder, and pulled her hips to his. He cared not whether she would feel the throbbing arousal that lifted between them. "I did not ever believe I would wed again," he told her, stroking his hand down the side of her cheek.

"Judith told me what happened with Nicola…and my father. I didn't know. Gavin…I am sorry that he should have been the cause of so much grief in your life….And Judith told me also of Gregory. She has long forgiven you, Gavin…'tis time you forgave yourself."

He sighed. "Ah, Judith. 'Tis ever she has the loose tongue!"

He pulled her again to him, again only to hold her head against his chest, to bury his face in her hair while the wind tossed around them, to allow himself the luxury of knowing only that moment… for that moment. Her breasts swelled against him and he enjoyed the knowledge that he would learn every part of those curves on the morrow.

"When we first met," Madelyne said, her voice muffled against his chest, "I saw you as a cold and driven man, seeking only revenge, and caring little for the sanctity of life. You acted foolishly during the fire—with honor, but with little thought for your safety. 'Twas as if you disdained danger, and relished the opportunity for death." She pulled back to look up at him, her delicate features shadowed by the mooncast. "I no longer see that same need within you, Gavin…and I hope that your need for danger and killing and war will ease with time."

"I have more to live for now," he told her, stroking her hair as it fluttered under his hand. "We will live together at Mal Verne with our children, and—" He stopped as she tensed within his arms, becoming completely still. "What is it, Madelyne? Verily you did not expect to be released from the obligation of bearing my heir?" Fear gripped him and harshness crept into his voice. Surely she did not expect that he would relieve her of the duty of filling his bed!

He held her away to look into her eyes and saw genuine fear shining in them, there under the moonlight. "You understand that I must have an heir, and that any man you would marry would require that of you!"

Madelyne nodded slowly, pulling from the grip he did not want to release. She stood with her arms crossed over her middle as though she felt pain there, and looked out into the darkness. "Aye, my lord, I know…and it was foolish of me to forget that. 'Tis only….Gavin, I have madness running in my blood! I am tainted… and will have tainted children!"

Relief, pure and bold, swept through him. "Madelyne…ah, Madelyne…." He cupped her face with his hands. "Listen, and listen well…." He delved into her eyes, searching them to make sure she saw his sincerity—and the truth therein. "Your father is mad, aye, but, Madelyne, there is nothing but sanity—beautiful, warm, sensitive, true serenity in you. I look into your eyes and I see naught of the madness that clouds Fantin's eyes or his actions….Madelyne, 'tis I who should fear tainting your goodness with my blood should we have a child!"

She stared up at him for a moment, then began to blink rapidly as moisture glistened in her eyes. "Gavin…thank you. Such beautiful words…and I see the conviction in your eyes, and know that you believe them. I can only pray, then, that you are right and that the madness will not run in the veins of our children."

TWENTY-FOUR

"IN THE name of God, let all know that this man and this woman are joined forevermore. Let none pull them asunder, and let them be one until death parts them."

Madelyne looked at Gavin, and he felt a surge of emotion as he grasped her hands tighter. He bent to press a chaste kiss to her pink lips, then another, and pulled away as the witnesses applauded in delight. Taking one of her hands, he slipped it into the crook of his arm and led his beautiful bride from the chapel and into the Great Hall.

They would feast and celebrate—the court had been waiting eagerly for this opportunity—and as soon as possible, Gavin would whisk Madelyne away to what was now the chamber they shared. He'd informed the king in no uncertain terms that there would be no bedding ceremony. "The sheets may be inspected in the morn, but I will not have Madelyne subjected to disrobing in the presence of anyone but myself or her maid."

The king chortled at his man's vehement comment, but acquiesced. "If I did not know better, Gavin, I should think you were well and truly smitten with the nun. Nevertheless, it will be as you say: no bedding ceremony…presuming you can abscond from the celebration in secret. I will not be responsible for the overzealous actions of your men and peers should they follow you!"

Gavin had agreed—he'd received more support from his king than expected—and now, as he sat next to his new bride at the high table, he had difficulty keeping his thoughts on the conversation he shared with Eleanor. When Madelyne had appeared to join him at the altar, he'd felt as though someone had slammed him in the stomach.

She wore a pearlescent gown of fabric that shimmered when she moved—the likes of which he'd never seen before. The undergown and over-tunic were cut of the same cloth, and both fitted to her body in a manner quite unbecoming a nun.

But she was no longer a nun.

Yet, Madelyne's garb was simple in its cut, and decoration. It was the fabric that made her look like a moon goddess, with her fair, serene face, pale pink lips, and long, glossy strands of hair the color of the blackest of nights that hung past her waist. A thin circlet of silver rested about the crown of her head, ineffective for holding her thick tresses in place, but perfect as a simple adornment that framed her face. A large pearl drop hung from the center of her forehead, suspended from the circlet, and long ropes of blue-white pearls wound around her neck and swung to the girtle made from silver links.

Gavin had never seen her hair completely unbound, and now, as it curled at the tips, falling over her shoulder as she bent to eat, he reached to touch one thick lock. He lifted it, feeling its weight, and wondered how soon they could leave the dinner.

He sipped at his wine and continued his conversation with Eleanor, even as he watched his wife chat with the king, who sat on the other side of her. Observing her, he could not believe that only one moon earlier, she'd been a shy, naive nun ensconced in a cloistered abbey. Today, she spoke more confidently, moved with more sureness, and most certainly was the most stunning woman he'd ever seen.

And she was his.

That was enough. Gavin rose from his seat, leaned to kiss Eleanor's hand, and said, "Your majesty, I have greatly enjoyed your presence…but I am off to enjoy my wife now. I must have you know that I am most indebted to you for urging me in that direction."

Eleanor smiled slyly and squeezed his arm. "You are quite deserving of that prize…and I am shocked that you lasted as long at dinner as you have!"

Leaning toward Madelyne, he whispered in her ear, "I bid you excuse yourself, madame, and have Clem escort you to our chamber. I will join you very shortly. I have had enough of this prattering and wish to have you to myself."

Her large, wide eyes turned to look up at him in surprise, but Madelyne did as she was bid. Gavin assisted her in bringing the bulk of her skirts from around the chair on which she sat, and, gesturing to Clem, sent her off in the right direction.

Now, the trick would be for Gavin to disappear without the revelers noticing and following him to insist upon the bedding ceremony. It was his plan to be well gone before any of them noticed.

Tricky awaited her mistress in the chamber, her eyes bright and her cheeks flushed with excitement. "There has never been a more beautiful bride, I vow," she gushed, helping Madelyne from her over-tunic. She unlaced the sides of her undergown and pulled it over her head, leaving her mistress clad in only a light chemise.

"The man is mad for you," Tricky continued as she helped her disrobe from the shift and then slip into a cream-colored slip of the lightest, finest linen cloth. "Would that Clem has come to his senses by now, but it appears that he is a bit more thick-headed than your Gavin."

Your Gavin. Madelyne fixated on those words. He was, indeed, hers now, and the thought made her stomach curl and flutter as she thought of what was to come.

All too soon, Tricky finished brushing her hair and, with one last pat on the head, hurried from the room, leaving Madelyne to herself. But no sooner had Tricky gone than a soft knock came and the door opened.

Gavin slipped in and turned to close the door, bolting it immediately. "I believe I escaped without being detected…but there is always the chance that someone saw me." He turned and froze when he saw her, standing next to the blazing fire.

"Madelyne…Lady Mal Verne…it is as if every time I see you, you grow more beautiful." He stepped toward her, resting the weight of his hand on her cheek and then reaching to smooth it down the length of her hair. "Since the moment I met you, I needed to see you thus…with your hair loose. I craved for days to know even the color of your hair…and feared you'd shaven it at the abbey. Now…I wish to see you clothed only in those black locks."

Warmth and anticipation skittered up her spine, and Madelyne felt the full impact of the effect she had upon the man who was now her husband. With a boldness she did not know she possessed—or how she came about it—she caught hold of her shift. Raising her hands above her head, lifting her unbound breasts under the chemise, and she felt the light linen scrape over them as she pulled the slip from her body.

When it fell to the floor beside her, she heard Gavin's intake of breath and saw the darkness surge into his eyes. His gaze heavy and dark, he strode toward her and gathered her into his arms. Her naked body fit to him, all along the length of him, sensitive to the roughness of his own clothing, the rise and fall of his chest, and the hardness of his arousal pulsing between them.

They kissed wildly, as one of his large hands reached between them to hold the heaviness of her breast, and Madelyne's bare feet settled atop Gavin's booted ones. The mixture of sensation between the coarse fabric of his tunic and the soft sensuality of his mouth, along with the demanding strokes of his thumb over her stiff nipple, caused a great shiver to tremble along her spine. Something swelled and dampened pleasantly between her legs.

With a deep breath, Gavin set her away from him and stepped back, placing both hands on his hips as if to keep them in control. "I believe it only fair that we should be on equal standing," he told her with a crooked half-smile. "Allow me to disrobe—if it please you, my lady—and we may commence with our desires then."

"It pleases me to assist you," she said, needing something to do, to focus on other than what was to happen.

She knelt at his feet, gathering her hair into a bundle and pushing it over one shoulder. Slowly, as the anticipation between them grew, she untied his boots, removing them from his feet. She unlaced his cross-garters, taking her time, sliding along the firm, muscled calves they enclosed. Madelyne felt the weight of his hand on the top of her head, and the firmness as his fingers tightened when she reached to pull down his chausses.

His legs now bare to her, Madelyne saw how thick and darkly-haired they were. She saw the ridges of muscle and the planes of his knees rising into massive thighs half-covered by his tunic. Heat pooled in her middle, sliding from her belly to the place between her legs, and she suddenly felt light-headed even as she reached to touch him.

As though sensing the effect he had on her, Gavin reached for her shoulder, lifting her gently from under the arm, so that she stood in front of him. "My tunic," he said in a rasping voice, reaching with both hands to gather up her breasts in the moment before she moved.

She obeyed, helping him to pull it up and over, stepping close enough that the tips of her upthrust breasts brushed against his thin *sherte*. Gavin's breath came faster, harsher now and he stepped back to yank the *sherte* from his shoulders—standing bare before her. His chest, broad and dusted with hair, rose and fell, rose and fell, and his bare, muscular arms hung, unmoving, from his defined shoulders.

Madelyne looked, saw that part of him that Peg promised would bring pleasure to her if she allowed it, and swallowed. Her dry throat constricted, grating in the silent room, and she stood still—unsure of what to do.

Gavin stepped toward her, and they were skin to skin, mouth to mouth, foot to foot. Before she realized it, he'd shifted them toward the bed and sank onto it with her.

The different textures of his body enticed her—coarse thatches of hair, rough callused fingertips, moist lips, sleek muscles, and soft hair—and Madelyne touched every part of him.

At last, he eased away, guiding her onto her back, and leaned over her to take one of her nipples into his mouth. He sucked gently, using the tip of his tongue to trace the sudden hardness there. She gasped at the sensation—a fire—that streaked through her, and her eyes closed as pleasure swelled and surged inside her.

"Gavin…." she breathed. With a brief, wicked grin such as she'd never seen before from him, he glanced up at her, then returned to his gentle teasing. Madelyne sighed in delight, shivering with a heat she'd never expected to know…and then nearly leapt off the bed when she felt the warm weight of his palm covering the thatch of hair between her legs. "Gavin, nay…what…." Her voice trailed off as a wave of throbbing heat started there between her legs and shot to the end of each nerve.

His fingers slipped in and through her private place in a teasing rhythm, gentle over the most sensitive nub that seemed to swell with every stroke. Madelyne found herself reaching inside, deep inside, for something that was…just…out…of…reach….And suddenly she was there, shuddering under his fingers and mouth and hands, sobbing with the shock of such pleasure, burying her face into the bedding to wipe the tears.

"Maddie, Maddie," he whispered, taking her into his arms and pulling her close to his solid chest. "My sweet, my sweet…you are so lovely." He kissed her on the top of her head, trailing gentle pecks along her hair and chin and to her mouth, where he covered her lips fully with hers. His slick tongue drove inside her mouth and he became more urgent, his hands pulling her hips, shifting them as he pressed her back onto the bed.

All at once, he paused, stilling in his position above her. "Maddie, do you know what is to happen?" he asked, his voice taut, his eyes searching hers. "Aye," she breathed, thanking Tricky—who, for all of her talk, was as inexperienced as her mistress—for broaching the subject with Peg. "Aye, I am ready, Gavin."

With a last, delving kiss, Gavin pulled back to ease between her legs. There was a smooth, sliding sensation and then, one sharp movement followed by a stab of pain. She gasped and he stilled, waiting for the surprise to pass.

He moved slowly, sliding in a sweet, warm rhythm. The pain ebbed, and as the numbness eased, something else began to take its place—that delicious, swelling sensation from before. Gavin's breath came more harshly and Madelyne twitched beneath him. He shifted into a faster, more urgent rhythm, and Madelyne closed her eyes as the pleasure grew, billowing into that explosion of beauty once again. As she gave a soft cry of surprise—*again!*—he arched back, fitting deep into her with one last thrust.

She felt him shudder against her and saw the naked beauty on his face in that moment of pleasure, and his low, rough exhalation. As Gavin came back to himself, she gathered him close, closing her eyes and smiling at an intimacy she'd never thought to experience.

How blessed had she become.

The morn came too soon for Gavin, but he relinquished the blooded sheets to a squire so that they could be displayed as proof of Madelyne's virginity and his own ability to consummate the marriage. There would be no chance of an annulment with such evidence.

Despite the fact that it was the day after his wedding, he was expected to attend Henry—and Madelyne to be present in Eleanor's court room—so they rose and went about their business during the day.

But when the evening came, and they ate in the great hall together, Gavin could not keep his attention from Madelyne…and from the rising color on her face, he presumed that her thoughts followed the same path as his. He could not remember ever feeling happier or more fulfilled in his life.

Even in his early days with Nicola—when he'd believed they might share a love betwixt them some day—this self-same sense of contentment and pure peace was never part of his life. Madelyne had brought that depth of serenity to him, and he'd spoken truthfully to her. Somehow in the last weeks since he'd met her, Gavin had lost his death wish, his urge to leave this earth, his sense of carelessness with his life. Now…he realized he wanted only to make a life with Madelyne.

The only thing that kept him from being wholly contented was the knowledge that Fantin de Belgrume was still alive.

Later that evening, as they lay nestled together in a cocoon of bedding, Madelyne was just drifting off to sleep. Gavin's hand stroked the length of her back while the other held her atop his chest. He toyed with her hair, and when he spoke, his voice rumbled deep within his chest, just beneath her ear.

"We shall leave for Mal Verne as soon as Henry gives his permission," he told her. "'Tis dangerous still for you to remain at court. I have set spies about and there's been no sign of him, but I know he has not yet given up the desire to take you. You will be safe at Mal Verne, and there you'll be able to settle into your new life."

She nodded against him, well content. Memories of the fortnight she'd spent at his *demesne* stirred pleasingly within her. "I look forward to working in the gardens, knowing that this time I will be there to see their yield." Her mouth curved against his skin.

"I shall see Henry on the morrow about when we may leave. Mayhap we can be on our journey before week's end." He wrapped a thick hank of hair gently around his wrist, loosening and then tightening it absently. "I wish also to bring the queen her gift before we leave."

"'Twas most kind of you to think of such a thing. She'll be pleased with the necklet, I am certain. I will be working in her herb garden on the morrow, but surely word will come to me of her delight."

"Aye. The queen does love her jewels as much as her husband loves his coin." Gavin stroked her hair, and she smiled under the comforting weight of his wide hand.

Madelyne basked in contentment. Her father had made no move against her at court, though she'd felt a bit worried that he might hear of her wedding and object.

Mayhap he'd returned to Tricourten, and to his experiments, and would leave them alone.

Twenty-Five

THREE MORNINGS after their wedding night, Madelyne was in the private herb garden tending to the five varieties of thyme plants when Judith came rushing along the overgrown path, calling her name.

"Maddie! Maddie, oh, dear God, Maddie, Gavin has been arrested!"

"What?" Madelyne staggered to her feet, tripping over her skirts and clutching at the apple tree for support. She must have misunderstood. "What do you say?"

Clem, who'd been sitting under the tree, watching over her in his master's stead, lurched to his feet. "What?"

Judith could barely catch her breath. Her face was white, and a lock of copper hair straggled into her face. Madelyne felt all emotion drain from her as her friend repeated the impossible words. "Gavin has been arrested."

"Why?" was all she could think to say. Her heart was suddenly slamming in her chest, and her head had gone light.

"He has been accused of attempting to murder the queen!"

How? Why? Madelyne could only stare at Judith. She could not even voice the absurdity of such a thought. "How…how can this be? Is the queen injured?"

"He presented a gift to her this morrow," Judith explained between short breaths as she tugged Madelyne toward the entrance of the garden. "In a wooden box, beautifully carved, and she did open it at once. But her head ached, and she passed it to Lady Therese, who wished to examine the necklet. When Therese pulled it out and placed it around her neck, she was pierced through the skin in three places. She became ill immediately, and, Madelyne, she has *died*."

Madelyne stumbled after Judith, frozen, shocked, disbelieving. She tried to make sense of what her friend told her, but the only thing that resonated in her mind was that her husband had been accused of attempted murder—of the queen.

"'Tis a mistake. 'Tis absurd." She muttered, at last standing alone and pulling from Judith. The king couldn't believe that of Gavin. How could he? He knew her husband. She shook her head as if to dislodge the impossible, the *absurd* situation.

"And the king wishes to speak with you. There were needles hidden among the wires of the necklet, and poisoned." Judith's eyes were wide, with tears sparkling at the corners. "Gavin is to be imprisoned—and he will be executed if 'tis proven he is the murderer."

Madelyne, followed by Clem, hurried after her friend. All the way, she tried to assimilate this news with her knowledge of the man she knew.

Nausea gathered in her middle. It was a mistake, she told herself. It was not true.

Gavin stood to the side in Henry's private court room, his arms bound behind his back, and a man-at-arms standing at his side. Madelyne fought the urge to rush to his side. Instead, she focused on the grave face of the king as she positioned herself in front of him.

"Your majesty," she curtseyed to him, glanced at her husband, then returned her attention to the man she'd believed was Gavin's friend as well as his liege.

"Lady Mal Verne, do you understand what is happening here?" Henry asked. There was no sign of the light humor that had glinted in his blue eyes before, and no evidence that he had ever been anything but a harsh ruler. Indeed, his face bore a haggard but steely set.

"Aye, your majesty. My husband is suspected of attempting to harm the queen. Forgive me, your majesty, but you know that Gavin respects her majesty and yourself and is devoted to both of you!" Madelyne knew she spoke out of turn, but she could not stand to see the proud figure of her husband restrained thus. "He would have no reason to wish either of you harm!"

"Lady Mal Verne," Henry's voice boomed. "We are quite aware of the circumstances. We would ask that you refrain from offering your opinion until it has been asked. Now we ask you, did your husband prepare a gift to be given to the queen?"

Madelyne drew herself taller and steadfastly kept her eyes from Gavin. "Aye, he commissioned a special necklet to be made for her in thanks for our wedding. The box in which it was contained was also created especially for her majesty."

"Aye. Created especially for her. With a poisoned pin-prick that would have sent her to her death if she had been the one to wear the necklet." His eyes pierced blue-gray into her gaze.

"Nay, your majesty. 'Twas a gift of thanks…not of death. Why would my husband deliver himself to the queen such a thing? Would he not know that 'twould point to him immediately? He is not *mad*."

But her father was.

A cold wave swept her.

Henry rose. He passed a glance over Madelyne, and she believed she detected regret in his expression. "Gavin, you must be imprisoned until this is resolved. I am sorry to do so, but the evidence against you is great and I cannot allow it to appear that I will not follow my own laws."

"Your pardon, your majesty," Madelyne spoke, stepping toward the king. "Please, your majesty, could it not be that someone who harbored ill against the queen—or my husband—prepared the poison?"

Henry swung toward her, a glower on his face that faded a bit as he recognized the concern in her eyes. "Of course that is possible. Did you think that possibility had not also occurred to me? Mal Verne…when did you receive the necklet, and was there a time where it may have been tampered with?"

Gavin glanced at Madelyne, then responded. "My lord…I cannot think of a moment when it could have happened, in truth. I should like to say otherwise, but I cannot. It was delivered from the town to my trusted man. And since that moment, 'twas safely hidden in my chamber until this morrow, when I took it to the queen."

The king swiveled to look at Madelyne, who felt her heart swelling in her throat, her stomach pitching with nausea. "'Tis enough for me to hold him, Lady Mal Verne, at least at this time." There was a trace of sympathy in his eyes before he returned to her husband. "Gavin, I do regret it, but you must be incarcerated until this is resolved."

One of the guards came forward at the king's gesture. Madelyne focused her attention on Gavin, though she stayed at the king's side. "Gavin," she said, her voice ringing clearly. "I will do whatever need be done to find out the truth."

He paused, forcing the men-at-arms to wait as he spoke. "Madelyne, have a care for yourself. I trust this will be resolved soon."

She watched after them, pushing back the despair that built within her. She turned to Henry and was surprised to see true regret in his eyes. "He is not a murderer," she told him boldly.

"We know that," was the king's response. "And I well hope that you can prove it, my lady."

Madelyne was given permission to visit with her husband while he was under house arrest. She reached through the iron bars to hold one of his hands.

"'Tis not so dirty as I'd feared," she told him, looking behind him into the dark cell.

"No rats," he replied, his eyes never leaving her face. "And a stool to sit upon…plus a small pallet on which to sleep. One cannot say that Henry is neglectful in his hospitality."

Despite his light words, she saw the weariness and concern in his eyes. Shadows flickered about them, cast by a torch slung on the wall behind her. "Do they feed you well? I will send Tricky down with some food and an extra covering for your pallet."

Gavin grimaced. "Madelyne, I have slept in much worse conditions. For now, I am most concerned about your safety. Please, remember to go *nowhere* alone. Not for one moment must you be unwatched. Keep Clem or Jube with you. I am sure this will be resolved quickly—Henry can't believe I've done this—and then we will go to Mal Verne, away from this place."

She touched his face, which was sticky with sweat and streaked with grime. "And a cloth and water I will send too, so that you can refresh yourself." She dropped her hand to hold his again. "Gavin, someone must have taken the necklet—before the metalworker delivered it to you, or mayhap after 'twas brought to you."

He pulled his hand away to grip the bars between them. "I removed the necklet from its box myself—if it had been tampered with before coming to me, I would have been pricked myself."

"Then someone has been in our chamber and has taken it, and made you to look like a murderer."

His head drooped. "Your head is much clearer than mine at this time—aye, Maddie. Have you talked to Jube or Rohan?"

She nodded. "Aye. They all have said that no one could have entered our chamber—as do all of your men: Clem, James, Antoine, and Peter. And they have seen no one about who should not have been there." She took a deep breath. "Could my father have done this? He hates you so."

He pressed his forehead against the bars, looking deep into her eyes. Her heart jolted out of rhythm at the soft, desperate expression there. "'Tis the most likely explanation. Your father is mad enough to do such a thing…all in the name of his work."

"My father. They say he has long believed that God speaks to him, tells him what to do—orders him so that he can finish his work." She lifted her eyes to stare into his, sorrow lining her insides. "Is it not a great irony that a man should use the love of our God, and his belief in Him, to justify evil? Whilst there are people—as Mother Bertilde, and others—who find only good in their love for God?"

A hand reached between and grasped hers. "Madelyne, you must take extra care now…He knows this accusation won't long stand, that I will soon be freed. It must be only a distraction, a way to detain me while he finds a way to take you. In his mind, you belong to him, you're still his possession. And, as with Nicola, he will take what he believes is his. I will not lose you as I did her. I couldn't bear it, Madelyne."

She swallowed, pushing away the fear that hovered beneath her calm exterior. "Aye, Gavin, you can be sure I will take care. And I will speak with every man and woman that I can to find out what they might know about these events." She thrust a hand between the bars, stroking the side of his face and tracing a finger over his lips. "Know that I love you, and that I will find a way to have the king release you."

"Maddie…" his voice was low and strained in the silence. He reached to clutch her fingers, bringing them to his lips for a soft kiss on their tips. "What good have I done to deserve you? I, who have lived in a violent, black world for so long…I do not deserve you. But I thank the Lord that you have been given to me."

Madelyne took care, as she'd promised Gavin—going nowhere without Clem or Jube at her side. Even when she was with Judith, one of Gavin's trusted men accompanied her.

In the mean while, she, Judith, Clem and Jube questioned as many people as they could who may have seen Gavin or Therese on that night.

Apprehension and worry hung in a heavy mantle over Madelyne. She startled at any large noise or shadowy movement, and tossed and turned in her empty bed at night. She knew that her father could wait around any corner, and the thought brought back nightmares that she hadn't had since leaving the abbey.

Gavin exuded frustration and anger when she visited him. He fumed over his helplessness, cursing everyone from the king to Fantin. They'd learned naught from any of the people with which they spoke, and time was moving on. Sooner, rather than later, Henry must bring Gavin to trial among a group of peers and, while not conclusive, the evidence was damaging.

"'Tis that or I will be imprisoned until I am too old to walk," he said angrily, snatching his hands back through the bars to pace in his cell. "'Sblood, Henry knows I did not do this! Why does he not release me to allow me the opportunity to bring your father to justice?"

"But can we be so certain 'tis my father who is behind this?" Madelyne asked. "You've seen nary a hair of him since you nearly strangled him out side of the king's court when he accosted me… could it not be that he has left Whitehall? Mayhap there is another who wishes you ill!"

"I should have killed him when I had the opportunity!" Gavin snapped, continuing to pace. "I do not know why I allowed you to sway me from my purpose that day. Had I listened to my instincts, we would not be in such a predicament and I would not be imprisoned thus!"

"Gavin, you could not have killed him in cold blood! You may be a soldier of war, but to kill a man in cold blood—mad or no mad—nay, I would not believe you capable of it." She reached through the bars, but he did not come back to her.

"'Tis a problem, then, Madelyne, if you do not believe me capable of such an action—for had it not been for you, I would have ended your father's life with little thought. If you believe otherwise, than mayhap the man you love is naught but one in your imagination." He slammed his hands against the brick wall with a dull thud and rested his head against the stones. "Please, go. I am weary of talking." He turned and walked back into the shadows of the cell where she could not see him.

Madelyne watched his figure dissolve into a mere silhouette, her insides twisting as her heart sank. Mayhap she did not know the man that he truly was, but she loved him nevertheless.

Silently, she blew a kiss to him—to wherever he sat and brooded in the darkness—and turned to leave.

"Clem, I am ready to leave," she said, stepping back around the corner of the passageway. Clem or Jube—whoever accompanied her—stayed away so that she and Gavin would have some privacy when she came to visit.

"Clem was called to assist Jube and Thomas with Rule." Rohan rose from the stool on which he'd been sitting. "I delivered the message and told him that I would make certain you returned safely to your chamber."

"Thank you, Rohan." Madelyne smiled at the young man. "What is wrong with Rule?" She knew how much Gavin valued his destrier, and even though she would not go near the horse, she appreciated its value as well.

"He's not been ridden since Lord Mal Verne was imprisoned," Rohan explained as he strode rapidly through the passageway. "Am I walking too quickly, my lady? This way, my lady. Thomas told me of a shorter route back to the hall."

Madelyne lifted her skirts as she hurried after him. He was walking very quickly, but she could keep pace. They rounded a corner and suddenly, something dark and soft descended upon her.

Her shriek was muffled as some heavy cloth enveloped her, stifling her cries and tangling her arms. Madelyne kicked and fought, but it was no use. Strong arms imprisoned her, and the dark wool smothered her nose and mouth. The air under it became hot and close and she felt herself slip into nothingness.

Twenty-Six

THE HOURS crawled by for Gavin as he paced in his cell. He'd been incarcerated for six days…and Madelyne had not been to visit him since the morning before, when he'd vented his anxiety and fear in such a venomous manner. Not that he blamed her for not wanting to interact with him when he acted in such an infantile way… but did she not know now much he longed to see her? How much he looked forward to her morning and evening visits?

He'd been a fool to speak so sharply, so spitefully to her when she'd done naught but treat him with warmth and understanding. Could he do nothing but drive women away?

He cursed himself and, holding to the bars, he pushed his face as close up against them as he could, trying to peer toward the right side, from which Madelyne would come. He missed the clean cloths and bowls of water she sent him every morn and night, and the bits of bread, meat, and cheese she wrapped up from her meals. Though he wasn't being starved, the fare served him was little better than peasant bread and watered-down ale.

Suddenly, he heard a commotion from that direction, and he pushed harder against the bars. Mayhap she'd come….

But it was Clem and Jube who burst around the corner, with the guard rushing after them. "Wait! Halt!"

"My lord, she is gone! She is *taken!*" Jube burst out as he and his mate came up against the gate. "My lady is gone!"

Gavin's world stopped. Everything went black.

"What do you mean she is gone?" he repeated, slowly, carefully…knowing that if he'd heard what he believed he'd heard he would surely go mad. Still, he kept his voice calm, low, slow. "How can she be gone when she is to go nowhere but with one of you?"

He gripped the bars, his breath increasing in speed, and saw the answer in their faces before Clem was able to respond. "She is gone? She is gone?" His voice rose and he shook the bars. "Get me the king! I must see him! Get him to me now!"

Sickness pitched his stomach and he felt the sweat springing to life all over his body, trickling down his back and face. "Take me to the king!" he commanded, staring at the guard, and reaching through the bars to grasp the man's tunic. "I must see him!" He pulled, slamming the man up against the bars with a clank. "Get me to the king."

He released the guard, who, with a terrified backward glance, rushed off. Gavin turned his attention to Clem and Jube, trying desperately to control the panic that screamed through his veins. "Tell me what happened, you fools! Where is she? How long has she been gone?"

Clem stepped forward, disease patterned on his face. "When last I saw her, 'twas yesterday morn when I brought her to visit you. I waited for her and whilst she visited with you, Rohan came to me with the message that Jube and Thomas required my assistance at the stables with Rule. He assured me he would return Lady Madelyne to her chamber."

Jube glanced at Clem and picked up the story. "I received a message from Rohan that Madelyne would stay with Lady Judith last night, so I did not think to find her until after the midday meal, when she did not come to eat."

"No one has seen Rohan and Madelyne since yesterday morn, my lord."

"Rohan. He is the one." Gavin spat the words, even as his mouth dried in fear. As he did in battle, he fought to collect his mind, to clear it from the dread that threatened to paralyze him. Calm and clear. He would remain calm and clear, for this was the most important battle of his life.

"Fantin has taken her to Tricourten, I would stake my life on it. You must go there, go after her…if the king does not release me…." His voice trailed off. He could not conceive of that possibility… Henry must let him go. "You must go! Go now!"

Gavin paced blindly after they left. Would Henry come to him? Would he understand the urgency? He stopped and grasped the bars when he thought he heard the sound of someone approaching, but no one came.

He paced more, feeling the rising tension in his chest. His heart thumped crazily, his breath came faster, in short, sharp pants as he tried to keep from imagining what was happening to Madelyne… what her mad father was doing to her.

But he could not keep his mind clear, and the bile gathered in the back of his throat. He retched in the corner, sagging against the wall, pushing his fingers into his eyes to keep the tears at bay.

Clem and Jube had to take the time to gather their things and collect the other men-at-arms from Gavin's retinue, and then they were off to Tricourten.

They traveled quickly, with one wagon carrying some basic supplies…and for transportation for Lady Madelyne, should they need it. The wagon would not keep their pace, but for the first leg of the trip, it would stay within a short distance.

When they stopped the first night, the wagon rolled into their camp only an hour after the men had dismounted. Clem and Jube sat with Thomas, Peter, Antoine, and three others around a fire on which a rabbit roasted. As he poked the meat with a stick to determine whether it was cooked, Clem saw an unfamiliar shadow emerge from the back of the wagon.

Bolting to his feet, he started toward it. "Who goes there?" he shouted, then stopped in his tracks as he recognized the deliciously plump figure of Patricka.

"'Tis I." She stepped from the shadows, planting her hands on her hips, and Clem felt a wave of disbelief wash over him.

"What in the bloody hell are you doing here?" he stomped toward her, wanting nothing more than to wrap his hands around her neck…and squeeze.

"I want to help. I may need to care for Maddie…" her voice wavered, but she continued. "We do not know how she will be when we find her…and I couldn't wait at Whitehall to hear from you. I won't be in your way, and I can help." Her hands remained on her hips and her chin thrust in the air.

"Woman, you are the most foolish, addlepated female I have ever met! You cannot go with us! You will return to Whitehall immediately!" He stuck his hands on his hips and thrust his chin in her direction.

Tricky stepped toward him, seeming to be unaware of the other men crowding around, watching the display. "And how will I get there? You cannot take me back, and I cannot go on my own. I will have to go with you, and Clem," as she spoke, her brown eyes grew wide, gleaming earnestly in the moonlight. "I will be no trouble! I won't slow you down, and I'll do as you say…but I must go. Please! I beg you."

Clem's tongue thickened in his mouth and he could not speak. His insides had melted into a puddle, and he was alternately desirous of paddling the wench and tearing off her clothes. But of course, he could do neither. The blasted woman loved Jube.

Instead, he swallowed, coughed, and, when he heard a snicker behind him, turned to glare at the man who dared do so. "All right." His words, gruff and short, were all that he said before swinging around to take his place by the fire.

At last, Gavin heard the sound of voices approaching. He prayed that it was the king…and his prayers were answered as the robust figure of Henry Plantagenet came around the corner.

"What is it that ails you, Mal Verne?" Henry bellowed, coming face to face with Gavin, with only the bars betwixt them. "You have been shouting the walls down here and nearly sent my guard to an early grave."

"'Tis Madelyne—she is gone, she's been taken by her father. You must release me and allow me to rescue her." Gavin strained against the bars again, bringing his face breath to breath with his liege lord.

"Fantin has Madelyne? How can that be? Did you not make arrangements for her to be guarded—"

"By *God*, man," Gavin breathed sharp and short, his teeth tight. "You know that I would not neglect such a thing! 'Twas one of my men who has betrayed me…and I believe 't has been him all this time, reporting to Fantin, that has enable him to best me so many times! 'Twas he—it has to be—who put the poison on the necklet! Now he has absconded with my wife and I must go after her!" He sagged against the bars, the cold metal a relief against his hot face. "Please, my liege, as I have served you well…please release me…."

Henry stepped away from the bars. "Release the man," he told the guard, watching impassively as Gavin straightened eagerly. "Go with God, Gavin…and this time, do you not return without de Belgrume's head on a platter."

Had he not been on such an urgent mission, Gavin would have reveled in the freedom of charging down the road on his mount's back. As it was, he had no pleasure in the moment. From the instant the bars opened on the door to his cell, Gavin had been in motion, frenetic and frantic.

Early the morning following his release—by his count, two days since Madelyne had been taken—Gavin overtook his men and their party. They were only hours from Tricourten Keep.

He barely registered the presence of the woman in the group, the maid Tricky, except to speak sharply to Clem to keep her out of his way, and then dismissing her from his mind. His focus, his life, his every breath was pinpointed upon arriving at Tricourten and finding a way inside the keep.

Gavin kept his mind from considering what he might find when they gained entrance. He could let nothing distract him from his goal of getting there, and finding Madelyne…and treating Fantin to a slow, painful death.

Twenty-Seven

MADELYNE'S THROAT was dry, but she dared not ask for water. She swallowed, again, wishing for just a drop of something for her parched mouth.

She'd arrived at Tricourten only a day before, but the hours that had passed since had been of such nighmarish quality that she dared not think on them. Instead, she allowed her head to fall back against the stone wall to which her wrists were chained. Her arms ached, extended as they were, and her fingers and feet had no sensation.

Bruises from the rough handling during her abduction and subsequent travel thudded painfully whenever she moved. The memory of her father's fingers fastened around her neck, thumbs pressing into the soft underpart of her jaw until she swooned, caused panic to rush anew through her veins.

Now, she watched fearfully as Fantin and his assistant Tavis, along with a pale priest, sat at a long, rough table in the underground laboratory at Tricourten. She had vague memories of this room from her childhood, prompted by the nauseating smells and evil-looking devices scattered throughout.

She saw the way her father's fingers opened and closed, opened and closed, like the mouth of a beached fish. "She will serve God here, with me. But she cannot do that if he has touched her and got her with child!"

"You must wait," the priest said to her father, his voice soothing. "All may not be lost. If she is not breeding yet, she can once again attain her pure state."

Fantin looked at her, and the expression in his eyes made her stomach heave. 'Twas not one of anger or evil…'twas one beaming with love—the love of a father. A *mad* father.

Prickles raced up her spine, covering her shoulders like a nasty cloak. "Aye…after we have exorcised every bit of Mal Verne's touch, and all thought of disobedience, she will be better prepared to serve."

Madelyne's stomach tilted. He referred to the day before when he'd beaten her with his hand and a thin leather whip until she collapsed on the floor, all bravado and strength disintegrating into blood and tears. She swallowed again, and closed her eyes against the tears. *Gavin.* She couldn't control the shaking of her body. It trembled against the cold, rough wall.

"Think, my lord," Tavis was telling her father. "She has been wed with Mal Verne for less than a fortnight…'tis only slightly possible that she carries his child. She may know the answer now."

Fantin swiveled toward Madelyne, his long face taut and white. "Do you carry that man's child?"

She could not speak. The words would not form. Madelyne tried to respond, but nothing came from her mouth. Fantin surged out of his chair and stalked over to her. Planting a hand on either side of her head, he stared into her eyes…and what she saw there was enough to make her light-headed with terror. They were empty: cold, blue, steel…*empty*…with tiny black pinpoints in the center.

"Do—you—carry—Mal—Verne's—child," he breathed, his stale, wine-tainted breath washing over her face. "Answer me, Madelyne, or I will pull that devil's child from you!" Quick as a flash, he brandished a thin, shining hook, waving it unsteadily under her nose.

"I do not know," she croaked, forcing the words from her trembling lips. "'Tis possible."

Fantin's shriek rang in her ears, and she instinctively ducked as he pivoted away from her. His hands slammed onto the table in rage, then wooden bowls and metal goblets tumbled to the floor as he swept his hand across them, knocking them awry. "Now what shall I do?" he howled, picking up a mortar and pestle and pitching them wildly toward her.

Madelyne did not move in time, and the wooden bowl struck her in the shoulder.

"Master, master…." Tavis's voice somehow reached through Fantin's insanity and served to redirect the man's anger. "We will simply wait until she has had her courses…and then you will know that she is ready for you. And if she does not have them in one moon's time…." he cast a sly look at Madelyne, trapping her eyes with his, "we shall rid her of the bastard's babe and then you might be assured she is pure once again."

"And then, when she is whole again, wholesome, she will devote herself to my work—praying and fasting in the name of God. She will be my link to the Father, and with her, I will find the answer."

Darkness, thankfully, washed over her and Madelyne slid into oblivion.

When she opened her eyes some time later, a man's face—one vaguely familiar—hovered near hers. As some of the cloudiness drifted from her gaze, and her mind began to focus, she realized that she was prone, on her back, and her arms, though still restrained, were not stretched as taut as they'd been.

The man brought a cup to her mouth and water—cold, heavenly, life-giving water—dripped between her lips. Her tongue slipped out to capture drops of it, and he tilted the cup so that it flowed more freely.

"Madelyne," said the man—an older man, of an age with her father, "I'm here to help you." He had red hair streaked with white, and calm gray eyes.

She tried to shake her head, but black spots danced before her eyes and she was forced to close them. It was an effort, but she forced a wan smile.

"You do not remember me…but your mother knew me well. I am Seton de Masin."

When he spoke, the remembrance renewed itself in her mind. Seton: the man who'd allowed them to escape Tricourten during his night watch. The man who'd kissed her mother with more than a chaste wish of peace. The man who'd come to the abbey in search of them all those years ago…and who duly reported to Fantin that they were not there.

"I cannot free you yet," he spoke quietly. "Fantin trusts me, and I must wait until the right moment. But I will do what I can to keep them from harming you further. I've sent word to Whitehall that you're here."

She tried to speak, to ask why…and he must have understood.

"As yet, I have no way to get you out of here…it will take a bit of planning. I have waited many years for a moment such as this, for I knew it would come. Though I always thought your mother would be the one in danger. Please, Madelyne, try to be brave for another short time…I will never be far from you…and I will get you free as soon as I can."

She closed her eyes, hope beginning to billow within. "Gavin," she managed to say. "My husband…he will come…."

Seton was already nodding. "Aye, I know. I have sent the message to him at Whitehall… But your Mal Verne is a wise man, and 'tis likely he already knows you are here."

Madelyne remembered suddenly that Gavin was not free to come and go….and despair washed over her. But she pushed it away. Seton was there to help…he had helped her mother before, and he would help her now. She made her mouth into a smile, and then drifted back into darkness.

Camped just out of sight of Tricourten's guards, Gavin, his men, and Tricky conferred in the wood. They didn't need a fire during the day, and at night would keep it very small so as not to alert the keep-dwellers that they were near.

"Fantin will be expecting us," Gavin commented. "We will be unable to gain entrance to the keep except by stealth. There must be a private entrance…but there is no way to find out."

His face felt tight and his eyes burned, gritty from lack of sleep. He'd barely eaten since leaving Whitehall—again, thanks to Madelyne for the robust meals she'd provided for him during his imprisonment, or he would be weaker. "He'll have his guards watch for a party of men attempting to come in…or staying in the village. He likely has scouts set out into the woods, here, as well, and so we must act before they find us. 'Twill not be an easy task to get into the keep, and I dare not besiege the place for fear he will escape with Madelyne…or worse."

Silence fell over the men as they digested this information. Their options were limited.

"I'll go. I'll go in and find a way to secure entrance for the rest of you. They don't expect a woman…and 'twould be simple for me to pass as a serf or villager."

Gavin stared at the plump little maid. His first reaction was to dismiss her offer, but the steadfast earnestness in her eyes gave him pause.

"Nay—you will not," Clem spoke angrily when his master did not. "'Tis too dangerous. We will find another way in."

Gavin looked from him to Tricky, a faint stirring in the back of his mind…but he thrust it away. "'Tis a ripe idea. I'll go with her," he said, nodding. "No one will expect mischief from a traveling husband and his wife—"

"Nay, my lord," Clem interrupted. "I will go with her. You'd be easily recognized, and I'll keep this wench from getting into trouble." He crossed his arms over his chest. "If the woman must go, then I shall be the one to accompany her." He dashed a glare at Jube, who'd remained silent, and then returned a steady look at Gavin.

"Very well, then, Clem and Patricka. We'll discuss it no longer, as time is of great import. You will enter the keep and find a way to let us in before the sun rises on the morrow. When you have ascertained your plan, you must send us a message that all is well and give us our instruction. How do you propose to do this?"

"We shall meet with you at that oak tree," Clem pointed at a strong tree hidden from the keep by a small hill and scattered brush. "As the sun sets."

Gavin gave a short nod, his face tightening. Grasping the forearm of his man, he squeezed tightly and said, "Go with God. Fantin may be mad, but he is no fool—and he believes he is in the right. He and his servant Tavis will be watching carefully." He turned to the maid, taking in the seriousness on her round, freckled face. "You are a brave girl to do this for your mistress. I'm certain that God will bless you." He grasped her by the shoulders, squeezed, and released. "Be off."

He turned, walking from the camp…needing to be alone while he waited…helpless.

Tricky and Clem arrived at Tricourten on foot. It would arouse too much suspicion if they rode in on a sure-footed destrier. He used a stick to walk, and affected a bit of a limp. They took care that their clothing was dirt-streaked, and Clem turned his tunic wrong-side out to hide the fine embroidery.

For all their pains, it was no hardship to enter Tricourten Keep. As Gavin had expected, the guards paid little attention to a man and woman—their attention would be attracted to a party of two or more men. Clem explained in a rough voice and poor grammar that they traveled to an abbey where his sister—Tricky—was to serve a great abbess, and that they merely needed one night's lodging. The guards nodded them in with barely a glance.

Tricky walked quickly alongside Clem, brushing against him as he limped along rather briskly for a man with an injured leg…but she forbore to point that out. She was as eager as he to complete their mission and allow Gavin and the others in…but at the same time, the excitement tripped her heartbeat up, and her nerves sang. And she was with Clem—who'd refused to let her go alone—who'd even ordered his master to stay behind so that he could accompany her. Mayhap the man was not so stone-headed as she'd thought!

They made their way across the bailey, toward what appeared to be the main entrance to the hall, when Tricky suddenly noticed a familiar figure leaving the hall. "Rohan!" she gasped, whipping her hand back into Clem's gut. Rohan—the traitor—would most certainly recognize Clem…and quite possibly recognize her.

Without a second thought, she grabbed Clem by the tunic and, using his own momentum, propelled him toward the wall of a building. He pulled her with him and she slammed into his arms, and suddenly their mouths were thrashing together. Clem moved, rolling along the wall, until she was pressed between his comforting bulk and the raw wooden planks of what smelled like the stable.

At last, he pulled free and turned his head slightly to look in the direction Rohan had gone. "I'd forgotten about him," he said between breaths. "Bastard. I've half a mind to take care of him right now…."

"Nay, Clem," Tricky plucked at his sleeve, "we must find Madelyne. We'll need to be mindful of Rohan, but I wish to waste no further time. We must find her and find a way to get Gavin into the keep."

"Aye," he replied, returning his attention to her. His eyes bored into hers. "Tricky, do you not think you have escaped my wrath for this harebrained scheme…I will have words with you after this is all over."

She could not help but smile up at him, and ticked at his nose with her fingernail. "Clem, sweetling, I should be quite disappointed if you did not follow through on such a threat…a tongue-lashing from you should be only one of many such repercussions of our relationship." Her coy smile and lilt to her voice sent a very different message than the one he must have expected. She swore his face tinged pink.

But now was not the time to carry this further. Tricky and Clem agreed to separate, explore the hall and the outside of the keep, and meet back at the stables within an hour.

"Have a care for yourself," he told her, his dark eyes boring into hers. Then, slumping over his big stick, Clem hobbled off to examine the stables and other outbuildings.

Tricky entered the hall, and found that serfs had finished clearing the food and platters of the midday meal from the rows of table. She tried to blend into the activity by picking up a tray, and following one of the other serfs, but her attention was caught by the two men who sat at the high table.

She paused, holding a wooden platter that oozed with grease, and looked at them. Tricky knew who they must be…Lord Fantin de Belgrume, the handsome man with the pale blond hair that rose from a widow's peak just off the center of his forehead, and his cohort: a slender, younger man with dark hair and soulful eyes who looked harmless. As she watched, de Belgrume laughed at some jest from his companion, and the beauty of his face, and the warmth of his laugh startled her. How could someone so beautiful be the monster that Madelyne feared so?

Suddenly, the other man—Tavis, Gavin had said was his name—looked at her and their eyes locked. Panic rose into her throat and she turned abruptly to take the platter she still held, but a peremptory voice made her halt in her tracks.

"You, there! You, with the red hair!"

Tricky froze, her heart pounding so hard it threatened to choke her. She turned slowly, waiting to hear a call for the guards to come down upon her…but instead the man called again, "Bring my master that wine!"

Thank the good Lord the man pointed to a table nearby that held several bottles of wine, else Tricky would have surely given herself away. With a quick bob of her head, she dropped the platter back onto the table where she'd picked it up, and hurried over to get the wine.

Her hands were slick with sweat and she nearly tripped over her skirts when she approached the high table, but de Belgrume didn't appear to notice. He pored over a curling piece of parchment while Tavis rested his elbows on the table.

"M-my lord," Tricky gave a brief curtsey and sloshed wine into de Belgrume's goblet. She was about to set the bottle down on the table when Tavis straightened up in his chair.

"I don't recall seeing you before," he said, his dark gaze sweeping over her. He was a handsome man, with slender fingers and a sharp tone in his voice.

She gulped, curtseyed, and stammered, "Me brother and I—we just become here this day."

A gleam that made Tricky's belly twist leaked into his eyes and he crooked a finger at her. "A shy one, are you?" He looked at her again, more slowly and with greater weight than a moment before. Tricky felt his attention pause at her generous breasts and then sweep over her hips and back up to her face. "You needn't be shy here at Tricourten. We treat our guests quite well…" he glanced at de Belgrume, who appeared to be in some other world, his lips moving as if in silent prayer, "unless they are family members." Tavis smirked at Tricky and his hand snaked out to snag her sleeve.

She allowed him to tug her toward him—what other choice did she have?—and this might be an opportunity to learn more about where Madelyne was. The next she knew, Tricky found herself settled on his lap. Mayhap she was foolish not to be afraid…but she did not believe anything Tavis might have in store for her would be worse than what Madelyne faced. Her resolve strengthened, Tricky managed a coy smile—subtle, for she did not want to appear too eager—and managed to squirm her generous bottom invitingly into his thigh.

"Family members? Aye, my lord, they can be trying ones can they not?" She purposely reached forward, brushing her breast near—but not quite touching—his arm as she grabbed the wine from where she'd placed it on the table. "Me brother is more bother than 'e's worth all the time." She straightened up, "Wine, my lord?"

He glanced at his master, and Tricky saw that the other man had begun to slump in his seat. "He'll rest for a time—he is weary from praying and fasting these last days. Now, soon, all will be aright, as he has found the answer to that which he seeks…aye, wine I'll have.

And that'll not be all I'll be having," he added, his eyes fastened to her breasts.

Tricky felt a roil of nervousness pump her stomach. Mayhap this was moving too quickly and she would find herself in a position in which she could not handle…best pull on a shy face for a time. "Of course, my lord," she told him. Rising from his lap—ostensibly to pour his drink—she shifted away and managed to remain standing and looking directly into his face.

When Tavis would have reached for her, she stepped lightly back. "My lord, I must find my brother…."

"Nay, not so quickly. He is likely chasing some other wench," Tavis told her with a sly smile, "and will not even notice that you do not attend him. You may attend me for some time…it has been long since I've seen such a comely wench here at Tricourten."

"Of course, my lord." She curtseyed again and watched as he drained his goblet. Mayhap if she plied him with enough wine…. She refilled his goblet as Tavis tugged her back onto his lap. Nervously, she glanced at de Belgrume. He had collapsed forward onto the table, his face planted in the center of the parchment that curled up around his ears.

Tavis slipped his hand, quick as a wink, down the front of her chemise and Tricky nearly leaped off his lap. His fingers sought her flesh and gave a firm squeeze before he extracted his hand and tweaked her chin with the same pinch. "Very nice. 'Tis glad I am that you travel with your brother and not a husband…else it would be rather uncomfortable for him." He smiled, and she was reminded of a wolf when she saw the way his eye-teeth gleamed.

"'Tis said that he," she tilted her head toward de Belgrume, "studies the great physicks…do you assist him in his experiments?"

Tavis drank more wine, slopping it over the side of the goblet when he set it down. With a quick glance at his sleeping master, he used a rag to wipe up the mess as he replied, "Aye, that I do. He is the master, chosen by God, to find the secrets of the ancients." He chuckled a soft, eager laugh and slogged his hand across his mouth. "He has worked for many years to find the answers, and now he has put the last peg into place. We shall soon be more powerful than even the king…even the pope. And I shall be at my master's side."

She filled his goblet, noticing that the bottle was nearly empty…and knowing that she would need more. "You are?" she prompted, fluttering her eyelashes even as he spewed wine-laden breath in her face. "You must be so very smart to do such things!"

"Aye, that I am…but my master…he is the gifted one. He is the one to whom God speaks." He stood so quickly that he nearly knocked her backward. "Come…I will show you our laboratory. He sleeps and will not mind." Tavis staggered over a dog lying beneath their feet, and cast another glance at de Belgrume. Gently, he raised the snoring man's head and settled him back in his chair, slipping a rolled-up cloak beneath his neck. "He must have his rest if we are to work this night," he explained, rolling up the parchment and slipping it under his arm. "I shall awaken him later, after you and I have had our…tour of the laboratory."

Tricky's chest tightened as fear and apprehension rose within her as Tavis closed his strong, thin fingers around her wrist and pulled her after him.

TWENTY-EIGHT

CLEM FINISHED his exploration of the bailey and outbuildings in short order, and decided to enter the hall to reconnoiter with Tricky if she'd completed her own search. He'd found something that might work for an unobtrusive entrance—a gate that was guarded, but with only one guard…and one guard could easily be disposed of from the inside once they determined the routine and schedule.

The great hall was nearly empty when Clem entered. At the high dais, a man slumped back in his chair, snoring comfortably… and 'twas the shock of white-blond hair that identified him to Clem. Fantin. He'd half a mind to put an end to this right then, and send the man to a burning grave with the help of the dagger that weighted his thigh…but that would be Gavin's honor and Clem knew that the time was not yet right.

He looked around and saw nothing of Tricky. Unease prickled his spine…where else could the woman be, unless she'd slipped from the hall before he came in? He'd make his way back to the stable where they were to meet.

With a frown and gusty sigh, Clem turned and came face to face with Rohan.

Tricky, whose hand was imprisoned within Tavis's grasp, hurried down a narrow, winding stair in his wake. She thought she saw a small shadow scuttle from a corner and dart beneath her feet, and she stifled a shriek.

Where was Tavis taking her…and what would he do with her once they arrived?

She prayed that at least her risk would come to fruition, and that she would see Madelyne wherever it was they were bound.

At last, they reached a small oaken door, heavily barred. Tavis released her hand, and, giving her an eager, sweet smile, said, "One moment, my dear, and you shall see what it is we have worked for."

It took him several moments to force the bar out of its metal slot, and with a grunt, he pushed the door open. Immediately, a putrid smell burst from the room and Tricky nearly gagged at the fumes.

"Come, my dear," he told her, drawing her into a cave-like chamber lit with an overwhelming number of sconces burning on the walls.

Tricky's eyes darted about and fastened on a long table near one end of the room. A figure lay on it, but was so shadowed she couldn't tell even if it was a man or a woman. When Tavis tugged her arm—the man was like a small child faced with a room of sweets—she was forced to follow him to the opposite side of the chamber.

The smell seemed to have lessened, so Tricky could breathe more freely…but when she was faced with the snake heads and skeletons of small rodents, and jars and bottles of foul-looking liquid and slimy solids, she felt her head grow light and she swayed against Tavis.

"What is it, my little chick?" he asked, leering down at her, one hand on either side of her hips, trapping her against the table. Suddenly, she felt very frightened and it was all Tricky could do to keep her face blank of fear.

"Naught'n, my lord," she told him. "I betripped m'self and nearly fell on your work here…." Swallowing hard, she reached up to trail a single finger down the side of his face. "I cannot believe you know all of this! Tell me about what you do with these…things."

It was the right response. Tavis nearly clapped his hands with glee and, towing her about the laboratory, pointed out everything from instruments of extraction—she did not ask what they extracted—and devices designed to boil and purge and grind and beat the ingredients to whatever potion they might be creating.

When they made their way over to the side where the figure lay, unmoving, upon the table, Tavis paused to look into Tricky's eyes. "This," he told her, a slim hand with one long fingernail pointing at the body, whose face was turned away, "will be our salvation. She will hear the Word of God, she will praise Him and serve Him and will be our salvation!"

He stared down at her, his breath rising and falling, and as if in a trance, reached out a hand to touch the figure that lay supine. Tricky stepped forward to get a look at her face.

It was Madelyne....and she appeared to be alive!

"What—who—is that?" she asked boldly, slipping her hand into the crook of Tavis's arm.

He appeared to shake from his trance and turned to look at her, the dreaminess gone from his eyes. "'Tis the daughter of my master. She is recently returned to us from days serving God in an abbey. My master has decreed that she shall serve God here, for the good of my master."

Tavis chuckled again, twirling against her in his glee. "She has been wed, and my master fears that she has been tainted by the touch of an impure man." Tavis continued, his face shriveling into a dark mask, "Despite her imperfections, now, my master will not allow me to touch her...though I burn to do so." He turned to look at Tricky again, lust glazing his face. "I shall have to settle for the likes of you...but I vow, 'twill be to your enjoyment as well."

Tricky swallowed, her tight throat dry and tasting of bile. Tavis, who appeared to have no concerns that she would carry tales, explained, "We wait only until she has been cleansed—exorcised— from the repugnance of coupling. My master has many ways of removing the evil from within her." He fingered a long, slender whip and looked at her. "She will not see the light of day again, for she must serve in silence and piety and for my master only."

Tricky blanched and terror clawed up her spine.

"He plans to wait for another moon to be certain she does not carry her husband's child…and if she does, aye, he must relieve her of that burden so that she might carry a more important one."

Tricky slipped from his grasp as he flung his arms wide to encompass the chamber, the realm, the earth…and she stepped backward. If there was any chance that she could sneak away….

"Where are you going?" Tavis turned, his voice booming in command.

He lunged for her and she side-stepped, crashing into a table and knocking a mortar and pestle to the floor. "I—I must find my brother…he will worry about me," Tricky said. "I would find him, then return to watch you at your work," she added, resting a hip suggestively against the table. Purposely breathing heavily, she forced her breasts to rise and fall just beneath his nose and watched as his attention floundered between her chest and the work in the laboratory.

"Nay…I will have a message sent to him. You may not leave yet." He reached and closed a hand around her breast, then his other hand pulled her toward him so that her hips slammed into his. She felt an unmistakable bulge thrusting between them and her heart began to race.

Before she knew it, she was pushed back against a table and Tavis had yanked her skirts up to her thighs. Panicked, Tricky began to kick and pound at him, but his weight, though slender, was strong, and bore her to the table. His groping hands pinched at her, causing great stabs of pain to shoot through her breasts. She began to sob, kicking, fighting, rolling her head from side to side as her legs were forced apart.

Suddenly, the door swung open and a voice boomed into the room. "Master Tavis! You are needed urgently up in the hall!"

Tavis paused only for a moment, then returned to Tricky. "Nay, I am occupied, de Masin….I'll be there in a bit."

"'Tis one of Mal Verne's men—he is here!"

That news caused Tavis to straighten and whip his head about to look over his shoulder. Tricky's heart pounded in her throat as she struggled anew. Clem! Did he mean Clem?

"Help me with this and I'll be up." He stepped away from her, and Tricky slammed her knees together and tried to roll away, but he held her firm. Leering close to her face, he said, "I will return to you, my little coquette….and you will not only watch us make history, but you will enjoy it as well!"

Tricky gulped under the hand that had closed around her neck and looked away from his eyes that had turned from soft and velvety to pure, hard lust. The other man came over and they tied her wrists and arms together, forcing her to slump onto a stool against the wall near Madelyne's still body.

Tavis raced out of the room, humming gleefully, but the other man stayed behind. Tricky watched as he approached Madelyne, stiffening as she saw him bend toward her face.

"Madelyne," he whispered, reaching to touch her face. "Madelyne…are you awake?" He glanced at Tricky and in his face she saw concern. "Do you not speak or I'll leave you here for Tavis," he snapped at her, then returned to the prone figure before him.

"Madelyne, can you hear me? Your husband's man has arrived…he's in the keep and has been found out." He glanced at Tricky, who gasped.

"Clem! They have Clem?" she asked, struggling to loosen her bonds.

The man strode over to her, glanced at the closed door, then glared down at her. "Who are you and what do you know about this? Speak, woman, for we haven't much time!"

"I came here with Clem…we were to find a way in and…." she stopped, gulping. Was this a trick?

"What, woman? What is it? If I am to help you, I must know all!" Angry spittle came from his mouth and urgency curved in lines about his lips.

From the table, Madelyne groaned. "Tricky?" Her voice was barely audible, but her maid heard and understood. "Seton?"

"Aye, Madelyne." Seton rushed to her side, stroking her face and offering her a sip of water. "Sweetling, they have one of your husband's men and will no doubt be scouring the keep for the rest of them. I must get a message to them...."

"Tricky...tell him...." she moaned. "He...can...be trusted. He...can...help."

Tricky glanced at Madelyne and then back at the man called Seton, who now stood glowering over her. She had no choice. Clem was taken. They would miss their meeting with Gavin...and this man might be able to help. Madelyne trusted him. "We were to meet Gavin and his men at the oak tree behind the hill on the west side of the keep at sun down," she told him. "We were to find a way to sneak them into the keep. I know nothing else."

Seton nodded. "There are more men. Aye, that is good." He returned to Madelyne. "What can I tell your husband that he will trust me? I'll meet him and bring him in. We will get you safe from here tonight."

Tricky could hear her mistress's sigh from her own perch and wished she could minister to her. What had they done to her?

"Quickly, Madelyne....they will come back at any moment!" He leaned toward her, and although Tricky could not hear what Maddie told him, he pulled back, nodding, and satisfied.

Just as he turned away, the door from the stairway flung open and in stumbled Clem, arms bound, followed by Fantin and Tavis.

Gavin paced in the wood just in sight of the oak tree, his stomach twisting in nauseating knots. The sun was nearly gone, and no sign of Tricky or Clem. He clenched his fists, knowing that their failure to appear was a sign that something had gone severely wrong.

The gray shadows were long and just turning to black when he saw the shift of a shadow from the hill beyond the oak tree. It was too slight to be bulky Clem, and much too tall to be Patricka. Gavin clenched his hands over his sword and waited, holding his breath.

"Mal Verne?" The sound of his name wafting over the cool summer air reached his ears. "I come to help."

Gavin did not move. He held his breath again.

"Mal Verne." The man moved closer to the oak tree, his hands held out in front of him so that even in the darkness, Gavin could see that he held no weapons. "Your man, Clem, is taken…and the girl is taken as well." He paused as though to measure any effect his words might have. Gavin remained silent, though he took a silent step forward.

"I've spoken to Madelyne," the man continued. "My name is Seton de Masin….she knows me from when she was a child…. Her message is that you may trust me. You will know this by the words I am now to speak: Madelyne gave you prayer beads made from rose petals when you first came to the abbey, and you still carry them with you. And she means you to know that she loves you."

Gavin stepped from the shadows, his suspicions allayed. He had told no one about those beads. Even Madelyne had not known he still carried them until after they were wed and sharing a chamber. "De Masin." He thrust his hand out and they shook. "She is alive? Is she hurt?"

De Masin hesitated, and Gavin's stomach pitched. "She is alive, she can speak, but she is injured. I could not keep them…from her…last night. She will be well if we can get her from that place."

Gavin struggled to control the frantic pictures and thoughts in his head. He must focus and stay clear headed if he had any chance of saving her. "Can you get me inside? I will have Fantin's head on a platter. Nay, he will die a painful death…slow and painful…."

"Aye. How many men do you have?"

"Five, plus myself and my man within."

Seton nodded once, then beckoned. "Come, let us go. We have very little time."

Twenty-Nine

MADELYNE FORCED her eyes open.

The acrid burn of candles, other smells she did not wish to define, and the throb of pain throughout her body assaulted her senses. The taste of the last bitter, putrid liquid that had been forced down her throat still surged in her empty belly. She couln't keep back a moan, and was rewarded when her father's face came into focus in front of her own.

Stifling a shriek, she closed her eyes and turned away from his face, the image now implanted on her brain: empty eyes with tiny pinpoints of black in the center, a wide, grinning mouth, and a mass of white hair as uncontrolled as the joyous laugh that erupted from his lips.

She was against the wall again, taken from her prone position on the table and re-strapped to the cold stone. The rough edges of the blocks behind her chafed her bruised skin, and her arms, stretched to their limits, had no feeling in them. She could barely keep her head raised, but with an effort she lifted it as Fantin's laugh stopped abruptly.

"What is it you say?" He turned and screamed at someone. "That cannot be!"

Madelyne tried to focus and looked around the room, her muscles cramping, her arms jerking involuntarily. She vaguely remembered speaking with Seton again, and talking of Gavin and her love for him…a sob clogged her throat that had naught to do with the pain in her bones, but the pain in her heart. She might never see her husband again.

As she looked about the chamber, Madelyne froze, staring in disbelief. Tricky? Dear Lord, how did Tricky come to be here? Her maid was slumped on a stool, her clothing mussed, dirty and torn, and her hair straggling about her.

Fantin screamed more profanities to some unseen messenger, then, with one last glance at his prisoner, turned to rush from the chamber—his robes flowing behind him. Tricky and Madelyne were alone and safe, for a time, from Fantin's rage.

"Tricky!" Madelyne hissed.

Her maid shook her head as though to clear the fog and slowly turned to look at her. "Maddie," she whispered. "Are you all right?"

"I am alive and thankful to be so," she returned. "And you? How came you here?"

Tricky explained quickly, and then gestured to a dark corner. "They have Clem over there. I cannot tell if he is hurt. He's not moved since they hit him on the head."

"Can you move on that stool?" Every word was an effort, but Madelyne forced them out. For the first time, she felt a ray of hope that escape might be possible. "Those shards from the broken bowls…mayhap you could cut…." her voice gave out, the words would not come…but Tricky knew what she meant to say.

"Aye." Tricky rocked on the stool, side to side, and managed to tip herself over. She rolled on the floor and Madelyne could not tell if she was successful in grasping a piece of broken crockery. Silence reigned but for the grunts and groans of exertion from her maid.

The sound of voices and heavy footsteps down the stairs caused Madelyne's attention to sharpen. "Tricky…they come! Can you right yourself?"

Gasping, Tricky rolled herself back to where she'd been and struggled to right her stool. The door flung open again, and Fantin and Tavis strode in, arguing.

Their loud voices, angry and shrill, sent greater shivers up and down Madelyne's spine. Where was Seton? Was there aught he could do?

"There is no sign that Mal Verne has entered the keep—he is no where to be found." Tavis spoke in an urgent tone. "You must concentrate on your work, Master Fantin…your time is so close!"

He flickered a look in Madelyne's direction, then, as his gaze swept back, it was distracted by the sight of Tricky on the floor, still attached to her stool. He trotted over, standing above her with his hands on his hips. "And where are we going, my little coquette? Surely you do not wish to miss our little demonstration anight?"

Roughly, he yanked her upright and reached to fondle her breasts. "Ah, such sweet rewards await me!" With a lascivious smile, he turned back to Fantin.

"Master…no one can enter this keep now without our knowledge. Mal Verne's one man gained entrance, but if there are others, they will be stopped by the extra guards we have posted. Mal Verne must still be jailed, awaiting trial for attempted murder of the queen."

"Aye," his master chuckled. "Even our king is not so foolish as to allow him loose in the wake of his little gift to that whore." Fantin appeared to be placated, and he swept over to Madelyne, fluttering his robe dramatically. He reached to touch her face, smoothing his cool hand lovingly along her cheek.

"Madelyne, dear daughter, feel you ill, or do you feel the strength of your cleanliness returning to you? The potions we have given you are only for your own health. We must eradicate the seed of that bastard Mal Verne if you are to attain your innocence once again."

Holding her breath, Madelyne turned her face away, afraid that even the little she knew would be betrayed on her face. God willing, Seton had found a way to bring Gavin's men into the keep….

Suddenly, the door to the laboratory burst open, and even through her haze, Madelyne recognized Seton de Masin as he pitched into the room, nearly falling to his knees. Blood smeared his face, and where he held his left arm with his right, more redness colored his fingers and clothing. He was followed by the priest, the white-faced, man with dark circles beneath his eyes. The latter prodded Seton with a sword to the back.

"Lord Fantin, you have a traitor in your midst," announced the priest as he stood proudly at the base of the stairs. Madelyne's head went weightless. Nay!

"What is this?" Fantin turned, his words soft, but the touch of his hand on Madelyne's skin turned heavy and still.

"This man has been feeding your daughter, and whispering with her whilst you work to rid her of the evil within her. He is destroying your ever chance of cleansing her!"

"De Masin, what is the meaning of this? Is this true?" Fantin whirled from Madelyne's side and faced his man, hands on his hips.

"Lord Fantin, 'tis not his only trespass," Rufus continued. "He strode from the keep and spoke with a man near the oak tree—in secret."

Madelyne dragged in a shaking breath, her body overcome with tremors. Oh nay…!

Fantin left her side as if propelled, leaving a force of shifting air in his wake, and a deep fear chilling her bones. "What are you about?" her father roared, snatching a gleaming sword from one of the tables, whirling to face his man.

"Your work will never come to pass," Seton told him, standing tall, though pain marked his face. "You seek to use Madelyne as the conduit for your work with God, but she will never fulfill that role."

"You know naught of what you speak," shrieked Fantin, his eyes wild and desperate. He swiped out with the wide blade. In his fury, he swung too wide, and Seton easily leapt out of its path…but the priest was not so fortunate.

Before Madelyne's eyes, her father's blade sliced through the neck of the little priest, leaving a deep, thick red line across his throat. He gurgled and slumped to the floor as Fantin stared in disbelief.

Then, as if some great power seized him, Fantin clenched his fists, flinging his arms wide and raising his face to the wooden ceiling above, and shrieked before launching himself at Seton. "You have killed him! My priest!"

"'Tis no matter, Fantin. Your work will come to naught," Seton told him, jumping gracefully from his path. He pivoted toward Madelyne, breathing heavily against his pain. "Madelyne cannot fulfill the role you have made her as your daughter. She is not of your seed."

Madelyne froze as Fantin screamed again. "*You lie*! She is my flesh, my only flesh and she was created with the woman God has chosen for me! She is my destiny!"

"Nay, you have been fooled all these years," Seton continued, taunting him, dancing around the table as his eyes flashed with purpose. "Madelyne is *my* daughter."

THIRTY

THE TIME had long come and since passed for Seton de Masin to open the small, side gate as he'd avowed he would.

Gavin pushed all emotion from his mind. He focused only on that gateway lit by flickering torches—watching the weathered with age, gray wood that kept him from his beloved—nay, he would not think on that.

Look only on the door. Wait for it to open. Count the knots, study the texture and grain of the wood.

It did not open.

Stare in the dim light at the splinters that form each plank.

It did not open.

His nerves screamed and yet he looked only there. He didn't hear the shuffling of his men. He didn't see them watching him.

He did not look at the night sky, studded with stars and a low moon. He knew only stillness, black stillness within—rage simmering beneath, struggling to erupt.

He did not allow it. He stared, grasping the hilt of his sword and still he waited.

And still the gate remained closed.

"Nay!" Fantin shrieked, freezing with his sword in the air. "Lying whoreson!"

Madelyne saw her own shock reflected in his face. Her body shook with chills and disbelief, yet something surged warm within her. She carried no madness in her veins. Her love to serve God came wholesome and from her heart…not from the twisted, skewed need of Fantin de Belgrume.

Seton continued to move, holding his arm, taunting Fantin. "All of these years, I have known she is of my blood and she has lived safely out of your reach. I have made certain it would be so. Why do you think I have stayed in your service for all these years?"

"Nay! 'Tis not true!" Fantin's voice reached a shrill pitch, then cracked into dryness. "Nay! Lady Anne would never have lain with one such as you…and you tell me tales with no truth, Seton de Masin! You will not sway me from my purpose, for *I am chosen*!"

Seton yanked up the sleeve of his tunic, baring his wrist, still dancing, moving ever closer to Madelyne. "See you here, Fantin—'tis all the proof you need. She and I have the self-same wrist-markings that my mother and her father have had before us. She is of my flesh. Madelyne is not your daughter, and she will not remain here under your care to live in the darkness of your world. I shall see to that."

With these words, Seton launched himself over the table, knocking bowls and dishes askew as he thumped to the floor next to Madelyne, banging into Tricky's stool and upsetting her onto the floor.

Seton reached for a long wooden broom and whipped it around, missing Fantin by only a whistle of air. He shifted his grip, settling the pole like a lance at his side, when something flew across the room and, with a dull thud, Seton dropped to the floor next to Tricky.

Madelyne screamed weakly when she saw the small, black ball that had smashed into her new-found father's forehead, and looked over to see Tavis, holding a leather sling.

"Master!" he shouted, horror crossing his face as he stared at Fantin.

Turning to look, Madelyne saw that her father had metamorphosed. While before, he had been animated, with fervor, and with eyes that glowed…now, his face curdled, darkening and shattering. His brows knit together and his eyes were slitted into angry black slashes. And his mouth…Madelyne swallowed when she saw the way his lips twitched and yanked, played as if a tiny thread tugged at them—as if they were controlled by some puppet master.

A thin stream of saliva leaked from the corner of his twitching mouth as it seized up and around in this silent, eerie movement.

At last, the mouth opened and a shriek of ungodly rage spewed forth, filling the chamber with such force that the bowls rattled. Fantin's face blossomed red and purple and his hands clutched at his middle as though he were trying to tear out his insides even as his feet stepped and jumped and danced on the stone floor.

The veins in his neck grew, swelling to blue and then black, as he screamed the cry of a dying man.

For Madelyne, in a moment of pure black fear and icy hopelessness, realized that his insides were dying…that he had naught left for himself, and that his mind died because his dream had been taken from him by Seton's taunting knowledge. She could barely comprehend that Fantin was not her father—it was unimaginable how shattered *he* should feel, learning that she was not of his flesh.

Fantin swept to her side, then, and before she could draw a breath to scream again, had the tip of a knife at her throat. His eyes bored into hers, burning, and his pupils were no longer pinpricks of black, but huge black saucers.

Madelyne closed her eyes, swallowing, and felt the tip of the knife cold on her throat as it constricted. She would meet her God now. The God *she* knew, not the one her father—nay! her father no longer!—not the God Fantin had fabricated.

Then the coolness withdrew.

She opened her eyes and found Fantin's face very close to hers, still crumpled with the destruction of his dreams, rasping a harsh breath from flared nostrils. "Nay." His single word, whispered, puffed on her face, stale and moist. Then he spoke, again, slowly, as though the words formed like perfect, single drops of water, dropping, one at a time, in his mind: "I loved your mother. She betrayed me."

He pulled away. The rage seemed to have subsided and though his eyes remained wild, his movements smoothed and slowed. "Nay," he said again, as if needing to convince himself. "She betrayed our God."

Those simple words, that coolness, caused a great, icy, fathomless fear to billow in her. Fantin's rages had always been a source of great horror and pain…but this—this calmness, this studied calmness, laced with purpose, caused her to shake with terror as never before.

If Fantin believed his God had been betrayed, then nothing would save her now. She held back a whimper. *Nay.* She did not live a life without hope.

And then hope, in the form of Tricky, seized her attention.

Madelyne saw her maid moving on the floor, wriggling, somehow no longer attached to her stool, no longer bound.

Quickly averting her eyes, she raised them to meet Fantin's. Mayhap….

"Fath—my lord," she said, struggling to keep her voice calm. "My lord, may—"

"Silence!" he shouted, spittle flying into her face. Madelyne reared against the stones, away from the sudden recurrence of rage.

He seemed to consider her for a moment. "What is it you wish to say?"

"The queen…."

Those were the only words necessary. "The whore! She yet lives, or so I hear from Rohan, my faithful man." He slammed his foot into Seton's unmoving body upon those words.

Madelyne's unspoken question was thus answered. "Why did you poison the necklet?" she asked, using every last vestige of energy to force the words from her lips, seizing upon anything that might keep Fantin's attention from the figure that slinked under the tables. A quick glance showed Madelyne that Tavis had not noticed Tricky's movements.

Nay, blessedly, he stared, enraptured by the exchange betwixt herself and Fantin.

"She is the greatest of all whores," Fantin told her. "She must die—'tis God's will. She must be purged from this earth, just as Mal Verne must be, just as his slut of a wife was, and as you shall be!" Red veins burst in the whites of his eyes as he screamed these last words at her, and Madelyne struggled to keep from bursting into tears.

He whirled from her, and Madelyne's heart froze. If he saw that Tricky was near the door and the stairs….Nay, he did not! He whirled back around with the same bloodied sword that had sent the priest to his death. She recoiled when he rose toward her, the silver blade glinting and dully blooded in a macabre pattern, and drew it back to swing.

She tensed, closing her eyes.

"Master! The girl is escaping!"

Madelyne's eyes snapped open in time to see the blade swipe past her, slicing harmlessly through her skirts, and clashing into the stones behind her.

"After her!" Fantin shouted at his man, who had already mounted the stairs. He turned to glare at Madelyne. "Do you not find hope in this," he sneered, "for she will not make it to your husband. If indeed he lurks about, she will find no way to allow him into the keep. You are safe here with me," he added, and laughed…that selfsame laugh that came with his madness.

He sank to his knees, there in front of her, and began to pray.

She had never heard anything more terrifying.

At last…at last.

Gavin heard the faint sound of scraping on the inside of the door. He need say naught, for his men saw the straightening of his spine and the tensing of his arms. They shifted quickly to their places.

The door eased open and they remained in the shadows, waiting.

"My lord!" a voice hissed.

'Twas unexpectedly a female voice, and Gavin moved, forgetting all caution. "Tricky?" he started, leaping through the open doorway, followed by his men.

Inside the gateway, he found himself surrounded by swords and chain mail.

Despite the surprise, Gavin did not falter, did not hesitate. He exploded.

His blade flashed and gleamed, striking out with all the strength he'd harbored these last days—these days of holding himself in check, of hell on earth, since Maddie had been taken. These men waiting him could be no match for his rage and need, regardless of their numbers. He would have them all for daring to stand in his way.

Gavin was barely aware of his own men behind and about him, brandishing weapons seeking to be as quick and deadly as his own, slicing through mail and flesh and clanging against more metal. His world was a blur, a mass of steel, noise, cries and grunts—yet Gavin saw with clarity every movement he made, every step and thrust of the blade, every shift and dodge and swing. They brought him closer to his goal.

He didn't know how many men he sliced or stabbed, but when at last no one raised a blade to him, he paused only for a moment, panting, yet not fatigued, and looked around.

Jube and two other of his men stood to one side, watching with wide eyes. They looked as though they'd been there for some time, watching some exhibition or contest. Their eyes fastened upon Gavin as though they weren't certain 'twas truly he…and Tricky, who'd been held prisoner by one of the Tricourten men at the beginning of the battle, now peeked from behind splayed fingers, peering from around a corner.

"What ails you?" Gavin shouted, infuriated by their immobility. "Why do you stand and stare? We must find Madelyne. Tricky— where is she kept?"

His roar prodded them into movement. It was only as Gavin started to follow the little maid and had to step over arms and legs and heads and feet—none of which remained attached to their respective bodies, but were scattered all over the ground—did he realize he had been afflicted with his own madness.

Fantin rose to his feet in front of Madelyne, still mouthing words of supplication. The sounds from above had made it known that some battle raged beyond the rafters of the ceiling.

His pleading, groveling, praising sent squirrelly shivers down Madelyne's spine and they coiled like snakes in the pit of her stomach. It was eerie and nauseating the way he continued to pray and implore God to help him, to show him the way, to give him the Stone.

He faced her, and what she saw there made her knees buckle as all strength drained from her body. His countenance glowed… shone with joy and light and fervor, even as the light in his eyes gleamed and his mouth continued to dribble the tiny trickle of wetness from one corner. His mind had truly gone, and madness—religious madness—blossomed within him.

What strength had he now? All the strength that comes with righteousness, and belief and faith. Madelyne knew the strength that came with belief. And when she saw it lining his face, she feared it.

Fantin flitted about the room, his lips still moving, moving bowls and jugs and jars, gripping his sword. He found a large jug and removed the cork, trickling its contents along the edge of the floor, along in front of Madelyne, around Seton's prone body and to the feet of Clem, who remained bound against another wall.

She smelled the rancid scent of pig fat, and felt its greasiness splash against her skirts, and watched in horror as a gleeful Fantin seized one of the many sconces along the wall.

"You and your father shall burn on earth as you will burn in hell," he told her, pivoting about as he swiped the torch through the air, leaving an arc of smoke in its wake. Fantin dropped the torch and the grease eagerly sucked the flames into its trail, instantly billowing rancid smoke into the air, and seeping along toward her.

"May God be with you," Fantin shouted gleefully, dashing on light feet toward the stairs after saluting her with his sword.

Madelyne watched in horror as he disappeared up the steps, and the flames began to eat the wooden trestle tables and the tapestries that covered the walls. The smoke grew thicker, the flames closer and hotter.

She pulled in vain at the irons that still imprisoned her arms. Her fingers had long turned to ice from loss of blood and the dampness of the dungeon-laboratory. Seton remained unconscious at her feet, and Clem, across the room, struggled with his own bonds.

The flames burned higher, and closer, and Madelyne felt the heat as it struggled toward her skirts. She kicked out and to the side, frantic, whipping her gown around her legs, trying to move away from the pools of grease that would soon be consumed by fire. There was naught she could do.

Gavin.

He would come soon. He must come soon.

She, too, had the strength of faith and belief.

A door—the door to which Tricky had been leading him—flew open, and Gavin suddenly was face to face with his nemesis.

"De Belgrume!" he cried, leaping at the man who'd emerged from a stairwell.

The man was prepared for him, and swung his blade as Gavin moved. Heat sliced down his arm, and Gavin shouted with rage and victory. Fantin had drawn first blood, but Gavin would take the last.

With a swift movement, Fantin slammed the door behind him and whirled, swinging his sword again. This time, Gavin easily dodged the thrust, and returned with his own blade, slamming against the man's side.

"Your whore burns below," Fantin gasped, feinting and then thrusting in one fluid movement. "You must go through me to reach her, but you cannot get there in time."

He laughed, then, easily, as though he'd had the greatest jest, and his blade met Gavin's. Chill raced up Gavin's back. He'd never felt such burning rage and taste for blood, but the man before him had a calmness…an easy humor, a glow, that bespoke of some inner strength—much like that which had attracted Gavin to the man's daughter.

Sweat ran in his eyes, and Gavin dashed it away as he rammed toward Fantin. The other man raised his sword and their blades clashed, pressing against each other as if frozen in mid-air, each man pushing with every bit of need and will he possessed. At last, the metals slid, and the swords moved, freeing them from the stalemate. Gavin didn't waste the moment by drawing back. Instead, he whirled, kicked, and thrust all at once, and suddenly, Fantin was away from the door, shrieking in unexpected pain.

Gavin propelled himself toward it, just as his opponent lunged forward. With barely enough time to block the move, Gavin whipped his sword and caught the downward stroke. He still had the door, and with a massive cry, he yanked it full open.

Fantin leaped toward him, and Gavin dodged, but misstepped, falling through the doorway and feeling naught but air beneath his foot. Off-balance, he began to tumble, and with one miraculous movement, snagged Fantin's tunic, dragging him with him.

The edges of the stone stairs slammed into his shoulders and legs as he tumbled down, letting his sword go to fall before him. Gavin thumped to the floor just after the clang of his sword, and had the moment to grab it then peer around the chamber choked with smoke before turning to face Fantin.

When he rose to his feet, the man had lost that aura of holiness. His face, streaked with grime, and his eyes burning in a face of pure fury reflected a loss of control, along with the self-same determination to win that Gavin felt.

Fantin's movements came, then, faster, harder, but more erratic than before. Gavin spared a look toward the wall where he'd seen a white-garbed form through the spirals of smoke, his heart sagging when he saw that it did not move. Fantin took that advantage and slammed his sword with such two-handed force that Gavin lost his grip and the weapon spun from his hand.

Now weaponless, he felt the surge of desperation and need, and launched himself to the side as Fantin drove what he'd intended to be the death stroke. Gavin flipped a stool toward his opponent, catching him in the gut, and with one sharp, swift lurch, snagged Fantin's sword wrist and gave a vicious twist. The bones snapped horribly.

Fantin screamed and dropped his weapon, whirling toward a sconce that flamed behind him on the one wall untouched by smoke, but Gavin moved too quickly. The sword was in his hand, and slicing into his opponent's chest before the man could snatch the torch.

Fantin screamed and sagged to the ground in a hopeless pool of blood and tattered clothing. Gavin yanked the blade from the bone where it had lodged, feeling the scrape against cartilage, and plunged it back in with two powerful arms. He took no chances that the man's deep strength should come back to haunt him.

As he turned to chamber, the sound of footfalls down the stairs alerted him. 'Twas his name being called, and Gavin shouted back between inhaling the thick, choking smoke. He had no moment to wonder what had taken them so long as Jube and the others stumbled down the stairs. They didn't need to be directed to the slumped man against the far wall.

Gavin launched himself over a table to Madelyne's side, where she sagged against the wall, her face turned into the sleeve of her garment in an effort to keep the smoke at bay. He registered the chains that bound her and the fallen man at her feet, shouting for help.

The wrist manacles kept his wife tight to the wall, and the flames licked only inches away. Gavin, his face so tight to his skull that he could barely form words with his mouth, gasped, "Madelyne, hold tight! Do not move!"

With every last bit of strength, channeling every iota of the desperation and fear he'd harbored, he seized his weapon with two powerful hands and brought it down onto the chains.

One of them snapped loose, and Madelyne sagged from the wall, toward, him, hanging only by her arm. He wrapped an arm around her waist, coughing into her hair, then released her to slam the sword down a second time. The stones held the chains more firmly, and this side did not release. The smoke clogged his nose and stung his eyes, and the warmth the flames made sent waves of sweat rolling down his back, dampening his hands.

"Dear God, help me!" he cried, and slammed the sword down again.

The reverberation sang through his arms, into his shoulders, and down his spine as the blade pulled the chain from the stone and crashed into the floor.

Madelyne fell into his arms, and Gavin swooped her up over his shoulder and turned to dash from the room. The flames had built higher, cutting a swath betwixt them and the stairs. By the speed of the fire, he realized his entire altercation with Fantin had been mere breaths of time rather than the long minutes it had seemed.

With a cry, one of battle and victory, Gavin tore toward the flames, dashing through them, feeling their heat sear them as he leapt through and stumbled to the stairs on the other side.

Jube stood there, waiting, and grabbed Madelyne from his master. They pounded up the stairs and collapsed on the floor in the great hall.

Gathering Madelyne into his arms, Gavin inserted himself betwixt her and Jube and pulled her to his chest. Kissing her head, her face, her mouth, he found himself murmuring wild things that made no sense…and at last had to pull himself away to look at her.

"Madelyne…." was all he could say before crushing her into his arms, folding her tightly to his chest. He shook, knowing how close he'd come to losing her…over and over again. "God, Madelyne, I love you. I died a decade of deaths when I learned that Fantin had taken you. I begged the king to release me, and he did, but—"

"It was Fantin," she told him, smothered against his chest, coughing softly. "Tricky heard him say it, and Clem too…he fixed the necklet for the queen, with the help of Rohan…the king will not say another word on it, I trow." She kissed him at the vee open-ing of his tunic, her lips warm on his skin at the indentation at the base of his throat.

"I hope you are right in that," he told her. "But I cannot help but agree—now that Fantin is gone, Henry will be much relieved."

"Gavin." Madelyne clutched at his arm, pulling away to look up at him, her sunken gray eyes like large moons. "I cannot believe this…but I have just learned that my father is not Fantin. 'Tis the markings on my wrist—Seton has them too, as his mother, and her father….I am the daughter of Seton de Masin, not Fantin de Belgrume!"

A rush of happiness and relief—for Madelyne, not for him-self—flooded Gavin. "Did I not tell you that there was no madness in your blood? Only the blood of a brave and intelligent man, my love. We have much to thank him for." He glanced at Seton, who, though slumped against the wall, appeared to be unharmed.

"He'll be overjoyed to know that my mother is not dead."

"Your mother?" Gavin stopped, staring down at her. "Your mother lives?" He saw the stricken look in her eyes, and knew that she'd forgotten the lie.

"Nay, she is not dead. I could not let the truth come out, Gavin…you understand why. But—oh, I've spoken treason to the king." Fear leapt into her eyes and she clutched at his arms.

"The king will not harm you for protecting her as you did. And if he should try, I do believe Eleanor would stay his hand." He kissed her on the cheek, amazed at the strength his little nun had shown over the last month of trial. "There is the matter of the land of Tricourten and whether you shall remain its lady…but I've wealth enough that should the king decide that you will not inherit, 'twill be no hardship."

"Aye, Gavin, and truth to tell, I should not care if I ever were to set foot upon the lands of Tricourten again."

"You will not, if you do not wish, my love. But I should not disavow the rents here, should the king allow us to keep the lands. I shall speak with him on it, my lady. My love."

Content with his response, Madelyne glanced over his shoulder and what she saw made her smile. "You may beg my forgiveness now, my lord," she said, nodding in that direction.

Gavin followed her gaze, twisting to look behind him, and saw Tricky and Clem entwined in a passionate embrace. He returned to his own love and gave her a rueful smile. "I beg your forgiveness, my lady…for doubting the prediction of your maid—it appears that she will have her way and her man."

He looked at her closely and saw, again, the bruises on her face and the streaks of blood dried on her cheek, and realized what she must have experienced at the hands of the madman. The pace of his heart picked up speed, and a shudder rushed through him. "Madelyne, my love….can you forgive me for letting this happen?"

She tilted her head back to look up at him. "Gavin, love, please do not speak of apologies to me any longer. You have a penchant for speaking them much too oft! Save them for when you neglect the anniversary of our wedding or forget to bring me a new herbal plant when you travel to London…But for now, just kiss me."

EPILOGUE

A LONE knight approached the ivy-covered walls of Lock Rose Abbey.

Dismounting from his horse, he raised a mailed fist to pull on the bell rope, remembering the day over a decade before when he'd done the same. The low, rolling sound of the tolling bell rumbled through the abbey, reverberating through the silent forest.

Moments later, the robed figure of an old woman, stooped and slow, approached the gate. "Yes?"

"I bring word to Anne de Belgrume that her husband is dead."

There was a pause, then the gate swung open silently, belying its age and the rust-colored bars. "You may wait here."

He took a seat on the bench in the center of a rose garden, after tying his mount to an oak tree.

When Anne de Belgrume stepped into his line of vision moments later, his heart stopped. She was as beautiful as he remembered—moreso, for the years had been gentle with her. He still could not believe that she was alive…having heard the story of her death when Madelyne went to court.

"Anne." He rose and reached his hands out toward her.

"Seton?" Gladness overwhelmed her voice and she rushed toward him.

Nothing had ever felt so good as when he folded her into his arms, heedless of the chain mail that that pressed into her. "Anne…

oh, my beautiful one…I did not know if I'd ever hold you thus again."

She pulled back to look up at him. "Is Fantin truly dead? Am I free?"

He nodded. "Aye, struck down by the husband of your daughter. Our daughter." He looked closely at her. "You did not tell her."

"Nay. I did not wish to burden her with that knowledge. Mayhap 'twas wrong, but I believed if Fantin should have learned it, he would have killed her. At the least, if he believed she was his daughter, he wouldn't harm her." She reached to touch his face, and the warmth of her hand stopped his heart.

"Aye. Our child…wed with a good man, safe now from your husband…and you are set free from this…sanctuary…should you wish to leave." His words were a question that he'd waited a lifetime to have answered.

"Leave? With you?" Anne breathed. "Aye, Seton. Always. Forever."

Lord Merle nodded at his guest, then turned to his daughter. "Maris, will you not show Sir Dirick where the men-at-arms lay their pallets? And any other comforts he may need."

Maris stood reluctantly, dismay by her father's innocent command. The last thing she wanted was to be alone with Sir Dirick. She'd felt his attention returning to her again and again during the evening, and had been unable to ignore the interest in his stare. Try as she might, she'd been unable to keep her mouth closed and her mind on her food—as her mother had admonished her many a time. Nay, if the man was to wed her, he'd know from the beginning that she had her own thoughts and opinions, and an interest in the world beyond Langumont's walls.

"Of course, Papa," she said in a voice that disguised her discomfort.

Obviously, Sir Dirick did not miss her mislike of the situation, for as soon as Merle and Allegra were out of earshot, he said, "Lady Maris, I am perfectly able to find my own pallet."

"Nay, 'tis my father's wish. I should not put a guest out," she smiled at him, swallowing the resentment she felt for being pressed into a marriage she did not want. In all honesty, it was not this man's fault—and he seemed pleasant enough now that he was not ahorse. "Have you bathed?"

"Nay," he shook his head, surprise flashing in his gray-blue eyes.

"May I offer you a warm bath before I direct you to your pallet?" she asked. "Gustave will bring the water. I won't take long, and you will soon be for bed."

"You?" Those eyes turned on her with a sudden intensity, and he looked at her for a moment, a very faint smile hovering at the corners of his mouth.

Maris's throat went dry and she nearly stepped away from him and the unexpected stirrings in her middle. The sudden image of this man, devoid of his chausses and tunic, settled into a tub that would hardly fit his large body, filled her mind. His dark hair, which now curled wildly about his face and jaw, would be sleek and dripping, his broad shoulders bare and steam rising from dark skin—

Maris bit her lip as her cheeks flushed with warmth. What was wrong with her? She'd never had lewd thoughts over such a mundane chore. "Aye, of course," she managed to say in response to the question she'd nearly forgotten.

"Nay," Sir Dirick rumbled after what seemed like forever. His smooth, low voice carried easily to her ears, even over the noise of the servants as they cleared off the tables and stacked the benches. "I do not believe I should put myself through such torture."

Her heart in her throat and her mind whirling—unsure as to what he meant by such a comment—Maris spun away to hide her discomfiture. "Then if you would follow me," she murmured and blindly began to make her way between the nearly-empty tables, anxious to be rid of her charge.

As they approached a group of rowdy knights, Maris paused, resting her hand on the shoulder of a burly, red-headed one. They quieted almost as if she'd commanded it. "Sir Raymond, how fares your shoulder? Is the pain lessening?"

The man's face nearly matched the color of his hair when he turned it up to look at her. "Aye, my lady. The pain is nearly gone." He moved his arm as if to demonstrate.

"You will come to the herbary on the morrow and I will check it again," she ordered. It wouldn't do for her father's best man to have an injured arm. "The last I dressed a wound for you, 'twas only once that you came to me—and look what has happened to it because of your carelessness!"

He grinned up at her, "Aye, my lady. On the morrow, I will allow you to torture me yet again. 'Tis only because your touch is so sweet that I can sit through the pain," he teased in the manner of a big brother.

Maris, who'd grown up with Raymond pulling at her pigtails and chasing her through the keep with spiders, planted hands on her hips as the other men laughed. "Aye, and you should keep such sweetness on your tongue, or I will put you through more tortures if you spread tales. Did I not warn you that some day you would pay for the frog in my bed?"

There wasn't a hint of guile in her actions, Dirick thought as he watched. She had no concept of what she did to a man, with those teasing golden-green eyes and vibrant smile—particularly the red-headed knight, whose besotted expression was not quite brotherly. Whatever reason she'd been in the village at night, it hadn't been for a tryst—he was now certain of it.

Dirick's skin still prickled at the memory of her innocent offer to bathe him, and he wondered if her father knew she'd made such a gesture. A sudden streak of heat shot through him at the thought of her scratched and stained hands soaping his body…but he thrust the thought away immediately. He'd do well to find a woman anight. Mayhaps one of the maidservants would oblige him.

Not for the first time that evening, he wondered why he'd heard nothing of the beautiful heiress of Langumont—from either Bernard or the court. Certainly a well-landed maid as comely as Maris Lareux wouldn't escape the notice of the unmarried, land-greedy barons at court.

Lady Maris's voice broke into Dirick's thoughts as she led him around into the area reserved for the men-at-arms and other important visitors. It was a large room, cordoned off from the rest of the hall by a heavy oaken door—much nicer than many of the men's quarters he'd slept in throughout England and France. A fire roared in the corner, and a serf slumped against the wall, snoring, with a stack of wood within reach.

"You may place your pallet anywhere you like, Sir Dirick," Maris offered. She handed him a pile of blankets, more than generous enough to keep one warm—especially with a blazing fire in the same room.

"Thank you, my lady." He took the bundle.

She paused for a moment as if contemplating her next words, and when she spoke, a small grin tickled the corner of her enticing mouth.

Her words, however, when they came, eliminated any hint of innocence. "Papa bade me see to your comforts. If your need is as great as 'twas yestereve, I will send a woman to you."

Dirick felt his face flush hot as he ground his teeth together in an attempt to maintain his dignity. Words escaped him, and before he could gather his wits, the little minx took his silence for dissent and whirled away down the dark corridor.

He could only stare after her, trying to decide whether he wanted to murder her or kiss her.

ABOUT THE AUTHOR

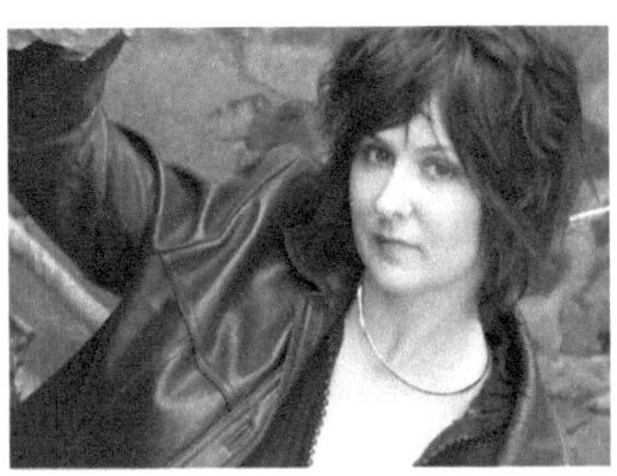 **COLLEEN GLEASON** is the international best-selling author of the Gardella Vampire Chronicles, a historical urban fantasy series about a female vampire hunter who lives during the time of Jane Austen.

Her first novel, *The Rest Falls Away*, was released to acclaim in 2007. Since then, she has published fifteen novels with New American Library, MIRA Books, and HarperCollins (writing as Joss Ware). Her books have been translated into seven languages and are available worldwide.

She loves to hear from readers, and can be contacted through her website at **colleengleason.com.**

www.ingramcontent.com/pod-product-compliance
Lightning Source LLC
Chambersburg PA
CBHW061529210726
48287CB00006B/1886